Crossroad Chronicles Behind the Iron Gates

Book One

Kikie P. Akers

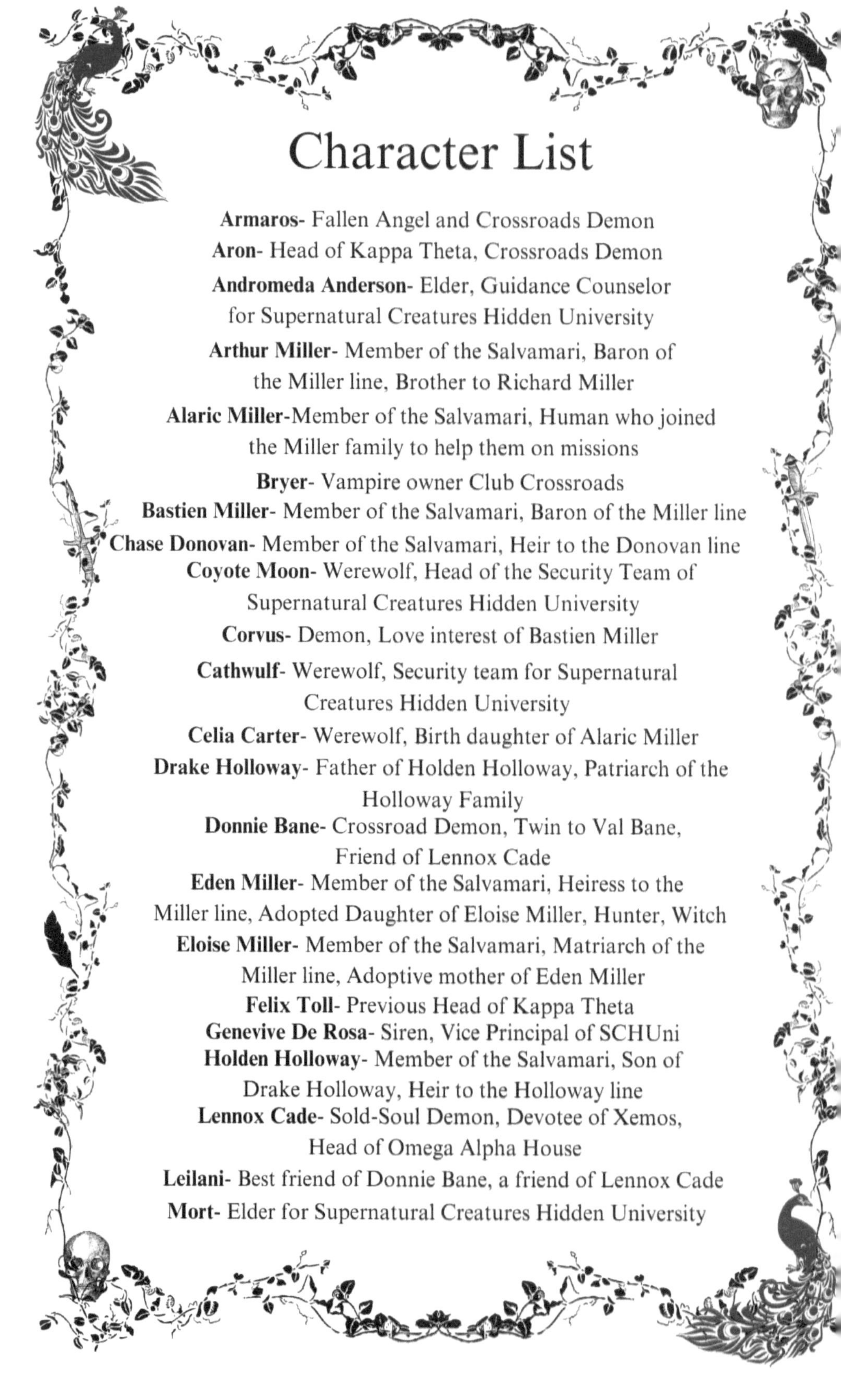

Character List

Armaros- Fallen Angel and Crossroads Demon
Aron- Head of Kappa Theta, Crossroads Demon
Andromeda Anderson- Elder, Guidance Counselor
for Supernatural Creatures Hidden University
Arthur Miller- Member of the Salvamari, Baron of
the Miller line, Brother to Richard Miller
Alaric Miller-Member of the Salvamari, Human who joined
the Miller family to help them on missions
Bryer- Vampire owner Club Crossroads
Bastien Miller- Member of the Salvamari, Baron of the Miller line
Chase Donovan- Member of the Salvamari, Heir to the Donovan line
Coyote Moon- Werewolf, Head of the Security Team of
Supernatural Creatures Hidden University
Corvus- Demon, Love interest of Bastien Miller
Cathwulf- Werewolf, Security team for Supernatural
Creatures Hidden University
Celia Carter- Werewolf, Birth daughter of Alaric Miller
Drake Holloway- Father of Holden Holloway, Patriarch of the
Holloway Family
Donnie Bane- Crossroad Demon, Twin to Val Bane,
Friend of Lennox Cade
Eden Miller- Member of the Salvamari, Heiress to the
Miller line, Adopted Daughter of Eloise Miller, Hunter, Witch
Eloise Miller- Member of the Salvamari, Matriarch of the
Miller line, Adoptive mother of Eden Miller
Felix Toll- Previous Head of Kappa Theta
Genevive De Rosa- Siren, Vice Principal of SCHUni
Holden Holloway- Member of the Salvamari, Son of
Drake Holloway, Heir to the Holloway line
Lennox Cade- Sold-Soul Demon, Devotee of Xemos,
Head of Omega Alpha House
Leilani- Best friend of Donnie Bane, a friend of Lennox Cade
Mort- Elder for Supernatural Creatures Hidden University

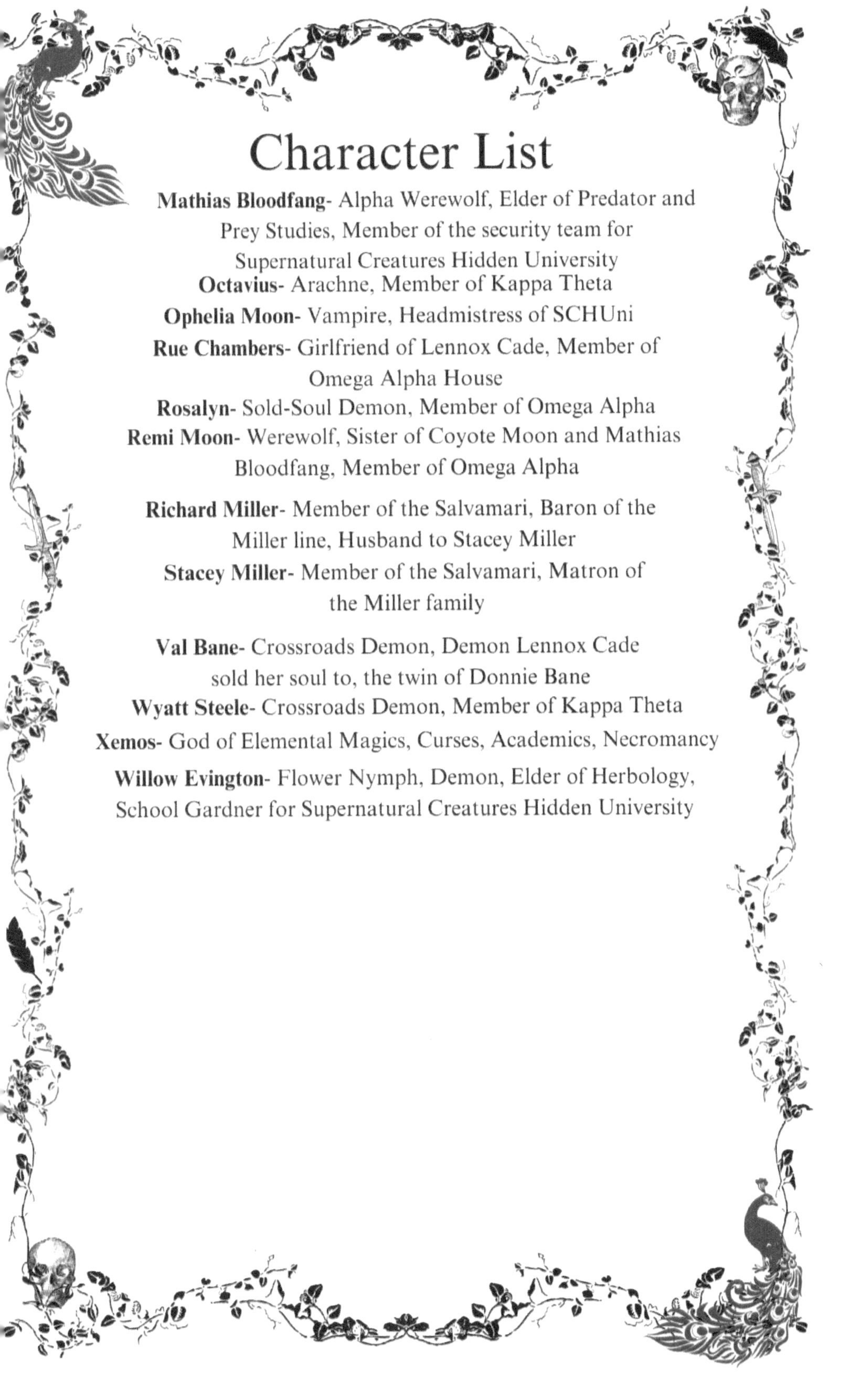

Character List

Mathias Bloodfang- Alpha Werewolf, Elder of Predator and Prey Studies, Member of the security team for Supernatural Creatures Hidden University

Octavius- Arachne, Member of Kappa Theta

Ophelia Moon- Vampire, Headmistress of SCHUni

Rue Chambers- Girlfriend of Lennox Cade, Member of Omega Alpha House

Rosalyn- Sold-Soul Demon, Member of Omega Alpha

Remi Moon- Werewolf, Sister of Coyote Moon and Mathias Bloodfang, Member of Omega Alpha

Richard Miller- Member of the Salvamari, Baron of the Miller line, Husband to Stacey Miller

Stacey Miller- Member of the Salvamari, Matron of the Miller family

Val Bane- Crossroads Demon, Demon Lennox Cade sold her soul to, the twin of Donnie Bane

Wyatt Steele- Crossroads Demon, Member of Kappa Theta

Xemos- God of Elemental Magics, Curses, Academics, Necromancy

Willow Evington- Flower Nymph, Demon, Elder of Herbology, School Gardner for Supernatural Creatures Hidden University

Playlist

Half of Forever- Henrik

Two Hearts- Maryjo Lilac

Dandelion- Gabbie Hanna

Family Tree- Rory

Figure You Out- Voila

Saints- Echos

Broken- Isak Danielson

Which Witch- Florence + The Machine

Army- Besomorph, Arcando, Neoni

Rescue- Lauren Daigle

Half Life- Livingston

Villain- Neoni

Alkaline- Sleep Token

Chasing Cars- Snow Patrol: Chapter 37

Black Out Days- Phantorgam

Fall For Me- Sleep Token

Talk- Hozier

Do or Die- Natalie Jane

Blood // Water- grandson

For the ones that refused to listen when the world told you who to be.

Welcome Home.

August

Prologue

Lennox

Life was just as it had been the last twenty-one years. Peaceful, surrounded by loved ones as a new semester was due to begin. With bags in hand, Lennox looked out the window and watched people in the streets. Their voices a low hum occasionally muffled by cars on their way to and from lunch. With a final glance to the left, she turned to the Eiffel Tower and let out a sigh at the sight. *Paris is beautiful- But she's all I need.* She then turned to face her girlfriend, fixating her violet eyes on Rue. A warm smile drifted onto her face as she watched her long brown curls sway gracefully before disappearing around the corner to the bathroom.

The woman muttered a list quietly to herself of everything they had brought. Lennox leaned against the nightstand, her hands on either side. Her chest filled with the warmth of love. Even after over fifteen years together she still had butterflies stir every time she caught a glance of her partner. Suddenly, Rue came to a stop, her golden brown eyes locking with Lennox's violet. With a raised eyebrow and smile forming across Rue's lips, Lennox's eyes distinctly moved up and down.

"What?" A laugh jumped out with the word as she tilted her head.

"Nothing, Love. I've just had a wonderful time, I don't want it to end." Lennox closed the distance between them and took her hands. A mirrored smile crossed Rue's lips. Rows of runes traced their way down the edges of her face and shifted slightly with her every expression.

"I wish we could stay too, but you already told Felix we were coming back today. You know he'll probably already be waiting at the arch by the time we get home. Besides, I don't think you'd be able to step away from Omega Alpha for more than a few months, and that's okay. It's one of the many things I love about you." Lennox faked offense as Rue wound an arm around her waist and kissed her on the cheek. "Do you have the key?"

"Of course I do, but I'd like to add I'd go anywhere with you," she added before taking out the familiar small iron key. Holding it up, the teeth weren't shaped into your average ridges, but were letters that spelled out 'SCH.'

"That may be so, but you are the happiest when you are there, and where you're happy, I'm happy." she teased as Lennox dropped her hands and started to grab their things.

"Let's go home."

Stepping forward, she put her key near the closet door knob which transformed to fit it and turned towards Rue. Taking a step to the side for her to go first, extending an arm and playfully bowing. As Lennox peered up, her eyes caught the white scars in the shape of intertwining chains and sigils flashed in the bright sunlight. The silver on her arm drew her attention momentarily, reminding her of her devotion to the God, Xemos when she was human. A soft smile formed as she peered at the intricate design, a small reminder of her freedom from the looming cloud of death for the last two decades. Rue took her hand once more and with a twist of the knob, the door opened.

A tall building about three stories high sat in the distance. The school made of light colored stones extended out on either side in the shape of a 'U'. Even from this distance, she could spot the Hellhound fountain in the center of the courtyard. The closest end to the arch was extended and inward into the back at least a hundred years before she arrived to house the bulk of the other students that attended the school, the whole thing set in the middle of a half circle of tall iron gates.

It was bright on the other side, the wind made the trees shake in the breeze. The couple stepped through the portal to return to Crucivia, Romania, and the grounds of Supernatural Creatures Hidden University. The moment their feet went through, they appeared in a large patch of grass on the edge of campus. Turning around she took the key from the door and quickly shoved it in her pocket as the magic door closed behind them.

"Well, there you are! I've been waiting here for you two to come back for the last hour!" Called the familiar voice of Felix. He made his way toward them from a tree he was leaning against a few feet away. His short blond, almost gray, hair tangled from the gusts of wind.

"Glad to see you too. You didn't have to wait here, you could have met us at Omega Alpha." Rue commented with a bright smile, hugging him.

"Where's the fun in that?" he asked, glancing at Lennox with his piercing blue eyes, moving over to her for a hug.

Opening her arms, she obliged, "After twenty-one years, I can't go one year without you waiting to welcome me back, can I?"

"Absolutely not! Did it since your first day here, it's tradition now,

Nox." he teased, lightly elbowing her in jest after letting her go.

Reaching out, he took a bag from each of them as they made their way toward the chapter house on the other side of campus. Their bags rolled loudly on the cobblestone path while Felix enthusiastically asked Rue all sorts of questions about Paris. Taking a second, Lennox's eyes drifted around the familiar grounds. The two chapter houses sat on either side of campus and a small road which led to where the Elders lived beside the woodland. The sun shone off the small lake off to the side of the Elder's homes. The summer still holding on before the winter took over.

"Good to be home, isn't it?" Felix asked them, Rue taking her free hand.

"It is," she agreed as they finally made their way up the stairs to Omega house.

"Are you too tired for our meeting tomorrow?"

"Not at all, I told you I'd be there early so we can plan out this year's events." Lennox glanced at him with a raised eyebrow.

"Good," he beamed as his phone started to ring when they reached the plum-colored door of the House.

Putting down their bags, he held a finger up for a second and answered. The couple laughed between each other, and after only about twenty seconds he agreed to something and hung up. Turning to him with a knowing look Lennox motioned for him to go.

"What? Some of the others from the main building's student dorms want to hang out tonight. It's ghost hunt night." He attempted to defend himself.

"Do whatever, I know you never say no and it gets you in trouble. Just don't be too hungover tomorrow." She shook her head.

"It's just a little hunt." His face twisted into false offense.

"Yeah, and knowing Barry he called Wyatt. Knowing Wyatt he's going to bring his suitcase which you're going to drink a bottle of rum from."

"You and I both know that's only the first and last day of classes." He took a few steps back toward the fraternity.

"And when someone dares you," Rue pointed out.

"Shut up," He wagged a finger at her as she laughed. "Look girls, no promises! I have to go get ready. I'll catch you guys later!" He waved at them and turned back down the path towards Kappa Theta House.

Rue faced towards the door and opened it for them. Lennox grabbed the bags and made their way through the frame. The simple two-story house sat on the edge of campus and as they opened the door they were met with the wall to the right. Photos of all the prior Heads of House and the years they held the position underneath. The long purple carpet in the middle of the entrance hall had the Greek letters of the house in bold white letters. *Just as we left it.* She knew that there were already a few others who had arrived back at the school, but they all must have been in the town as it was silent.

"Let's go unpack." Rue took Lennox's hand and led her toward the two flights of stairs. The first went straight to the landing and then went right to the floor above where their room was. Lennox nodded and allowed herself to be pulled, with a love-struck smile across her face.

The night filled the dark room, only dimly lit by lights outside. Vines swayed in the breeze that came in through the open window. Lennox and Rue slept through the peaceful night back to back in the bed they'd made by pushing two mattresses together. Lennox shifted many times through the night as dreams of Felix laying in the middle of Kappa Theta. Her nightmares were only interrupted when her phone lit up and buzzed demandingly by her head. With a groan, the pink-haired demon rolled over and reached for her phone. As she did, she looked out her window and saw the night still outside. *What the hell, what time is it?* She rubbed her eyes in the light of her phone. Lennox squinted to finally see three ten am with a new message from her friend and Co-Head of House's name. With an exasperated groan, she went to her messages as Rue slept deeply beside her.

Felix Toll-

Hey, We were out late- Meet closer to 10?

-Sent 3:09 am

Lennox Cade-

No problem, get some sleep. You're gonna wish you had when I get there to plan the party at Club Crossroads.

-Sent 3:10 am

Felix Toll-

Okay Mom

-Sent 3:11 am

After a scoff at his response, Lennox placed her phone back on the nightstand. Rolling over and sliding through the sheets, she inched closer to Rue. Carefully, she wrapped an arm around her waist and pulled her into her chest. Lennox closed her eyes and the world went dark once more. The images of Felix at the feet of a shadowed figure soon returned to her dreams.

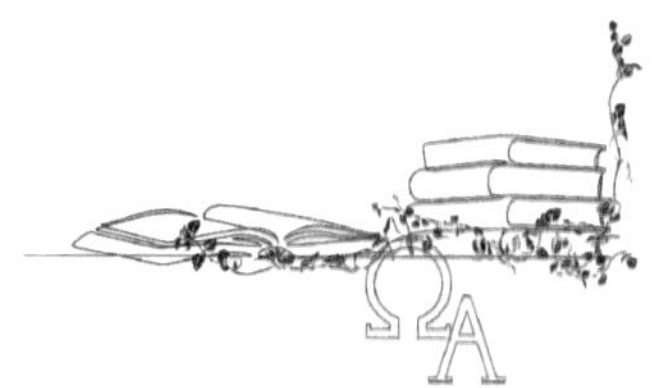

At nine forty in the morning, Lennox woke up once again. This time to the sound of footsteps of the early arrivals moving up and down the halls. Stretching a little, she rolled over and buried her face in her pillow and felt Rue move. She felt a hand on her back in a silent request to not get up. Turning her head to the side she gave Rue a sleepy smile.

"No more sleeping half the day," Lennox told her in an early morning rasp.

"You don't have to go yet, I'm sure Felix is still sleeping?" She asked hopefully, peering at her with a smile.

"If I don't show up at ten, he's never gonna let it go. Even if he still is, I'd rather avoid a semester of being called, tardy tom." Lennox laughed.

They both knew Felix well, the three of them were thicker than thieves. Viewing him as an older brother since the day she walked into the school. Before Rue could stop her, Lennox moved from the covers and got out of bed. With a dramatic flop to her back, Rue let out a sigh as Lennox started to get ready. Slipping into a lavender sweater and jeans she looked into the mirror in her closet. Short wavy hair tangled into a mess on the top of her head welcomed her in the reflection. Attempting to run a hand through, she started looking around for her comb. Internally, she cursed herself for always putting it down half asleep. She started to rummage through the drawers inside the wardrobe.

Pausing, Lennox was unable to hide her smile. Quickly, she glanced to the side. The wardrobe door completely blocked her from Rue. Her smile grew as she looked at the purple velvet box hidden among her notebooks and pens. Inside she knew there was an emerald cut, three-stone ring with a deep citrine. The center matched the golden hue of Rue's eyes that she had searched years for.

Absorbed in the little box she didn't notice the long ivy vines had started to snake across over from the bookshelf. It wasn't until one of the ends of the vines wrapped around the handle of a comb in the open drawer and held it, waving it a little.

"Ah! Thank you Ampelos!" She gently took it from the vine. After taming the mess on the top of her head, she turned back to Rue and grabbed her phone from her nightstand.

"I'll see you after I make sure Felix isn't cuddling with whatever he was drinking last night."

She smiled, staying under the covers. "Have fun! Take a photo for me if he's using a bottle as a stuffed animal."

"I will!" She called back.

Lennox bounced down the two flights of wooden stairs. With a smile, she waved to a few housemates she saw on her way out. When the door shut behind her, she walked down the sidewalk to the path that led to their brother house. The end-of-summer breeze was still warm As she walked she drew in a long breath of fresh air as the warm sun brushed her skin. Her thoughts drifted to the coming winter months. She wasn't a fan of the snow that came with it. As she crossed the familiar campus, she saw various Elders moving around their rooms through the tall windows along the large main building. The University grounds reminded her of a cross between a castle in Ireland, which Lennox hadn't been to since her Aunt Arya took her on a summer trip. The second reminder was of the school she went to in her human years in upper New York. Large, old but strong. As if it has always been a part of the world.

It only took a few minutes to get to the front door of Kappa Theta. The building was completely still. Felix and Wyatt would be the only ones there since none of their other housemates had more than likely returned to campus. Reaching up, she used the bronze knocker on the door and hit the panel three times. Lennox paused and listened closely for footsteps that never came. With a quick debate on how annoying she wanted to be, she brought her phone out to get to the keys she carried. She selected the one on the keychain for the Chapter House.

He must really be hungover. She put the key in the lock and turned it only to hear the lock click into place. It had already been unlocked. With a frown she turned it again and turned the doorknob.

"Felix! You know it's not a good idea to leave your door unlocked. How many times have I told you!" She called, making her way into the entranceway.

The house was silent as she listened again for Felix to make his way downstairs. A big banner hung above the stairs with the Greek letters for the house in white. Light tunneled in and reflected from the open door against the hunter-green background. Scanning the room, Lennox noticed one of his school sweatshirts on the floor and paused. In seconds, she decided to ignore it and went past the line of photos of the previous Heads of House. The wall was almost identical to her own house. *It's so quiet.*

Keeping her attention forward she stepped closer toward the main living room until her feet stopped moving. Lennox's stomach turned as the hair on the back of her neck stood. Internally, she pulled at the green thread of magic. Her arms heated as she kept the flow of power dulled, the glow from the chains would give her position away. Regaining herself, she pressed forward as the sound of her heart started to pound in her ears. There was a sudden, loud crunch beneath her foot that caused her to stop once again. Moving her foot to the side, a cell phone now with a broken screen laying underneath. Recognizing it as Felix's and rolling her eyes, she scooped it up before she entered the next room.

"Dude! You have to stop getting so drunk you leave your shit everywhere! Your housemates are gonna think you like to decorate the floor with your belongings. Now I owe you a new screen."

She had her eyes on the broken phone as she walked in. *He has to be somewhere down here. Looks like it was more than just a ghost-* Bright red colored the floor right in front of her. Her heart fell into her stomach as her eyes followed the trail of blood straight to two people laying on the floor. The red stained his almost silver hair and the Elder's, Narcissus was laying on his stomach, his face away from her but she recognized the others long brown curls now also stained. *This has to be one of his pranks, there's no way this is real.*

"Come on, this isn't funny… Toll, get up, you're the one who wants to have this meeting every year." Lennox scolded him, frozen to her spot a few feet away. Her eyes darted around the room for anyone who could be recording her reaction, "I don't know how you convinced an Elder to join you in this, it's not funny."

She made her way over to the Elder first. Once she was close enough to look at him she leaned over to get a better look at his face. Putting a hand on his shoulder and shook him, but found he was nothing but dead weight. She moved to his other side and knelt down to get even closer. Lennox felt the contents of the puddle surrounding him seep into the fabric at her knees. Glancing at the blood she thought was fake she noticed a long cut on his side coupled with another s-shaped cut on the side of his face. Lennox looked at her hand which was now red from her attempts to move him and felt her heart rate spike in seconds.

Dropping both phones, she stood. Every hair stood on end and her heart leapt into her throat. *This isn't fake…* Her eyes shot back to her hands then to Felix lying on his back. His eyes on the ceiling, unmoving. His once bright eyes were empty. Vertical sigils on his chin and right eye weren't the usual ashy black color, but silver. She knelt down beside him, tears and pink strands of hair blurring her vision.

"Felix?" His name came out with a dry whisper of disbelief. When she shook his shoulder, she could see that he was gone. His skin was already starting to lose its warmth and she could see a large wound in the center of his chest. Frozen to the spot her mind raced. *Wyatt, Wyatt should be upstairs.* "Felix... Wake up! WYATT! Wyatt, please! Where are you?!"

Silence. Complete and utter silence followed her broken screams. Another wave of panic sent shivers through her bones. *No... No no no. You can't be gone too.* Placing blood stained hands on the floor, Lennox gripped and pulled as hard as she could on the internal vine-like tether to her magic. The glow from the silver chain markings that wrapped her arms illuminated Felix's face. She tore her eyes away from him and closed them. Lennox reached into the stone the house was built out of. Anchored by the earth she momentarily felt the heaviness of each room. Searching, she found Wyatt and Felix's room. It felt the same as the others, empty. *He's not here... He's okay. Thank, Xemos.*

The sense of helplessness washed over her as for once she had no idea what to do. *Only one species of demon has a beating heart, and it's not his. CPR wouldn't work.* Her fingers went cold and she was suddenly deeply aware of the thudding of her own heart. Standing, she rushed to her phone, struggling to unlock it due to the blood on her fingers. She growled in frustration at her shaking hands.

She leaned against the doorframe and slid down the wood, wiping her hand on her jeans. After what felt like an eternity, it worked. She found the security team's contact and tried to ignore the tinted red fingerprints left over the glass of her phone. After pressing the call button, she put the phone to her ear. The other side rang a few times before someone finally picked up.

"Security desk, Cathwulf speaking." The familiar voice asked on the other end.

"I don't know what happened," she gasped. The realization their blood was all over her clothes came tumbling on top of her. "They're gone- I don't know what happened."

"Miss. Cade? What do you mean? Where are you?"

"Felix... Narcissus ... They're dead." Her voice broke as she said the words out loud.

"Wha- okay, it's okay. Lennox, I need to know where you are."

"Kappa, please- Just come."

"We will be right over, stay on the phone with me, okay?" The sounds of rustling and her talking into a walkie-talkie could be heard on the other end.

Within ten minutes campus security and the principal were at the frat house, the squeaking echo of the door sent a shiver down her spine. Out of the corner of her eye she saw them step through the entrance hall to find Lennox still planted against the doorframe, phone in hand. No matter how much she tried, she couldn't pull her eyes away from the red that stained their bodies, that stained the floor and now her very heart.

The Headmistress of the school, Ophelia Moon, glided over to the girl with a look of worry and fear along the sharp angles of her face. Lennox noticed the vampire's pause but didn't react as she still attempted to wipe the blood from her hands on stained jeans.

"Lennox, darling. Are you alright? What happened here?" Principal Moon asked calmly, her silver eyes watching her expressions.

Though she knew of the Headmistress's presence, the edges of her mind were coated in red as her thoughts spun. Lennox jumped at the sound of the woman's voice by her right ear. Dropping the phone in her hand once again, her heart raced as she turned her head towards the voice where she locked eyes with Ophelia. The Head of House stared without truly seeing.

"I- I thought it was a prank. They- He was..." Her words came breathlessly, not really hearing what she had asked but explaining. Denial. "He can't be... I saw him yesterday... He texted me hours ago..."

"It's okay, are you hurt?"

None of the woman's words made sense in Lennox's mind, tears welled up again as the demon choked out. "I- I don't know... I walked in and... There's so much blood... Felix... Elder Greene."

A hand met her shoulder, the touch sent adrenaline to course through her at the touch. "It's okay, you're safe now."

"NO! IT'S NOT OKAY! I DON'T CARE ABOUT ME, HELP THEM!"

Lennox screamed as rage suddenly took hold and got the better of her. *How can she not see it? They need help.* Her usually purple eyes flashed with a bright green glow as the magic fought to come out, confusing her grief for danger. She could feel her arms start to heat from the confined magic. The ground beneath them started to shake, and some branches from the bushes out front tried to worm their way in the door.

"Coyote and Cathwulf have it, breathe darling." Ophelia instructed calmly but with a strict undertone, turning to see the branches out of the corner of her eye.

When she realized what was happening, Lennox focused her attention on calming the storm brewing inside of her. She pushed clouds of grief down and looked into the woman's eyes as she encouraged her to breathe evenly. The security team, two werewolves easily spotted by silver streaks in their hair, walked past the two women over to the bodies. Head of security Coyote, bent down to Narcissus and Cathwulf made her way over to Felix. The demon's gaze drifted toward the scene to see their faces drop causing the tears to spill over again.

Deep down she knew they were gone, she had felt their cold skin and saw their empty eyes. However, she still rejected the idea that in a place she thought was so safe, there were now two people dead. Blinking to clear her vision once more, attention falling to the pools of red Coyote and Cathwulf were stepping around carefully.

"Darling, You don't need to see this-" She put her hands on either side of Lennox's shoulders trying to get her to look away from the sight of the two men, "-Come, let's go get you cleaned up."

"No," she refused to look away from the team, each talking quietly into their phones. *How could she expect me to leave? I can't leave him now, he wouldn't leave me.* She strained to hear who they were talking to.

"Miss. Cade, please." She asked kindly as Lennox finally met the Principal's eyes.

"I won't leave until they do." She wanted nothing more than to look over and see Felix laughing at her. *I'll never hear that sound again.*

Pausing, Principal Moon nodded seeing the determined look in her violet eyes. "We don't have to leave them yet, but let's go wait in the entranceway."

Finally she gave in and the two stood and Principal Moon took off her jacket, using it to replace where her hands had been. Lennox felt the gentle guiding push Ophelia gave toward the door, she allowed the action but tore her eyes away from her best friend only after they were out of sight. As she waited in silence with Moon she tried to make sense of what had happened here. He had texted her in the middle of the night, so he had to have been fine then, right? Was that him who sent that, or someone else? *No, it had to be him- the mom comment was something he did quite often. How did the hunters even make it here? Why were Felix and Elder Greene targets? How did they manage to kill two people **on** campus?* Sure, most everyone here was running from someone or something, but for them to just show up and start targeting peaceful people? It didn't make sense.

It was a while before a plain white van parked in front of the door to Kappa Theta. Two uniformed men got out and unloaded a pair of stretchers from the back. As they approached the stairs, Coyote and Cathwulf moved forward to meet them. Everyone on the scene was respectfully quiet and only spoke in hushed voices when words were necessary. Lennox was numb as she watched them enter the threshold. Her eyes followed them as they vanished into the common room. *I can't believe this is happening.*

Time passed slowly until they made their way back out. Sheets covered both men's faces. There was gut turning silence as they were loaded up and the van rolled away down the gravel road and drove through the iron gates into town. Lennox hadn't noticed Coyote and Cathwulf had stopped beside them and watched the van drive off. Letting her eyes drift to them, she noticed the slightly shaken expressions on their faces, the rage in Coyote's eyes. As far as she knew, this never had happened in the history of the school.

"Okay, I'm ready now…" She agreed to leave almost so quietly that the others almost didn't hear her.

With a small nod and a second to the security team, Principal Moon and Lennox made their way back out the door and to Omega Alpha. A few of her housemates were still milling around when Lennox entered with the principal. The red on her clothes peaked out from under the jacket she was given, catching the attention of one of them. Her housemate, Lealani, a faun-like creature stared from the doorframe of the common room, like she had sensed the unrest. Lennox pulled the borrowed jacket closer to her. Her eyes dropped to the floor as she tried to ignore the unwanted attention.

"Go wash off, I'll wait for you here. I'm going to have to talk to you in my office as soon as possible. I'm sorry." Principal Moon instructed softly.

Without a single word, Lennox made her way up the stairs to shower and change, thankful Rue was already in the main building to help some of the Elders with various chores before the first day.

An hour later Ophelia, Lennox, and Coyote all sat in the principal's office. The morning light drifted in through the open windows as she kept her eyes fixed on the grounds. Below her gaze fixed on the chapter houses, people walking in and out, either moving in or meeting with others still blissfully unaware of what had occurred. *How am I going to tell everyone?* Faces of her friends each with various reactions whipped past her mind's eye ending with Rue. The images of their faces almost brought Lennox to tears once again.

Her eyes followed the window ledge to the dozens of plants lining the windows where the principal had books tucked between. With a deep breath, she reminded herself of the task at hand. *Where was Wyatt? Whoever did this didn't kidnap him did they?* The sound of the man as he shifted beside her broke her thoughts as Coyote sat uncomfortably in his chair. The man was much too tall for it. Tension built within the silence while he quietly watched her face. Both he and Principal Moon sat with their attention on her. It was almost as if no one knew where to start.

"I need you to tell me everything you know and saw." The werewolf told her matter-of-factly with a hint of compassion layered underneath.

"Have you guys found Wyatt?" The question shot out, worry plain in her eyes.

"Yes, he was found in one of the dorm rooms in the main building. He's safe." Coyote confirmed quickly. "I know this is hard, but please. I need to hear your side."

"When Rue and I arrived at the school yesterday, he told us he and some friends from the main campus were going off for a ghost hunt. I-I know they always drink so I didn't think it was that suspicious when he texted me to meet a bit later." She stopped and took another breath. "I went back to sleep... I should have-"

Principal Moon stopped her next words. "If you would have gone a few hours earlier we could have lost you too. There wasn't anything you could have done, my dear. I'm sorry. "

The words burned in her mind, denial still strong in her system. There was a long list of things she could have done if she had shown up to Kappa Theta instead of going back to sleep and the three of them knew it. Principal Moon herself had helped when Lennox had begun being summoned by various witches for help, protection. She had watched Lennox take down other demons and creatures when parties became too rowdy. The words that burned like embers sent a wave of anger beneath her calm demeanor.

"I could have saved them."

"You can't save everyone, Miss. Cade. something I've also had to face the reality of." The woman's voice held a deep sadness only someone a millennia old would know.

"I can and I will. Every time." There was a short pause as the three of them looked between each other again. "You're more than welcome to check my phone…. Wherever it is."

"We have it, I just need the code to get in." Coyote spoke up once more. "You heard nothing after that?"

"No, not a word after that-" She shook her head knowing she would be a suspect until she was cleared. "It's 7373."

He nodded before leaning towards Lennox. "Now, tell me everything that happened this morning. Please don't leave out anything. You never know what could help in a situation like this."

Lennox started at the beginning, first when she was woken up in the middle of the night to Felix's text message. The room listened intently, Principal Moon couldn't seem to hide her emotions as she recounted walking into Kappa Theta. The pools of blood she thought were fake. Screaming for Wyatt and hoping he was okay. Ophelia looked at her in the same way she did when she entered the chapter house. Fear and sympathy was written in the lines of her exhausted gaze. Grief that caused Lennox's voice to break occasionally. Every word stung, each image so clear in her mind that she had to force herself to not break at the memory of the blood that had stained her only an hour ago.

Coyote seemed much better at hiding how he was feeling as he took notes, but she could still discern the sadness in his eyes. She drifted off her retelling when she made it to her calling for them. She had put up the wall between her emotions and magic before entering the room, knowing that her grief could cause the branches from the trees below to find their way inside. Lennox's now empty eyes peered at the Principal, as she finished as if she were miles away from the office.

"I'm going to have to ask your housemates to confirm you were in the house all night," he told her, putting his pen down.

"I understand…"

"We will find who's done this, I promise you," Coyote reassured her.

Lennox nodded, "Is that everything you needed?"

"Yes, I think so darling, why don't you go get some rest?" Principal Moon urged her. "We will inform the Chapter Houses in a bit, I sent word to have Rue meet you at Omega."

The room fell back into silence as Lennox stood and made her way out of the office. She was more than happy to retreat to the seclusion of her and Rue's room. She wanted to go back to sleep. Wake up to Felix texting her again, no matter what time it was. Walking back down the empty halls she felt her emotions starting to get the better of her again. Embers of hot anger burnt their way through the walls of her mind.

Her feet stopped just around the corner from an empty classroom and her heart started to race faster than her thoughts. *If I had just come to the house at the originally planned time… Maybe this wouldn't have happened. I could have been there in time. I could have stopped the hunters, they wouldn't have been prepared for me to show up to check on him.* She felt the coolness of the wall behind her, her arms wrapped around her as she slid down. Tears found their way back to her eyes as grief consumed her once more.

There was a familiar deep voice of the god of elemental magics, curses, academics, and necromancy in her mind that spoke, *"You would have been dead as well… Your time is not over. We have much work to do, the people here need you, Little Phoenix."*

Throwing her hands up, she fought with the voice out loud. "I don't care, I could have done something!"

"No, you couldn't have-"

"Then what use is my magic, huh?! Why does anything I do matter here?" She yelled loudly over his voice. "Then why am I called for help? It's all I've ever done, help people and I couldn't even help someone I loved! You promised me at my devotion to keep those I loved safe!"

"From the curse... You are devoted to me for a reason, Lennox. Everything will be revealed in time. The school needs you this year. You have this magic for many reasons, and I will keep you and your loved ones from your curse as is our deal."

"You didn't stop Val from breaking our deal early..." She accused the voice, it was a low blow and mostly unrelated, but she couldn't think straight.

"That was the end of your human life, my child. You were needed here. Now, remember that you represent me. Do not act irrationally. Your rage will lead you down the wrong path. Put your trust in me as you always have, Little Phoenix."

She paused as the familiar, comforting presence surrounded her, knowing when he called her by the nickname she wasn't to question what his plans were. Her deal with the voice replayed in her mind's eye, the promise of devotion she had made to the god for magic back when she was human. She didn't expect that deal to follow her in death, but it had. He had even come to save her from being stuck in hell after her death.

"I brought you here after I retrieved you from hell, you wanted to study as part of your devotional acts. Now go back to Rue. I will be with you."

His presence faded away on the next breath. After taking a few minutes to pull herself back together, she stood and made her way back to Omega Alpha. She opened the front door and hoped that everyone would pretend she didn't exist. Word of her coming home blood stained had to have made its way around the house by now. However, she came back to find Rue sitting on the stairs in the front entranceway, her head in her hands, waiting for Lennox. When she walked through the front door she saw her head shoot up. Rue stood quickly, the same look in her eyes as Principal Moon had earlier.

Lennox stood motionless in the doorway. Her eyes scanned over Rue for any injuries, paranoia taking momentary hold. Her deep golden skin was untouched, unstained from their best friend's blood, and for a moment it was as if her own hands were still coated. Rue's chest rose and fell steadily, calming her nerves as the world tumbled in. Neither of them spoke for a moment as Rue closed the distance and slowly wrapped her arms around her.

They paused in the entranceway before she felt a gentle guide from Rue toward the stairs. Without complaint she allowed herself to be directed to the stairs, down the hall and into their room. Rue opened the door and let Lennox go in first and closed the door with a soft click. She was already stopped in the middle of the room when Rue approached and gently pulled Lennox into her arms once more. They both cried, for how long she didn't know, but she didn't stop until tears refused to appear.

Rue put her forehead to Lennox's and ran a hand through her hair. Lennox lifted her eyes to peer into Rue's dark golden eyes, leaning her head into her palm a little. As the two held their gaze, she could see the tears still forming streaks down the edges of her face.

"I know you think there was something you could have done, but I don't know what I'd do if I lost you too."

"You would find happiness again."

"Not until I destroyed whoever tried to hurt you." Rue's voice dipped lower, a threat.

"As I would you… But I don't think I could ever love someone like I love you." Lennox let her hand drift to Rue's waist, pulling her closer. She was safe, here in her arms.

"You would, I'd want you to." Rue's hand slid to the small of her back, returning the desire for closeness.

Lennox paused, not wanting to think of a life without Rue. "The real question is who did this?"

"We will find out, love."

"I swear, I will personally drag whoever took him from us to hell… If it's the last thing I do," She vowed venomously.

Nodding in agreement Rue held Lennox still, neither of them letting go. She could feel the deep sadness emanating off of her, and knew that this also wasn't the first time she had lost someone she considered family. *Now a broken family of what once was five now down to four.*

"Did you tell Rosalyn?" Lennox asked, voice breaking.

"I called her, she and the others will be on the grounds in the next couple of hours."

"Thank you… I- I don't know if I could have been the one…"

"I know, but you've been through enough today. Someone has to care for you once in a while."

Lennox paused, watching the sad smile cross Rue's face. "You don't have to hide how much this hurts from me." Lennox whispered.

"You don't have to either." Rue led her over to the bed and put her hands on her knees as she bent down to sit. "You don't have to hide from me."

S tanding in front of the mirror, Lennox's gaze trailed over her attire. An all-black dress with a matching knit cardigan. *He would
hate all the black.* Adjusting the hem of her dress to cover more of the
black tights she was wearing she peered up to her reflection. Her empty
gaze blinked back at her. She had gotten good at pushing her grief aside
over the last few days. Pushing down the tears to only let them fall after
the sun did.

Students returned to the school a few days earlier than normal to
attend Felix and Elder Greene's funeral and wake. She had gotten her
phone back from Cathwulf the next day. Rosalyn and Wyatt had been
spending the majority of their time beside Rue and Lennox, the four of
them leaning on the other. Wyatt had stopped every morning to drag
Lennox out of bed with some new task they had to do within the house

or main building. It was annoying but she appreciated the distraction he was trying to give.

"Lennox, love? Are you ready?" She called as she peered around the open door.

"Yes, coming," she turned away from her reflection and opened the door to go downstairs with Rue.

When the two made their way to the edge of campus where the iron fence met the woods, they were met with a number of chairs set up with two photos and two closed caskets. Elder Greene on her left and to the right was Felix, each with a large photo on a stand at the head. Lennox's eyes fell on the photo of his bright smile frozen in time, the last few days hadn't felt real. Even now it was as if her mind could still convince her it never happened.

Everyone that had been at the school, Elders and students alike. All who had known the pair over the last few decades were in attendance, dressed in all black. Cathwulf was milling around the edge of a group of past Elders by the back row. Her eyes darted over the various groups. People were looking at the dozens of flowers that were brought by guests to the place by the photo. Lennox's eyes follow an Elder who had left the school over fifteen years ago and smiled sadly. *I wish it was for a happier event.* Quietly, Coyote came over and opened the two lids to allow others to place things beside the Head of House and Elder. She watched and didn't realize she had stopped as the Elder placed forget-me-nots at the base of each photo.

Lennox felt a soft tug on her arm as Rue led them to the photo of Felix. After a group of his housemates walked away to sit in the chairs, her eyes traced the photo for a moment before her gaze fell to her right. Felix laid in the casket, appearing as if he was asleep. The only reminder of his passing was still within the once deep markings, now as ashy gray as his skin. For a second the edges of her vision went red as she remembered the pool around him. Lennox wasn't stupid. The story of her discovering the two had spread around the small school. People would soon have their own theories, many too scared to admit that there could be Hunters on the grounds of one of their safe havens. The very threat most of them had come to escape.

The rage she had pinned under her grief fought to make its way to the surface. With a pull on the green thread of her magic, Lennox used the red in her memories to color the flowers she grew from the ground. The blooms moved their way up and over the edge of the casket. Slowly dozens of bright red poppies bloomed and she became aware that the drowning of quiet voices had softened. In the soft hum around her, she heard someone come up behind them and was met with the face of Coyote. His yellow eyes were filled with a much deeper sadness than when he had arrived on the scene. He didn't speak for a few seconds in which she let her attention drift back to the red poppy petals.

"When I came here, I promised I would protect everyone here... I failed this time." He told the two in a barely audible voice. "I will do everything in my power to make sure you're safe."

"We appreciate that, Coyote." Rue thanked him.

Lennox peered back over to meet his eyes, which watched her carefully as if worried. "Thank you." She told him and managed the slightest smile.

Without another word, he returned the smile and turned to meet Principal Moon who made her way to the podium. She had pulled her long silver hair into a tight bun paired with a long black dress that moved in the wind gently. The two men didn't have much family as was the case with most around here. Felix had Rue, Rosalyn, Wyatt and Lennox while Elder Greene as far as she knew was dating the Herbology

Elder, Willow Evington. The two had been together since well before she had arrived at school. Glancing around, she searched to find Elder Evington in the crowd masking tears. Her gaze was fixed on the photo of Elder Narcissus. Squeezing Rue's hand and letting go, she made her way over to Willow as Rue went to the front row to join their friends.

"He was a good man," Lennox told the Elder as she stood beside her.

Without moving, Elder Evington responded, "So was Felix-"

Before they could say anything more to each other, Principal Moon spoke up to the crowd. "Alright my darlings, would everyone please find a seat?"

Everyone started moving to their seats at the sound of the woman's voice. Lennox joined Rue and took her seat between her and Rosalyn. The weight in her chest became heavier as she saw the tissue clutched in her best friend's black lace gloved hands. Her short black and red streaked hair was curled away from her face. Her deep crimson eyes brimming with tears. Wyatt beside her had traded his usual graphic t-shirt for a matching black button up and tie under his usual black leather jacket, his long messy hair tied back in a bun.

"We have all come here to mourn the loss of two of our own. Head of House Felix Toll and Elder Narcissus Greene. We come to celebrate their lives and spend some time as a community to heal." Principal Moon started. Lennox was listening until her eyes fell on Felix's casket. The speech was nothing but chatter in the background as Lennox remembered her first day at SCHUni.

Twenty-four years ago Lennox had walked into the iron gates of the school for the very first time. Xemos had just rescued and brought her here from Hell after she was released from her deal with Val. It helped to be the god of curse-breaking in cases like this. Easy to walk into Hell and reclaim a soul already devoted to him. He told her about the school where supernatural creatures went to hide, study and live normal lives.

When she walked behind the iron gates for the first time, there was another demon with short silver hair sitting under a tree about ten feet away. When he heard the gate squeak open he looked over, smiled and immediately made a beeline for her. As he approached her gaze trailed the telling 'X' of a crossroads demon on his temples, coupled with some sigils going down one eye and on his chin.

"Hey! I've never seen you before. Coming to apply to the school?" The demon called over with a large smile that seemed plastered to his face.

"Actually yes, I didn't imagine such a warm welcome." She had felt Xemos vanish from the grounds once she crossed the gates.

"Yeah well, as long as I'm around someone will welcome you home."

"Pretty presumptuous I'll get accepted."

"Are you on the run from the law?" His smile faded into concern as his eyes darted around her.

Lennox turned to follow his gaze, her stomach sank as she thought maybe Val or Armaros would go against their irritated grovelings for a now broken deal. When she saw nothing but empty grass she looked back at him. "Uhhh- No I'm not."

"Good! Then you have no reason not to be approved. Felix Toll, Head of Kappa Theta." He held out a hand.

"Lennox Cade, you have a fraternity here?" He took her hand for a moment then dropped it back to his side.

"Of course we do! We got everything the humans do!" Felix smiled. "Why don't I show you to Principal Moon's office? Unless you already know where you're going."

"Actually that would be perfect, if you have the time,"

"My plans can wait, let me show you." Felix said with a swift turn on his heel and led her deeper into campus.

Her memories were interrupted by Rue who slid her hand into Lennox's with a gentle squeeze. As she peered over and met her concerned gaze and gave her hand a squeeze in response, a silent 'I'm here' as she returned to the moment. Rue gave her a small smile, tears stained her face as she returned her eyes to the front where Principal Moon was just finishing up her speech.

"I know we are all nervous with the recent events, however, we will make sure everyone here is safe and we will find who did this," Ophelia promised everyone in attendance. "Thank you all for coming today, please feel free to meet in the cafeteria for food or go back to your dorms to prepare for the first day of classes tomorrow."

The couple stood from their chairs as people started going in different directions and resumed their chats of memories. Glancing over to Wyatt and Rosalyn, Lennox could see the same desire to go home in their eyes. With a nod toward the Chapter House the others all turned silently to make their way back to Omega Alpha. Wyatt reached his arms around the group from between Rosalyn and Lennox as they went home.

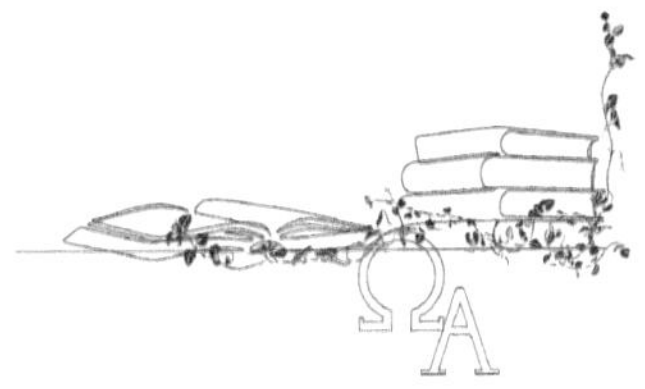

The four of them were holed up in Rue and Lennox's room over the next few hours. The friends drank, shared old stories, and occasionally let out a few more tears. Outside the window, the sky turned dark and the moon rose in the sky. Light from the lamp posts created constellations across the grounds outside the window. Wyatt had pulled out

Uno cards from Lennox's desk and started dealing when the demon stood with a small stumble. The others laughed at her stumbling as Rosalyn threw down a card in the center of their circle on the floor. She found herself genuinely laughing for the first time in days but quickly declared she was going to get tea from the kitchen before doing her nightly duties.

A dull thud echoed with each step down. The iron rail was cold under her fingertips. As she ran a free hand through her hair and turned into the kitchen to see Eden Miller stood at the granite counter. The high fae girl stood with her back to Lennox as she waited for the water on the stove to boil. She had her long midnight hair swept up into a bun, her long pointed ears sticking out the side. It seemed she had just returned from a late night run as she was dressed in tight black athletic wear, her face was slightly flushed.

Eden had arrived the previous year to join her family who taught in the human studies side at the school. Elder Eloise Miller, her mother as Lennox understood, taught Business Studies. While her two Uncle's Elder Richard and Arthur Miller taught Sociology and Engineering. The school hadn't seen such a large family unit in decades. Though high fae usually traveled together, it was exciting when the last Miller rejoined the family on the grounds of SCHUni.

"Hey, how was your summer?" Lennox asked with a small smile. "Did you and Bastien go on your trip around the world?"

Eden turned and gave her a polite smile, her amethyst eyes meeting hers. "We did. He just had to go hunt down the best pizza the world had to offer. How about you and Rue?"

"Good, we made it to Paris as you suggested."

"I'm sure it was beautiful as always." Eden answered as the kettle started to whistle. "Did you want any?"

"Please actually, lavender and mugwort if it's in there," Lennox requested.

"That's actually what I was already making," Eden told her and shook the jar of lavender.

She scooped out the mixture into two tea infusers, each into their own mugs and poured the boiling water in. The mug scraped against the countertop as she pushed the steeping tea across the counter. The woman leaned against it, her eyes searching the Head of House. Lennox knew she looked almost ghost-like. Rosalyn, Wyatt, or Rue hadn't said anything however she had seen her reflection. She knew exactly how her eyes revealed how haunted her nightmares were. How during daylight hours her gaze was glazed with grief

"Are you not sleeping well?" Her face changed to one of worry. "I knew you and Felix were pretty close. I couldn't imagine losing any of my family like that... To be the one to find them."

"I still see them, even when I close my eyes-"

There was a brief pause as Eden ran her finger nail over her thumb. "The faces of our dead loved ones I think remind us how important it is to focus on the living."

"Have you lost anyone?" Lennox's words came out almost too quiet.

"The faces of the dead haunt my dreams... I don't think that will ever change." Her eyes went to her mug.

"What do you do to help?"

A few pieces of hair fell from her bun as she remained quiet for a minute. The silence gave her the answer. She had found nothing that helped. "Maybe the tea will help you sleep better.."

"Cheers to hoping." Lennox smiled a bit at the girl and raised her mug.

The demon brought the cup to her lips and took a sip of the familiar earthy blend. She peered over at the open doorway as people passed getting settled in for the night and remembered it was time to close down the house. Returning her tired eyes to Eden and took another sip before speaking.

"Thank you for the tea, I have to get a few more things done around here. I'll see you in the morning for the First Day Breakfast Mixer." Lennox nodded to her concealing the pang she felt in her ribcage at the thought Felix wouldn't be there.

"Of course, I'll see you in the morning," Eden replied, making her way back to her room.

Lennox made her way around the house sipping her tea as she started doing her new nightly checklist. Lock the windows, check the backdoor, and make sure the balcony doors are locked. Lastly, once darkness fell over the grounds she locked the front door for the night. The process took all of ten minutes in which she finished her tea and went up the stairs once more. When she opened the door, she found the group still sitting in the middle of the floor with abandoned cards laid in front of them.

"Shit, Wyatt- I forgot to tell you the doors to the houses were about to be locked." Lennox placed her cup down on the table.

"It's fine, I'll crash with one of you guys tonight if that's cool?" Wyatt downed another shot as he finished his question.

"How about a group sleepover? First one of the new semester." Rosalyn suggested and stood to go grab things from her room.

"That's a great idea, you all can sleep here if you like. I'll go get the air mattresses." Rue agreed and made her way over to the closet by the bathroom.

Within twenty minutes, Rosalyn brought over extra blankets, pillows and a set of Wyatt's clothes from the last time they partied together. Lennox inflated the air mattresses with the help of Rue and everyone settled into their sleeping arrangements for the night. Wyatt posted closest to the door with Rosalyn at the foot of the bed. Crawling in beside Rue, Lennox pulled the blankets over them and wound an arm around her future fiancé's waist.

As her eyes closed, Lennox imagined all the ways she could propose, still not having found the perfect way just yet. With dreams of possibilities she fell into a deep sleep. However, soon after the sound of her alarm played loudly. Her violet eyes shot open and found the night had faded already, light streamed in through the window. She rolled over to face Rue but was met with a wall and vines between where she normally slept. Her eyebrows met as she touched the wall. Tiredly, she pulled on the green thread of magic and tapped the barrier to command it to move. Silence on the other end, not a single leaf twitched. With a sigh, she forced the branches aside to find Rue's spot empty.

Sitting up she checked her phone, nothing from Rue. It was odd. Usually, if Rue was up before her she would text her some sort of good morning. She moved from the bed and picked up her cardigan from the back of the pink fur computer chair on the way out, noticing Wyatt and Rosalyn were now gone along with any signs they were ever there. For a second she listened for any movement outside her down however the house was completely silent. Walking into the hall, her gaze drifted around the halls and noticed that a few of the photos on the walls looked a little crooked. Carefully she went through the hall to the stairs. Holding her breath, she stopped halfway down the stairs and peered around the corner to the front entrance. The door was wide open, the early morning sunrise illuminating the bottom of the stairs.

Quickly, she made her way down and slammed the door shut. It popped back open with a loud and low creak as it moved back toward her. Her gaze drifted to the lock to find it completely busted with what looked like a hammer. Lennox's heart sank into the pit of her stomach. Her head snapped behind her and she could feel her heart trying to leave her chest.Her screams for Rue echoed through the house as she peered around the entranceway for any signs of her. No reply came and her feet carried her forward. Everything seemed to move in slow motion as she went into the main common area.

Rue lay in the middle of the floor, surrounded by a pool of bright red blood, the same way she had found Felix. Running over, she knelt down feeling the same dampness in her jeans from less than a week ago. Red stained her hands as she shook Rue, ashy gray replacing the black markings on her face.

"No... No- No! Rue!" Lennox rolled her on her back, looking into her blank eyes.

With a panicked gasp, Lennox sat up in bed. *Where is she?!* Her eyes searched around the dimly lit room for her, trying to get her bearings. A set of arms suddenly wrapped around her and pulled her in. Her whole body started to shake as the tears spilled over. Rue held her tightly to her, whispering reassurances into her ear. After a few minutes her body finally stopped. Lennox looked up at her with an agonized expression.

"Hey- You're okay," Rue's voice came from beside her.

"It was you."

Rue's face fell a little barely seen in the darkness. "You don't have to worry about that."

"But I do- Anyone could be next," she argued, barely louder than a whisper.

"I know, but it won't be one of us. We will make it out of this. Remember that time we got away from those Italian hunters?"

"If it wasn't for you, we'd still be down there."

"We have absolutely nothing to worry about. Between the both of us, we will help keep everyone in Omega Alpha safe." Rue paused. "I'm sure whoever is going to be appointed as the new Head of Kappa Theta will do the same."

"I hope it's not some new guy, honestly. I'm sure they'll offer Wyatt the spot?"

"If they did, there's no way he would have not said anything. Unless Principal Moon thinks that maybe a fresh start would be a good thing." Rue suggested with a yawn.

"Well, whoever it is has a lot to live up to… The last thing Kappa needs is some party boy as a Head of House. He's going to have to take all of this seriously, especially with Hunters around."

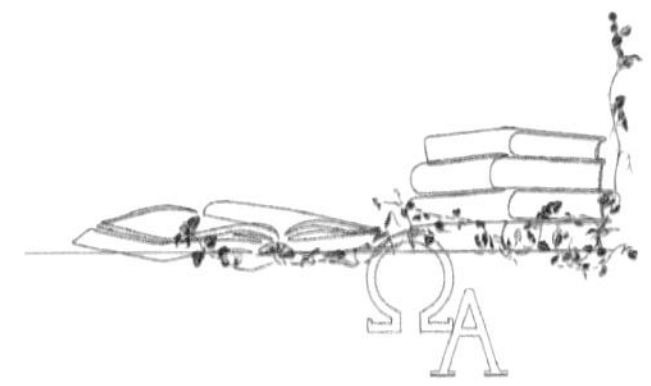

The two made their way downstairs hand in hand to start the yearly tradition of hosting breakfast for the First Day Breakfast Mixer. The first-day tradition had started three years after she arrived and became Head of House for Omega Alpha. Felix had come to her and asked if she had any ideas for new gatherings the houses could do. He had explained the two two needed to get to know each other more as at least half of each had started pranking the other. She had remembered a tradition from her human life with her Aunt Arya and explained how she would always cook a big meal for her and friends on the first day of school. Felix had loved the idea and instantly set to work in the kitchen beside her the first day of classes. This was the very day Lennox met

Rue. A new student and member in the Chapter House that Lennox couldn't keep her eyes off of. Felix had coaxed her to sit beside her and instantly she found herself with butterflies.

As the memories of their first meeting flooded her mind, Lennox felt the pang of grief she was growing accustomed to settle in her stomach. Only a gentle squeeze on her hand made her remember it was time to set to work as they turned into the empty kitchen. Usually, Felix would have made his way over by now to help set tables and Wyatt would help recruit the people in Kappa to come to eat all the food. However, this time it would only be the former doing that job. *I guess whoever is the new Head didn't get the text I sent.*

Lennox moved to grab her phone to check the message where Wyatt had given her a number. It seemed he had it memorized since there was no name listed with the numbers. She followed Rue instead when she called her over to start the coffee. The three machines bubbled as they brewed full pots. As steam wafted up, she got to work on the scrambled eggs and the pancake batter while Rue set the tables.

The smell of breakfast wafted through Omega, which drew people down from their rooms easily enough as they woke to go to class. The room slowly filled with her housemates and Lennox smiled as Eden was the first to come down and take a plate. She was quickly followed by her roommate Plague, horsemen of disease. Next one of Lennox's friends came down. Donnie Bane, Crossroad Demon and twin to Val Bane, the one who made the deal with her that sent her soul down to Hell. *The very demon who was too lazy to torture me herself.* Their similarities had been difficult for Lennox to deal with, but after two semesters she stopped jumping when she saw Donnie out of the corner of her eye.

A knock echoed from the door, which Rue answered. A drove of students from Kappa Theta found their way in and straight to the food.

They still came, even after the rumors. The sight caused a smile to tug at Lennox's lips. Bastien Miller, Eden's cousin, made his way over to her. He pushed his chestnut hair out of his matching eyes and joined the other Omega's. A bright smile crossed his face as he was followed by his housemates and her friends Wyatt Steele, Octavius Whitlock, and a new guy she had never seen.

Letting her smile widen, she accepted the side hug Wyatt offered as he was the first to close the distance. Lennox's eyes followed him for a moment, noticing the jean jacket and red bandana that kept his dirty blond hair from his face. The look was finished off with a snarky smile which made him look like a typical human frat boy. *Don't judge a book by its cover.*

Octavius followed from the back in attempts to give his long spider-like legs some space as they tried to tug into his back. The newer members of Omega Alpha watched wearily from their seats. Octavius, the black widow-human hybrid with skin as dark as the night sky and warm star-like undertones, always brought up people's most common fears. His narrow face and high cheekbones highlighted his handsome features and kind lavender eyes.

Wyatt on the other hand caught plenty of attention with his plethora of tattoos, above average height, and stormy irises. That very storm suddenly drifted past Lennox which sent her attention behind herself. Eden sat beside Bastien as he spoke excitedly about something Lennox couldn't hear. She glanced back to the Crossroads Demon who seemed to only have eyes for the woman. She had seen the look only a handful of times on the man's face. Eden Miller would be the next person he would try to win over. Though Eden herself had never been seen flirting with anyone and had turned everyone down at parties when she did attend them.

"Hey there Nox! Look who I brought! How are you doing?" Octavius asked as he peered around the room for Rosalyn, Lennox guessed, while Wyatt stared and the new guy continued to speak, not noticing his friend's distraction.

"Hey!" Wyatt's gaze broke from the raven haired girl. "I got them all out of bed!"

Octavius folded his arms over his chest. "Yeah, well I helped get them out the door."

"It doesn't matter, as long as they came to eat the food." Lennox smiled. "Thank you for bringing them... Felix, he- He loved this tradition."

"I know, and we'll keep it going- No matter what- Right, Aron?" Wyatt swiftly seemed to try to bring things back to a positive note which dulled the pang in her chest.

Oh, yeah totally!" The new guy, Aron, ran a hand through his hair and let out a chuckle as he spoke. "I don't think anyone would hate on some free food to start the day."

Lennox's eyebrow twitched as from the corner of her eye she saw Octavius spot Rosalyn and vanish over to her table. From beside Aron, Wyatt's gaze had found its way to Eden once again and appeared to be deciding how he was going to talk to her. Doing her best to hide her distaste for the comment since that's not what any of it was about, she allowed her smile to remain in place.

"How are you enjoying Kappa Theta? Have you met your Head of House?" Secretly, she was hoping this man had some information on this mystery.

Aron's half smirk turned further upwards as his eyes lit up. "Everytime I look in the mirror, actually."

"You're the new Head of House for Kappa?" Lennox failed to bite back her words.

"Don't sound so surprised," he puffed up his chest slightly. "I may be new but I think I can handle it. Where is your Head of House?"

"You've found her."

"You're Lennox Cade?" He sized her up for a moment. "Let me guess, your bite is bigger than your bark?"

"Don't sound so surprised," she tossed his words back, her gaze darkening.

"Spunky, I like it." He smirked deviously.

For a moment, neither of them spoke as his forest green irises darted over her face in attempts to discern what kind of demon she was. Her face remained an unwavering smile as it was quite normal upon meeting another demon as their stories were usually marked across their face in some way. Aron's gaze followed the six dots split into two sets of three at the outer edge- top and bottom of her eye sockets. Then to the marking in the center of her forehead, the symbol of Xemos. A trident shape with a horizontal line in the middle with three dots down either side of the points. It appeared after she was released from her deal with Val. Lastly, to each of the four white X's, set two under the corner of her eyes near her nose. The other set at the top of her cheekbone marking her as a sold-soul demon. The four markings had previously been deep black, however, when Xemos pulled her from Hell, they faded into something close to scars.

She did the same, her eyes following the black line from his forehead to his chin with three stitch-like markings going down the bridge of his nose. The line crossed over the center of his face where two more sets of three stitches lay. At the end of the line sat the markings she was looking for, a set of tilted crosses at the top of his cheekbones. *Crossroads demon.* Lennox shifted to her heels and felt her heart rate pick up, Wyatt and Donnie were the only two she had been able to trust in this lifetime. The others she had found were just as ill intentioned and conniving as Val was.

Aron's eyes lingered on her pale scars for longer than she preferred. She cleared her throat to break his attention from the part of her story she hated the most. His eyes snapped back to hers and she realized curiosity sprung to life, his smile faltered as he seemed to notice her shift in demeanor. Wyatt must have taken notice as he stepped beside Lennox, looping his arm through hers catching her attention. The moment she looked up to him, she felt peace return and a more genuine smile appeared.

"I think it's time we all get some food?" Wyatt smiled and pulled her toward the food table, the others followed suit behind them. Momentarily, she felt his head next to hers as he whispered in her ear. "Give him a chance Len, he cares about people. I know he's not Felix but I've known him for a while and he's a good guy."

Another pang- Another flash of Felix laying in a pool of blood- Lennox flinched and kept her eyes on the coffee pot in front of her. "I need a partner that will help me protect everyone in these houses, can he do that?"

"I can, and I will." Aron's voice came from her left side as he stood beside her, waiting for his turn for a cup of coffee.

"Will you?" Lennox questioned before anyone could stop her. Images of Elder Narcissus and Felix flashed in her mind's eyes. "Because it seems you're only here for the free food."

His forest eyes filled with shadow. The previous smirk was wiped from his lips as he looked down at her. "Look- I know what I need to know about what happened to the previous Head of Kappa. How you were the one to find him and as I understand the grieving process.

What I don't appreciate assumptions made about me. So, of course Lenny-Boo, I will help you protect everyone here but first you need to get over whatever is going on here."

For a moment, Lennox was rendered speechless. Flames dully sparked to life inside his pupils as his smirk returned at her lack of comebacks. Lennox bit her tongue and pulled out a mug and filled it as Aron spoke once again.

"When I was asked to be the new Head of House I got a list of everyone here. Although, when I read your name I didn't quite expect *this*. When I asked Wyatt about you, he painted you quite differently. I hope to meet that version of Lennox Cade next time."

"How did Wyatt paint me?" She asked and met his eyes again.

"Much more accepting- not judging a book by its cover. Though the spunk he told me about is definitely still intact. Maybe once that chip on your shoulder towards me falls off we'll be able to get to know each other on a more... Personal level?"

This time, her face flushed as annoyance bubbled to the surface as his tone turned soft and flirty. *He is not trying to hit on me right now.* From the corner of her eyes, she noticed Wyatt looking between them, seeming to deliberate on intervening or letting the entertainment continue.

"I do not have-" She started to speak, venom leaking into her voice as someone approached behind her.

"Grief and tragedy do strange things to people." Rue's light voice came up behind her and Lennox felt her arm wind around her waist.

The man eyed the couple, his flirty demeanor shifted in seconds when he noticed. "Lenny Boo has a girlfriend? NICE! Good choice, she's cute."

His eyes returned to her and he lifted a hand for a high-five. When Lennox didn't return the gesture he put his arm back down to his side.

"Got it, we are serious."

"Don't worry, she'll come around." Wyatt reassured Aron.

"You two seem to already have kindled a friendship." Rue commented, turning to Wyatt.

"We actually have known each other from various deals over the years." Wyatt explained quickly.

"Yeah, we met in Texas when we both turned up at one of the crossroads." Aron reached over and fluffed Wyatt's hair.

"Sounds like destiny that you're here together! Glad you made it safe to SCHUni." Rue smiled.

The group made their way over to the food where Lennox took a few things before they went her way over to an empty sitting area in the common room. Aron and Wyatt both had tall stacks of pancakes on their plates and were already locked in conversation as they ate. The hum of conversation filled the silence.

"How are the pancakes?" Rue smiled at the two men.

"The pancakes are good... ummm-"

"Rue," she answered his unspoken question.

"Aron, new Head of Kappa."

"Oh, well good to meet you. Hopefully you two will find your groove eventually." Rue shot a look at Lennox.

"I think eventually she'll see I'm not as bad as she thinks." Aron finished the last of his breakfast.

"She's right here." Lennox spoke up.

"I'll talk to you when you're ready to play nice." Aron stood from his chair and turned to Wyatt who was finishing his coffee and watching Eden and Bastien out of the corner of his eye. "I guess I'll see you love birds around, I'm grabbing some to go coffee before class. Gotta go meet all your Omega's. Maybe I'll catch a few numbers. Wyatt? You want some coffee and a wingman?"

Wyatt's eyes snapped to Aron. "I got your back, I'll catch up with you later Nox, Rue!"

Aron winked as he turned away and made his way into the kitchen with Wyatt. Lennox peered at Rue with an annoyed expression. Before she could get up to go to class Octavius, Donnie, Bastien and Eden all came over. Though Lennox kept Aron in her line of sight as he talked to a group of women by the coffee pot. After only a few seconds she noticed that Wyatt kept peering over at Eden who had her back to him. *Normally if someone catches his attention he's not so shy about it, I wonder-.* Octavius's voice caught her attention.

"Pancakes are supposed to be round, dude."

"They can't be all perfectly round!" Rue argued.

"Why are you even complaining about the shape of them? They still taste the same," Donnie rolled her eyes at Octavius.

"Because I can!" He took his seat and started into his food shaking his shoulders to adjust where his legs would sit against the back of the chair. "Besides, who says I'm even complaining?"

"Sounds like your problem," Bastien told them from his spot at the table by Eden.

"Yeah, you should be happy there's even anything left." Eden teased, motioning to the almost empty area of food.

"Yeah yeah yeah-" Octavius waved one of his free spider arms nonchalantly

They all laughed as people finished their breakfast and started making their way to the school. Slowly, each person stood from their chairs and made their way out. When it was just Rue and Lennox, Rue turned to her. Her once hidden concern now reflected in her eyes.

"Are you sure you'll be okay here cleaning up?"

She nodded and pulled her hair into a small bun at the top of her head, pieces falling out at the bottom. "I'll be fine, don't worry about me, love. Someone has to clean up."

"Okay, if you need me, remember I'm a text away." Rue smiled and kissed Lennox before making her way to her first class.

Lennox went over and put away the leftovers and washed the dishes. The house was silent and she found herself lost in her thoughts as she had often been recently. Shaking her head, she turned on the music. She started to sway to the music and found herself finally feeling relaxed for the first time in days. Sliding the dishes into their spots Lennox went over to the corner she had put her bag in earlier and went out the door to go to her first class, chemical sciences with Elder Lucian Clyde.

Eden

Five empty boxes sat on the top of a single bed against the wall. Eden placed jars of herbs on the small dresser that she had brought from her family home on the other side of campus. The sounds of chatter of a few of her housemates trickled under the door. After placing the last jar down she eyed the box she had accidentally dropped on her way up. Thankfully, none of the shattered glass had found a way out.

She moved to the bed and opened her phone. It was her third mission mostly alone. She had trained to be a hunter almost every night for well over a decade with her adoptive mother, Eloise Miller. Now, they were on one of the biggest missions The Salvamari had attempted in their generation. Exterminate each of the seven supernatural schools and societies from within.

When she was sixteen, Eloise had brought the family to the grounds. Every night for five years Eden prepared to walk among the community. Eloise started teaching while her brother, Basiten attended classes on an assignment for The Salvamari. Eden remained inside the house where she would prepare for her next step as the next Matriarch with her grandmother, Stacey. During those five years, Eloise would tell the others she wasn't interested in attending due to her "desire to travel." Where in reality, she wasn't old enough to fit in as a college student. It wasn't until she was almost twenty she joined Bastien. With only five years between herself and Bastien, they acted and were viewed more like siblings.

After all the years of training, the family fit in well. They allowed four years to pass to gain trust among the others on campus. The Salvamari had planned the mission to go slow and now that every member was settled in place it would be time to start moving forward. It was easy enough with a common name like Miller to cut off any connections to the well known hunter clan.

The Millers, a matriarchal family within The Salvamari, with a widespread reputation of being some of the most heartless of hunters around the globe. Each with their own Head's of Family, their unit was run by Eloise. Eden, her only child, adopted or not, was next in line for the position of Matriarch. She had trained since the age of seven to take over for her mother at a moment's notice as was tradition. The Salvamari were mostly made up of various families, and occasionally others who had been hurt in some way by the supernatural world.

In 1852, the Miller family started hunting independently when

Eloise's great-great-grandfather, Roy Miller, died leaving his wife and daughter behind. He had been fishing on the nearby coast when a siren happened to cross his little boat and lure him into the water. Roy's death caused his wife, Ethel Miller to start trying to get revenge on any siren she could find, which soon progressed to all supernatural creatures. After twenty years of hunting, Ethel met Atlas Holloway during one of hunts for werewolves with her daughter, Astrid. The two families had built a name for themselves by being called to several towns to rid them of dangerous creatures.

The Salvamari wasn't created until the second chance meeting of the two families when a town had called both to deal with demons and vampires plaguing them. It was after three weeks of working together that Ethel and Atlas decided they would be able to accomplish their missions and protect each other as a unit. From then on, Atlas, his wife Nymeria and children traveled beside Ethel and Astrid from town to town. For ten years the families offered five more spots to spread themselves further than anyone had done before, their cruel ways being sung about in taverns and followed them everywhere they went. Thus, upon the death of Ethel, Astrid and Atlas created The Salvamari with three matriarchal families, Donovan, Miller, and Reyes, and four patriarchal families, Holloway, Belmore, Sullivan, and Moore.

Eden walked over to her desk and scooped up the intel notebook she had kept over the years. The red spiral spine held together well however the pages were well worn after all the notes from Bastien. Opening the book, she scanned the names she had taken down. Each with a note beside telling what species of creature they were. *The next target could be anyone of these.* As she continued to flip through the book she spotted the list she kept of all her victims. Her amethyst eyes fell on the most recent name, Felix Toll.

Her hand brushed over the underside of her left wrist where lay a matching tattoo to the rest of her family. The Compass, an all black needlepoint star with a curved letter "S" tilted vertically along the center. One one curve sat three dots and on the opposite side sat four more to represent the seven families. Originally, it was designed with magic by Atlas when he learned families had become separated during missions for multiple days and made an easy way to reunite with each other. This would only be given by each Head of Family when the next generation reached the age of fifteen. The oath lasted a lifetime as did the connections through The Compass. That was until the first Heretic, Nikoli Miller, son of Matron Astrid Miller and Baron Sterling Welsh. As she knew the story, the man had helped to free an angel that had been caught by Cyprus Cade and the Miller's. The night Nikoli was banned from the family, Stacey the Matriarch at the time, grabbed his wrist. He had let out a scream of pain and a large "H" appeared over his tattoo. His ability to track the family, lost.

When Eden arrived at the family home, she and Bastien became all but attached to the hip. They spent their years being trained by Eloise, Stacey, Richard, and Arthur. Each had their roles to prepare for and as Bastien a Baron he would train to fight alongside and protect Eden during her duties before and after becoming Matriarch.

Flinging herself onto the bed, she stared at the ceiling as scenes from the other night played in her mind. Felix with his head poked around the corner to find the Elder already shackled and yelling for the student to make a run for it. She however, had been faster. With a tug of the internal blue thread, she blocked his exit with a gust of wind. Suddenly, Eden's phone buzzed demandingly from her bedside table. As she looked to see who it was she saw her mothers name flash across the screen.

Mom-
Meet me at Crossroads Coffee Shop in 15?
-Sent 10:21am

Eden Miller-
Sure, I'll be right there
-Sent 10:22am

Eden approached the coffee shop just outside of the school gates. The small gray building with large red windows spelled out the words 'Crossroad Cafe' in big white letters on the glass. It sat between a local bookstore and convenience shop. The windows were barley covered by a few trees and bushes in front of the windows. The raven-haired girl opened the door and peered around the shop for Eloise. There were only a few small tables spread around the shop, her mother sat in one off to the side. The woman was easy to spot no matter how much she tried to blend in. Her medium length brown hair as per usual was tied into a bun. The look was paired with her classic royal blue turtleneck and black jeans. All that was missing was the weapons belt that only left her waist when she was inside the school. *The perfect blend into the wall outfit.*

Eden made her way over to the table and sat across from her, allowing a smile to come to her face. Eloise read over the menu in front of her as she turned the black star sapphire ring on her finger. Set in yellow gold with a beaded halo around a dark stone that showed its beauty in the light momentarily before it returned to the regular onyx color. The Matriarch's ring looked as ordinary as any other jewelry however. Set inside the ring was the very stone stolen by Ethel. A treasure won from the siren who killed Roy. A trophy. One that held the ability to give the wearer magic. Now, the Miller line used to give them magic. It was only a few seconds before Eloise peered over the rim of her black framed glasses.

"A few minutes early, good." Eloise praised as Eden sat across from her. "How are you settling into your new dorm?"

"Good, I've met my dorm mate. Plague, Horseman of disease. Although some of my herb jars seem to have shattered in the process of the move."

"We'll get you some new ones." The Matriarch waved her hand. "Such accidents are bound to happen."

"It's how we pick up the pieces." Eden quoted her mothers words back.

"What can I get you two?" A male voice asked, halting their conversation.

Eloise looked over as the young centaur stopped at their table. She quickly put on a fake smile which Eden knew disguised disgust. "Coffee black please."

"I'll have a macchiato, cold with extra espresso." Eden requested.

"Coming right up," he smiled at them and made his way back towards the coffee machines.

Eden turned to Eloise, happy to see her. Each had spent the summer on separate missions in various countries with other members of The Salvamari. Her mother was usually pretty cold towards everyone, except for her. Even then, her softness was only in her eyes as she watched over a spell or training. This was a stark contrast from Greer Donovon, the Head of the Matriarchs. Eden had spent the summer with the family a few years back. Greer had a kind demeanor. She was surprised at first. However, it was soon stifled when they went on their first hunt of the summer the day after she arrived accompanied by her daughters Victoria and Rosemary.

Eden knew where her mother had gotten her demeanor from. The apple never fell too far from the tree, especially in this family. Her Grandmother and Matron of the Miller family, Stacey, wore the same neutral expression permanently on her face. That was however until she saw Eden. The Matron had retired from most hunts allowing Eloise to take over. Though, much to her daughter's distaste visited often to check on the family. During her visits, she would make it bluntly obvious Eden was her favorite. She had even come in to check on her while she was with the Donovan family to see how her training was progressing, always excited to see her magic transform.

The centaur made his way back over to the silent table with their coffees and swiftly left. Both women lifted their coffees and took a few sips. Eden glanced at her mother and noticed she was deep in thought about something. It was then she started to connect the dots. This wasn't just your average catch-up. Something had happened and Eloise had to tell her something she didn't want to. Eden opened her mouth to speak but Eloise raised a finger. The black stone momentarily glowed dully. The world around them fell into mostly muffled silence.

"Do you have your silver knife?" Eloise questioned her as if this were a test.

Eden kicked her leg lightly and motioned toward it with her head. "Has something happened?"

"Are your mental wards secure?" Another question, another attempt to avoid the topic.

"They are iron clad. Mother, what-"

"Everyone is fine, Eden I-" Eloise's face fell. "This is the year we start the mission."

"I know, we've already started." Her eyebrows joined in confusion.

Eloise paused, her eyes scanning her face. "Have you seen anything of interest?"

"Aside from the new Head of Kappa? I thought everyone here was of interest to us."

Before she spoke Eloise let out a long breath, watching her daughter's eyes intently. "There is someone of interest here. Specifically to you- Your *birth mother*. She attends this school and I think it's time, due to the mission at hand...And she'll be a target... You should know."

Eden fell silent for a moment, the words birth mother hit her like a smack in the face. Every person she had met over the last year in Omega Alpha ran through her mind. *How does she know? How long has she known?* She felt her smile fade, replaced by shock as she shifted in her seat.

"If she's here... That means she's one of them-"

"Yes Eden, I'm afraid she is." Her tone was flat but Eloise shifted as if uncomfortable with the conversation, looking at her almost apologetically. "I did some digging some years after I adopted you and found her... Well, *it*. Come to discover, it was a crossroads deal gone bad."

That only leaves a handful of possibilities. Eden's eyes didn't move from her mothers face. She'd always known she was adopted. Everyone within The Salvamari knew it too. It was something Eloise never hid. But this she seemed to have known for years until it was necessary to be told. Her stomach turned with the taste of betrayal but quickly shoved it aside. *Eloise isn't a woman of many words, she has her reasons.*

"Who is she?" Eden asked, unsure if she wanted the answer.

After a very short pause she gave her the name, "The Head of Omega House, Lennox Cade."

Her body went stiff and she sat back in her seat, clenching her jaw as she looked at her mother. She had always wondered who had abandoned her at the orphanage, even though Eloise had always been her mother in her eyes. *How could she allow me to go to school here for a full year and not say anything?* At first she had wrongly assumed that whoever it was had just arrived. A good excuse as to why this never mattered before. Now, she came to understand it was because she had walked past Lennox every day. Eloise had purposefully left this fact out of the briefing they had the day before going after the Elder and Felix.

Eden grew up knowing most demons were self-interested, soulless manipulators and nothing more than a void. However, with all of this knowledge she had, she couldn't help but feel slightly conflicted. Lennox didn't seem like one of the bad ones. In fact, she had never seen her mad even when Felix hid every one of her textbooks across campus. Although, her mother had always told her they seemed normal until they came across a human to manipulate.

"If you found her... Do you know why she left me there?" Eden asked, only allowing her tone to break on one word.

"Honey, she's a demon now. If that tells us anything it is that she's selfish now and was selfish then. She is a Sold Soul demon. The most self-serving, conniving species of them all. I think we should be thankful she left you instead of corrupting an innocent soul. You are a human dear, *I* made sure of that. As far as I know, your father was also human but died before you were born. However, for your mother, I believe she's also some kind of witch which is why your magic came so easily to you."

Eden chose her next words very carefully, knowing how some of this might seem. The sensible part of her screamed at her that none of it mattered. No matter how much she wanted to go ask Lennox everything she ever wanted to know. Every why and get out all the pent up anger she hid from being left. Eloise was right, she should be grateful, and she was but her curiosity got the better of her.

"What if she's not like them? Is there a chance she's different? I mean Lennox has never done anything to hurt anyone there."

The Matriarch's eyes darkened. "I thought I taught you better than to question me like this? I've given you all of the information I've gathered, there's nothing more and I don't think we need to go digging further."

"I- Yes mother. You're right... Thank you." Eden nodded looking at her coffee still sitting between her hands.

"Now, onto the smaller fish to fry. You have a housemate named Rue, yes?"

Her heart sank into her stomach as guilt made its way to the surface. "Yes-"

Eloise shot a glance around the room before giving her daughter a satisfied look, with her compliance she spoke again. "That's the Eden I know. This could be your revenge on Lennox. Crumble her world to the ground before we go for her."

Get your target alone, they will never be able to win against the many. Eloise's words reflected in Eden's mind. This was her chance to prove that this new information wouldn't shake the morals that had been trained into her.

"I won't let you down, mother." Eden agreed to the mission without pause.

"Good, I'm sure you won't," Eloise said approvingly while drinking her coffee. "Now, what classes are on your roster?"

Eden pulled out her phone thankful for the switch in conversation. "I have Predator and Prey Studies, Witchcraft and its Applications, English Literature, and Psychology."

"Smart choices," her mother sipped her coffee. "I have a feeling they will come in handy this year. Especially after the stunt you and Bastien pulled at Kappa Theta. Maybe you'll be able to do it, cleaner. You know how to lead, I've shown you that. You should have taken charge and made Bastien help you move them to the woods."

Eden's words caught in her throat as well as the coffee she was drinking, *shit.* She had told Bastien they needed to move to a different location. However, they had seen the security team close by and didn't want to risk being seen. She wanted to defend herself and Bastien but she knew it wasn't any use. They had killed them right inside the dorm where anyone could have come in to discover them. The scent of fresh blood or even a locked door could have drawn the werewolves to them.

"Yes, Mother- it won't happen again,"

"Good." Her mother finished the rest of her coffee. "I'm sorry to leave you but I have to go to my class room and finish setting up my classes. I will see you tomorrow."

"I understand." She eyed her own barely touched coffee, under-standing she was expected to sleep at Omega tonight.

The woman stood and made her way out of the coffee shop, heels clicking lightly on the floor. A few people took notice as Eloise passed them. She always walked with her eyes up, moving with an air of confi-dence and power. The bell at the top of the door sounded as the woman left. Eden let out a deep breath and went back to her coffee. *I can't believe this... I need to tell someone.. But who can I trust?* Her head spun and she needed someone who wasn't her mother. Within seconds she had her phone out, her fingers dancing across the letters.

> Eden Miller-
> Are you alone? I need you to meet me somewhere.
> –Sent 11:28 am

> Bastien Miller-
> I swear if you're just trying to get me to move something in your room, I'm going to smack you. I'm not on campus but I'll be at the house around 4, is that okay?
> -Sent 11:32 am

> Eden Miller-
> Fine, I'll see you then.
> - Sent 11:40 am

Eden took her coffee and left to get back to the Miller home. Swiftly, she made her way through the gates to campus, past the chapter houses and main building, to the street leading to the Elder's homes. Each house was slightly different but made from the same fieldstone and brick of the school. *What if he doesn't believe me? What if someone else hears us?* All the thoughts of how this could go wrong filled her mind. However, their home was the safest place for this conversation despite the potential risks. *What if he thinks I'm not human?* The thought shoved its way to the forefront of her mind causing the hair on the back of her neck to stand. *Death.* That's what it would mean.

She shook her head fighting off the thoughts and turned to the last two-story house on the tiny street. She made her way past the garden and up the three stairs to the red front door. With a quick click of the lock, she pushed the door open. Eden took off her shoes and went to the stairs, avoiding the paintings clustered all over the hallway of various members of The Salvamari. The smooth wooden handrail slid under her hand as she went to the first door on the right, slipping into her room.

Walking in, her eyes drifted around to the various gold frames, mirrors, and candle holders on shelves along deep blue walls. She snapped her fingers and the candles around the room sparked to life with soft light. Shells she had brought back from various countries shone light off their smooth surfaces. Coupled with the light from the windows, it was bright enough to see clearly. Eden turned to her desk and opened her laptop which sat between two large gold candles. An extra large selenite tower easily seen from behind the screen, her favorite in her collection.

A feeling of calmness washed over Eden as she put in headphones turning on her favorite playlist. The music finally silenced the racing thoughts that threatened to overtake her. Within seconds, she started to daydream about what her life would have been like if Lennox wouldn't have left her at the orphanage. Would they have been happy? Would she have ended up a demon as well, doomed to repeat her mother's mistakes? Would Lennox even have made that deal? Shoving the questions aside, she focused on the lyrics of her favorite masked British alternative metal band. She felt the air warm a little as she slowly relaxed and was able to start her studies on her next target, Rue.

The meeting room with paintings of various generations of the family was lit by her mother's favorite chandelier that was brought back from a hunting trip in France. Eden examined the dangling crystals as she waited for Bastien to meet her. The utter silence sent her thoughts in circles as she attempted to reconcile everything she knew. The things she had been taught growing up didn't meet what she knew about Lennox. After only a few minutes he entered the room with a skeptical look on his face.

"Oh Heiress Miller, your knight has arrived!" A smirk appeared on Bastien's face.

"More like the Bard," She taunted half-heartedly.

"Better add Bard to my title."

"Bastien, the Baron Bard, singing his songs as he puts a silver knife through a werewolf's heart. I suppose there's a ring to that."

His chestnut gaze traced her face, his eyebrow lifting. "Why did you really call me here?"

Eden's eyes drifted to his and she drew in a shaky breath. There was no dancing around the subject now. "Eloise told me who my birth mother is..."

"Who is it?" His face changed instantly and he moved next to her. "By the look on your face I don't think I'm going to like the answer."

"Lennox Cade." She let the name hang in the air, watching his reaction.

"Shit... OH SHIT!" His voice raised, looking at her in surprise.

"HEY! SHUT IT!" She scolded venomously. "All I need is someone hearing this I don't intend for."

"I know," he tried to calm the situation, keeping his tone even. "No one else should be home right now."

She didn't break eye contact with him, waiting for any reaction. His expression was neutral until she noticed the fearful look that made its way into his eyes. *No... I knew this would happen.*

"I'm sorry, I just didn't expect this- Are you both sure?"

"Eloise seems pretty sure." Eden felt the tip of her pointer finger dig into her palm.

"Are you okay?" He asked, his hand going to her shoulder.

Eden debated her next words. "I'm conflicted... We were taught that these creatures were nothing but trouble, but I've never seen Lennox or her girlfriend cause anything."

"Don't let my sister hear you say that." He teased, a smile finding its way back onto his face. "You know better than to trust a demon, Eden. They're all nothing more than snakes."

"I know that... That's why I'll be getting my revenge with the next pin to knock down. Rue."

"And you're okay with that? Killing your birth mothers partner because Eloise told you to?"

"I don't really have much of a choice. This is the final year of the mission. What I want doesn't matter right now. What matters is taking down these schools and protecting humanity from these creatures."

Bastien's hand dropped back to his side. "Has Eloise put you up to this or are you doing it because you want to?"

"Both."

The sudden sound of footsteps on the wooden floor echoed down the hallway. The sound was quickly followed by the front door being opened and shut. The response was immediate from Bastien. In one fluid motion he had his gun from the weapons belt hidden under his clothes and had it trained towards the sound. His full attention locked on the doorway to the entrance hall as he stepped beside her. He paused waiting for Eden's instructions. In the absence of Eloise, she was in charge. The heiress already had her own gun pulled from her own hidden belt when she silently caught his eyes, a storm building within her irises.

"What was it you were saying about no one being home? Go-" She instructed, motioning to the door.

He moved forward towards the door and Eden followed close behind. He put his hand on the doorknob and swung the door open, aiming his weapon as he turned the corner. She followed and was met with empty space and dropped her guard after she heard nothing moving inside the house.

"Great, Bas. Whoever that was probably heard us."

"Or not, we can't skip to the worst-case scenario."

"Don't tell me how I should react to this," Eden snapped.

He put his hands up, pointing his weapon to the ceiling without thinking and running a free hand through his short brown hair. "Eden, I'm sorry."

She paused as she realized her hand was shaking. She still had her weapon trained on the front door where he stood. He took a cautious step towards her. He slid the Glock into his belt with one hand, putting the other on her wrist. As soon as his hand made contact with her skin she quickly shoved her gun back in its holster and turned away. *Get your shit together, someone could have walked in and gotten shot. Worse yet... Who heard us?*

Allowing herself all of ten seconds she turned back to her uncle. "It's okay. We don't say any of this to my mother, got it?"

"No, of course. This is between us as always." He promised. A strange pause followed his words until he decided to change the subject. "What are you wearing to the party at Club Crossroads tomorrow?"

"I'm not going," she folded her arms over her chest.

"No, no you're going. I refuse to let you sit in your dorm all alone this year. You are going to live some of your life and not just for Eloise.”

“I live my life,” she frowned and put her hands on her hips.

“Eden, Eden, Eden, you are a people pleaser. For once, let's go have fun even if we are surrounded by *them*.”

“I am not, how dare you suggest that… Although, I do need to go after her girlfriend, Rue.” She paused considering her options.

Bastien let out a scoff as she spoke. “Living for Eloise.”

She rolled her eyes and moved to turn toward the stairs. “I can do both.”

“Fine, I'll distract Lennox and the others while you get Rue alone, BUT!” Bastien held up a finger to her, “Party FIRST kill AFTER.”

“I'm not making any promises,” she retorted.

“Party FIRST, murder AFTER!” He repeated himself looking exasperated. “If I see you wearing some uptight outfit I'm not going to speak to you.”

“Well, I don't really have party clothes-”

“Wear that skirt you hate and something fun on top. I'll even let you borrow my leather jacket to go with it.”

“But it's too tight around the legs!” She complained.

“That's the whole point of it, it's a pencil skirt,” Bastien's phone started to ring. “I have to take this but I'll see you after classes tomorrow,” he started making his way toward the kitchen.

“Wait, Bas! How am I ever gonna do anything in it?!” Eden called after him. “You can't just walk away!”

“Hold on-” He told the person on the other end. “Yes I can, figure it out, you know you can text me but only if you really need help not looking like a prude.”

Soon he was up the stairs and out of sight. Eden turned back towards the door and sighed. She truly didn't want to go to the first traditional party, but the two houses at Club Crossroads would probably be the best way to get Rue alone. Eden turned toward the front door, remembering she was supposed to be sleeping at Omega. Picking up her backpack from the side table, she slid out the front door. *At least I get to steal his favorite leather jacket.*

September

The next day, Eden made her way down the hall with phone in hand. Confused, she looked around trying to find her last class. It was then she realized her next class was upstairs and across the building. *Well, that's inconvenient.* Switching directions, she went up the stairs to the magical studies section of the school. Every specialty was mostly separated into its own areas Humanity courses from the Magical courses. Quickly, she found the right room, Magical Practices, and their applications.

Pulling her bag a bit closer to her she stepped through the door. Eden blinked in surprise as she discovered that she wasn't the first one to arrive. A young man was already sitting at one of the desks distracted by his phone until she walked in. Eden remembered him from the previous year. He was someone close to Lennox and Felix. Last year the two hadn't spoken more than a handful of times. Wyatt was one of the many Crossroads Demons but was among the more popular ones that attended the school. He had the traditional crossroad markings on his cheekbones, several tattoos, mostly on his neck; what she could see of his arms, and dark as coal hair.

She didn't stop walking as she went over everything she knew about the man. Demon, past Curse Creator in Hell, Graduate as a Crossroads Demon with a current major in Necromancy, a minor in Witchcraft, and member of Kappa Theta. His long waves were tied back into a messy bun. His leather jacket slung over the back of his chair. His gaze lifted to meet hers. She only allowed herself a moment to scan his reaction to her entrance, stormy eyes glinting with curiosity.

He leaned back in his seat, seeming deep in thought for a moment as she moved to a desk a few seats away. Eden pulled out one of the elemental magic books stashed in her bag and started to read. That was, until a voice interrupted her thoughts.

"Ahhh- Good morning Sunshine, I must say you are almost glowing. Is that a new moisturizer?" He asked in a charming, slightly raspy voice.

Surprised someone was suddenly calling her sunshine, she looked up and raised an eyebrow at the demon. "Must be the lights in here."

"No darling, I know lights and this-" He waved his hand in a circular motion at her. "Is it a new cream or what is it you ladies call it? Ah! Foundation! Though your beauty is far beyond skin deep if I do say so myself."

"You hardly know me and if I recall the last time we spoke I'm pretty sure you were wasted. I'm surprised you even remember my face."

"Oh, I could never forget someone like you, Eden Miller." He put his chin in his hand.

"Did you get here early to harass the first girl to walk in?"

He leaned in his chair a little to see the book she had pulled out. "Actually, I was waiting for my destiny to show up and here you are! The one and only Little Miller."

Turning towards her in his seat, he let his blueish-gray eyes drift over her. *Destiny? More like blind to the truth... But if he was human, I might actually consider him.* She fought off the disgust at the thought of a being with a demon. Admittedly, he was attractive. Piercing eyes, inviting smile, and sharp jawline only pulled her in more. If only he knew who she actually was. He would avoid her like the plague knowing she could be his end.

"I don't believe that destiny is the word you're looking for." She attempted to return to her book.

"How's the cult- I mean family? Kinda seems like a fae trap. One of you is always just around the corner."

She pulled her sweater around her legs suddenly self continuous about the way her skirt fell when she sat. Her hardened exterior dropped a little when he called her family a cult, she had never heard anyone refer to them in such a way. For a second, she imagined tossing him into the basement simply for the cult comment. The whole thing had been renovated into something close to a jail with two holding cells and multiple hooks with demon chains. Finished off with a weapons vault in the corner to contain and get information out of creatures like him. As much as she wanted to, she only had personal reasons to do it. That wasn't enough, yet.

"Miller is actually a very common last name... Besides, fae travel together, remember?"

"Ah yes, but I would assume after the third Miller that maybe mommy dearest would slap a condom on the old man." Wyatt stood, leaving his bag at the desk and sat beside her.

Her obvious distaste for him seemed to egg him on rather than get him to stop. At this point, it was a game of cat and mouse. Eden kept her eyes on the pages as he joined her. Her heart fluttered at the proximity and the hair on the back of her neck automatically stood on end. *He's a predator.* She kept her face expressionless until she felt his hand slip into hers. Ever so gently he slid the book down.

Eden's eyes hardened as she fought to contain her anger. "You think insulting my family is a good way to flirt?"

The smile on his face faded ever so slightly as he seemed to realize he had started off on the wrong foot. Everything in her screamed to rip her hand away. However, warnings about demons played like a broken record in the back of her mind. *No sudden movements.* She stayed still but glanced down as his grip tightened slightly. Her hand looked so small inside his. She was met with a traditional style black rose tattoo on the top of his hand. Something within her stirred as her eyes traced the tattoos she could see leading into his sleeve.

"I'm sorry, I didn't mean it like that." Wyatt apologized. "I've been told my humor isn't the best at times. Let me make it up to you with a drink."

She scanned his face for lies but found none. "No, thank you."

"What's wrong sweetheart? You are far more attractive when you don't look like you want to kill me."

A scoff escaped her as his fingers slowly started to walk up her arm. "Trust me, I could."

"I don't doubt that for a second. Honestly, I'd be interested to see you go for it."

"Just tell me when and where, beautiful." Eden shook her head and tried to ignore her stomach doing somersaults. A sigh escaped him.

"I would think eventually your cold, mile high iron walls will fall... It seems I just have to be patient enough for that to happen."

Anger reared its head.

When his fingers reached her shoulder, Eden grabbed his wrist. Her grip tightened hard enough to leave a light bruise. She moved fast, the smirk on his face replaced with surprise. Her amethyst irises cut into his with piercing anger, sizing him up for a fight. Within a few seconds, the room dropped a few degrees. A spark of understanding lit in Wyatt's eyes as her threat clicked.

"My walls are stronger than you think, Wyatt. I wouldn't waste your time on me. In all honesty, you would probably regret meeting."

His eyes darted to his wrist as she was still holding it up and away from her. As he spoke, Eden could see his breath in the air. "Careful sweetheart, your bark may be big but I promise you my bite is bigger."

"Is it? Are you so sure about that?" She challenged with a small smile. He was playing a more dangerous game than he realized. One that could potentially end with a dagger to the chest.

He jerked his arm back from her grip and rubbed the spot. Leaning in he was inches from her face and his eyes grew dark for a second. "You really shouldn't underestimate me. I'm very good at getting exactly what I want. What I want is you, my Little Viper."

Eden's expression didn't change when he leaned toward her once again. Instead, she shifted her leg closer to her hand where she could take out her knife if need be. It wouldn't kill him, but it would be enough time to knock him out. Wyatt didn't know it, but after the discovery of Lennox being her birth mother, Crossroad demons held a special spot in her anger. They had been the reason Lennox hadn't reminded human. *Alive.* Lennox was stupid, they could have lived out a happy mortal, normal life. Instead, she had to be selfish, leave her child and end up here. She was determined to never end up like her.

"See! I knew there was something about you, you have spunk. Besides, lucky for you- I am immortal and all."

"Lucky me." She reached for her bag trying to put some space between them, but his leg was blocking her from it.

His eyes followed her hand down. "Are you wanting something, Little Miller? You could ask nicely, I think the word you're looking for is please."

"I think the words I'm looking for are 'personal bubble.'" Her hand twitched toward her leg to sink her knife right into his chest. *Maybe that would get him to leave me alone.*

"You have entertained me, darling, there is no personal space now." Wyatt slid his foot aside. "You should know one thing about Crossroad Demons. Once we grow an attachment, good luck shaking us. Unless you're willing to make a trade, but those are only for my customers. You are more of a guilty pleasure now."

"I would never make a deal with a crossroad demon. I've heard about too many sideways deals." She opened her bag and pulled out one of her books, Crossroad Demons and Deals.

Wyatt leaned over a little more, peering over her shoulder when a laugh escaped him. She jumped in surprise as he snatched the book from her and reached into his pocket. Her hand was inches away from the hilt of her knife when he pulled out a pen. A cocky smirk appeared across his lips as he cracked his knuckles and started to flip through the pages.

"Now, where is it?" He muttered to himself. "If you wanted an autograph all you had to do was ask. I'm all about giving back to my fans, after all. You know, this whole game was unnecessary if that's what you wanted."

Eden's mouth stood agape for a second before twisting into anger. "What the hell are you doing? I am *definitely* not one of your fans. If you have so many of these so-called fans, shouldn't you be flirting with one of them?"

"Why would I? They aren't the ones I'm interested in. Wait, there it is!" He clicked the pen and signed his name and phone number on a page that featured him. He closed the book and handed it back to her. "Take care of that number, you never know when you're going to want to use it."

She snatched it from his grip, her face burning. He was so irritatingly into himself, thoughtlessly confident yet there was something about him that drew her in. Her thoughts drifted to the family gatherings with every member of The Salvamari. All the times one Heir specifically would catch her alone. Their flirtations, secret meetings, a strange draw to each other neither could explain before things got too complicated due to their training. Wyatt reminded her ever so slightly of him-Eden shook the thought away.

"I can't think of any reason I would want to text you."

"Give a man mercy, Little Viper. Maybe you'll need a date to one of the house parties, or maybe the big party tonight at Club Crossroads?" He raised an eyebrow.

"I don't drink and I don't go to parties. I prefer to use my time productively."

"Don't do parties? That just won't do, especially when you have the party master as your date!"

"You sound like my cousin, besides, you're being very presumptuous, soul digger." She lied about how she was related to Bastien and shot back the insult. It was something she had picked up last year, knowing it was a common slur when it came to Crossroad Demons specifically and would hit where she needed it to.

"Ohhhh- Ouch, that one hurt a little," Wyatt teased. "But I forgive you. That is if you agree to let me take you out."

Tilting her head down a little, she eyed him incredulously. His eyes studied her for a few seconds. The storm in his eye burned into hers as he searched for what she didn't know. Taking a moment to check the guard around her thoughts Eden didn't look away. His gaze was unyielding as she put a mental hand on the walls around herself. Not even a whisper of any attempts. Before she could say anything, his smile fell a little into a look of seriousness.

"Tell me, why are you so hell bent on pushing me, and I imagine others like me, away? What did my kind ever do to you, Eden Miller?"

Caught off guard by his question, she opened her mouth to respond but quickly closed it. She took a moment to gather her thoughts before giving out more information than she was willing to. "That's a story for another day, Steele."

"That's fine, just gives me more time to steal your heart. I will show you I'm nothing like other demons." He dropped the question. "Now for that date you owe me, how about I come to your place. Since you don't like to party. Have a little party of our own and get to know each other? Eight thirty on Saturday?"

"I don't owe you anything. Even if I wanted to go on a date with you I'm not sure my place is appropriate. Besides, I have to study for the papers I've already been assigned."

He leaned back again, peering at her thoughtfully. "You're right. I don't mind a little drunk study session. But there is one thing you should know about me, I don't give up easily."

"I don't crack easily, Mister Steele."

"Good! Then I'll see you Saturday to hit the books!"

"Now hold on, I didn't agree to-"

It was then the door to the classroom opened once more. A group of students followed by the Elder teaching the class entered. The sounds of low muttering filled the air. Eden let out a small breath finally relaxing a little. *Saved by the bell.*

"I'm not done winning you over yet, my little viper. I'll see you at seven." He whispered beside her ear before returning to his original seat before she could even tell him no again. *Dammit.*

The other students made their way to their own seats, a few of them peering over at the two. Elder Alden, a vampire with magical capabilities made his way to the front and started to set up. Writing quickly on the board, elemental magics and their everyday applications.

Eventually, the class ended and Eden was eager to get out of the room before Wyatt could try to talk to her again. As soon as the Elder dismissed them, she was out of her chair and half way out of the room. She pulled out her phone to text Bastien. Her fingers danced as she told him she had met Wyatt and he seemed to have taken interest in her. Only to receive "Lol" in response minutes later. Luckily, she could head back to her dorm to have some dinner before dragging herself out to the party at Club Crossroads.

Making her way back down the halls, other students went about their days. She swore she could feel someone slowly making their way up behind her. A Elder approached her. Alaric was looking right at her with a bright smile, his shoulder-length dark hair in a tangled messy bun. She relaxed slightly when she saw her fellow hunter.

"Hey there, cousin!" He beamed. "Good to see you. How was your summer?"

Thankful for the save, she stopped to talk to him, feeling the person behind her stop too. "It was good, how about you?"

She leaned over and gave her 'cousin' a side hug, taking the opportunity to see who was following her. Wyatt was standing five feet away and opened his mouth to speak. Out of the corner of her eyes she saw the look given by the Elder. He swiftly turned the opposite direction. Alaric watched the boy walk away from them and peered back at Eden, now alone in the hall.

"I see you have a shadow," he teased once everyone was gone.

"Unfortunately- but I don't think he'll be much trouble. He'll get bored."

"Good. Can't have any distractions this year, Eloise made that clear."

"Ew- Like I'd ever get with one of those creatures, Alaric. Besides, what about your little adventure with the security team? What did my mother say about that?" Eden crossed her arms over her chest.

"I was just trying to be helpful, see what they know." He shot back.

"What are they going to think when they ask to see your wolf form then, hmmm?"

"Eloise says she can make a potion to help hide the whole human thing for a few hours. Do what I gotta do I guess."

"Yes, since you got yourself into that situation. Making friends doesn't help keep a cover."

"I see we disagree on that subject."

"Remember, getting attached can only lead to trouble... Remember who these people are- I'm sure your fiance wouldn't forget." Eden walked past Alaric making her way out into the courtyard and to the path that led to Omega Alpha.

E den stood in front of the mirror in her closet, eyes drifting over the uncomfortable outfit Bastien had suggested. She fiddled with the bottom edge of the tight light leather skirt and attempted to pull it down in hopes for more cover. A discarded pair of tights lay on the edge of her bed as she found the skirt kept riding up with every step. *Damnnit Bas, why does it have to be a party? How the hell am I supposed to kill the girlfriend if I can't even move?*

Rolling her eyes, she turned to the mirror. The gold satin crop top was only held on by a loop one either side of her rips and two strings from the very top. Eden was grateful for the jacket she would be borrowing. As she moved, the small metal beaded fringe brushed along her sides. Her long straight hair fell over her shoulders to the bottom of her ribcage. Eden started to pull into her regular ponytail but before she could wrap the hair tie around it, she heard Bastien complaining already. *Let your hair down, it's a party, Eden.* With a sigh, she let it fall and turned away from her reflection.

She made her way out of her dorm and down the stairs. A few people were still getting ready to head out for the party. She nodded to a small group standing in the common area before she went out the front door. Almost immediately, she regretted her outfit even more as the cold wind bit at her. Her eyes scanned the grounds as she waited for Bastien. It was only a few minutes until he appeared from the long path that connected the two houses. His eyes traveled up and down her outfit as he approached. Bastien made his way up a few stairs to the porch, holding out his jacket to her.

"Looks like you are going to actually need this, a little cool to be dressed like that."

Eden snatched it from his hand and wrapped it around herself, glaring. "Don't even start with me- You told me to wear this."

"Take a joke for once, Eden. You look great." He rolled his eyes, turning back towards the steps. "Come on, half of Kappa is already there.

With an exaggerated sigh, she followed him onto the grounds. The grass and path were illuminated by the light of the full moon, the trees by the lights from the main building. The two made their way to the school's large iron gates. Thankfully, they were left open for the members that would be going to the yearly party. The chains that held them open rattled in the wind.

Bastien rambled about his housemates the entire way. Quietly, he fed her more information he seemed to deem useful about the others around campus. Eden was only half listening as she went over all the ways she could get Rue completely alone. She trusted that after it was done, she would be able to find him so they could leave. *I don't really feel like being here longer than I have to be.* Then the very probable possibility that she would run into Lennox slammed to the forefront of her mind. She hadn't seen her since Eloise told her the truth. Dread and anger filled her as she saw the demon's annoying smile in her mind's eye. *She's so happy here, it's like none of it even happened.*

"What do you think?" Bastien asked her, breaking her from her thoughts.

"You should definitely avoid them."

"I should avoid all my classes and kill every demon in the school? Definitely not. I knew you weren't listening." He elbowed her in the side.

"Okay- I wasn't. What did you say?"

"I said, I've been keeping a close eye on the head of Kappa, Aron. I think there's something there we can eventually use when Eloise sends us after them."

"Oh? What do you think that would be?" she asked.

"His heart, he's a good guy to the others. He cares too much already and that'll be his downfall. I heard him complaining to one of his buddies about Lennox though he seems to care about her. I also heard Donnie and Lennox talking about Aron as well. If there's two things those two can agree on, it's their dislike for each other and the fact they wouldn't let anyone else be harmed, including each other." he smiled, proudly. "Besides there's just something about him that screams I have a secret. He's almost too carefree."

Thinking for a moment, she nodded in agreement. "That's good, we could use that. Just have to find out more about his past."

They stopped talking when they made their way toward Club Cross-roads. The lights in the bar and dancing area were off and colorful flashing lights illuminated most of it. Thankfully, the music wasn't blasting yet, she could still hear herself think. Eden's eyes drifted around to see who was there. Bastien was right, a lot of Kappa Theta guys had already arrived and started drinking. Over the music she caught the sound of Lennox's voice causing all of her attention to snap to where the annoyingly bright pink-haired demon stood. *You really know how to stick out in a crowd.*

Lennox stood beside Rue. The couple was in a group of two others, a man with a red bandana and a deep red-headed demon with curled horns. Her eyes followed the markings on her face. A set of black X's under the outer corners of her eyes gave her away as a Crossroads Demon. She didn't recognize her but she did know who the first demon was. Aron, Felix Toll's replacement. *How bold to take on the job of someone who was just killed.* Without saying anything, Bastien started making his way toward the group. A bright smile across his face, his usual facade, Eden following close behind.

"Hey, guys! The party can start now that I'm here!" He said cheerfully over the music.

Aron's attention turned from the group and his face lit up, "Hey! Good, this party was getting a bit dull. What's your poison?"

"A double shot of Tequila and a cranberry vodka for Eden."

"You got it," he turned to the bartender.

Using the moment of distraction she scanned the small group until Eden's eyes were locked on her target. Lennox and Rue were chatting in each other's ears with drinks in their hands. Seeing Lennox caused her stomach to twist. Talking to the demon would be different from every time they had spoken. Now that she knew who she was and what she had done, the hunter had to hold herself back from immediately taking her to the basement. *Enjoy your last year here.*

It only took Lennox a few seconds to notice her. "Glad to see you here."

"Thanks- it's not really my scene, but my cousin insisted." She shrugged.

"Well, we will make sure it's a good time. You guys got here at a good time, don't have to fight for any drinks yet." Rue smiled.

"Oh, it's already a good time," the vaguely familiar red-haired demon said. The biggest smirk Eden had ever seen appeared on the demon's face as she looked at Lennox. "Especially with, what did you call her, Aron? Lenny-boo?"

She decided to watch closely at whatever was going on between this girl and Lennox. Even though she didn't know her name, she did look almost identical to her housemate, Donnie. They even had the same horns and similar markings with the classic tilted crosses on their cheekbones. *Eloise just had to claim the school with the only Crossroads program.* Seeing the look on her birth mother's face was all the confirmation she needed. They had a history.

"Lenny-boo, Leonard, two of my favorites so far." Aron smiled at the woman.

"Maybe you could actually learn my name." Lennox shot back.

"Oh, but this is just so much more fun. Especially when it seems to piss you off so much." He nudged her and turned to the redhead. "I like you, what did you say your name was?"

"Bane, Val Bane," she held out her hand and took a step closer to him.

"Well, Bane- I think we are gonna have quite the night."

Lennox had a disgusted look on her face and went to speak but was cut off by Rue, "Oh look, more drinks are here!"

Rue turned and took the drinks from the bar and handed them to Bastien and Eden. She had been fully absorbed in the conversation between Aron and Val while Lennox watched them from the corner of her eyes. *I wonder what's going on with these two?* She nodded in thanks as a drink was handed to her. Aron took Val's hand, talking in her ear.

"So, Eden. How was your first day of classes?" Rue asked her over the music.

"Actually quite normal, until my last class." She entertained the conversation, deciding she could lure her away at some point by acting friendly.

"What happened during your final class?"

"Well, this guy decided I was his next Rapunzel." Eden told her.

"Rapunzel! Rapunzel! Let down your long hair!" A familiar voice yelled behind her.

An unexpected hand was suddenly wrapped around her shoulder. As soon as she felt it, Eden turned into whoever had appeared. In one movement, her hand clenched into a low fist aiming for the person's stomach out of reflex. Without missing a beat, Wyatt's free hand stopped hers. His fingers wrapped around her first, holding it tight enough to hide the action. Her gaze shot up to him. Wyatt hadn't even broken his jester-like demeanor as the storm locked with her narrowed eyes. A smile plastered to his face, Wyatt held her there for a moment before he leaned down.

The music gradually became louder but seemed to drift into the background as a look of surprise filled her eyes. Something fluttered deep inside Eden. Only for a moment, she was frozen to the spot as she forced herself to not get lost in the way he was looking at her. *Get your shit together. He's only a soul snatcher, annoying too.*

His expression softened contrasting with the rasp in his voice as he held her there, "Something wrong, my Little Viper?"

"Absolutely nothing." She pulled her hand back from under his rose tattoo, shifting so he had to remove his hand from her shoulder.

"You're looking quite lovely tonight. I didn't know you liked leather." He teased, running a hand through his hair. "I thought you weren't into parties?"

"I don't- Bastien dragged me out."

"Well, in that case, I guess I'll enjoy your company while you're here." Wyatt smirked at her, confident from their little moment. "Let me grab a drink to keep up with you."

He stepped past Eden to order a drink from the bar as well. Rolling her eyes, she turned back to the group just in time to see Aron taking Val by the hand away with a wave. It didn't seem like anyone had noticed their little exchange. Until her eyes fell on Bastien who had a devious look plastered on his face. She knew the look well. It would appear whenever he wanted to encourage her to do something she shouldn't. *Dammit, Bas, it's not what you think.*

The others were watching the pair make their way out and an almost angry look drifted into Lennox's eyes. Another demon soon replaced the two that left for the night. This one was slightly taller than Lennox when she stood beside her. Lennox peered over at the girl and her anger slowly faded away into an exasperated look. After watching the many members of Omega House, she knew Lennox and the demon, Rosalyn were best friends. They had been for decades since being locked up together in Hell according to Donnie when she asked last year.

"Here all of ten minutes and he can't wait to get out of here?" Lennox said so quietly, Eden almost missed it.

"Come on girl, ignore him! He'll catch up in no time." Rosalyn lifted her drink to Lennox.

"He's just having a bit of fun, Nox." Wyatt commented with a smirk after ordering a few more shots for the group. "Loosen up, even though I know how hard that is for you. We are in college after all!"

Bastien stepped beside Eden as Wyatt distracted the others. The look in his eyes from earlier still on his face and nudged her. "Seems like you've got a shadow tonight. Maybe even for the year."

"You're not the first person to say that. But don't even start." Bastien opened his mouth. "We both know what you're thinking."

"Come on Eden, live a little. He's not a target and what Eloise doesn't know can't hurt."

"Just because you like to ignore the rules, specifically not fraternizing with supernatural creatures, does not mean I should. You know how that goes in our family." She glared daggers at him.

He put his hands up, he laughed a little. "Alright, I'll drop it, for now."

Others from the two houses slowly started filling the space and the music was mostly too loud to talk. Wyatt passed out his round of shots to the whole group and held his glass up, yelling over the music. "Here's to a year to remember!" The others in the circle raised their glasses. Eden followed suit, chasing hers with the drink Bastien ordered for her. Trying to hide the face she made, she put her glass back on the bar. *Oh, it definitely will be.*

Two girls started making their way up to the group, Donnie who looked eerily similar to Val except she was dressed in bright clothes and seemed much more friendly with Lennox. The other, Leilani. The creature had antlers like a stag, purple hair with markings similar to a demon. Eden knew the two from last year. Leilani didn't speak. As far as she knew it was due to a run-in with a hunter. The demon fawn smiled at her housemates as Donnie looked over to Lennox to hear their conversations. She had to get closer than she would have preferred due to the volume of the music. Thankfully, Wyatt was distracted by Bastien who after winking at her, was throwing questions at him relentlessly.

"I saw her over here, you okay Nox?" Donnie asked with concern in her voice.

"Yeah, forget about it. Let's just have fun." Lennox shrugged off the conversation, clearly uncomfortable with the subject. *Noted.*

"Then let's dance," Rue held her hand out to her with a soft smile. Lennox took it and looked at the others in the group to see who would join.

Bastien held out a hand to Wyatt who laughed, eyeing Eden for a moment before taking it. As he pulled him towards the dance floor he grabbed the other drink he had ordered. Her eyes met Donnie and Leilani's before they also made their way to the dance floor. She made her way over to the bar but kept the group in her peripheral vision. Just before she could sit, Bastien came up behind her and tugged her backwards by the back of her jacket.

"You're not gonna sit in a dark corner and wait. You look like you're sulking. Party first- duty later." He scolded, taking her by the arm and pulling her away from the stool.

"I'm not here for the party, and you know that."

"And you know that I don't care! Pep up, do your job and look like you're here to have fun before someone gets suspicious. What's gotten into you? It's like you forgot how to hunt." He started dragging her towards the dance floor. "You've got a hot shadow, you know? I could imagine many things I'd like to do with him. But for some reason, he seems only interested in you. Odd isn't it? He's always been so wound up with half of the women in the school."

"I have absolutely no interest in getting closer with that Soul Snatcher." She pulled her arm back from his grip.

"He is a demon, and you are a fae. At least that's what you tell people, remember? " Bastien whispered in her ear and pushed her towards Wyatt.

With a huff, she almost bumped right into him which would have made both of them spill their drinks. Surprise filled his face and his eyes shot to her then to Bastien who motioned to go on with his hands before he turned back to the group. Eden watched him go with disdain as he sent another wink her way and seemed pretty happy with himself.

"Well I guess it is my lucky night, I didn't even ask him to be my wingman. Though it's nice to have your cousin's approval already." He smirked at her and held out his hand. "Care to have some fun?"

"No thank you." Eden turned to join Bastien.

"I'll make you a deal, we dance and I won't call this our first date."

"Because it's not a date, a date is *both* people agreeing to meet."

Wyatt smirked and leaned closer. "Technicalities. Be that as it may, would you at least allow me to show you a good time? I'll keep it PG of course... Unless you decide otherwise."

"There is a zero percent chance I will change my mind."

"Give a man some mercy, Little Viper." He motioned to his hand with his eyes. "I'll be a perfect gentleman."

"No funny business, Steele."

"None at all," he pulled her to him as the music took over the entire club.

After two more drinks, Eden started to notice the world spin occasionally. For a few seconds she started to lose herself in the music. The beats. The way his eyes sparked in the strobe lights. However, she quickly pulled herself out of it when she caught a glance of her target dancing over his shoulder. Wyatt was annoying, however, he was respectful in where he placed his hands as they danced. When they all had finished their round of drinks, Lennox went off to go get more.

A buzzed Rue made her way over to Eden, "Would you tell Lennox I went to the bathroom?"

"Actually, I need to go too. Bastien? Would you mind?" She tapped him on the shoulder and handed him her half-finished drink.

With a nod he took it, and she felt Wyatt's hand release her side. "No worries girls, have fun powdering your noses."

She opened the door, the light flicked on almost blinding her for a moment. As her eyes adjusted, Rue made her way to a stall while Eden quietly locked the door behind them. She pulled her phone from her jacket pocket, quickly texting Bastien to meet her outside. It was absolutely perfect, they couldn't be interrupted here. The best revenge was making your target watch as their world fell apart before their final day. Putting it away once more, she rolled up her skirt an inch and pulled out a dagger made by Eloise. The handle was covered in carved lilies, the stems winding down the blade down to the point, charmed exclusively to end Rue's life. *Any second now, I will be one step closer.*

"You know, I've never seen Wyatt be so enthralled by anyone before. He was telling Lennox and I about you earlier. He's a good guy like Felix was, you should give him a chance." Rue's voice came from behind the door.

"That could be but he's not really my type. Besides, my mother wouldn't approve." She admitted turning towards where the demon had gone in and waited.

"From what I've heard of Elder Miller, she doesn't like many people. No offense." The sound of movement came from the other side. *Any second now.*

"No, you're right. She doesn't and neither do I." Rue opened the door. "The whole reason we came was to get rid of monsters like you, like Felix."

At Eden's words, she saw Rue's face shift from the usual polite smile to shock as the dagger was forced in between her ribs. It slid in smoothly until she felt metal meet bone. The sudden force sent a reverberation through the hilt and into her palm. Years ago she would have shuddered. Now, she wrenched it back out warm fresh blood pooling from the blade to her hand. She took a step forward as Rue staggered back, eyes locked on Eden. Before the demon could fight back, she clamped a hand over her mouth and backed her into the stall. Using her strength she pushed the woman against one of the side walls. Her eyes flickered with the type of betrayal that only comes from trusting someone you shouldn't have.

"Scream, and you'll regret it. I'm making this easier for you than I have on others." Eden slowly removed her hand.

"Why?" Rue's voice broke as tears formed.

"Because, it's my job, and I want revenge... Now don't talk. It'll hurt more." the hunter answered her quietly.

"What did we ever do to you?" Rue gripped her wrist.

Easily moving her hand back from Rue's grasp, she used her knee to jab it into her target's side. She felt her victim's weight slowly shifting towards the ground as. She bent down with her halfway until Rue slumped the rest of the way. She stayed there for a second looking her in the eyes.

"It wasn't you... You're just a pawn in my plan." She stood taking a few steps back out of the stall.

The sound of coughing was all that came in response as the woman slowly succumbed to her fate. As what was left of her life slowly drifted away. The markings on her face dimmed just as Felix's had done a week ago. She waited for the feeling of temporary peace to wash over her. But it didn't. She shook her head and turned away and went over to the sinks. Quickly, she washed the blood from her hands and tucked the dagger back into its hiding spot. *It will come when I see Lennox's reaction.*

I have to get outside. She shrugged off the feeling of regret that stirred with every kill since she was a kid.

Glancing at her smart watch as it buzzed with a notification, she saw a text from Bastien confirming he was outside. Unlatching the window, Eden stood on the counter and crawled out after glancing around to make sure no one was around. After confirming the coast was clear, she walked around to the other side of the building where he had told her to meet him. Her Uncle was sitting on a bench with a cigarette in one hand and a drink in the other hand looking much more intoxicated than she was. *He was obviously having much more fun.*

She joined him and peered over. "I was having fun with your boy toy. He's got moves."

"Then why don't you try and find your way into his bed?"

"I tried, he doesn't seem interested in any other Miller but you. But it doesn't matter, did you do it?"

"Of course."

"How do you feel? Did you get the revenge you hoped for?" Bastien questioned, taking a sip of his drink.

"I did, for the most part. I'm sure it'll sink in once she's discovered. I-" She was interrupted by a voice calling from nearby. She turned towards the sound and saw a figure moving quickly toward them. "Eyes up."

She was on her feet in seconds as the person got closer. At the command Bastien was already beside her, moving his hand closer to his hidden weapons belt. From the street lamps, she was only able to catch a glimpse of who it was. Recognizing her gray-haired grandfather, Richard Miller and relaxed briefly. Until she saw the look of disgust on his face and a dagger in hand. She felt Bastien brush her as he stepped in front of her left shoulder, his gun half out of its holster. A training technique the men of the Millers were taught when one of the members of the matriarchal line was potentially in danger.

"Father- What are you doing?" Bastien asked.

Richard's rough voice boomed in response as he pointed the dagger directly at Eden. "Why are you protecting that?!"

"What do you mean? This is Eden!" He trained the weapon on his father.

"No, it's not. I don't know what it is! I heard you two talking yesterday at the house. Her mother is one of the monsters we are supposed to be getting rid of!" He snarled and got a foot away from Bastien.

The older man moved faster than either of them could. He quickly grabbed Bastien's gun and pointed it back at the ground before pressing on his hand to make him let go. With a clatter, it dropped to the ground. He shoved his son away from Eden who took a step back. There was no stopping him as he gripped her arm, forcing her back towards the bench. She struggled beneath his grip, unable to break it she lashed out and sunk her knee into his thigh. The man wound his arm back and with all his strength punched her directly in the left eye. Pain exploded in her face, filling her vision with black and rendering her useless for a few seconds.

He used it to his advantage and shoved her back down into the seat. The metal of the blade caught her eye as he held the dagger to her chest. Panic filled every inch of her body. She knew exactly what the dagger was supposed to do. Though it would have the same base effect however it wouldn't quite do what the man seemed to expect.

"I don't know what my daughter's brought into this family, but you're not one of us." His eyes were locked onto Eden's.

"You know I am nothing more than human!" She squirmed, trying to get her leg under him. "How has Eloise not told you!?"

Her knee was met with just the right amount of force in the perfect spot from his elbow that sent a wave of pain down her leg forcing it back. She let out a cry of pain, not wanting to use magic on anyone in the family. She knew exactly what kind of danger she was in. Richard may not have ever held a high title within the family but he was well-trained with much more fighting experience than her.

"Even if that's true, you will end up just like that filthy demon. The apple doesn't fall far from the tree. You and I both know that you have never fit in with this family. Now I know why. You're nothing more than a trained pet my daughter brought home. You bring shame to this family with your tainted blood. You will never lead this family, not as long as I can help it."

His words hit Eden harder than his fist. Her vision was still blurry, clouded even more as tears formed. She was so focused on his words she didn't see he had his dagger pulled back to strike until she heard Bastien yell. Suddenly, the force that held her down vanished as someone dragged the man off her.

Looking up she saw the familiar face of her mother illuminated in the low street lights. Eloise was peering down the rim of her glasses at Richard who was lying on the ground. Fire and brimstone raged in her eyes. Bastien was standing to her front left shoulder, just as he had done with Eden holding his gun beside Eloise's directly at the man. She had only ever seen her mother this enraged once in her life. When she was very young, Eloise and Stacey had gotten into a very loud argument about something in Eden's past. Looking back, it now made sense what they were fighting about. Her lineage. After it had taken her grandmother several months to start speaking to Eden. After a few years, they'd ended up growing close, Eden being her favorite.

"Are you okay?" Eloise asked without taking her eyes off the man and motioned Eden to join them.

"I'm fine," She answered and stood to the right of Eloise, clenching her hands into fists to prevent them from shaking.

"What the hell are you doing, father? Eden is next in line, our future and you are trying to kill her!? She is not a demon and to suggest otherwise is going against this family. Without her, we don't continue our legacy!"

"I heard the two of them talking yesterday. She is tainted by demon blood. I'm not as easy to fool as Stacey," Richard shot back.

"How dare you talk to your Matriarch like this! She is the product of a human who only cared for herself and was abandoned. Miss Cade wasn't a demon at the time of her birth and if you were really listening you would have known that. Now, I'll let you up but you will not be hurting her. We will go back to the house and I will tell you everything I know." She turned to Eden, her knuckles turning white but her hand steady. "I presume you've done what you needed to here?"

She nodded, "Yes Mother."

"Good, you and Bastien will go make yourselves look like you've been there the whole time." Eloise turned her attention to Richard. "Not a word or I will make you a Heretic here and now."

Eloise put her gun back into her belt and Bastien followed suit. Richard stood roughly, looking like his pride was wounded. In the light from the club, the Miller family crest reflected the silver and blue enamel peacock on her right hip. However, she knew he wouldn't disobey what Eloise said. No matter how much it pissed him off if he wanted to stay within the family. Without a word he started to make his way back the way he had come and Bastien turned to Eden. Reaching up, he fixed her hair moving it to cover the big red mark that was slowly starting to darken

"You need to not look like you almost just died. Are you okay to go back in?"

"You heard Eloise, we need to finish the mission." She avoided the question as he finished with her hair. She wouldn't show weakness now. "I'll go back into the bathroom and lay there like the attacker knocked me out. The eye will help the story."

He looked her over once more, his worried expression softening. She cursed at herself internally. He could always read her like a book. He nodded in agreement and turned back to the entrance. Shoving the panic that had filled her when she saw the dagger down for the moment, she made her way to the window and slid back in. Eden hastily went over to unlock the bathroom door and cringed a little as she lay down on the bathroom floor and closed her eyes. *This better work.* Her body still coursing with adrenaline couldn't relax as the minutes ticked by while she waited for the unfortunate soul to come across the scene.

Her mind filled the time with images of Richard, his dagger getting closer. Of Rue and her dagger sinking into her ribs. Blood that covered her hands with each death. Finally, to Lennox. The whole reason she was a hunter, a Miller, an Heiress. Her stomach turned as each face crossed her mind only to be broken by the door opening. The person's footsteps came to a brief halt before they went carefully around her to the stall Rue was still lying in. The woman let out a gasp and Eden felt her shake her shoulder. "Hey, can you hear me?" Eden didn't respond as she got closer. "Okay, okay, you're breathing. It'll be okay, I'll go get help."

The sound of her footsteps receded. *It worked.* From the bathroom, she could hear the woman over the music.

"Someone help! Someone's dead, the other isn't responding!"

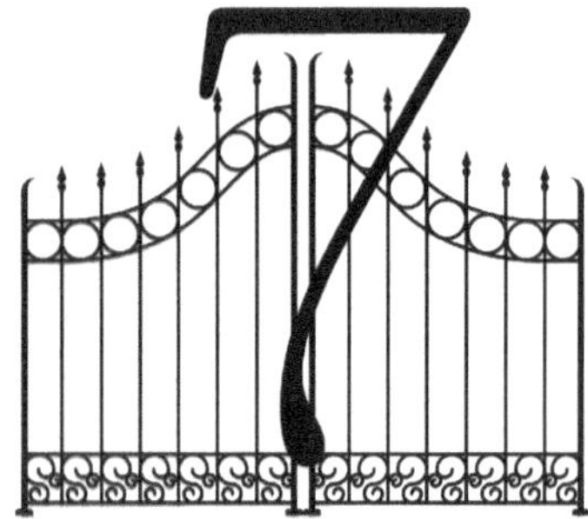

Lennox

The music cut off and the entire room turned to her. There was a brief pause before chaos broke. Some people started to rush out, others pulled out their phones calling for help as they followed the flow of people out. The woman who was still standing at the door of the bathroom screamed again begging for help. Her screams sent pins and needles through Lennox's body. Her own screams echoed in her mind. Her previous loose demeanor quickly shifted to seriousness, sobered within a few seconds. Her instincts kicked into gear as she pulled at her internal vine. Her eyes bearing a dull green glow as they darted back and forth from her friends and the woman. She looked to Wyatt and Rosalyn after a head count on the group. The two stood beside her seemingly waiting to see what they could do, both looking worried.

"Help me get everyone out, now." She directed Rosalyn before turning away from the group. "Wyatt, call the security team and find Eden and Rue."

Both nodded and started directing others while Lennox moved towards a group of Omega Alpha members surrounding the girl who had screamed. The girl was a vampire, her housemate Percey. She closed the distance, moving past the others as calmly as she could manage. Percey still had her hands over her face. Lennox bent down to her and held out a hand. As she did, memories of Felix laying on the floor flooded her mind. *No, no. Not right now.* Lennox shook her head and forced herself to focus on the panicked eyes of Percey. Grief threatened to overwhelm her and rage would win if she allowed her emotions to take over.

"It's okay, let's get out of here, the security team will be here any moment," she promised, watching her carefully. "Take my hand?"

The blonde-haired girl examined Lennox's face before nodding. "Yeah-"

She didn't take her hand but stood and started making her way towards the door. A few of her friends walked beside her, Percey with a blank stare in her eyes. After they were out of sight her mind wandered to where Rue was as her feet carried her towards the bathroom door. Every hair stuck on end as the thought crossed her mind. *No, she's fine. She's probably taking care of someone outside.* With each step her heart began to pound louder and louder in her ears, until a hand grabbed her wrist. The sudden touch caused her to jump and whip around just before the closed door.

"The staff at the club have it, Len. We need to go outside too." Wyatt's voice pulled her from her thoughts.

"I have to help, it could have been one of my girls..." Her eyes looked without seeing at the door where voices echoed.

"You can't look at another dead friend. Whoever it is-"

"Whoever it is, they are alone. They may be gone but they are alone!" Her voice slowly got louder. "They are my responsibility, Wyatt. He was *my* responsibility!"

Wyatt moved in front of Lennox and placed his hands on her shoulders. Every movement was distinct, slow, unthreatening. Her eyes glowed dully as anger threatened to boil over. Instead, he only raised his eyebrows. He was rock steady just as he had been since they became friends. The two had their fair share of combat against each other to know they were matched.. "Do you trust me?"

She paused and finally met his stormy eyes. "Yes."

Without a word he pulled her away from the door and past the members of club staff. Wyatt pulled her into his side and arm holding her tightly against him.Lennox let her head fall on his shoulder for a moment. The smell of his leather jacket mixed with whiskey brought her back to the moment. The two stepped outside and he released her to join the others. Her gaze swept over each of their faces, Bastien, Donnie, Lealani, Wyatt, and Rosalyn each safe. Whole. She forced herself to remain outwardly mostly calm though it was almost painful as she wondered about the fates of the other two.

"Has anyone seen Rue or Eden?" Lennox attempted to keep her voice as even as possible.

"I haven't seen her, but I'm sure she's safe." Rosalyn spoke up. "Do you wanna go back to the house and see if she's there?"

"No, I think I should stay. I have to know if it was one of my girls or one of Fel..." She paused and looked away as Donnie reached a hand to her shoulder. "Aron's boys."

"It's okay, Lealani and I will go check for you." Donnie offered.

"Thank you, text me if you find her please." Lennox nodded as the two went back to campus.

It took a little longer than previously for Coyote, Cathwulf, and a new member of the security team to arrive. Everyone parted for them. The newest member was much taller than the surrounding crowd. The man stood about seven feet tall. A long scar was drawn down the right side of his face over a single milky white eye. A long white stripe in his hair on the same side as the scars marked him as a werewolf. He walked around the crowd trying to get everyone organized. Lennox herself had just managed to get herself together when they approached her. The sounds of whispers in the air.

"Is everyone out here alright?" The man asked, looking down at her.

Lennox cleared her throat, evening her voice. "As far as I know, we don't know who the victim is. I'm missing quite a few people but I don't know who was in the club and who's back at the houses."

"Okay. Can you get a list of all the names here? Is there anyone at the house you trust to get a list together?" He asked as Lennox's attention drifted back to the doors of the club.

"I can." Rosalyn quickly offered. "Mister... What's your name?"

"Thank you. Oh, sorry. I am Mathias Bloodfang. I'm here to help Coyote."

Just then Coyote came over on his way into Club Crossroads. Fang only glanced over. "We will go in. Come on, Fang. Cathwulf will stay out here and make sure nothing else happens."

Wyatt turned to Lennox and met her eyes, his eyebrows raising slightly in a silent question. Nodding, Lennox wordlessly told him she would be okay and turned to the door. She glanced around for Rue one last time but didn't spot her. Pulling out her phone she motioned for

Rosalyn to do the same as they spread out to gather what they could. Between typing out names, she was sending texts to her asking where Rue went off to Lennox did her best to keep her mind busy. Coyote and Fang had been in there for well over twenty minutes. There was a nagging feeling in the back of her mind. *What if she's not at Omega? What if... No, she's fine.* She fought with herself trying to keep herself together to keep everyone else calm. After another few names, she took a second to call her phone, hoping she would pick up.

It rang *once. Twice. Three* times. Lennox watched everyone start to head back to the grounds, her back to the door. *Fourth* ring. The door to the club opened. The sound of a phone ringing from within drifted on the air before going quiet when the door shut. Lennox turned around to see Coyote walking toward them accompanied by a familiar woman with raven hair and purple eyes wrapped in his jacket. *Fifth* ring. *Why does he look like he's just seen a ghost?* Lennox turned to see him as he weaved through the crowd towards her, his usual even expression already shifted into sadness as he met her eyes. Her throat tightened and every hair once again stood on end as it went to *voicemail.*

"Eden?" She rushed forward and her gaze scanned over her face. Her eye was swollen, slowly deepening in color.

Before Lennox could ask any questions, Wyatt appeared beside her his hands reaching out to Edenand his voice leaking with venom. "Viper, what happened? Who hurt you?"

"I- I don't remember. Someone came in and." Eden looked away as Wyatt's hands hovered just over her arms. She seemed to hesitate for a moment but seemed to shift toward him to allow the contact. "I was talking with Rue then... Everything went black until the Security Team arrived..."

Wyatt looked like he was going to hit someone but steadied himself with a breath. "They better hope I never find out who they are."

Leannox's breath caught in her throat at Rue's name. "You... You went in with Rue."

For a moment the world seemed frozen in time, her violet eyes drifting to Coyote. In seconds it settled as to why he looked so sad when he walked out. He started to speak but stopped abruptly. That was all the confirmation she needed.

"No." Ringing started to fill her ears.

"Lennox, I-" Coyote stepped toward her.

"I was right... All along. I was right." Lennox's voice broke as the world started to pick back up.

"You don't need to see-"

"SHE'S ALONE AND YOU ALL HAVE KEPT ME FROM HER!"

In seconds the rage she had buried since Felix's death burst through every mental and magical wall she had created. Internally she gripped the blinding thread of magic. Power, hot and hungry echoed through every limb. The sigils on her arms glowed. Vines of ivy found the small holes she had created the the backs of all her clothes for times like this. The vines grew thick and twisted themselves together, allowing a few to drape at the bottom of ten foot long wings that stood taller than her.

Her feet started to carry her forward but Coyote stepped in her path. "Miss. Cade. You cannot go in there."

"You think I give a shit what you say I cannot do?" The demonic side of her had started to take over. Lennox's voice was unearthly, dissonant. A clashing and jarring melody.

"Not right now, no." He growled.

"Glad we are on the same page."

Lennox took a few steps forward, ignoring the stare of the others. The sound of Wyatt and Rosalyn calling to her. She tried to shove past the man who still seemed unfazed by her display of grief to get to the club door. Coyote reached out and wrapped a single arm around both her shoulders. His grip was gentle yet firm around her as her body shook. Red. There was only red. She blinked away the tears that threatened to obscure her vision. He may have been bigger but if it came down to a fight, she was sure she could get past him.

"Let me go." The ground beneath the two of them shook lightly.

"No. I'm just trying to protect you." He told her in a soft, strict voice, irises turning a bright yellow.

Her wings stretched behind her. Coyote tried to keep his grip but was forced to release her. "I don't want your protection. I protect others. I failed to keep Felix safe. I failed to keep Rue and Eden safe."

Coyote moved forward to attempt to stop her once again. Lennox lifted her hand and with a simple tug on the thread shook the ground under his feet. He came to a halt as he almost lost his footing. Without looking she pressed on. She was right. The whole time she had been right. She should have listened to her instincts and went to see who it was. Which one of her loved ones was laying on the bathroom floor. Lennox's jaw tightened and her face twisted as her mind conjured an image of Rue on the floor. It had been her all along. Rue, alone. Cold, alone. Dead. Alone. Lennox had broken every promise she made. The hunters had taken someone else she loved. The sounds of Rue's voice, her laugh, she would never hear it again. This felt personal.

Rosalyn stepped forward and Lennox felt a hand grip her wrist. Her head spun around to see her best friend looking at her with sadness in her garnet eyes. Her wings flared and stretched up as she saw the molten veins that flowed up her arms. Heat to counter the heat in Lennox's chains. For a moment, the red in her vision started to return to normal. Until suddenly the door to the club opened and shut once again. Fang stepped out of the door and his eyes drifted around the crowd. Finally, they fell to Lennox and Rosalyn who stood only a few feet from the entrance.

"I heard something, what's going on out here?" He asked looking at Coyote for a second before returning to her.

She locked eyes with him as if to challenge him as well. "Let me through."

"No, but it seems you already knew that." He said in a deep, gruff voice.

She stepped to the side but was blocked again by Fang. She growled in frustration as her eyes turned pitch black. With another tug at the thread she lifted her free hand and sent branches toward the man as a distraction. He didn't look away from her as she felt the connection of magic to the branch suddenly temporarily cut off. The man's eyes also glowed a bright yellow but opposed to Coyote there was magic behind his next words.

"Don't come any closer."

She felt a strange sensation wash over her and she couldn't focus enough to keep using her powers. The anger she previously felt started to be forced to the side as he looked at her with a glow in his eyes. *No.* Lennox tried to rebuild the mental barrier in her mind, brick by brick. The magic within her mind was familiar from her studies. Lennox had never met him but she had done enough essays on werewolves. There was a very small pool of Alpha wolves and this was one of their special tricks. Creating confusion within magic users to neutralize them. Deep down she could feel the embarrassment, but that didn't matter right now.

"Nox, you don't want to go in there... Just breathe for a moment." Rosalyn choked out.

"I should have been with her." Lennox lamented.

"We'll wait right here until she comes out. Like you did for Felix."

"No." Lennox persisted weakly. "No... I won't. I don't need protection. Not from this. I was going to propose to her, she was the love of my life and I'm going to stand beside her until my knees give out. Then I'll kneel at her body until my eyes won't stay open. I will sleep on the floor. Beside her. One last time. She will not be alone until she's put in the ground."

Wyatt walked over with an arm around Eden. "Just let her through, man. Sometimes we have to break rules... Lennox never breaks rules so this should tell you something."

The man looked at the group of them before finally stepping aside.

Lennox's wings folded in as she stepped through the doors. As soon as she entered, her eyes darted around the empty club.She completely ignored Rosalyn following close behind. Her feet carried her toward the bathrooms but quickly found what she was looking for. A set of white sheets had been laid on the floor, another on top of a person. There were a few spots of fresh stains around the torso. She quickly closed the distance and bent down. Lennox's heart pounded in her ears as her fingers touched the top edge of the sheet. With a shaky breath in she lifted it to uncover her face. Rue looking merely asleep. Her markings, gray and ashy. Tears blurred her face as she broke. Her elbows gave out and her forehead rested on Rue's. An inhuman sob released from her chest as her left wing stretched over her body. It rested ever so gently, completely blocking the two from view. Tears dripped onto the floor as she sobbed. Her body wracked with grief at the loss of her soulmate.

"I'm so sorry I couldn't protect you."

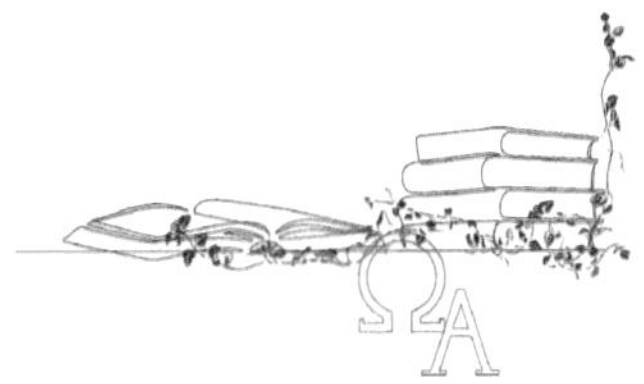

Lennox kept her promise. That day she hadn't left Rue's side. She had remained on guard from the moment the mortician came to take her body until Rue was laid on the table. When the man brought up paperwork, Rosalyn quickly volunteered. Lennox had stood for hours going over the last fifteen years they shared. True to her word, Rosalyn found her knelt beside the table beside Rue's head. Her wings wrapped all the way around the table. A shield while Lennox's back was turned. Rosalyn hadn't said a word but brought a chair. She hadn't asked her to come home. She only waited until Lennox passed out, her head on her arm by Rue's cold hand.

She had awoken in her room beside a note that told her they were all taking shifts to stand beside Rue. A few days passed as the school prepared for another funeral. In the meantime, Lennox visited the mortuary every few hours. Grief overcame her the moment she stepped foot in the now empty feeling room. So to escape it she would go fill out paperwork and choose the casket for her to be buried in.

Her friends Donnie, Octavius, Rosalyn, Wyatt, and Lealani all took turns checking in on her between classes until the day of the funeral. It was sweet, but once they were gone she found herself lost in thought of all the things she could have done to prevent this just as she had done when Felix passed. Although, this time Rue wasn't here to bring her back to reality. Occasionally, her grief would be replaced by anger. She would daydream about what she would do if she ever found out who had taken them from her. By the end of her raging, vines would attempt to crawl their way toward her through the window. Lennox would quickly send them away to hide her grief.

Saturday morning. Lennox sat on her bed lost deep in thought as she looked at Rue's stuff hanging in their closet. Coyote had informed her she needed to pick out something for Rue to be buried in. She had tried for days and others had offered but she had refused. Now matter how determined she was to open the closet, he couldn't bring herself to go in. Until now- an hour before the service. *If I had just gone to check on her.*

Lennox was already dressed in the same outfit she wore to Felix's and Elder Greene's funerals. The only black clothes she owned. Taking a step towards the closet, she touched one of Rue's favorite shirts. The soft fabric ran through her fingers as memories of her wearing it in Paris flooded her mind's eye. Gripping the sleeve, she fought back the sadness in vain though she had run out of tears the previous night.

Suddenly, there was a knock that caused her to jump. Frozen to the spot, Lennox watched someone slide a note under the door. Squinting to see what was written on the top she saw her name in familiar hand-writing. She had seen her fellow Xemos Devotee and mentor, Mort's, handwriting hundreds of times. She let out a long breath and moved toward the door at the same time footsteps receded. She picked up the envelope from the floor and cracked the door. Mort was already gone however the smallest smile found its way to her face. Two loaves of her favorite lemon lavender and sage pull apart bread greeted her. Lennox brought it into her room and quickly read the note he had left.

Lennox, you are not alone. My door is open to you as always. May wisdom guide you in the darkest hours.

Warmth started to flow through the heart she thought had been frozen after Rue's death. He had found her the day after her arrival.

According to Mort, Xemos had told him he had dropped her off at school. She walked over and put the bread away and made her way to the closet once again. *Let's try this again.*

A second knock interrupted her thoughts. "Who is it?"

"Rosalyn, is it okay to come in?" Her soft voice wafted through the door.

"Yeah." She moved her hand in an unlocking motion. The lock on her door flicked with a small click.

The young woman walked into her room. Her eyes fell to where Lennox stood in front of the open closet. Peering up at her, she saw Rosalyn was ready to go in her more formal black attire. With a soft smile she joined Lennox. The weight of her hand on Lennox's shoulder almost brought tears forward once more, only to stifle it with a small sound of sadness.

"I know today is going to be hard but I'm here, okay?" She gave her shoulder a light squeeze.

"I know... You have been since we met... I don't think I could make it through without you, Ros."

"We went through hell and escaped. If they try for me next, I'll take them down and throw them in our old cell." Rosalyn told her, confidently.

For a moment, the memories of how they met played behind her eyes. She had just died after her deal and was taken to a cell in hell. Since everything else was full, she had been chained up beside Rosalyn. They had spoken in whispers between being tortured by the crossroads demon Rosalyn made her deal with. Armaros, a fallen angel turned demon who was known to be among the most powerful and cruel. He had lived up to his reputation in less than a week and they bonded in their hate of him. In the end, the lighting scared demon walked in and set Rosalyn free. Lennox on the other hand stayed for a while until Xemos came to hell and rescued her from Val, the demon she had sold her soul to.

"I'm very grateful for you." Lennox told her with the first mostly genuine smile she'd managed in days. "If anything ever happened to you...Wyatt-"

"Girl, don't say that shit. You'll always have me and the others." Rosalyn scolded as she peered into the closet. "Have you found something for her?"

"I- I haven't been able to pick." She stuttered looking back at the shirt she still had her hand on.

"How about that white sundress she wore to last year's send off party?"

Lennox said nothing but nodded as she pulled it out and turned to Rosalyn. A somber silence fell between them as Lennox followed her to the door. The two silently turned and went into the hall. Half way down the front steps she found she couldn't take her eyes from the dress. The memory of how she had wanted to propose to Rue when she next wore it sent a pang into her stomach and a knot in her throat.

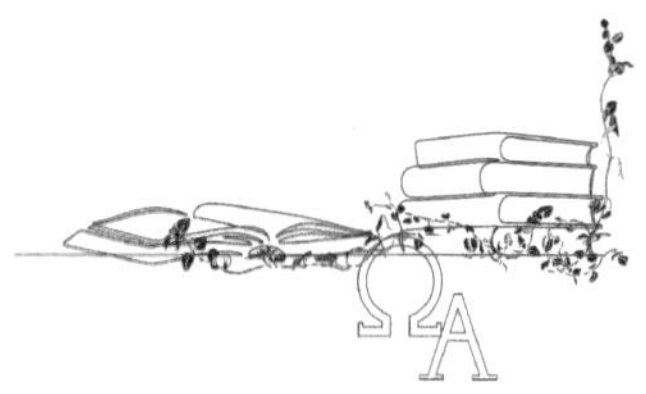

The smell of lilies filled the air as Lennox gazed at the casket that stood beside the newly dug hole. Everyone in attendance was already slowly walking away from the rows of chairs after each put a single orange lily around the open earth. Finally, she was left completely alone beside the casket. Her violet gaze locked on the dark wood of the coffin tracing the gold trim as she tried to will herself to stand. The white lily in her hand felt like a pin holding her to the spot as her thoughts drifted. *This is the last time I'll ever be next to her. She didn't even know I wanted to promise her forever... I never thought the end of eternity would come so soon.*

Her chest heaved as her emotions sprang to the surface, the crushing weight of grief came down harder than ever before. The sight of the coffin started to blur as every attempt to breathe in was rejected, her lungs refusing to expand. The flower in her hand shook as the mask fell. Her face dropping into her hands, uncontrollable sobs racking her body. Death for demons was final. There was no coming back in a new life. The knowledge that not even some version of Rue would be out there to find again one day hammered the already broken pieces of her heart.

After what felt like an hour, she finally gathered herself once more. Wiping her eyes and looking at the flower in her hand she rose to her feet. Her eyes drifted to the photo of Rue smiling beside her body. It was a photo Lennox had taken this summer while they were in Paris sitting outside a coffee shop. She let her feet carry her to Rue's side, stopping in front of the casket. Slowly, she placed her flower on top of her chest as the closest loved ones of the deceased did. The snow-like lily stood out among the almost dozen orange ones which caused her breath to hitch for a final time. Drawing in a shaky breath she leaned over and brought the lid of the casket down. Her hands shook as her eyes locked on her eternally sleeping face for the final time. With an exhale, Lennox placed a kiss on the wood, resting her forehead there.

For a second she pulled the green thread her magic, resting her hand on the wood. Seconds later it started growing and blooming hundreds of other white lilies from the top all the way down the sides, completely engulfing the casket in bright white flowers. Once it was completely covered she stood upright, not taking her eyes off of the lilies.

"This goodbye is forever, but I will never forget you, my love."

Gathering her strength, she turned and started walking back up towards Omega. Though she came to a brief stop as her eyes caught a group of people standing together by a tree ten feet away from the furthest chairs. Donnie, Leilani, Wyatt, Rosalyn, Bastien, Eden, and Octavius were waiting for her. Each was respectfully looking anywhere but at her whispering among themselves. A grateful smile crossed her face as she slowly made her way over to them.

Donnie was the first to turn and see her approaching. In the sun she could see her face was also glistening with tears. She closed the distance once Lennox started walking again and had made it close enough to the group. Her friend scooped her into a tight embrace and she saw the others turn to face them at the sudden movement. There was a second set of arms as Rosalyn joined them, her own grief apparent in her eyes.

"You stayed," she said just loud enough to be heard.

"Of course we did, we need to stick together. You aren't alone, Nox." Rosalyn assured her.

Looking up, Wyatt and Octavious came over as the others stayed a few feet away, waiting. Wyatt fiddled with the sleeve of his classic black leather jacket as Lennox was released now fully facing him. Her own sadness was reflected in his stormy eyes as he wrapped his arm around her shoulder.

"Through thick and thin, Len." He smiled in his usual, trying to lighten the mood, kind of way.

"We are your family, Lenny. We aren't going anywhere," Octavius agreed, putting a hand on her shoulder.

"If there's anything we can do, you can always call us and we will be there," Rosalyn offered.

"Thank you all, but I think I'd like to head back to my room."

"Let's head home then." Wyatt said, offering his arm to her.

Octavius quickly moved to her other side and did the same. With the most genuine smile she had in days, she put her hands on their arms. Turning to view the casket one more time. Feeling Wyatt start to walk away, she let her eyes drift to the ground as they made their way across campus.

"What you did was beautiful," Octavius whispered to her.

"Thank you... She loved lilies, they reminded her of sunsets." Lennox told him.

Once she was finally alone Lennox changed out of her funeral dress as quickly as she could. From the drawer she took out a pair of sweatpants and a t-shirt and quickly shoved them on. She approached her desk to her laptop in an attempt to distract herself. It took a conscious effort to convince herself everyone would be fine in their rooms tonight. She pulled up her latest essay and started to type with the hope that a little work would tame her thoughts. As much as she wanted to begin a hunt for Rue's killer, Rosalyn and Fang had talked her down. Lennox's attention wavered in and out as she wrote about practical ways to use magic during certain star positions. After about two hours of work, the sun had already disappeared and the moon had taken its place in the sky.

Her gaze drifted around her darkened room. She stood roughly from her fuzzy pink computer chair and walked a few steps over to the small altar she had dedicated to Xemos. After striking a match, she lit the handful of candles she had spread out across the table. The soft glow of the candles on the small desk illuminated the room just enough for her to see things clearly. Her eyes stayed on the dried purple asters placed in sets of six on either side. Her offering cup once full of whiskey, now dry. The flames danced out in her peripheral vision. In the back of her mind the images of flames winding their way up vines from her back as a man with lightning scars held her wrists. The sound of her own screams echoed from within her memory.

The silence in the real world was almost deafening despite the screams in her mind. She hadn't realized it until now just how loud it was. High pitched ringing filled her ears slowly getting louder as she stood motionless. Until her name was called. As if underwater, it took her a moment to register. *Lennox?* It sounded like-

"Rue?" She spun around.

The dark room was empty. For a moment she could almost see Rue sitting on their bed and Felix in her chair, spinning with a drink in hand. The vines around her room shook a little as if trying to get her attention. One of the branches wound its way over and tapped her on the shoulder. Smiling softly, Lennox's face softened.

"Thank you Ámpelos," she sighed, taking comfort in the little companion she had created when she arrived. The ivy had grown all over the room over the last twenty years and even taken on its unique personality over the years. "I guess it's time... I should clean out her clothes."

Turning towards the closet, she let herself take a breath before stepping over and opening the door. Lennox reached in and started to pull each item off their hangers one by one. Memories surfaced with most of them. Trips they had gone on, nights spent in, parties they had gone to with Felix. When she pulled down a pair of sweatpants and accidentally knocked the ring box from her jacket pocket that was hanging on the back of the door. It fell to the floor with a soft thud and her heart jumped as she quickly bent down to pick it up.

A wave of new emotions overcame her as her eyes were glued to the box. *This wasn't supposed to happen... I was going to propose... And they took her from me. Took them from us.* The rage she had pushed down all week started to rear its head. This time there was no pushing it away, no fighting for control. Anger filled her every thought down to her core. The vines around her shook again. This time much more aggressive than before as the candle flames grew taller. Vines started to wind their way around the room like snakes, covering the door and locking her within. She had the window cracked for air. Ivy had found it and started to grow out the window and down the side of the house.

Unable to find anyone to blame for the tragedy, her mind circled to her human life. All the death that had always seemed to surround her wherever she went. The curse. The whole reason she was here in the first place. *I thought I escaped it when I died. It must have followed me.* The vines stopped as the faces of all her friends standing by the tree earlier crossed her mind. *First, Felix, now Rue, and the others... they are all in danger. Anyone I love... Is in danger... It's my fault. I can't be here, I have to leave.* The guilt caused her feet to carry her toward her door. The vines over the door spread apart for her. Lennox quickly made her way down the stairs and into the night.

The cool wind blew across her face as she made her way down the sidewalk toward the large iron gates. Lennox had nothing but the clothes on her back as she managed to get to the entrance of the school without being spotted by the security team. She placed her hand on the cold iron and paused. Her stomach twisted as she turned to face the school, a lump forming in her throat. *I can't leave without telling at least one person, they might think I was hurt like the others.* Not wanting them to worry more than they had to, she thought about who might be the least likely to talk her out of this. Anyone in Omega would stop her and she knew it. It was then she remembered the very demon who had made the very curse she was scared of now. The face of Wyatt Steele came to her mind's eye. Her heart sank deeper down into her stomach as she could already see the sadness in his eyes. *He has to understand why I need to leave. He hates that curse as much as I do.*

She slid her hand off the gate and started the five-minute walk over to Kappa Theta. She cursed herself for not sliding her phone into her pocket as she walked the grounds for what she thought was the last time. All the while she considered various ways to get Wyatt's attention without waking up the rest of the house. Lennox glanced around the area once she arrived and found a handful of small pebbles. Taking a few steps back she tossed one at a time at his second-story window every few seconds. After about five pebbles that hit the glass with a loud thud, the window opened and Wyatt popped his head out. When she saw his eyes fall on her she waved sheepishly.

"Lennox? What the hell? Hold on, I'll be right down!"

With a nod, she wiped her face with her sleeve after he disappeared. *Maybe he won't notice I've been crying- Maybe this will be simple... Who am I kidding?* She walked around to the front of the house. After about five minutes the front door opened and the demon stepped out stretching and rubbing his face. His hair was a mess in the bun on the back of his head dressed in a band shirt and sweatpants. He walked down the two steps off the porch and made his way over to her, concern clear on his face. Lennox could see every emotion written across his tired face. Even though she woke him up, he seemed happy to see her.

"Well well, look what the cat dragged in at two in the morning. Little Miss Nox, I was having the most wonderful dream about my future wife! Wait- What's going on?" The smile on his face dropped when he finally got close enough to see her. He pulled her into a hug and took a small step back in attempts to catch her eyes.

Lennox looked at her hands and avoided his eyes knowing that her face was still flushed from the rush of emotions. *This is it... It's over and this will make it real.* She took a deep breath in, wishing she wasn't about to say what she was about to.

"Wyatt... I'm leaving, I couldn't go without telling someone."

Silence followed her words. Lennox squeezed her eyes shut in attempts not to cry. The full weight of her words caused a lump to form in her throat again. Feeling his finger under her chin, Wyatt used a single finger to lift her face to meet his gaze. She opened her eyes to look into his. Clouds of confusion and sadness, his grip tightened slightly as if he was trying to hold her there. *I don't want to go.* Her heart shattered at the thought. Heartbreak was written in her eyes as she bit back the words she wanted to say.

Wyatt's eyes darted between hers as if to decipher what was inside her head. His gaze caused her breath to hitch in her chest and a few tears to escape. She remembered how much she hated him when she found out he was the reason behind a four-generation curse that had passed on to her. Wyatt's expression softened. He took her face in both hands and ran his thumbs over her cheeks, wiping away the tears trailing down. "Why? Lennox, this is your home, you can't leave- Not now." His voice broke as he dropped his hands. "Just... Come inside and we can talk about this. I'm here for you."

Her eyes went wide at the thought of stepping foot inside Kappa

Theta, the memory of Felix still fresh in her mind. "I can't... I should get going before someone notices I'm not in my room. I didn't want anyone to think something bad happened."

She turned to leave but he grabbed her hand lightly. "Wait. Come just sit on the porch with me. One hour, that's all I'm asking for."

She sighed, evidently wrong about Wyatt not trying to stop her. "One hour, but then I have to go."

He moved to stand beside her as she carefully made her way towards the stairs to the porch. Doing her best, she averted her eyes away from the dark green door and pushed the face of Felix from her mind. Stepping up they sat on two chairs the other members of the house had left out. She peered over at him and slowly relaxed enough to even herself out as he patted her knee. As Lennox's eyes met his, a sad smile appeared on her face and her heart tore a little more at the break caused by grief.

"I've known you for seven years, Len. You've always said how happy you are here. What's changed?" He asked.

She paused and considered her answer. She knew the moment she told him the true reason it would become real. In the seconds that followed, memories of the last seven years followed freely. The first time they met in the courtyard after their many fights over the decades. Principal Moon and Felix had to pull the two apart. Once expulsion was threatened, she avoided him. Until he drunkenly shared his biggest regret. The creation and release of her curse. It had taken over a year for her to begin to forgive him. Multiple nights of long conversations laced with anger. Eventually, the night he won her trust.

"You know, I hated you for that first semester."

A tense laugh escaped Wyatt. "Until I helped you get that Witch to safety from her mother trying to drown her."

"I would have died in that undercurrent if you hadn't pulled us out." A shiver ran through her spine as she remembered how her wings had been twisted in the current and scraped the river bed.

"You're stalling."

"I have a whole hour, right? Won't you miss our late night chats?" Lennox tilted her head toward him.

"I won't- Because you're not going to leave." Confidence laced his raspy voice.

"Wyatt, I-"

He stopped her with a simple hand. "You had every right to hate me... Every right to still hate me."

"You're not the demon who threw that curse out into the world for fun anymore."

Silence drifted into the air briefly. His lips turned up a bit more and gratitude filled his eyes. He didn't need to say it, Lennox knew how hard he had worked to change. When he had come to the school he had told her he was on a mission to become better after meeting a demon in Texas. *A demon with a red bandanna... Aron.* A new piece clicked into the puzzle and regret stirred in her stomach. Wyatt had only ever spoken highly of the Crossroad Demon who helped him realize he may find peace here at the school and drove him to be a better man. *I judged him too harshly.*

"Len," His voice broke her thoughts. "What's really going on?"

"The curse... It's back."

Wyatt's face shifted from a comforting smile to ghost white. "That's impossible, Nox. Xemos himself told us it was broken when he took you out of hell."

"Look at all the signs, Wyatt. Felix and Rue, a friend and a lover. Die under mysterious circumstances. You designed it to kill anyone the victim loved." Her brows furrowed.

"I did, but it couldn't have come back. You told me your daughter didn't have the mark when she was born. That's all thanks to you." He told her gently, his expression softening in understanding. "I never told you, but- When you were worried about Rue when you two met, I went to Xemos by myself. He told me it's a one in a million chance of it coming back."

"For all you know, it's been lying dormant within me! It's trying to, I don't know, reactivate?" Lennox's voice rose and broke and the bushes shook beside them. "First it was my mother, Olivia, of cancer. I was three... My father, Cyprus, was in a car accident. I was ten... His sister Arya took me in and was murdered a month before I turned eighteen. Then Mason months after I found out I was expecting Gemma... Now hunters have come and randomly targeted people I care about? What are the chances that even just the mark on my right shoulder didn't act like some sort of magic bad luck beacon and the single chance is happening? What if you're next? Rosalyn? Octavius? Eden? Donnie? The pattern is continuing again and I seem to be the only one seeing it."

Wyatt took a deep breath as he watched Lennox. Silence fell between them. His expression shifted into regret and seemed just as upset as she was at the thought. She knew it was the darkest spot in his past and she had just brought everything to the surface for both of them. His hands covered his face for a moment, the black rose on his right hand standing out in contrast against his pale skin. Slowly he ran them down his face before he peered at her apologetically.

"I'll never forgive myself for releasing that curse into the world." He paused and watched her face. "If there's anything I know, it is broken. All traces are gone. You are not cursed anymore, Lennox."

She shook her head, incapable at accepting his words. "Why don't we test it? I leave and if they follow it has to be back right?"

"If the threat is here, what is leaving going to do? You will be gone and we will still be in danger, but if you stay you can fight." He countered in an attempt to reason with her, and tilted his head down.

She stood from her chair and turned to him, desperation in her eyes. The edges of her vision threatened to burn red. *He can't see it and I'm going to have to bury more people.* Her next breath hitched in her chest and her hands shook as she broke from his gaze. *I have to go.* Her feet started to carry her toward the stairs.

"I am the reason they are here. If they are targeting me, they will follow me."

Wyatt quickly reached out and took her hand, giving her arm a light tug which caused her to face him once more. "My hour isn't up. Stop, take a second. Think about what you want to do. Do you want to run? Or help us protect everyone who's still here?"

She stood there frozen to her spot, locked eyes with the storm inside. All of the previous lightness lost, tinted with a wave of dark anger just beneath the surface. Wyatt's hand was still wrapped around hers, completely encasing it. Her eyes fell to the rose as he pulled her toward him. Lennox decided to meet his eyes once more as he seemed to search for the reasonable side of her. Gently, his other hand took hers and he held them to his chest.

His lips parted to speak again. "These hunters have taken two of my best friends already. I'm not about to allow the loss of anyone else. We need you- I need you."

It was all he needed to say and he knew it. She could never walk away from someone who needed her, no matter the cost. "Wyatt-"

He's right, you know. The deep voice of Xemos echoed in her mind, outwardly her determination wavered. Exhaustion filled her as the God moved easily through her mental barriers.

You said there was a chance. She tossed back as Wyatt watched her closely. It wasn't the first time he had witnessed the two mid conversation. He only looked mildly annoyed as he waited. She didn't take it personally as she knew the two hated each other.

That chance has not come to pass, nor does my Sister. Rest easily, about that. Xemos reassured.

"What if I just cause more pain?" Lennox said aloud to both of them, her voice broke slightly.

There it was. Her fear from her human life laid out on a platter for him once again. She had watched Mason's parents cry at their son's funeral. To this day she could still hear the woman's sobs as he was lowered. The woman's words to her as she left. *I'm sorry you didn't get to say goodbye. He loved you more than I've seen anyone love another person.* The grip he had on her hands loosed slightly as she was brought back to the moment. Wyatt's eyes softened as he brushed a piece of her hair from her face and released her hands finally. With a long sigh Lennox stepped back over to her chair once more, soon joined by him once more.

"You won't, the only pain you'll cause is to the people who did this. Besides, even if they do follow you, do you plan on facing them alone?"

Lennox's eyebrow rose. "Why would I put you guys at risk?"

"You don't even know how many of them there are. The crazy cult people tend to run in packs."

"I've taken on hundreds of humans." Lennox folded her arms over her chest.

"Hunters? Trained supernatural assassins? How many at a time? Two? Four? Nine?"

"Two, Rue and I-"

Wyatt held up his finger. "That's with Rue, what about completely alone?"

"... No."

"If you are outnumbered and you're too far from the grounds we won't make it in time. If you die, there's nothing stopping them from coming right back here and picking each of us off."

His last words shook her as she saw the image of each one of them dying, herself already in the ground unable to stop it. The spark of the calm, rational version of her ignited. It slowly illuminated the dark edges of her mind. Guilt pierced her heart as she met his eyes for the third time. Whether he knew it or not she had subconsciously blamed him.

"It's okay," His voice came out softly. "I understand why you feel the way you do, why you would only believe this to be the only rational explanation."

"I'm sorry-"

"Don't be. As long as we are together, we can take on anything. You will *not* have to bury anyone else... Are we in this together?"

Lennox nodded as words refused to come out. Her entire demeanor shifted as her body untensed. A smile appeared on the man's face followed by a long exhale. His tired eyes lit up with his usual spark as he patted her knee.

"Thank you for coming to me. For trusting me."

"I couldn't let you guys think the worst." Lennox admitted.

He nodded and pulled on his leather jacket as he stood and offered his hand to her. "How about we go back to Omega and hang out with Rosalyn for the night?"

"I've spent so many nights there already. I don't want to intrude."

"Well, you could come up to my room if you wanted."

"Aren't yours and Aron's rooms conjoined?" She asked, her nose wrinkled slightly.

It was his turn to raise an eyebrow at her. "And?"

"And, I don't want to see him... Not yet, I- I have an apology to make but I'm not ready for it yet." She paused and considered her options. "Why don't you spend the night in my room? If you are okay with that."

"Nox, I love sleepovers and I'm already dressed for it."

Wyatt offered his hand to her and this time she took it. Lennox stood easily from her chair and followed him toward the dark grounds, back to her home. The whole way back she explained how the whole night had ended up this way, from her summoning to the moment she found the ring box in Rue's jacket pocket. Wyatt had swung an arm around her shoulders and offered to help clean up with Rosalyn's help in the morning which Lennox gratefully accepted.

The only sound Lennox heard as she walked down the hall. Vice Principal De Rosa began her day with a mass email about an assembly. The sound of occasional sets of footsteps echoed as other students walked past her. In typical Lennox fashion she walked down the hall fifteen minutes before asked to arrive. As she turned left down the hall, her eyes remained glued to her phone.

Lennox-
I hope you checked your email this morning.
-Sent 2:14 pm

> Aron-
> Of course, I did Leonard. Don't worry your little pink head, I'll be there.
> -Sent 2:16 pm

With a scowl, she shoved her phone back into her pocket. Lennox turned the corner to go down to the first floor to the auditorium. With each step down the first flight, her bag hit against the side of her leg which almost hit another student as they passed each other. The woman was tall with long brown hair and a silver stripe framing her face who looked lost. *Werewolf, maybe new? I've never seen her around. Although, she does look vaguely familiar.*

"Looking for something?" Lennox asked.

"Yeah, I was told there's a meeting today. I got to Omega Alpha yesterday and I'm still learning the area. I'm Remi Daniels- Uhhhh, excuse me, Remi Moon."

An amused smile crossed Lennox's face. "You seem more confused than I thought. I'm Lennox Cade, Head of Omega Alpha House."

"It's a long story, but I met my brother for the first time yesterday and I'm still getting used to the idea." Remi admitted.

"That's great, who's your brother if you feel like sharing?"

"Coyote Moon, he's on the security team here as I understand it." The girl smiled nervously and continued to rant. "My uncle is Mathias Moon, but everyone calls him Fang. He's new this year too as the Predator and Prey Elder and a part of the team with Cathwulf and Coyote."

It all clicked quickly once Remi explained. She looked a lot like her brother and the new Elder. Lennox had heard of the werewolf before she had seen him, though never saw him in person or photos. From what she had read, he was the last of an Alpha werewolf line. Now with new information she realized Coyote and Remi were a part of it. *Well, I guess that explains why they are all so tall.*

"So that's why I thought you looked familiar. Coyote has been here for a good amount of time. Congratulations on finding your family. This place has a way of bringing people together. Your Uncle has quite a reputation in our world."

"It seems to be. I guess we'll be seeing each other quite often since you're the Head of House."

"I'll be around. If you ever need anything you can always reach out. Do you want me to show you where the auditorium is?"

"That would be helpful, thank you."

The two of them made their way down the stairs, toward where the meeting was to be held. Lennox looked at her schedule and pointed out a few common classes as they passed by. She gave her as much information as she could about house events and some of the Elders.

"There's quite a few Elder Miller's here so some of them go by their first names. Elder Alaric Miller, Biology and Elder Richard Miller, Sociology. You have Elder Eloise Miller for Business Studies."

The demon stopped as they approached the entrance of the auditorium. The enlarged canvases from the funerals with flowers beneath that sat beside the door. The faces of Elder Narcissus Greene, Felix, and Rue knocked the wind from her chest. Her still broken heart cracked open again and she stood frozen to the spot. Her violet stare locked on Rue's eyes- Her smile.

A voice tried to break through her haze of grief, but they sounded so far away. She could see Remi staring at the photos and then at her out of the corner of her eye. Lennox was busy clutching memories of Rue's laugh when three more voices joined. They paused and one of the people came to stand on her right side. A hand on her shoulder brought her back down to reality. When she glanced over, she saw the face of Rosalyn looking at her with a knowing look in her eyes and a kind smile.

"Are you ready for the meeting?" She asked, with a silent 'are you okay' with a slight brow raise.

Lennox let a false smile cross her face, she wouldn't want to draw too much attention. "Yeah, I'm fine."

She turned to see who else was around them and her eyes fell on Vice Principal Genevive De Rosa, Aron, and Rosalyn. They had joined herself and Remi, chatting amongst themselves. Lennox watched them for a moment and noticed Aron sneaking uneasy glances at Rosalyn who peered over at her for a moment. She forced herself to push aside her grief and turned toward the group. *Rosalyn and Aron have very similar markings.* The stitch-like pattern on their noses and cheekbones was almost identical. Something felt familiar in the back of her mind, but at the moment she focused on the assembly as the red-headed woman turned towards her with the usual neutral expression.

Her bright blue siren eyes fell on Lennox, "Good to see you, Miss. Cade."

"Likewise Elder De Rosa," she nodded as a smirk formed on Aron's face. "What do you find so entertaining?"

"You're so formal Lenoard, take a chill pill." He insisted, his smirk turned into a full smile.

"And be a little more like you?" She shot back. "Maybe I'd consider your advice if you actually used my name."

"Where's the fun in that? Besides, no one can be like me," Aron winked, amusement written across his face.

"These guys seem to not like each other." Lennox heard Remi whisper to Rosalyn who stifled a laugh.

"If only you knew the half of it," she whispered back.

She couldn't help but let out a small chuckle as Aron looked over to the other two. She watched his smile falter when his eyes fell on Rosalyn again but seemed to quickly recover. The Vice Principal's back was turned while she was busy with the lock on the door to the auditorium when her strict voice trailed behind her.

"Alright you two. You're supposed to be working together." She turned to look at the two Heads of House as she opened the door for them.

"Yeah, Cade-" He was cut off by Rosalyn moving between them.

"Alright, I'm heading in." She hooked Lennox by the arm. "Let's go, I wanna get good seats."

The group made their way in and took their seats. The other students in the school slowly started to file in as classes ended early for the day. Aron went to sit with some of his friends at Kappa, while the three girls sat beside each other. Wyatt saw Aron and the others first as he walked in. The two smiled at each other and started to talk. *Are they planning something I need to be worried about? It doesn't matter, not my circus, not my monkeys... Well-*

Her thoughts were interrupted by Wyatt's voice calling over. "Hey! You made it too! We'll join you guys!"

Aron shot him a look. "Why don't we go over with the guys?"

"Naw, come on. I bet Eden will be over here shortly. Help a guy out and be my wingman."

"Only because it's you," the blond-haired demon agreed. Lennox watched him all but drag him back over. She noted it was slightly odd he seemed to be avoiding them. Usually, she couldn't escape him trying to push her buttons.

After twenty minutes the last of the Elders, Eden, and Bastien all made their way in. She was surprised to see every single teacher in the back row. *Must have been required for them too.* Normally, Elder Eloise Miller never showed up to school gatherings. Eden and Bastien were also usually a toss up. However, they made their way to sit in one of the middle rows when Wyatt motioned for Eden to join them. Lennox noticed Eden's eyes dart to her cousin for a moment before he elbowed her with a bright smile. Basiten excitedly pulled her over to the group and took their seats filling almost the entire front row now.

She turned back towards the front where Elder De Rosa stood with the three members of the security team. Cathwulf was a little taller than the siren. However, still small standing next to Coyote and Fang. The hum of whispers filled the area which blocked her from her attempt to listen in.

Finally, the siren turned to address the room, "Alright, it's time."

As she spoke the room got quieter. The creaking of the older wooden seats echoed while people shifted in their seats to pay attention. A few final whispers drifted around as the Vice Principal proceeded with an almost angry undertone.

"We all know that the school has had many losses this semester. Never, in the history of this school have we been attacked in such ways, and I promise we will get to the bottom of it. The security team has called in Mathias Bloodfang Moon to join in their efforts to keep everyone here safe. That being said, I will allow Coyote to speak on the new procedures that will be in place during these uncertain times."

Elder De Rosa took a step back and Coyote took her place. He scanned the room before speaking with a serious look in his eyes. "Thank you, Vice Principal De Rosa. This semester we will be instating a curfew. All students must be back in their dorms by eleven. We will be doing extra patrols. If we find anyone out after then, you can bunk by the security office for the night and trust me none of us want that... Please do not walk alone if you can avoid it, travel together in pairs or better yet sets of three. The security team's cell phone numbers will be distributed. If you feel unsafe, please don't hesitate to reach out to us. If you see anything that looks suspicious, the office is located down the stairs from the main entrance of the school. One of us will always be there."

Coyote paused as he looked around the room. It was so quiet you could have heard a pin drop. Everyone waited expectantly, the looming weight of unspoken questions hung in the air. The man let out a sigh as he read the room. A knot formed in Lennox's throat as he started to speak again.

"I can't hide what's happening from you all... We have every reason to believe Hunters have hidden themselves among us. Unfortunately this means I have to give you some tips to spot them. Humans will ask a lot of questions about you and your life. They will usually be intimidated by you. As well as be more apprehensive of indulging in the seven sins. We are doing everything in our power to find the imposters. These Hunters have learned our way of life... Our strengths, our weaknesses; we do not take this lightly. Please follow the guidelines we have set and stay on alert. That is all unless another Elder would like to add anything?" The room stayed quiet. "Have a good evening everyone."

He turned away and everyone started to get up. Lennox heard Rosalyn chatting to Wyatt while Remi stood to go talk to her family. Elder De Rosa turned towards Aron and Lennox with a finger held up just as he attempted to sneak out.

"You two, I need you to stay for a few minutes."

"Ohhh, the Heads of House are in trouble?" Wyatt teased them.

"Naw, can't be. Lennox doesn't break rules." Bastien chimed in.

"Very true, at least not too often. It's been years since the last time." Wyatt let out a small laugh.

"You mean to tell me, Lennox Cade has broken a rule?" Aron asked, cocking an eyebrow.

"You know I'm right here," she put her hands on her hips.

"Once or twice since I've known her. Oh, Len, it's just all in fun." The tattooed demon tilted his head to her before turning to Eden. "Let's get out of here sweetheart."

"Don't call me that," her brow furrowed in annoyance.

"Oh, I'm sorry Little Viper." He leaned against the back of one of the chairs.

"Little Viper?" Bastien eyed her. "I like that, it's fitting."

Lennox laughed a little as Rosalyn started to shoo the others out once everyone else was gone. Soon, it was Aron, Remi, Elder De Rosa, the security team and herself left in the large quiet room. The two students made their way over and joined them as the Vice Principal looked between them. Aron smiled at the very tall man, Elder Fang, who he seemed to know already.

"What can we do for you, boss man?" He asked, crossing his arms as Lennox listened closely.

"We are hoping that sharing the information with the school will put the Hunters on edge enough to make them pause long enough to find them. We need you to make sure that everyone in your houses is inside at curfew. If anyone is missing, we need to know as soon as possible." Fang told him, glancing at Lennox.

She nodded when Fang met her eyes, "That's not a problem."

"You two need to figure out how to work together. You're a team and we trust that you can keep your eyes out for your fellow housemates, even on each other." Elder De Rosa turned to her with a serious look on her face. Aron's playful demeanor shifted when her piercing blue eyes fell on him.

"Can't make any promises for this one, but I will do my best." Aron flashed a smile.

"Of course, Elder De Rosa." Lennox nodded and noticed Coyote take a long breath in.

"There's something else." Coyote spoke up, "With all of the deaths, we don't believe they were picked at random."

Lennox's heart fell into her stomach, his words sent her hair on edge. *Do they know about my curse? No, they can't know. Wyatt or Rosalyn would have never told anyone... They are the only ones left alive that know.* Her eyes still drifted towards the ground as she hoped they hadn't somehow figured it out.

"We have reason to believe all Elders and you two have a greater risk for being targets. We think any of you could be the next victim. Lennox due to Rue's death and Aron due to the target that seems to be on any authority figure." Quickly, she raised her eyes back to him and tried her best to hide her surprise. "Don't worry, we will be making sure you both remain safe. Lennox, Remi has agreed to go with you if you don't have anyone to walk to the main building with from Omega in the mornings. Aron, if you don't have anyone, Fang will accompany you."

As he spoke, her thoughts started to drift slightly. *They've been working their way to me, taking out everyone close to me. He's right. Aron and I might not be close but he could be used to get to me.* She nodded in agreement, it would be annoying but it was understandable. As for working together, she still owed him an apology. Though now wasn't the time as he would probably make a scene of it. Once Coyote received a nod from both of them he seemed to relax a little.

"Alright, head back to the houses for the evening." He told them before he turned away as the Elders and Remi made their way towards the stairs.

Aron looked over to her with a mischievous smile spread across his face, his green eyes lit up. He hooked his arm through hers, "Let's go home, I'll make sure you get there safely!"

"Okay, mister Boy Scout." She shook her head as her jaw feathered.

"What's a Boy Scout?" Aron asked while he pulled her along.

Forced to go with him as he escorted her back toward the exit of the auditorium, she felt her face heat up as her annoyance bubbled. The photos from earlier were still fresh in her mind. Lennox's jaw clenched as her mind dragged the image of Felix to the forefront of her mind. Aron made a joke about Fang being the new sheriff in town. Every nerve slowly started to ignite. The red hot rejection filled her flowing into her stomach. *They should still be here, this place was supposed to be safe. They are gone but somehow it's all still the same?* As they passed the doors and the trio of photos Lennox's hands had balled into fists. *It's not right... it's not fair.* She finally spoke up as grief buried her once again.

"This isn't funny, Aron! People are dying, that's why we have to do this! You could be a target! Don't you care?" Pulling her arm from his, they stopped in front of the display.

He stopped and looked at her. The usually plastered smile whipped off his face replaced by surprise. He kept his tone even as he frowned at her and seemed almost hurt yet again. "Of course, I care."

"Really? Because I haven't seen you take any of this seriously. You skip classes, I think I've seen you at two over the last few weeks? Everything is always a joke to you. How am I supposed to believe you?"

"Just because I skip classes, doesn't mean I don't care about the safety of everyone here, Lennox." Aron told her with his brow furrowed.

"Well, you definitely don't show it." Lennox folded her arms defensively. *Looks like someone does know my name.* "Look- I don't blame you if you don't want to be involved with all this with everything that's going on."

"Are you done?" He asked harshly, his eyes burning into hers. She opened her mouth to speak before she was stopped. "You think I'm going to leave everyone now? You guys need the help and I'm not going to let anyone get hurt. Do you forget I have friends here too? It's only been a few weeks but I will not walk away just because of a little danger. If I leave, how are you going to protect anyone if they get to you? You don't think I haven't already put all of this together? Out of both of us, you're the one they're going to target."

His frustration slowly started to fade as he looked into her eyes, revealing the smallest hint of worry. It was her turn to be surprised, he had come off as a frat boy who only wanted to party. It was odd to think that only after having been at the school for a few weeks yet he was already so attached. *There's a sensible side to him? I didn't think that was possible... Maybe it is time for that apology.* She dropped her arms as she realized he must have put it together after Rue's death. Tragedy seemed to circle her like a predator to prey. She was grateful he didn't know anything about her curse as she sighed avoiding his eyes.

"See there's more to me than you think," his voice still carried a mildly irritated tone.

"You're right- I'm sorry... When you came, everything happened so fast, I didn't give you a chance- but to be fair, you didn't give the best first impression." They fell into a brief silence.

"Thank you, I do understand. I like to push people's buttons, it's fun. However, I do have a *heart*... I do understand grief more than you think." Aron said, his voice softening slightly, a smirk crossed his face when she said he was right.

Lennox looked over to the door, not wanting to be in front of the photos anymore. She finally met his eyes again and nodded her head towards the door. Maybe they could work together, the thought sent mixed feelings through her but she knew she had to try for the sake of the ones left from the attacks.

"We should head back and start getting a list together for both houses for nightly checks and a checklist for at night and in the morning."

She took a few steps towards the door. With a nod, he followed her out of the main school building. They made their way onto the grounds, the warm afternoon sun contrasting with the cooler breeze. Aron rambled on about the curfew and Lennox was still thinking of things she could do to help keep everyone safe at night after the lockdown. *They got into Kappa in the middle of the night, there's nothing stopping them from just walking into either house.*

"We need to work together to protect everyone. Even with the curfew, it won't stop them from unlocking the doors to wherever they want to go."

"What do you have in mind?" Aron asked. "Security cameras?"

"No- the school has plenty of those. The office is far enough from the houses. Even if they were in their wolf forms, I don't know if they would get there fast enough..."

As she thought for a moment, she remembered the vines in her room. Lennox knew that using the same magic to cover the houses every night would take a lot of energy to create but it would be worth it. If someone tried to get through them, she would know immediately.

"I can use magic, I lean mostly towards earth elements. I can grow vines around the windows and doors of both houses right after we make sure everyone has made it before we lock everything down."

"You can do that?" He asked as they kept going down the path. "Wouldn't that drain you running it all night?"

She ran the theory in her mind. "Not unless they were more like motion detectors instead of active wards. Yes, they could take a lot to create, but I would sleep much better knowing if someone is trying to come in, I would know. I can handle waking up tired as long as I can get some peace of mind."

"Passive magic can still become overwhelming if done for extended periods, Lenny-Boo. I know someone like you knows that." Aron pointed out.

"I don't see many other options." She shook her head as they got closer to Kappa house.

"I do, I can help. I don't use passive magic as much but I can hang out around the houses at night, lay a little boobie trap around the perimeter."

"Hold on, what kind of perimeter?" She questioned, eyeing him suspiciously.

"Well, I lean towards fire, they walk over it, it'll start a controlled fire around the house and it should draw enough attention before they can get through it." He explained.

"Are you sure it's controlled? Could it catch the house on fire?"

"About as controlled as I am," he joked. Seeing the look on her face, he put a hand on her shoulder. "No, the house won't burn down, it would be far enough away. Geez, have some faith in me."

They approached the front of the green doors and Lennox eyed them nervously. Every time she got too close, she remembered the morning she last walked through them. *You know it's not a good idea to leave your door unlocked.* Her words haunted her nightmares along with the pools of red that had covered the carpet. Red that covered her hands and clothes. Stained them beyond repair- Stained her very core. Lennox couldn't bring herself to walk through the door still as she expected Felix to come out still. She couldn't bear to look at the place he had taken his final breaths. Aron stopped when she did, she could feel his emerald gaze on her.

"You can come in if you want. You can call someone to walk over to Omega inside if you want." He offered.

"I- umm, no thank you, I'll wait outside for someone." She pulled out her phone and texted Rosalyn and Donnie to ask them to meet her.

"Are you sure?" He asked as they went onto the deck.

"I'm sure," she told him a little too quickly.

"Okay, I'll be inside if you need anything. I'll email you the list of the Kappa guys." He watched her carefully and obviously didn't believe her.

"I'll email you the nightly checklist I've been doing later, I'll start with the vines tonight and we can switch off every two days. Change it up every once in a while so they won't catch on."

With a freshly printed checklist in hand, Lennox and Remi made their way to Kappa Theta house right at eleven. They discussed how the vines would work, Lennox going over two theories on how to make it not so draining as they approached. Just before they turned the last corner, Lennox's phone rang in her pocket. Looking at her watch her heart leapt into her throat as she saw who was calling.

"I have to take this, give me a few?"

"Of course." Remi nodded and continued around the corner.

Quickly, she pulled her phone from her pocket. She had called the The Wardens of Wisdom, Xemos's special research and defense unit, the day after she almost ran away. The death of Rue had pushed her far enough. To protect everyone else she had to make sure everyone was right. That the curse was still dormant. Her last resource, The

Wardens. Each were a different supernatural species turned Phoenix. Ruana, Satori, Osian, and Nathaira. Across the screen was a photo of a woman with short ginger hair and bright lavender eyes in the middle of a large library. Satori's large tan mouse ears perked up toward the camera. Lennox smiled as she imagined one of the other's sneaking up on the Library Mouse. Answering and putting her phone to her ear, she heard the woman's normally quieter voice berating someone beside her.

"No, that scroll belongs on the top- Well hey there Len!"

"Hey Satori, you got back to me quickly." Lennox laughed lightly.

"Well it was pretty urgent. Can't have curses runamuck. Now what's up?"

She shook her head. "Little Mouse, you called me."

"Right! Yes, well I went over some of the old journals from your family line. Nothing there still. However Ruana offered to go try and break into Steele's old office."

"She may be a demon, but that door has a blood lock. The moment they spell Wyatt's blood, every demon within a mile radius will come sniffing around. They know he's abandoned his position. Is it really worth the risk?"

"If it means finding a true cure for you and possibly Renas? Of course it is." Satori's voice hardened.

"You know they aren't the same curses. It could be a dead end."

"It's worth the risk- What do you mean? You were onboard last night!" Her voice faded slightly. "Cade's curse is the closest thing we've seen to Renas's. If we can get our hands on the ingredients we could- Fine."

Lennox spoke before Satori could. "It's okay, I'm not looking for a curse. I'm looking for confirmation. Is it still in hibernation?"

"We talked to Xemos." Osian spoke up. "He said the only way it can be reactivated is if you ingest Mournwood Powder on a full moon. So unless you have one of the rarest herbs in the world in your tea collection, it is dormant."

With a long sigh of relief, she ran a hand through her hair. She let her gaze drift to the lights on in the student dorms in the main building. "I do not, thank you Osian."

"We'll keep you updated, Len. Keep your eyes out okay? Come visit us soon. Echelons Elysium needs a spot of color." Satori's voice came back.

"I'll try to after the semester is over. If I make it that long."

"You better or I'm coming over there and bringing your ass back myself."

"I'm not a Phoenix, as much as you want me to be." Lennox started to walk to where Remi disappeared.

"Not yet!"

"In your dreams, talk soon everyone." She pocketed her phone after Satori hung up.

She rounded the corner to Remi who stood there on her phone. When she came into view, the wolf looked up with a smile and continued down the path without asking many questions. Finally the house came into view where Wyatt and Aron stood out front. The two were locked in some debate about a Taylor Swift record they were fighting over.

"It's my turn with Taylor's Debut!" Wyatt complained.

"If you can find it!" Aron laughed.

"My guess is under his pillow." Lennox teased as the two approached.

Wyatt turned and smiled brightly before going down the few stairs. His arm wrapped around her in a side hug. "There you are! Are you sure this is going to work?"

"It has to," she hugged him and looked over to Aron. "Did you lock all of the windows and doors and do a headcount?"

"Yes, everyone is all tucked in and ready for their bedtime stories. Would you two want to join?" He winked at her, running a hand through his hair over the red bandanna.

"I'll have to pass this time, unfortunately."

"If my brother catches out after curfew he'll have us mopping the school all night. I don't know about you but I value my sleep." Remi added.

"Oh I'm sure big brother will understand if you're a few minutes late." Wyatt commented to the werewolf.

"I'd rather not test that." She shook her head.

"I'll see you two in the morning to lift the vines from the house," Lennox told the group."You should go inside now if you don't want to be locked outside."

With a nod, the two boys made their way back up their stairs to the door. Just before she turned to start to grow the vines around the house, Aron looked back and caught her eyes. To her surprise, his forest green irises were filled with concern. Lennox gave him a soft smile hoping to reassure him and in a way herself for such an intricate spell.

"Be safe, okay?" He seemed to be speaking to both of them, but it almost felt directed at her.

She nodded, holding up her phone. "I'll call you if anything goes bump in the night."

With a nervous laugh, they went inside and locked the door behind them. Lennox took a few steps closer to the building and closed her eyes. Internally she pulled at the green thread of magic and allowed it to flow freely from the source. She felt her arms heat. The glow of the chains and sigils illuminated the other side of her eyelids. All at once, her connection to the plant life around the house entangled itself with the flow of open magic. The bushes and trees beside the house shuddered as she created new vines from the few already climbing up the cobblestone.

In her mind's eye, she saw the vines creeping to the windows and over every entrance. At the same time she felt the energy slowly drain. The heat on her arms started to sear. It was about five minutes until the last vine was over the back entrance. When she opened her eyes, Lennox was met by the very ivy vines she had pictured. They covered everything only leaving bald spots of stone peeking through every so often. Her success hummed within her. The illuminated chains and sigils had dimmed leaving only the sigils alight from the consistent flow of magic. A smile crossed her face as she could feel the alert that she and Remi were nearby.

"Good job, Poison Ivy!" Aron called from the window, making Lennox and Remi laugh.

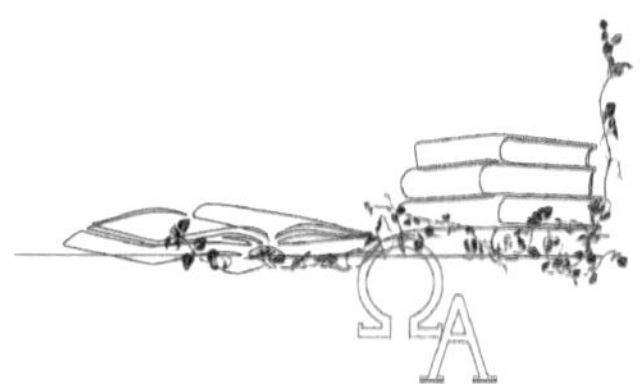

Lennox opened her eyes as a sharp pain spread from her side. Her screams added to those that could be heard over the clanking of metal. As she peered above her and found the source. Her arms had been securely shackled with thick chains over her head. A familiar voice came from beside her which blocked out the iron clanking.

"Leave her alone," it yelled at someone.

Her eyes shot over to her side, there was another demon with short choppy black and red hair chained up beside her. A combination of dried and fresh blood was mixed across the side of her face. She peered worriedly back at Lennox with a knife that stuck out of her right leg, her chest shaking with every painful breath. *I'm in hell, the first day... When I met Rosalyn.* She knew what would happen next. She looked down to the right to find a knife handle exactly where she knew it would be buried. At the realization, a wave of life-like pain burned through her torso and caused her to lose her sense of rationality. *What the hell? I've never been able to feel in my dreams like this.*

With her jaw locked and a grimace on her lips. A familiar charred black hand was holding it there. Her nerves caught fire as she felt the presence of her worst nightmare looming over her, just as he did that night. Lennox's eyes followed the burned skin trailed its way up from his fingers beyond the rolled sleeve of his pitch-black suit. The pressure faded as he released the handle. A pained groan to escape her. She tried to lean forward but his fingers held her jaw up forcing her to meet his gaze. It took a second but her eyes focused on the man with shoulder-length black hair and eyes dark as midnight whose only color came from the glowing green irises set inside the center.

His face bore the marks of his story. Lighting scars stretching from his right forehead down to his left jaw, appearing again on the left side of his neck. A mark from being smited from heaven as she understood. Tattoo-like markings lined his face. An unholy trinity of reversed crucifixes on his forehead and each cheek. Stretching from each ear down his cheekbones were blackened lines, dark and thick blurring down his jaw. Identical lines lined each side of his neck almost connecting to curve out at his collar bones, with three dots between them at the base of his neck.

He leaned until his face came within inches of hers. Large tattered bat-like wings shifted behind him as he kneeled in front of her. Their gazes hadn't broken, locked in a game of determination. She pulled down on the shackles making them clatter loudly as his hand suddenly clasped around her neck. He squeezed just enough to cut off most of her air. His free hand wrapped around her wrists, forcing them to stay still. A wicked smile plastered across his lips as he looked deep into her eyes like a lion eyeing up its next meal. A tingling sensation filled her now cherry red face as she gasped to get any air she could.

"There's so much fight in you," his deep voice echoed along the walls. "There must be something worth fighting for. I want to see."

His hand drifted from her throat to her bright pink hair. The demon's fingers winding their way through gently as if he was trying to move it out of her face. That was until he suddenly gripped it at the roots which left her nowhere to go. Mental fire had sparked to life under his palm. Lennox's barriers were weaker, easy to invade. There was no mercy, no softness, just fire as memories of her daughter, Gemma, newly born wrapped in blankets burned across her vision. He laughed looking over to the woman.

"I see! You have a daughter- but you gave her away. Do you hear that my dear Rosalyn? She lived your dream and denied it!"

Her eyes followed his to a barely conscious Rosalyn who had a single tear running down her cheek. Her heart sank for her newfound friend as the woman passed out from her injuries. The world started to go blurry from the intense heat of the fallen angels' continued search. At the same time she felt a tug at magic she didn't think had followed her into this life. Instinctively, she pulled at the thread, the flow of magic started to rapidly heat the iron. A look of surprise crossed his face momentarily as he took his hand off hers. His grip on her hair vanished finally making the fire inside her mind sizzle out. She gasped finally able to breathe again and coughed as she peered back up at him. His lapse brief, soon replaced when his eyes lit up with excitement.

"Well well, would you look at this? A bitch has some magic in her. I must ask, where did you acquire it?" He demanded while Lennox caught her breath. When she refused to speak his eyebrows furrowed in frustration. "You may speak- Now."

He seemed to be counting down in his head as he waited impatiently. With an irritated growl, he took his hands and placed both hands over hers completely encompassing them. A light orange glow illuminated his face as fire trailed its way over his exposed forearms to their joined hands. She screamed again feeling the fire seer her skin. Her throat was raw from the hours he had been there. The man seemed to enjoy her pain as his smile widened.

"You want to play it like this? You have fight in you but you're weak and you know I am stronger." The fire in his hands only heated more. "Where did you get your magic from?"

The pain felt like nothing she had ever felt before. Her arms shook as she looked at the demon. After what felt like ten minutes of refusal to give in to what he wanted. She motioned to the silver scar-like markings on her arms with the hope the information wouldn't be used to get someone else hurt.

"The Cult of Xemos! I joined before my deal, and in exchange I received magic!"

"See that wasn't that hard, was it?" The fire dulled as she answered his question. "Xemos, that's some ancient power young lady... Serious stuff."

He shifted even closer to her. His midnight tie brushed the side of her face as he examined her skin. His hands slowly slid down her arms before the demon wrapped his hand around her forearm and moved it in the dull light to see the chain and sigil scars. His fingertips traced their way between the scars and now fresh burns.

"I can hear your heart racing, Miss. Cade... Don't tell me Xemos didn't teach you how to deal with a big bad demonic fallen angel like me? You didn't come across it in your studies?"

"What would you know of Xemos?" Lennox challenged letting her eyes go to his wings. The last few black feathers clinging to various parts to confirm his words.

"Well, after being alive almost as long as he has, I've come across my fair share of Gods and Goddesses in the world. I happen to know exactly what he has to offer his devotees... Which leads me to wonder, how much power do you have?" The demon grinned as his black eyes sparked to life once more. "I wanna see."

His hands quickly moved up and gripped her shackles once again. FIre caused white-hot embers to melt down her arms. Her legs kicked out in an attempt to fight back but he shoved his knee on top of her leg and applied almost crushing force to make her remain still. "Stop moving," he commanded in a low growl beside her ear. *Don't let him win.* She fought for a second as she started to pass out from the pain. Suddenly she gripped the internal thread and the connection to her magic locked into place again. Long ivy vines started twisting their way from her back forming into the shape of wings until taking on their final, ten foot span. Various loose vines hung from the tips and edges as they forced their way between the two which sent the man backward.

He fell back a few feet from her, her whole body collapsed forward only held up by the solidified chains as the wings encircled her. Her heart pounded in her chest and ringing filled her ears as the dangling vines started creeping toward the demon. They wound their way around his wrists and up arms like snakes that constricted them to prevent his approach. In the moment of respite, Lennox tried to recover from the burns. She looked up just in time to see him bring his hand up to his face to examine the plant life. An irritated grimace crossed his face as angry red bumps formed into his skin. He pulled against them but they wouldn't let go. The smallest smile found its way to her face as he seemed completely thrown off.

However, it didn't last long. His hands erupted with flames once more. This time, fire trailed its way down the plant life and caused it to ignite like wildfire. In a matter of seconds, the flames made their way straight into her back. Permanently burning the skin from one shoulder blade to the other. At this moment, she wished he would just end her, the pain all-consuming.

The final scream wracked her already raw vocal cords. She arched her back and pulled down on the chains. With the barrier gone, he pushed a hand against her shoulder and slammed her against the wall. The feel his hand on her face wasn't gentle as he forced her to look him in the eyes again as hers started to close from the drain of power and the overwhelming pain.

"I'll be back to see more of that lovely baby of yours, maybe one day she'll want a deal like a dear old mummy." Lennox tried to muster the energy to speak but the world faded into darkness once more.

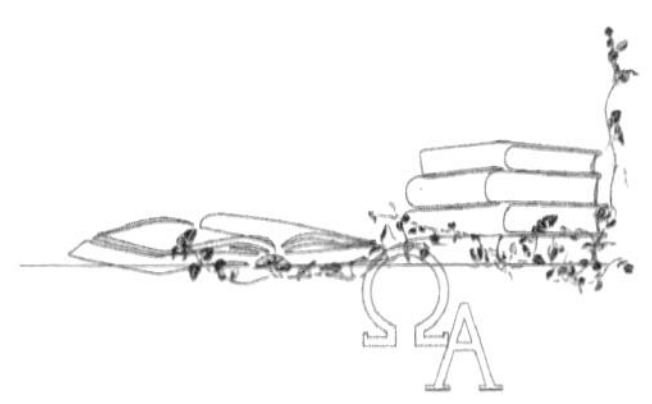

She shot up in her bed and flung off her covers. At the same time Lennox's gaze shot around the room as her lungs reached for air. For a moment she could have sworn that she felt the cool cell floor under her. When she ran a hand through her hair, she found her hair was damp with sweat. *It's not real, I'm not there.* She wrapped her arms around herself in an attempt to find comfort. For a second she looked beside her for Rue, only to be met with an empty bed once again. Momentarily, she had forgotten what had happened. Within seconds it crashed back and her face fell into her knees. Behind her lids, the face of the demon from her nightmares haunted her. That malicious smirk of enjoyment. Her eyes flew open and she looked out the window. It was completely covered with thick vines that blocked out the night. After what felt like an eternity, her heart slowly stopped racing, replaced with a heaviness deep inside her chest. *It's been fourteen years since I've dreamed of Hell... Why is it all coming back now?*

Her hand searched the sheets for her phone until she felt it under her pillow. Three ten in the morning. Lennox dropped her phone back into the sheets and rolled onto her back she stared at the ceiling. Her nightmare repeated like a broken record as the weight in her chest slowly started to consume her thoughts. *Armaros has nothing to do with the curse... This doesn't make sense.*

Lennox stood from her bed, her arms around her still as she made her way to the door. A sharp pain burned momentarily white hot between the top center of her shoulder blades to the back of each shoulder. With a grimace and a soft tug at the green thread, she brushed two fingers at the candles around her room. They sprang to life as she opened her closet and turned her back towards the mirror. Slowly she pulled down the shoulder of the school t-shirt she wore to bed and peered over her shoulder. Lennox cringed internally, her fingertips already wet with something as the fabric peeled off injured skin. Long, deep scratches decorated the top of her spine and shoulders. Fresh blood dripped over long healed burn scars. Scars from *him*.

Her brows stitched together as she reached back and touched it in disbelief. Another flash of pain went down her spine as her fingertips brushed the sensitive spot. Her gaze darted to her fingers where she saw the evidence, blood under her fingernails. *Did... I do that?* After another glance at herself she wrenched her eyes away and cleaned herself up before she turned back to the door.

Within seconds she made her way down the darkened hall on the other side of the house to Rosalyn's room. Lennox hesitated when she stood in front of the door and debated turning back to attempt to sleep. However, every time she blinked the demon's face remained there. *Do it, she'd want to know.* Rosalyn was the only other person in the school who knew exactly who he was. Knew the horrors of the nightmares. With a deep breath, she lifted a hand to the door and knocked on the door just loud enough to hopefully be heard by her friend.

After a moment of quiet, she knocked again, "Rosalyn?"

"Is the house on fire?" Her tired voice responded.

"Not quite, it's not urgent but it is serious."

"Lennox?" She asked before she could hear the sound of a bed creek and footsteps approaching the door.

"Yes, it's me," she called back as the door opened to reveal a very tired-looking demon.

Rosalyn's garnet eyes fell on Lennox and her expression shifted to worry. "What's going on, Nox?"

"Can I come in? It's about our time in hell-" The weight of the words hung between them.

"I-" She blinked in surprise and moved aside for her to come inside. "Come in"

The two sat on her bed and Lennox told her about the nightmare memory that wouldn't let go. As she recounted the whole thing from her point of view, she found herself picking at the skin next to her nails. Rosalyn had fallen deep into thought as Lennox recounted every detail. Toward the end, she placed a hand on top of hers gently to stop her from going too deep.

"There's something else-" She started nervously and shifted to face her back towards Rosalyn. Lennox turned and pulled the back of her sweater down just enough to show the top of one of the deeper scratch marks that had finally stopped bleeding.

"What happened? Did you do this in your sleep?" She felt her friend move closer to see.

"Yes... When I was in the dream but it almost felt real. Like my back was on fire again." She turned once more, adjusting her sweater back to its place.

"It was probably when you were scratching at it..." She thought for a moment. "Armaros vanished years ago, Len, he has no reason to come here. The day he let me go, it didn't seem like he would ever try to find either of us again. He seemed so... Haunted. I think he went into hiding."

She looked into her friend's eyes and found that she also seemed a little worried as well. "That's just it, no one knows where he is or has seen him. Why would I start dreaming about him after so many years?"

"It has to be a coincidence. I wouldn't blame you if you didn't feel safe here. I know it's hard to believe right now but between the security team and your vines, we are safe in here, at least for the night."

"You're right... I'm sorry to have woken you up, Ros." She stood from the bed to make her way back to her dorm room.

"Wait, I know how hard it is to forget when it comes up again. Do you want to spend the rest of the night here?" She offered with a kind smile, sleepiness creeping back into her eyes.

She did her best to push aside the image behind her eyes. Rosalyn would know more of Armaros after having been his victim for just over eighty years. Lennox took a second to consider the offer and nodded knew she didn't want to be alone. She moved the sheets aside for Lennox to join her in the bed as there was no couch or extra bed in her dorm. She pulled the sheets back and went under the blanket. As she had done many times before, she settled in and rolled to her side with her eyes on the door to the hall. It took a while for her to drift off, but the image of Armaros slowly faded into black as sleep took over.

Eden

Eden's dorm room was mostly quiet except for the sound of a page-turn every few minutes accompanied by the tapping of Bastien's foot. With her nose buried in her magical theories book, she hadn't noticed the darkness of night had fallen outside. She peered up after finishing the chapter she was on and her gaze fell on her uncle who had his phone hidden in his book, then to the window. *Where did two hours go?* She peered over to her laptop which read eight o' four.

"Since when was it eight?" She asked him and closed her book and stretched.

"Since four minutes ago." Bastien taunted without looking up from his phone.

"You actually stayed quiet for two hours?"

"Actually no, I tried to talk to you but you were practically dead to the world. I thought I might need to call Wyatt to snap you out of it if you didn't come out of your trance soon." He closed his book with a smirk.

"Never call him," Eden rolled her eyes. "I'm sorry Bas, what did you want to talk about?"

"When do you think you'll go after Lennox?"

She paused for a moment before responding to him. "Not until Eloise gives the green light. We have time and with the new wolf we have to be even more careful."

"You can't tell me you haven't thought of confronting her," he tilted his head down while lifting his eyebrow.

"Of course I have, but I don't think I'm ready."

"Well, if you need backup, I'm always there." He reached over and elbowed her lightly as he stood.

His phone buzzed against the pages of the book as he received another message. Eden stood and peered over his shoulder. Immediately she recognized the name on the phone. Corvus followed by a red heart. The demon was Bastien's most recent fling that seemed to be lasting a bit longer than just the usual one-night stand.

"I can't wait to see you tonight, wink emoji." She read out loud as she reached for his phone. "What are you doing? You never have hearts next to their names."

Bastien held it above his head out of her reach and looked down at her. "Not that it's any of your business, nosey. I'm just having fun with one for a while, got a problem with that?"

"I'm just saying-"

"Yeah yeah, don't get caught by Eloise," Bastien said with an exasperated sigh.

She rubbed her temples and pulled her long black hair into a bun on the top of her head. Eden tried to push away the feeling that something more was going on. *If Eloise finds out he's hanging around with that demon too much, she'll make him a Heretic.* It was the worst thing to happen within The Salvamari. Usually those who were cast out it was as if they never existed. Personal items destroyed, photos, record, all communication cut. Eden raised her eyes back to him to find the gears turning in Bastien's eyes while he seemed to sway the conversation.

"Are you okay, after the whole Richard thing?" He asked sincerely.

"Yeah, I'm fine." She lied and turned away to look in the mirror as she messed with her hair. She had been having small panic attacks at night when walking the house, not that she would tell him.

"You don't think that I know how to tell when you're lying?" In the reflection she watched him cross his arms over his chest. "Anyone else would buy that, maybe even Eloise and Stacey. Not me- When you try to lie to me, you know if you look me in the eyes you'll break. Oh, and you dig your thumb nails into your fingertips when you're nervous."

"Okay, there's no reason to call me out like that."

"As there's no reason for you to be in my business, Little Viper." Bastien threw back at her with a bright glint in his eyes.

She froze when he called her Wyatt's pet name. "How do you-"

"Mr. Steele is not very quiet about his interest in you."

"Of course, he's not... Isn't that a little hypocritical? You seem to be in my business." She put her hands on her hips as he started to make his way toward the door.

"Not when he comes to me to ask how to win you over," he opened the door and started to make his way down the hall.

Eden followed close behind to get the last word in, "Well you tell him-"

"I'm not telling him anything you say." Bastien stopped and fully turned to her midway down, putting a finger up to stop her. "If you have something to tell him, you know where he lives, but I do believe he said something about a study date tonight?"

Her face flushed as she realized that she hadn't been able to tell Wyatt no to his drunken study date idea. Eden had refused to use the number he left inside her textbook and avoided him in the halls. She sighed as she pulled her phone out to check the time. Eight twenty-one, he would be there much sooner than she would have preferred. *Maybe I can find a way out of this?*

Out of the corner of her eye, she saw Bastien's smile grow, "Don't worry, the whole causal look works for you."

"Why didn't you say anything sooner? Now I have to figure out how to get him to not come over!"

"Okay, stop. How many more times do I have to tell you to enjoy your life?" He placed his hands on either side of her arms with a grip. His chestnut eyes bore straight through her as he tried to break through the walls she clung to so tightly. "This guy seems genuinely interested and even if he is a demon you are allowed to have fun before we take our next steps toward going after Lennox. It's a great cover and it'll keep you close enough to know anything they know about who the hunters are. Besides, it's not like you have to sleep with him."

"Eww, Bastien." Her face scrunched as he said the last words and started back down the stairs. As she continued down she couldn't help but admit to herself how right he was. "Fine, but I'm not making it easy for him."

"Of course, you won't. Just give him a shot?" He reached up and pulled the clip from her hair. Quickly, he shook his hand through it and made it fluff up with an entertained smirk. "Don't worry, you'll be fine. I know it's your first date ever but just play nice and you'll have yourself a great cover."

Eden reached up, fixing her hair as he made his way into the entranceway. "I don't know how much I can do, but I'll entertain the idea."

"Well good, 'cause I see him making his way over now." He nodded towards someone moving up the path from Kappa with a small suitcase rolling behind them.

"Oh goddamnit."

"God can't help you now! Besides, which one?" Basiten gave her a final exasperated look.

"Eloise says there's only one!" She called as he went toward the fraternity.

"Stop living for Eloise!" He called, causing her face to turn red.

Eden peered as the demon approached the house and moved quickly as she went to shut the door before he could catch her. That was until his voice calling her name drifted over and brought the annoyance with it. *Shit.* She paused for a moment as Bastien's words echoed fresh in her mind. With a sigh her look of mild disgust faded into a more appropriate annoyed expression. Eden stood in the doorway and waited for him to approach with a giant smile plastered to his face. She reached up and ran a hand through her hair again in an attempt to still look presentable even in her hoodie and sweatpants.

"Little Viper! Too late, I saw you!" Wyatt called from under the streetlamp closest to the door.

"Well, look what the cat dragged in." She leaned against the doorway and crossed her arms, the cool night breeze blowing across her face.

"Well, you never called to cancel so I just thought maybe you were looking forward to our date." Wyatt shrugged as he met her in the doorway in his usual all-black jeans and a t-shirt with a leather jacket.

"This is not a date, but I guess you can come to study for an hour. One hour, then you're gone long before curfew, got it?" "Gone before curfew, sure can do!" He exclaimed, walking past her dragging the small silver suitcase behind him.

Eden looked down as it rolled past her feet and closed the door behind them. *He has no intentions of leaving here sober.* As she closed the door she watched Wyatt look around the mostly empty house. Most people were either hidden away in their rooms or somewhere in the town before they all had to be back. He didn't miss a beat as he made his way toward the kitchen to go unpack. His confidence showed he had made the place a second home. He moved to unzip the suitcase and Eden quickly reached out to stop him.

"Why don't we go study in my room?" She asked her hand on his arm.

He raised his eyebrows and peered down at her hand for a second, "You actually want me to come to your room? What are people going to think, Little Miller?"

"That we were studying. I prefer to not have interruptions when I'm reading," she told him simply. "Just come on." *I can't have Eloise knowing he's hanging around me yet.*

Without any retaliation, he picked up the silver case with ease as the sound of bottles clattered from inside. She started to make her way up the stairs while he followed close behind. His footsteps slowly became closer as she showed him the way to her dorm room. Eden lifted her hand and pulled at the blue thread within her to unlock the door. Out of the corner of her eye, she noticed him put his free hand above her head and lean over her from the doorframe. Something fluttered within her which caused heat to fill her cheeks as the lock clicked.

"Never thought I'd get invited in on the first date." Wyatt comment- ed when she went to turn the doorknob.

She turned her head to look up at him and saw the sarcastic side smile on his face. "We are just studying, nothing else. When are you going to stop calling this a date?"

"Sold-Soul demons may be the only ones with beating hearts but when it comes to you... Until my heart starts beating again." Wyatt shifted even closer to her, almost a mere five inches away.

Eden rolled her eyes in annoyance, she shook her head. With a huff, she twisted the knob and went in. Wyatt was left standing in the door- way for a few seconds before he joined her once more. The black-haired demon looked around her room. Her gaze followed his to her various potion ingredients and magical practice books. Carefully, she watched him from the corner of her eyes as she went over to her desk and sat opening her laptop to open an assignment.

As she moved one of her books beside it, the knife which was usually tucked away in her sleeve, slid from the table and toward the floor. A flash of silver metal in the low light of her room made her heart skip. Eden quickly caught it just before it hit the floor. Wyatt took his eyes from the photo of a black cat she used to own as Eden slipped it into her sleeve. With his suitcase still in hand he made his way over to her and started to take out a few bottles.

"So I brought whiskey, vodka, and rum. I didn't know what you liked so I also brought wine coolers, you know in case you want to work up to the stronger stuff."

"I think the wine cooler is enough for me, thank you."

Reaching in, he pulled out one for her and held it out to her. "Why don't we make this a little more interesting than just working on as- signments? We quiz each other on practical magics and when we get one wrong, it's a shot. We could even play our own twenty questions, the quizzer gets to ask a question with each shot and the other must answer honestly. I think it could be a fun way to get to know each other."

Eden paused for a moment and considered his proposal. *What is he trying to do? Could he just be trying to get me drunk to pull something... Or worse, is he on to me? This could end up really bad for me if he asks the wrong things. No- he can't be, he would have brought the security team if that was the case. Besides, if he tried any funny business I can still fight.* Eden opened her drink and let her eyes drift back to the demon, his eyes glinting in the dim lamp-lit room. Her gaze trailed him up and down in an attempt to decide the best way to bring him down if need be.

Wyatt waited patiently as her eyes met his again. The storm pulled her in briefly. She even felt something in the back of her mind begging her to move closer. Until Eloise's voice echoed in her mind. *Never trust them.* A sudden sting from The Compass caught her attention before she brushed it off. Now wasn't the time. *Focus, he's your cover.* However, if she said too much, she would have to take care of it. Which in turn would bring more unwanted attention her way. Though under it all lay a strange pull to trust him the longer she looked into his eyes. The feeling caught her off guard which must have registered across her face as his expression shifted to amusement.

"What do you say?" He asked, leaning his left hip against the desk.

"Fine, I'll play your game."

She put her drink down and pulled out her Magic Basics book. As Eden flipped through the pages her long black hair fell in a curtain into her face. Quickly, she shoved it back and weaved it into the previous messy loose bun with long strands hanging out. While she skimmed to find something they hadn't covered yet, her eyes caught a page on elemental magic. The clang of glass on glass filled the silence and halted her search which caused her gaze to shoot in his direction.

Eden watched his hands closely as the sound of the seal snapped open on the evidently new bottle. *It's new, he couldn't have put anything in it.* She fought with herself as paranoia got the better of her. *He's trying to prove he's different. He won't actually do anything. But... Can I trust his words?* She blinked in an attempt to clear her head as he poured out two shots of rum and left them on the counter before he picked up a wine cooler. *He's starting off slow too.* Her attention returned to the book. Eventually she found a chat of correlations between the first types of elemental magic.

"What matter of magic is used when practicing thermal sensory magic?" She propped her right foot up on the seat of her chair.

"That's a trick question. It's not just one, it's all three. Earth, air, and water all combined for the user to be able to read the temperatures around them or control said temperatures." Wyatt stared at her and turned to sit on her desk. Unable to hide her surprise, she felt her face shift and started to explain. "I graduated from the Crossroads Demon courses hundreds of years ago. Then I came back and continued seven years ago for fun. Magic basics is at least once every new major."

"So that's why you're rarely in classes."

"Only a few things about magic change every few years." Wyatt shrugged.

"Then why do you even stay?" Eden questioned.

"Because I have found a home here. As have others. It's one place we don't have to hide who we are and feel safe... At least it used to be." His words faded off for a minute before he peered over at her once more.

Surprised at his response, she leaned back in her chair. Something about the discovery that creatures she had been taught to hate had the desire to find a home never occurred to her. *They are more like humans than I thought...* Eden had considered the thought more and more since she arrived at the school. However Eloise had kept her training schedule full outside of classes. Wyatt broke her thoughts when he reached toward her and motioned for the book in her hands. The gesture made her eyes dart to him, his eyes still locked on hers almost as if he never looked away. *Did he notice me checking out for a second there?*

"I believe it's my turn to quiz you?"

"I didn't think you would need the book, Steele?" She taunted.

"I don't, but it makes it easier." He motioned for the book again.

Eden handed it over, she tilted her head at him. "Just don't leave your number in this one."

"Well, I wouldn't need to if you passed your phone over and I left it there." He winked at her as he flipped through the pages before he seemed to land on something. "True or false, growth magic is a form of the elemental magic of creation."

"False, it's a form of life magic as well as necromancy and love magic."

"Very good, no shots for either of us just yet. Let's try a switch since you seem to know your fair share. How about basic magic principles?" He held the book out to her.

"You're on." Eden agreed and took it from him.

They continued back and forth for a few rounds. Both answered correctly each time. Over the course of ten minutes, they had each finished their first drinks. Wyatt knew more than she had initially thought. The challenge of who was going to take the first shot was a much more fun game than she assumed. For the first time in a long time, Eden found herself relaxed with a true smile on her face.

Wyatt crossed his legs on the top of her desk where he was perched.

Looking over she saw the dirt from his shoes get onto one of the books. "What is the Latin word for fire?"

"Hey! Get your shoes off!" She laughed and lightly hit his foot before she answered. "Impes."

"Wrong, little Miller! It's ignis, impes is attack." He smirked and quickly put his feet down.

"Shit."

"You know what that means." He motioned to the two glasses he had poured.

"A deal's a deal." She sighed.

Eden put aside the book and stood to follow him. Her eyes followed his movements as he pulled the leather jacket off. His shirt came with it and for a moment she caught a brief glance of the bottom of a moon phase tattoo that went down his spine. The sight sent heat flooding to her cheeks, her attention fixed until his t-shirt covered it again. She took advantage of the extra time he took to hang his jacket over hers by the door to compose herself and force her heart to settle.

Just as Wyatt turned to join her by the bottle she had regained the mask she put on tonight. The glint in his eyes reminded her of stars that peaked out of a cloudy sapphire sky. The beauty almost caught her off guard. He was less than two feet from her with both glasses, one held out to her. She was the first to break their gaze as she took the glass from him, her eyes lingered on the small hourglass shaped tattoo on the side of his wrist. The top was fully shaded in black, the other just an empty outline. *As above, so below.*

"To you, Little Viper. May you see the truth of my intentions." His voice dipped lower, the rasp suddenly stronger than usual.

They both downed it quickly. Eden felt the burn of the alcohol encase her throat. Her face twisted as she put her glass down and looked back to see he hadn't even reacted to his own drink. Quickly, she attempted to fix her face before he saw, even though more than likely he already had. "That was cute," he laughed lightly as the smirk grew across his face. "You really don't drink, do you? Don't you know that's what college is for?"

"No, I don't. Some people actually enjoy learning."

"Only for the first few years, then the novelty wears off." He admitted and shook his head. "Well, for everyone but Lennox. Over twenty years and somehow she's still excited to learn something new."

A small silence fell between the two for a moment as he spoke about Lennox. *He obviously has no idea that she is my birth mother.* Eden's attention was drawn back to the moment when Wyatt took a step towards her. She froze and watched him closely, her breath caught in her chest for a second. *He's going to try something.* Eden shifted her body ever so slightly so she had easier access to her knife.

His stormy eyes softened as he looked into her own violet ones; a crooked half smile pulling at his lips. He was no more than three inches from her when his starry gaze drifted behind her as he bent down and reached toward the silver suitcase on the table behind her.

"Do you want another one? Before I get to ask my question?" He asked, his arm grazed over hers.

"Sure," she agreed. Her voice more of a whisper as the sounds of glass clinking together filled the room.

He was quickly back in his original spot and placed another drink into her hand. Surprise filled her as her heart fluttered back into rhythm. It took a few seconds to realize her paranoia had almost gotten the better of her when it seemed he was just flirting. He was respectful of her space for the most part and seemed insistent he was going to show her he wasn't like the demons. *Is that something they are even capable of?* Some of the things Eloise had taught her since joining the family had come into question the longer they were at the school. She cleared her throat as he held out a wine cooler. Eden took it and waited for whatever question he was about to ask knowing this could go well or quite terribly.

"Alright, Little Miller for my first question, what is the last lie that you told?" He asked her closely.

She took her time to open the bottle and considered the question. She was constantly lying about who she was, not that he needed to know that. "Well, I told Bastien that his favorite boy toy was waiting for him in his room when I wanted to be left alone."

The black-haired demon laughed a little, "My, my Little Viper. I'm sure he wasn't happy when he went to his room and probably found otherwise."

"He definitely wasn't. But he was fine the next day." She shrugged and started to move back toward her desk.

She placed her drink beside the book they were reading out of, picked it up, and started to graze the pages once more. She could hear his footsteps follow behind her before she felt him peer over her shoulder. Eden peered to the side and saw his eyes trace over the page she had opened to.

"You know, if you're looking when I ask the next question it's cheating. I think you could add that as a reason for another shot and a question." She taunted.

"Oh no, another shot." Wyatt put the hand with his drink over his forehead and took a step back. "Whatever shall I do?"

Wyatt turned on his heel, made his way over to the bed. He sat crossed legged on top of the blankets. Eden frowned at him again and motioned down with her eyes at his shoes. For a moment the expectant look on his face remained before his smirk faded and he looked at his feet.

"Oh, sorry!" He quickly kicked off his shoes. Each one hit the floor with a dull thud as he recrossed his legs.

"How about a topic change?" She asked, putting the book down once more.

"What did you have in mind, my dear?"

"Demonology," she challenged him to facts about his own kind. Little did he know, she had spent the last four years studying at her mother's insistence.

"If you insist. I don't think you know what you're in for, I've been around awhile."

"Even demons who have been around for thousands of years can get a question wrong."

"Alright then, do your worst." He tilted his head toward her expectantly.

"How does a Sold-Soul demon get their powers?" She asked as she took a seat in her computer chair and lifted her bottle for another drink.

Secretly, this was one of the many questions she couldn't find an answer for when it came to Lennox. She had spent hours in the family library reading through recovered journals from missions to find where her apparent earth magic came from. The day she had walked into Omega she had seen the ivy vines that trailed around the demon's window. Over the last two years, she hadn't met another demon who seemed as capable with their element as Lennox.

"Easy, from the demon who they made their deal with. Though there are special cases of interference such as Lennox. Demon, but Protector of Witches. As a devotee to Xemos her elemental demon power was amplified three levels up the scale to match a Crossroad Demon." He answered confidently and quickly shot a question back at her. *Well that was easier than I thought it would be.* "What offerings are recommended to bring to the crossroads?"

"Your most prized possession and any bottle of booze to share," she recounted her studies with a genuine smile crossing her face. "Come on, that's an easy one."

Wyatt paused for a moment as his eyes lit up when she smiled. "Alright, let's up the difficulty. Show me what you've got."

Eden considered her options not too keen on another shot. She landed on a question only demons with personal experience would know the answer to. She shifted in her seat and put her elbows on the back of her chair.

"What happens when a demon is stabbed with a cursed knife that isn't theirs?" His face shifted and he fidgeted with the snake ring on his finger. *So he's never come across that one.*

"I know a stab wound from the correctly cursed knife would kill a demon, however- I believe it would leave a mark on the intended demon, but not kill them."

"You don't seem so sure." Eden pointed out

"Well it doesn't happen very often." He shrugged. "Lennox would probably know."

Eden's curiosity got the better of her. "How did you two become friends?"

Wyatt let out a genuine laugh. "Well, we weren't always. She rightfully hated my ass for years."

"How come?" She leaned her cheek on her hand.

"Our history is complicated but... She started to chase me down a few years after she got out of hell. Almost killed me a few times." He shrugged and pushed his hair from his eyes. "Seven years ago I was just starting to become who I am now."

"How did you two go from that to best friends?" Eden frowned.

"I showed her how sorry I was for what I did. Lennox, she's someone who will never stop giving second chances. Even after everything she's been through."

The silence that followed was loud until his expression slowly softened. His brow was still furrowed and he let out a sigh. In one motion, he downed a shot and poured a second for himself.

"Are you okay?" She asked quietly.

"Yeah, I just don't like the thought of anyone I care about getting hurt."

"I couldn't imagine losing anyone in my family." Eden peered into her hands as guilt weighed her down.

"You won't." His matter of fact tone caught her off guard. "You don't have to worry about that, Eden. I would never let anyone hurt you."

She moved her hands to her hips. "I'm perfectly capable of protecting myself."

"I never said you couldn't." He kept his velvet voice even as he stood from her bed. "I'm just saying you don't have to worry about it."

"Shouldn't I worry if you're not around?" She allowed her voice to match his with a smirk as he got closer.

Wyatt stood a few feet away from the chair. "I'll find a way to be watching even when I'm not there."

"Pretty creepy if you ask me." The laugh that escaped her was louder than even she expected.

The sound of his accompanied hers. *Have his eyes always been that blue?* Eden saw the storm clear for the first time as he laughed with her. "You're right. I think just a way to let me know if you'd ever need back-up."

"I could call you, we have phones."

"Oh but that's not as much fun." He winked. "Maybe a nice Nazar outside your door?"

With a dull thud, he placed the glasses on the edge and poured another set of shots for them. For a moment, she eyed the one that she had been drinking out of and decided a little more couldn't hurt the situation. As the alcohol went down, her nerve seemed to strengthen as her previous drinks started to invade her thoughts. Regaining her nerve Eden placed the empty glass back on the desk as he perched back on his spot on the back corner of her desk.

"I believe it's my turn to ask the next question." She broke the quiet and turned toward another one of her books to switch topics once more. Suddenly, his hand was on top of hers, stopping her from picking up the book.

"I'm done studying... I want to know more about you." He insisted with a velvet tone.

"Like what?" Eden asked with a raised eyebrow.

"Things like your biggest dream, your favorite animal, maybe even how to make you smile. I do enjoy seeing you happy, it's not too often."

He ever so slowly started to close the distance between them. She saw his gaze trace over her as if he tried to memorize them. Feeling a strange flutter she had only felt with one other person. Slowly, she took her hand from under his and fiddled with her sleeve. *Maybe Basiten is right... Could I give him that chance outside of being a good cover? Not that Eloise could ever know it's more than that...*

"I like peacocks actually. I like what they symbolize."

Wyatt leaned against the wall, his lips curled back into a smile. "Confidence, awakening, and royalty, very fitting for my favorite Miller."

"What about you?"

"Huskies," he told her excitedly. "They are high energy and fun."

"I think that's also pretty fitting for you, Mr. Steele." The flutter she tried to suppress earlier made its way to her chest behind the walls she held so tight. *Maybe he is who he says he is.*

Eden lost track of time as the dizziness set in, and slowly relaxed as they took turns asking questions. Wyatt was more than happy to share many aspects of his life with her and old stories of drunken nights with friends. The room was light-hearted and fun until the markings on his face reminded her who he was. A demon. Though at this moment he slowly started to look more... *Human.*

"Your mother looks like she'd kick a puppy out of the way if it was in her path. Is she always like that?"

"You mean closed off and direct? Yes actually, though she does care." Eden tried to explain her mother without coming off the wrong way. However, when it came to Eloise, she didn't present herself in the best light.

"Only about anyone with the last name Miller. What made you guys come here anyways?" Wyatt started to pour another round for them.

"She heard about how secluded the place was, she's not a fan of large amounts of human interaction." She laughed at her terrible inside joke. Once he put the bottle down again they both took their fourth drink and shook her head as the burn started to dull once more. "White flag, I need a minute."

"Having a hard time keeping up?" He asked, his hand placed beside hers where she put the shot glass down again.

"Go easy on me, it's gonna take time for me to even try to go shot for shot with you, party boy." Eden taunted.

His smile brightened as they went back to the bottle to pour the next round. His hand drifted to hers and fingers brushed the top of her hand lightly. She glanced down at their hands as they hovered just over one another over the bottle, then blinked up to see his gaze on her for a reaction. She didn't move her hand away. His hand gently brushed over the top of hers. Looking into his night-like eyes she decided having to hang around an attractive man, even if he was a demon, wouldn't be the most terrible thing she would have to do.

"Thank you for letting me in, I'm glad you didn't cancel," Wyatt told her genuinely.

The first real smile Eden had in a while tugged at her face. "It's been nice actually."

"I told you, I'd break in eventually." He beamed.

"You moved a few bricks," Eden corrected.

"I'll take it, one at a time is fine with me. I'm a patient man, Miss. Miller- Remember?"

Suddenly, alternative rock played demandingly from his jacket pocket. A frown replaced the smile and he stood from his spot on the side of her desk. With an apologetic look after he glanced down. Eden shrugged off and motioned for him to answer. He picked it up after a few seconds and put it to his ear.

"What Aron? No, I haven't been looking at my phone... What do you mean it's five minutes till curfew? No, I don't have anyone to walk back with to Kappa... Okay, I'll see you two in three minutes." Eden heard his words and turned to the window behind her to discover night had encircled the grounds into pitch-black except for the few lamps. The soft thud of his footsteps behind her drew her attention away from the moon. "Gone before curfew, that's the deal right?"

"That was the deal... I don't have anywhere for you to bunk for the night." She nodded fighting with herself internally. She knew she should want him to go but a part of her didn't want him to.

"It's fine, I don't mind sharing a bed with a pretty woman. But I'm taking it slow. I want you to want me here. So for now Aron and Octavius are on their way over." Eden stood with a nod and handed him the bottle they were drinking from while he started to pack. He held up his hand. "Keep it, when you drink you'll have something to remember tonight by."

"I'll put it in my afternoon coffee." She joked and put it back down as he closed the silver suitcase.

The pair started to make their way toward the door until Eden stopped him and opened it. She poked her head out to see if anyone was in the hall. There was no one there but voices. The sound of a few voices trailed up the stairs and she felt him bend beside her ear.

"Don't want me to be seen coming out of your room, huh?"

"I'm just not ready for any questions." She turned back to him and felt the red creep into her face as she stepped aside for him to leave. "I'll see you in class."

"Or you could text me?" He asked, winking at her.

"I'll think about it." She told him, letting him move past her into the hall.

He shook his head and took her hand for a final time, squeezing it lightly. "I hope you do, Have a good night little Viper."

Aron and Octavious's voices wafted up the stairs from the entrance hall intertwined with the voices of the other Omega girls. The door closed less than a minute later as the boys went back to their own house. Quietly, Eden shut the door and locked it behind her. With her back against the wood she let out a long, deep breath. Thoughts fluttered around her mind which caused more confusion than ever.

For a moment she considered an attempt to call Bastien but knew most nights he was busy. A yawn pulled at her and the world still spun slightly from the alcohol. It would be much easier to tell him everything that had happened once she was sober in the morning. Eden took the knife from her sleeve and laid it on her nightstand, pulled the sheets back, turned on her favorite nighttime playlist and crawled into bed. That night as Eden lay there, she considered her emotions and her duty to the Miller legacy. If she fell in love with a demon, it would end in his death and she would be marked a Heretic.

The next evening, Eden stepped through the front door of her family home. The open curtains let in the last hour of daylight and illuminated the dark green walls. Even though it was a weekend, Eloise had texted everyone in the family to meet at the main Miller home for a family meeting. Since this wasn't out of the ordinary, Eden took her time as she went down the hall while her amethyst eyes trailed along the faces of generations of Miller hunters framed in gold. It started with the first members and creators of The Salvamari and ended at the back with the current members in one large photo at the end of the hall.

She let herself take in the annoyingly traditional portrait. Her grandmother Stacey with long gray hair that faded into charcoal black. Glaring smokey eyes staring daggers down at her, sitting in a chair in the center of the group. Her husband, Richard looked just as he did the night he almost stabbed Eden, standing to her left beside his brother, Arthur, who looked eerily similar to Richard. To her right stood Eloise who stared at twin daggers from behind her glasses, her pin-straight chestnut hair pulled into a tight bun as usual. Young twelve-year-old Eden stood between them, taking a second to really look at her past self her eyes grazed over the angry look in her eyes. Long black hair that fell over her shoulders with Stacey's hand over top of hers on the arm of the chair. *Are you a Miller? Or are you a pawn in their hunt?* She asked the younger version of herself almost angrily as she realized just how much this place had started to attempt to tear down her walls.

She tore her gaze away from the portrait after she remembered she was expected in the next room. Her shoes didn't make noise while she walked and fixed Bastien's leather jacket around her as the sounds of a few voices caught her attention. Eden took a deep breath, her nose filled with the scent of lavender, and exhaled as their words became more clear as she approached the room. *Mom must have been nervous and burned incense.*

"What do you think I am, dumb?" Alaric's voice questioned loudly. "I know what I'm doing, I've lived with a werewolf before."

"How were you planning on shifting into a wolf form then?" Eloise's annoyance flooded her voice.

"I was hoping you could... Help me out with that? You're fantastic with potions."

Eden turned the corner into the dining room just in time to confirm her mother's annoyed tone with the sight of her narrowed eyes and crossed arms as she glared at Alaric. The squeak of a chair that scraped along the floor echoed in the silence which caused her to peer over at the source of the sound. Bastien sat in his normal chair on the left side of the rectangular dinner table and flashed an entertained smile at her as he motioned for her to join him. Quietly, as to not interrupt the two Elders, she made her way to her spot on the right side beside the head of the table. As she took her seat, Eloise started to speak once more, her maroon heels clicked on the floor.

"Of all the dumb things you've done this is by far the most inconvenient. Fine, but I'm only helping you because I don't see a way to dig you out of this one." Eloise crossed her arms over her chest, messing with the necklace over her turtleneck shirt as she went into deep thought. "Since you've gotten yourself onto the security team, you'll look too suspicious claiming to be a wolf but never being seen as one. Now, take your seat so the others don't think I'm not able to handle things here."

The man took his seat, and Eden noticed he attempted to stifle a smile. She checked to see if Bastien caught the same thing and met his hazel eyes until he nodded slightly. Eloise sighed and made her way over to her chair next to Eden, put a bag down and pulled out papers from folders. No one spoke as the sound of the front door echoed through the house. Her eyes drifted toward the entrance of the dining room as she waited for the others to join them from their own home down the street. Within a few moments, three people turned the corner and entered the dimly lit room. Stacey, Richard, and Arthur all to their own seats. Stacey was at the other end of the table opposite of Eloise, Richard to her left beside Alaric and Arthur to the seat beside Eden.

"Hey there, young buck, squirt!" Arthur smiled brightly at Bastien and then at Eden as he moved to his seat, and patted her on the shoulder. "It's good to see you."

"Glad to see you too, Baron Arthur." Eden said with a friendly smile.

"Hello, Matron Miller, Baron Richard and Arthur," Eloise greeted.

"Hello, my dear..." Stacey nodded to her daughter and turned toward

Eden, a kind smile forming on her face for a few seconds. "How is my lovely granddaughter? Your training and studies? Have you been able to keep up with everything?"

"They are going well. Mother and I have another training session tomorrow morning." She answered with a small smile as she knew she was Stacey's favorite as the up-and-coming head of the family.

Eden noticed the look on Eloise's face out of the corner of her eye, she saw the earlier annoyance return. The Matriarch cleared her throat to draw attention back to her and within a few seconds everyone turned their heads to face her.

"Now, we are here to discuss some new developments that have been brought to my attention by my brother, Eden, and Alaric. They have informed me that the newest member of the security team could pose a genuine threat to our plan. The one they call Fang I have discovered through my research that his full name is Mathias Bloodfang, the last remaining Alpha wolf."

The room fell into silence as most of the older hunters shared a look of knowing between each other. Through her studies, Eden knew how powerful the wolf would be if it ever came down to a fight as she had seen just how tall he was at the school assembly. She spotted several magical items the man seemed to have, he must have gathered them of the last several centuries.

"How do you intend on taking care of the dog?" Stacey's voice came from Eden's right.

"Alaric here has joined their team and has discovered some things about each of them. As we know, werewolves are fierce when it comes to family. I say we take them on from there." Eloise responded, and tilted her head towards her mother.

"What information have you found, Alaric?" Richard chimed in and turned toward the man.

Alaric looked over at the man and choked on the sip of water he had taken. Eden heard Bastien snort as he did, which in turn made her break for a few seconds as a laugh attempted to escape. Eloise shot the pair a glare. Quickly, she turned back toward the other end of the table. The bearded dark brown-haired man awkwardly stood from his chair as he was addressed.

"I have discovered that most of the members of the security team have connections to each other that go beyond pack members. The head of the security team, Coyote Moon is Bloodfang's nephew as well as Remi Moon. Who as I understand, they have been looking for over the last three hundred years. Cathwulf is also dating Coyote at the moment, I see plenty of opportunity to slowly start to chip away at the threat. I've even spotted Fang with Elder Andromeda Anderson." Alaric explained to the room.

Her eyes fell on her grandmother who looked at Alaric in disgust with each name he listed off. Eden took a second to consider the possibilities, she leaned back in her chair. *That means the siblings are at least half alphas themselves. Probably also very proficient in magic as well.* Thoughts of her own magical abilities and how she could potentially take down even a half-alpha wolf let alone a full. *I could put all the water in his body into his lungs... But how much strain will that put on me? Could I even continue to fight after doing something like that? He would probably fight back; if I'm too weak to defend myself. Magical toll doesn't affect them in the same way as me.* Her thoughts were broken by the gruff voice of Richard and flinched as he spoke, Eden forced herself to peer over at him.

"I say we go after each member over the semester starting with Cathwulf."

"I say the solution is simple. If the dog is an issue, put it down."

Stacey's exasperated voice spoke over her husband.

"We can't just go after him, you of all people should know that he is something we don't want to upset until we know how to handle him," Alaric interjected.

"Who are you to tell us what we can or can't do? You're not even a real Miller, you're just borrowing the name." She shot back at him, glaring at him.

Eden could feel the tension rise quickly in the room as the two stared each other down for a moment. The rest of the Miller men shifted in their seats which made them creek in the silence like a guitar string pulled too tight. Richard's jaw clenched, Bastien's hand went to his side, and Arthur glared at Alaric, almost dared him to disrespect a Miller woman again. Papers shifted beside her as Eloise leaned forward and rested her palms on the table, and glanced over her glasses at Alaric.

He looked taken aback, the man started to sputter out words, "I- I misspoke, apologies."

The room seemed to calm down as he tried to diffuse the situation. Stacey nodded in acknowledgment of his apology. "Though it is up to my daughter, I believe we should be keeping an eye on this Andromeda. What do we know of her?"

"She is the Elder for demonology, Guidance Counselor, and a high-ranking succubus I've heard," Eloise answered the question.

"Nothing we can't deal with then." Stacey peered around the table and finally landed on Eden. "Nothing dear Eden here couldn't handle if need be. We need to know how to weaken him, and it may be the perfect way to throw things off."

"And until we are ready to act. She will be ready, right my dear?" Eloise turned to her.

With a quick nod, she agreed. She couldn't tell her mother no. "Yes, I'll be ready."

"Good, until then find a way to get close to her so you can keep an eye out."

"What about Cleo Anderson?" Eden spoke.

"What of her?" Eloise's eyebrow rose.

"Do you think she'll be able to recognize us with the magic on our disguises?"

"No, some of our more defining features have been clouded so she won't be sure it's us."

"Even if she did, we'd take care of it. In the few encounters we've had with her, we are confident we could overpower her quickly enough." Stacey added.

Eloise turned back to the room and glanced at each person for a moment. "Does anyone else have anything?"

For a second, she could feel something or someone burn a hole straight through her. The sensation sent a wave of nerves over her as Eden looked over at Richard to find him staring back at her with fire behind his eyes. The two of them hadn't been in a room together since the night at Club Crossroads the previous week. From beside her, Eloise stepped behind her chair and she felt her mother's hands on either side of her shoulders. Neither of the women broke eye contact as the man opened his mouth.

"I think it's best to hold your tongue, Baron." Eloise warned darkly. "We've spoken and you are alone in your opinion."

"Do you not realize how terribly this could go?" He spat back. "Where do you think she got her magic, huh? That cursed demon blood runs through her veins!"

"She is on our side, and the future of this family, Father." Bastien interjected, his anger showing on his face.

"Hush boy!" His voice echoed along the walls as he slammed his fist down.

Anger filled Eden as they all started to yell at each other. Her hair stood on end and her ears went hot. She tilted her chin down ever so slightly. Internally, she pulled on the blue thread causing the room to go cold as she glared at the man.

"You will not speak to him that way!" Eden yelled over everyone. "You will talk to your family with respect as we have. I don't care what you think of me, this has been my family and I have given the last fourteen years to this family and become one of you. I have proven myself time and time again. You will not intimidate me, you will not tell me who I am, and you will accept me because you have no choice."

Her hands shook in anger as she spoke and she leaned forward in her seat. Once again, the room was thrown into a heavy silence, although this time due to speechlessness. Eloise squeezed her shoulder and as she attempted to even her breathing, she could see each in the air which caused a smirk to make its way across her lips. The fear that spread across the man's face fueled Eden as it seemed he had realized he was cornered.

Richard went to speak once more, but Stacey shot him a look. The man huffed and crossed his arms and dropped the subject. The feeling of victory washed over her knowing he couldn't argue anymore. Not when all the Matriarchs of the family when they banded together. The room returned to a normal temperature as her mother spoke again.

"That seems to be everything. I'll see you all next month for our next family meeting."

The sound of chairs along the wooden floor echoed followed by light chatter between various members of the family. Stacey started telling off her husband, and Eloise turned to Eden, with a hand on her arm. When she faced her mother, Eden searched her face for her reaction to her outburst she found a smile had formed on the woman's face and her eyes beamed. With a slight nod, she dropped her hand back to her side and Bastien made his way over to them.

"That was badass, Eden! I've never heard you do something like that!" He told her excitedly.

"It just came out. I don't know what got into me."

"Do you want to go to Club Crossroads for some drinks? My treat."

"You both have class tomorrow." Eloise scolded her brother.

"If I'm being honest, I really would like to go back to my room." She shook her head.

"Fair enough, I'll see you in class," Bastien saluted Eloise and made his way from the room.

"I'll see you in the morning, Mother." Eden said tiredly.

October

*E*den *Miller, this is an order, you don't get to disappoint this family, do you understand me?* Eloise's voice rang in her mind from her dreams the previous night. The memory was old, something she hadn't thought about in years, that happened when she was no more than eleven.

Eloise, don'tcha think you are being hard on her? She is only a kid, only been with the family for four years, maybe just ease up on her a bit? A sixteen-year-old Bastien asked his sister as he peered at the younger version of Eden sympathetically.

No. You and I both know in order to survive we must eliminate; we must act first before they do. Eloise scolded harshly with a glare at her brother.

I-I can't Mother... W-What if he is innocent? We don't know for sure that they are all bad, what if there is some good in him? I don't want to kill anyone.

Tears streamed down her face and her chest heaved as Eden looked at the wolf they had chased down and tied to a tree. Eloise had demanded she lift the revolver with a silver bullet inside at the restrained boy, Bastien had backed off when she pointed her own weapon at his foot.

You will not interfere, Baron. The Matron had walked up to her daughter, raised her hand and swung so quickly that the only thing that could be seen and heard was air followed by skin-on-skin contact. There was a dull thud as Eden's body hit the cold and damp ground.

Do not test my patience again little girl, I am doing what is best for you, hell what is best for us! Why can't you just do what is asked of you?

Eloise rubbed her hands together to stop the sting from the slap as the child sat back up. Eden brought her hand to her cheek and felt the heat from the slap along with something wet and slick. Pulling her hand down her amethyst gaze slowly fell to meet the color red. Unwillingly, from the pain and embarrassment tears started to find their way to her eyes. Underneath boiled anger, a deep anger she never quite understood. A frustrated sigh was the next sound to be heard from Eloise.

Stop crying, emotions are a weakness we can't afford to possess. Dry those tears and for the love of god, you have dirt on your face. You have a job to do and you need to be quick, quiet. This family doesn't need to be on the radar anytime soon.

She shook her head to disperse the memory and pulled on her training clothes, black leggings and matching turtleneck shirt. Eden reached for her waist and adjusted the fit of her weapons belt with two holsters, one empty and one with a combat nine millimeter on her right hip with her peacock badge. Empty weapon bags on the left.

She peered around the room before she made her way out in case she had left something behind and as she did her eyes fell on the bundles of herbs she was drying above her bed. She stepped closer to discover mold trailing across her bundle of lavender and rosemary below it which caused her eyebrows to knit in frustration. Quickly, she walked over and pulled them down from the wall and threw them into a bag before she went downstairs.

"Dammit, that's why I was having nightmares."

Her light steps sounded louder, in the mostly quiet house as she went down the stairs. She moved past the family portrait and to the kitchen to throw away the moldy herbs before her gaze fell on the light wooden basement door, the sure sign that her mother had made it down before her. Without breakfast, she went to the door to meet Eloise and went down into the dimly lit area. She let her attention drift around the room until it fell on the three empty barred cells installed years ago against the far left corner of the wall.

Her gaze trailed over to the opposite wall, past the sets of charmed iron shackles and found her mother at the weapons cabinet while she pulled down two of the many various guns that sat inside. She was dressed in the same black pants and a turtleneck, paired with the belt Eden wore. Both their peacock crests sat on their right hips to show their statuses within the line of succession. The request of long sleeves meant one thing- *Great, we're training outside today.*

She took a deep breath in preparation and approached the table with two blank bullets, two sets of throwing stars, and two smoke bombs. Her hand hovered over the choice of weapons before she picked up one of the sets of throwing stars and examined them closely. The metal flashed in the light from the few lights above and the sharp edges had been filed thinner at the request of the Matriarch, who was peering over at her with a hint of a smile.

"Ten minutes early, perfect."

A small click reverberated around the room as Eloise cleared the barrels of two Glocks and joined Eden at the end of the table. She placed them down and picked up her own set of stars before she put them securely in a small bag attached to her belt. Eden followed suit and put them in one of the empty pouches to her left on her own belt. A slight sinking feeling filled her stomach as thoughts that hadn't plagued her in years started to surface. *These are designed to kill the very creatures that have started calling me a friend... More than a friend.*

Wyatt's goofy smirk crossed her mind, then Octavius and Rosalyn who had seemed to be getting closer the more she watched them. Remi and Celia who seemed to have their own thing going on and what that could be. Lastly, Aron and Lennox, the final face of the woman who left her as a defenseless baby, the one who seemed to have moved on so easily and wore the mask of selflessness. Her right hand balled into a fist, her nails dug into her palm and her ears went hot. Eloise cleared her throat which caused Eden to bring her attention back to the moment.

"Today we are going to be going over stealth in hand-to-hand combat. We will be going out into the woods on the farthest side of the lake, off school grounds, and playing cat and mouse. The rules are, you can only use the weapons on the table and there will be no magic use from either party." She stopped for a moment to watch Eden's reaction.

She nodded in agreement and picked up one of the Glocks. The chamber slid open easily to confirm it was empty; she took one of the blank bullets to load. *Two of everything, one for each of us.* Quickly, she finished with her weapon and put it in the empty holster on her right hip.

"No outside weapons, no magic." Eden confirmed and pulled her regular weapon from her hip, released the clip and placed it on the table.

"Good, pick up the rest, and let's head out to the woods." Eloise attached the other Glock and the smoke bomb to her left hip and started to make her way back toward the basement stairs. Doing the same, Eden followed her up the stairs and out of the house.

The dawn illuminated the road that attached all the Elder homes together. Each was almost an identical copy of the other with only a few slight modifications. Made out of the same field stone as the fraternity and sorority houses, only this time with red, blue, or the odd yellow door at the end of the street. The brisk morning air bit at Eden's face and gray clouds loomed overhead to mark the impending snow. *It's October, and we are training outside hours before it's supposed to snow?* She hid her annoyance at the thought as the two women walked in silence, at least until they reached the woodline that ran along the lake behind the last Elders house.

"Eden, we need to discuss what happened in yesterday's meeting." Eloise turned to her with her usual serious face, and watched her over the rim of her glasses.

Nervously Eden ran her thumbnail across her fingertips, she peered back at her mother. "I know I shouldn't have let myself say the things I did."

"No, Eden dear. I'm proud of you." She told her softly and only briefly allowed a small smile to show.

"You are?" Eden's eyes widened.

"It showed you can hold your own one day as the head of this family. I saw your strength, Eden. I have the trust that one day you will make a great Miller Matriarch."

Eloise raised her hand and placed it on Eden's shoulder as they made their way along the lake woodline. She allowed herself an appreciative smile directed at her mother, pride filled her chest as she had won her approval even if only for a while. After Eloise dropped her hand, Eden felt the cold air blow her hair from her face, birds flew overhead to make their way from the grounds for the coming winter. The two fell into a conversation over what had happened after Eloise took Richard from Club Crossroads, she discovered more of what had happened that night.

"He had overheard you telling Bastien about our conversation. Your grandfather decided to take matters into his own hands without telling anyone."

"You mean he didn't know about Lennox being my birth mother?" She asked.

"No, the only one I told once I found out was Stacey. She sees you as a great leader one day. You could bring the Miller family to places even we never dreamed of. Richard on the other hand didn't see it that way that night. As you know he can get very eccentric when it comes to the unknown. His distaste for demons is a lot more extreme since he got back from that mission in Peru with Lucifer's two assistants that got to Arthur."

"Lumina and Silas? They are on Earth? They never come here unless Lucifer sends them." She took a moment to consider the situation, though to many this wouldn't be too concerning to the Millers it was definitely something she would need to keep an eye on.

"They couldn't figure out why they were here, but they got ahold of Arthur and for some reason were asking where this school was. By the time Richard got there, Arthur wasn't in the greatest shape. So when they got back and he heard you, it sparked something that seemed to scare him. He seemed to think that the two were coming here for you once he heard one of them discuss a human girl on the campus."

Momentarily she considered the theory, Richard could have been onto something despite the off hand comments. Though she had no demon blood in her, that might not stop two demons from the high ranks of hell from thinking just as he had. She always knew she was different from the rest of her family, though they could use magic it never came across like hers. It was stronger and easier to access for her and she could learn new skills quicker. They were looking for the school and using a Miller to try and find it. *Everything points to it...* Her stomach sank in her as they fell back into quiet as they approached a very small clearing on the other side of the lake.

By the time they had made their way to the training spot, the sun was shining brighter, making the cold air warm every so slightly. Frozen dew on the trees and surrounding grass glimmered in the morning light. With a quick step in front of Eden, her mother's expression returned to neutral while Eloise's eyes darkened. The hair on the back of her neck stood on end and the unspoken start to the session commenced. The rules were simple enough, the game they were playing was nothing new to her, now it was a question of who was chasing who.

"I want to know if you can keep up the strength from the other day, as the prey." Eloise's left hand rested on the handle of her gun as she answered the unspoken question. "Run little mouse."

With the three words, she took a few steps back so as to not take her eyes off the woman and made her way toward the tree line. Eloise soon did the same on the other side of the clearing so they would both enter a different part of the forest. Finally she turned her back, Eden picked up her pace and searched for higher ground. Occasional twigs under her feet broke as she stepped lightly, being careful to not make too much noise she followed the path that the various animals had created over time. The moss that covered almost half of the ground and up rocks helped to keep her steps quieter. *I need to leave enough evidence to lead her where I want her.*

She reached up to a branch above, she pulled down on it which caused it to snap loudly. Birds flew from the treetop in her area and she turned, running to the right. Quickly and quietly she scanned the area and found a nearby fallen tree with a large three-foot pit where it was torn from the earth. The roots stuck high up from the ground and provided enough cover if Eloise was to pass by on the other side but left her front open. In seconds she decided to use the cover until she knew where she was, Eden ducked into the pit, her back against the damp roots.

The morning woodland was eerily quiet as she listened for footsteps in response to her breaking the branch. She took in her surroundings for a place to lead Eloise until the glint of iron caught her eye. About ten feet to her right stood a mostly standing stone arch with four panels of iron gates that hung from the arch precariously. *That's odd, I thought the school only had the gates around the campus.* Before she moved Eden's eyes darted around her before she stood from her spot. As she did, a sudden warmth washed over her in the morning light until to her left a sound of something flew beside her ear.

A yellow and brown speckled moth fluttered by her head and landed on the gate. Her eyes followed it as well as her feet as she moved branches aside and approached carefully. She squinted as she caught a glimpse of a white shape on the back, the skull distorted with the graceful movements. *A Death Head Hawk Moth... The grounds have magic all around, this could be some sort of trap.* Completely in the open, she tried to be as quiet as she stepped over a few long fallen branches, damp with the frosted moss. Adrenaline flooded her system and suddenly the training session felt much more real, like the only threat wasn't Eloise. *Was this set up by Mother?* Eden paused and considered her options, the sudden lack of cold air sent nervous shivers down her spine, and the feeling of someone behind her pulled her attention away from previous concerns.

Eden remained motionless for a breath, then she moved in one fluid motion to face whatever could have been behind her, gun in hand pointed at the source of the energy. A man with charcoal black hair stood almost ten feet away, dressed in black pants, a deep purple button-up with a moth the same as the one that had passed over her head seconds ago where his tie would have been. He watched her with up-turned clear water eyes. His thin, almost angelic face calm, unmoving to the threat of a weapon trained on him. *What are you?* Eden took in his features quickly as she went over her creature studies to decipher how much danger she was in. The man let a small smile cross his face as their eyes locked for a few moments before he put his hands up and showed no fear of the weapon in her hands.

"I didn't come here to hurt you, I have come to help." His deep velvet voice echoed among the trees.

"Why would I believe you?" Eden challenged.

"You have no reason to, but I have no weapons." The man slowly put his hand in his pockets and pulled them inside out, after he lifted his pant legs to show there was nothing there. "I know you don't trust many people so I know I'm asking a lot, however, it's about your family."

Eden still stood frozen in her spot between the trees, gun still pointed at him. *Why is he so interested in my family?* With a quick adjustment of her grip, she waited for him to change tactics, however he only looked back at her and allowed the silence to join them. Curiosity started to overwhelm her as she attempted to make sense of the situation at hand.

"First tell me who you are and maybe we can talk." She demanded with a raised eyebrow to play off her nerves.

The man smiled again, "I am Xemos. God of elemental magics, curse breaking, academics, and necromancy. I am here to offer you answers and a deal."

Her eyes scanned the god's face for lies, however, his expression didn't change in the slightest. His ocean-like eyes bore into her own with confidence, his right hand outstretched to her as he motioned toward the forgotten gate behind her. The moth on the collar of his shirt fluttered its wings. *It's alive.* Her breath caught in her chest and slowly the black-haired woman lowered her weapon, rendered speechless of where she had found herself. A god was something she had never been taught to deal with as Eloise didn't believe there was more than one.

Xemos started to walk toward the gate while he allowed a small distance between them as he turned his back to her. *He's not even worried about a gun. If he really is a god, he might have answers... He might be my only shot.* Cautiously she followed behind him and closed the distance between the trees and the gate. As they approached, the other moth took flight, circled the two of them, and vanished into the morning. Once he was close enough, he leaned on the remnants of the stone archway beside the distorted iron. Eden stopped a few feet from him and crossed her arms expectantly to hide the tightness she felt within her chest. *Could he be working with Lumina and Silas?*

"Will you give me a chance? A chance that you'll trust me? I could give you some answers, though you may not like them"

The thing she craved the most, she shook her head. "I'll decide when you tell me what you want with my family."

A smile crossed his face as the moth flew to his shoulder. "Ever skeptical, Miss. Miller."

"As a God, I'd think you'd know that." Eden shot back.

"Oh, I do. I must admit I know more about you than I think you or Eloise would prefer... Before you were Eden Miller, you were Gemma Cade, daughter of Lennox Cade. Lennox, as you know, left you at the orphanage to later be adopted by Eloise Miller. Later she died due to a deal with a crossroad demon."

Every muscle in Eden's body tensed, flinched slightly at the name she was given at birth and her eyes went wide. "How the hell do you-"

"I am a god of academics. It is in my nature to know things about my devotees and their kin."

The trees swayed in a sudden breeze and she felt bumps form across her skin despite the warmer air around her. The blue thread of magic pulled as her thoughts ran wild. The final few words caught her attention. *He knows Eloise or Lennox, but Eloise doesn't believe in the old gods so that only leaves Cade.* Eden's hand drifted to her belt where she remembered there was nothing more than training tools. Her gaze never left him as he seemed completely unperturbed by her action.

"You never wanted to be a hunter, let alone a Matriarch. If I recall correctly, you fought tooth and nail for years."

"I did, but Eloise said sometimes it's just harder to adjust, it was normal to have a period of time like that as a child."

"Because, you were never meant to kill innocents, Eden." Xemos lifted his head ever so slightly.

"You probably don't even know what I'm meant for."

"I don't know the answer to that, Little Moth, because it is not for me to decide."

Her nose wrinkled at the name. "Then whose is it?"

"Yours, the decision will always be yours. You just have to act on it."

Eden rolled her eyes. "You know everyone says that. Besides, no one gets a say when their fate has already been decided."

"Is that what you believe, Eden? Your life boils down to one path and there's no way to change it? Maybe you're not ready."

His words struck a chord with her, and her hands went to her hips. Over the last few years, Eloise had said those very words to her which caused anger to boil up into her chest while her thumbnail ran across her fingertips.

"I'm never in control of my own life, why would I believe you could change anything?" She asked as suspicion took hold.

"Because I know you're questioning your family's values. You're not getting the truth from Eloise and as a God of academics, I believe you should have all the facts before you decide where the rest of your life is going. You are next in line to become Matriarch, but you have another choice here. I believe the time is coming soon for your decision to be made."

Eden laughed, his words echoed back in her mind. *You have a choice here.* For a few seconds the anger was pushed aside, replaced by disbelief. "No, I don't, I owe it to Eloise to stay with the family, I'm the only one who can continue the family and if I don't... I have a duty to the people who took me in. Besides, what other choice is there?"

"You could get to know Lennox and her friends, maybe even that boy Wyatt Steele. Your uncle seems more than happy around them." The god clenched his jaw as he said Wyatt's name, an obvious attempt to try and hide his distaste for the man.

"Are you sure about that?" She raised her eyebrow at him. "You don't seem to like Wyatt that much. Did he follow you around like a lost puppy too?"

Xemos chuckled. "No he did not. We just have a... Long history."

"Well, this I have to hear," She crossed her arms over her chest.

"Another time. Eloise is drawing closer. Now tell me, do you like feeling like a dog on a leash?"

"Excuse me?" Red hot rage flashed in Eden's eyes as the string of magic tugged for her attention.

"The Salvamari Compass? It's basically a magical barbaric tracking shock collar."

"I-" Eden paused as Xemos shifted his weight to the other foot and he motioned to his left wrist, where The Compass lay under her own sleeve. He was right, but she wasn't about to admit it. "I am no one's dog."

"No you aren't but why do they treat you like one? Send you away on little missions to gather things or sick you on a creature of the night. Yet somehow, you have seemed to catch the eyes of the one I least expected."

"I'm aware. Maybe he should mind his gaze instead of being so focused on me."

"Unfortunately it's in his nature. Mister Steele is a very determined one. However, that's neither here nor there. What matters is what you want."

"And what exactly do you think you can do to help me?"

"You have a choice and I can lead you toward the right paths, guide you to where you want to be. When your mother made her promise to me, she received powers that were also passed to you. I add to the power and assist in tapping into it. For your devotion and learning from my other devotees, I would be there when you need me. You don't have to give me an answer, but I hope the information I gave you is enough to maybe gain a little bit of trust."

Eden knew she shouldn't agree to anything with a man she didn't know in the middle of the woods. He seemed reasonable, he didn't force a choice unlike anyone else in her life. *Why is everyone bringing up Wyatt? What does he have to do with any of this? First Bastien and now this god?* Before she could ask what was so special about Wyatt or answer, his eyes went to the treeline behind her, and he nodded before he suddenly vanished in a gust of wind. The heat sucked out of the air and sent a cold breeze directly into her face, which sent a shiver down her spine. Before she could move, there was a soft click of Eloise's safety being switched off behind her right ear. *Shit, I have to give myself enough time to get back to my gun.*

Quickly, she reached behind her head, her right hand came into contact with the smooth fabric of her mothers sleeve. She gripped Eloise's wrist, she pressed her fingers into the center and with a clatter of metal, it dropped the muzzle and dug itself barrel deep into the ground. Eden brought her other arm up, gripped higher up her mother's arm and dropped to the cold wet dirt. She swiftly drove her weight to the ground and used the force of her action to make Eloise fall head-first over her. As soon as she could, she released her and put as much distance as she could between the two of them. *There was no thud.* See turned her head, she watched Eloise still on her feet and was already half way back the few feet she had created.

Suddenly, her feet stopped and a sense of confusion and anger swelled up into her chest. The lies Eloise told her about why Lennox had left her echoed through her head. *Honey, she's a demon now, if that tells us anything is that she's selfish now and was selfish then.* Her anger at the lack of information her mother was willing to share about her past started to take over. The long-asked questions of her family's motives had planted the seed of doubt which had only grown over time, and blossomed this year. This created nothing but rage as she was looking Eloise in the eyes.

She drew in a sharp breath, Eloise had taken advantage of Eden's emotional stumble. Her hand came into contact with her daughter's shoulder with a tight grip and a dark gleam in her eyes as she pushed her toward a tree. Her body shook as the magic fought to come out as red filled her vision. For only a moment, Eden opened her mouth to speak her thoughts. *How could you lie to me? How is anyone going to trust me to lead the family when you kept so much from me? Who am I supposed to believe when I've been lied to all my life?* The words almost came out, however, none would dare come out. Once again she silenced herself.

Eden moved as she had been trained, Eden forced her arm up into her joint and made the grip break once more. She reached up and grabbed ahold of her attacker's wrist again and forced her arm out to the side, and bent it behind her back. With all of her body weight, she shoved Eloise, who stood about three inches taller than her, forward. It was then Eden remembered the purpose of the training session was close combat, she had been completely distracted from the purpose she was here due to the interaction with Xemos. She attempted to regain herself and saw Eloise fall to the ground again with a smile on her face.

"That was a very poor choice standing in the open," Eloise commented, moving to her feet as if they were done.

Eden's chest heaved as she waited with her hand on her gun for her mother to stand. "It was a trap, and it worked."

"Was it? You seemed pretty distracted," Eloise raised an eyebrow at her daughter.

In the blink of an eye, her hand moved back to the left pocket of her belt, and the flash of a silver star whistled past Eden's head. It was a warning, she reached for her smoke bomb and pulled the pin off.

A singular large white cloud filled the space between them just tall enough to hide her once more. She turned on the ball of her foot, and ran toward the trees once more. *This is a test, this is all a test.* Despite the thought, her heart raced as if in real danger.

She made it all the way to a patch of frost covered pine trees before the cloud dissipated. As she slid between the branches, needles brushed her clothes and face. In seconds she found the base of the large tree and took cover with her back to the bark. Her eyes darted around the branches, and she listened for Eloise to come through after her. The sound of the Matriarch's cough could be heard as Eden assumed she had started to search for her once more.

Now was her chance to level herself before she started moving. She allowed herself three breaths before she turned her attention toward the sound of the footsteps that seemed to go back to the gate. She stepped out of the tree and saw Elosie's back to her as she hunted. Eden approached from behind and pulled the Glock from its holster, aiming it at Eloise who was going to retrieve her gun from the dirt. *If she gets her gun back I'll lose.* In quick succession, she took the safety off the sound which caused her to stop.

"Do I still seem distracted, mother?" Eden asked with victory in her voice.

"No, you don't, which is good," Eloise turned around slowly, unlatched her belt, and placed it on the ground to prove to her they were done.

With a click the safety was back on and slipped back into her belt. She moved back to the gate and picked up the Glock still in the ground before she rejoined her mother. With a nod, Eloise picked up her belt once more and the pair started to walk back toward the house as people would wake around the grounds soon.

"I think you'll be a fit Matriarch, Eden."

The lightness of validation filled her, "Thank you, Mother. I just want to make you proud."

The day passed uneventfully once they got home. The other members of the family were off on their own around the house as Eden made her way back down to the kitchen. She could hear Bastien and Stacey's voices trail up from downstairs during their training session before she turned the corner. For the second time today she was met with her mother, this time she was cutting an apple into quarters. The woman didn't look up at the entrance of her daughter, but instead put some of the pieces in a bowl and pushed it to the other side for Eden to take. With a soft smile, she moved to the bar stool in front of the bowl and gratefully had a piece.

The two women were silent as the muffled voices of the training session trailed up the stairs. Even though they weren't very loud, Eden could hear the frustration in Stacey's voice who told her son off for another smart comment. Eloise picked her knife back up and continued to cut some honeydew with the smallest entertained smirk.

"Bas really has no concept of how to hold his tongue," Eden shook her head as he retorted about how he threw the knives and how they still hit the target despite his wrong grip.

"He never has, that's why men will never run the family."

The two shared in the entertainment for a few more minutes as Eloise finished with strawberries and some bananas. They left the bowl on the center of the table for anyone in the house and she peered up at her through the thin wired glasses and deep amber eyes.

"Eden, there is something I think it's time for you to learn how to create daemonium pugionem."

She blinked in surprise, "You really think I'm ready?"

"I do, you're stronger than you know. Eat some more and then meet me in my study." Eloise instructed and went around the corner.

After a few more pieces of the apple, the black-haired woman stood from her barstool and made her way around the corner her mother had disappeared behind previously. As she moved down the hall, past the family portrait to the door on the far right corner of the hall. The door stood open for her and as she walked in, she found Eloise place three black candles in the shape of a triangle on the wood floor. The late afternoon sun streaming in the window was the only thing that illuminated the room aside from the flicker of the flames. On her desk sat five jars from the family's supply of herbs, four of them with a small supply of the needed herbs for the spell. *Pomegranate seeds, witchgrass, and wormwood with an herb that is related to the demon.* She gazed at the other two jars she saw a single ivy leaf and a jar of mullen.

Eden noted the herbs and swiftly came to the conclusion of who they were for. *Lennox and Aron.* At the thought, something inside her sank into the pit of her stomach. *If we are making these, that means it's only a matter of time until we go after them. There's so much I still have to find out. I have to find a way to talk to her before I kill her. And Wyatt... If he finds out.* No matter what her mothers reason was when she left her at the orphanage, she was still angry deep down and needed to see Lennox prove that she wasn't the monster she thought her to be. So far she hadn't lashed out about the deaths inside her closest circle, *but masks can only be worn for so long.*

She turned her attention to the other items on the desk, she had witnessed the ceremony a handful of times and knew to check to make sure they had everything. Her eyes fell on the two different knives on either side of the jars. On the right sat her mother's favorite knife for magical workings, the left two black-handled daggers in the style the family normally used when creating the weapon that would change within the flames to represent the demon they were made for. A set of small pieces of paper and pen was set off to the left corner of the desk. Once she was done with her checks, Eloise walked up behind her and pulled out a small black silk bag. "Do you know who they are for?" Eloise questioned and held it out to Eden.

"Yes... Lennox Cade and Aron."

"Begin when you're ready," she coached as she stepped behind her desk to oversee the spellwork.

She opened the bag and moved to the front desk and opened each jar one at a time and poured a little into the silk pouch. She stopped and started with Lennox's dagger with the addition of the leaf inside with the first round of herbs. She picked up the pen and quickly created a sigil for the demon with her full name written at the top. *Lennox Esther Cade.* Quickly, she folded the paper away from her and placed it among the other contents of the pouch tying it closed.

Eden turned towards the candles on the floor and concentrated on the use of her magic to ignite a small fire in the center. Sparks snapped after a few seconds and flames started less than an inch from the floor. The flames were so intense they burned blue and snapped as she held the mixture over it, heavy between her fingers. *No going back. For the family, to protect others.*

Without a sound it dropped into the fire, Eden turned on her heel and picked up Eloise's knife and one of the black-handled daggers as she made her way back to the candles. Easily she placed the dagger into the flames and held her left hand over the fire. She took the knife and placed it in her palm. The blade was angled over the middle of her hand as she pressed it into her skin which left one long cut and caused her to grimace as she did so. As she waited for the blood to pool in her hand she shifted her focus on the face of the pink-haired demon. Her eyes so much like Eden's she wondered how she never caught on, the little white crosses on her cheeks showing somehow she had escaped her deal with Val. The thought of her face made her hand shake in anger which caused her blood to start moving too much. With a breath she steadied herself and once there was enough blood she tilted her palm down and allowed the blood to fall into the flames.

When she was satisfied, she peered at her hand where a dim blue light illuminated the skin around the cut. Like water that flowed back together, her skin weaved itself back perfect, her magic automatically healed minor injuries. Out of the corner of her eyes, she saw the flames grow and turn a bright crimson color.

"Good, now reach in and pull the dagger out." Eloise instructed.

With a nod, Eden reached into the fire with the help of her magic to create a barrier around her hand, and felt for the handle. Once her fingertips came into contact with it, she pulled it out and examined it closely. The metal had darkened from its previous silver to a light gray and there was lettering going down the center of the blade. The name *Lennox* was etched into the metal. Just above it was intricate designs of ivy as if carved into the steel which wound into the blade.

Eden took in her work, she knew it had worked, the feel of magic inside that buzzed in her hand. *Once this comes in contact with her blood, it'll be over.* She turned to face Eloise and went back to the desk as the fire went out. She placed the knife down in front of her mother for inspection. Eloise picked it up and looked at it closely before she looked back at Eden and nodded. "Good, now for Aron's."

Pride swelled up in her chest as she moved back to the jars and picked up the next bag Eloise had placed for her while she worked. Easily she began to do the same steps from before though this time with the mullen and joined it with the herbs. She picked up the pen once more and started to write his name down.

"Stop. Write his true name." Eloise interrupted as she slid a piece of paper over to her.

With a raised eyebrow she picked it up and read the name to herself. Her eyes widened as she read and her attention shot back to her mother. "He... He's here? He's Aron?"

"He is. Make the sigil for his true name," she stated simply with a dark smirk.

"Yes, Mother." Eden complied and quickly continued with the same ceremony as before.

This time the dagger that emerged from the fire was mostly black. On the pommel was a large metal rose with leaves and on thorn covered branches followed smaller roses twisted among the vines going down the grip. An elegant bypass crossguard connected the hilt to the blade where the true name of the demon was carved in elegant letters vertically down the fullet.

After the creation of the daggers and Eloise was satisfied with the results, she dismissed Eden. Without a word, she had turned and left the study with the decision it was time to go back to Omega for a few days. *At least I have a place to get away from my family.* This year she found herself grateful for the escape as she walked down the street of Elder's homes, the slightly warmer breeze contrasted the one she felt this morning in the woods causing her to pull her hood up on the sweatshirt she had grabbed on the way out.

She went up the front steps, to the door, and stopped. Loud country music came from the other side of the wood which easily told her there wasn't an easy way of getting by unnoticed entirely. *Great, a party. I was hoping to avoid people.* She rolled her eyes, opened the door, and closed it as quietly as she could so as to not catch the other's attention as she made her way down the short entrance hall. With a quick glance around the corner, curiosity got the better of her as she looked to see who was having a party at dinner time. She was met with a familiar group of six people that all sat on the leather couches with a board game on the coffee table.

Wyatt yelled over the music at Rosalyn and Octavius who were in the middle of some sort of line dance. He had ditched his leather jacket and replaced it with a flannel and black cowboy hat. His brows furrowed in concentration as he corrected them. Her attention was drawn when she saw Bastien, who must have joined the party while she was with Eloise, sat beside Aron and Lennox on the other couch.

She watched the two demons as they sat across from each other, they had no idea she had just sealed their fates. Adrenaline coursed through her as her gaze fixed on the back of that bubblegum hair as she prowled from around the corner. They were completely unaware of what was on its way, a sense of future victory played within her mind which overshadowed the initial anger at the sight of the woman. Wyatt stepped to the other side of Rosalyn right where Eden stood in the middle of the doorway. Instantly, his eyes fell directly to her face and his smile widened as if he had hoped she would show up. *Shit, I'm caught.*

"Little Viper! There you are!" His voice boomed which drew everyone's attention to her.

"Hey! There you are, the teacher's pet!" Bastien called from the couch, a smirk crossed his face at the inside joke.

"I am not a teacher's pet, she's my mother." Eden retaliated. "I was just going to my room, don't let me bother you guys."

"You're right, that's Lenny," Aron spoke up as he jerked a thumb to the pink-haired demon beside him.

Lennox opened her mouth to retort but was cut off by Wyatt. "Come on, Nox. You can't deny it."

"Fine, I won't argue." She put her hands up and turned to face Eden, their almost identical eyes met. "Why don't you join us, Eden? You're not disturbing us."

"I'm okay, you all seem to be having enough fun." She attempted to make her way to the stairs as there was no way she wanted to be around Lennox more than she needed to be.

With her back to the group, she didn't hear the footsteps that came closer as the music continued to play loudly. A hand suddenly came into contact with hers which caused her to stop in her tracks and swiftly turn around still on edge from the day's events. The grip on her hand tightened gently just enough so her hand wouldn't slip from theirs though she tried to pull away. Eden's gaze fell on none other than Wyatt Stelle who had managed to close the distance between them unnoticed. The storm in his gaze was calm as he peered down at her with the usual flirty look as he squeezed her hand. Eden felt herself hesitate for a few moments as she tried to tear her eyes from his.She blinked and felt herself come back to reality just before she smoothly pulled her hand from his grip.

"You could stay, I'm just teaching them the copperhead line dance," His deep velvet voice was just loud enough for her to hear. When she pulled her hand away, his expression didn't fall instead, he seemed unphased.

"I don't want to interrupt your fun."

"You're not interrupting, there's always room for more." He ran his right hand through his hair, the black and white rose hand tattoo placed there caught her attention before he extended it to her once more. "Please join us, Little Miller."

Eden peered past him for a moment to see Bastien who didn't attempt to hide his blatant stare as the others talked and laughed. He raised his eyebrows and gave her a quick go-on motion. *He just wants to see me with Wyatt.* She turned her attention back to the man who still had his hand outstretched to her, his eyes almost pleading for her to join them.

"Fine, fine. Just for a little bit." Eden agreed as she turned to walk past him, until his hand slid into hers once again. Before she could retaliate, he closed his fingers and pulled her into the common room.

Everyone smiled as Eden took a seat beside Bastien who elbowed her after Wyatt went back to Rosalyn and Octavius and line danced. With a swift glance around the others she could tell they avoided her eyes purposely as if they hadn't all just seen the moment in the hall. Her eyes fell to Wyatt as he seemed distracted with multiple stolen glances her way as he corrected Ocatvius.

"It's not so bad having friends you know," Bastien leaned in close to her.

"I know, I've just never really had this many, real or as a disguise." She pointed out.

"You had a boyfriend though, why not give it a try?"

"Holden doesn't count... We weren't official and you know that."

"Yeah yeah, duties come first- As usual." He taunted.

Her eyes fell to the chilled bottles laid out on the table and picked up one of the wine coolers. *These aren't friends,* she reminded herself and her eyes drifted to the two heads of house chatting between each other. *I'm so close to her, I could just get her away from the others and ask my questions... I have to wait till the right moment. If I'm the reason Eloise's plan fails I'm dead.* Desperately, she wanted nothing more than to hear the truth from Lennox but she fought with herself instead. As much as she had to find out if it was Eloise or Xemos who told her the truth she couldn't be the reason they had to pick up and go before she could get what she wanted. She felt her adrenaline pick up the longer she looked at the woman who had left her, she turned her attention back to Wyatt.

"No no, cross the right foot over the left." He scolded Octavius.

"I'm trying!" He argued over the music.

"Come on, it's not that hard!" Aron teased.

"If it's so easy, you do it." Octavius countered.

"With pleasure," He placed his hands on his knees and stood from his seat confidently as he joined Wyatt who lit up with a shared look.

As Aron walked up, Eden noticed his eyes dart towards Rosalyn. His jaw feathered as he passed a few feet away. With a quick note of his discrete movements, she peered beside her at Bastien and wondered if he had caught it. A tap against her foot from him confirmed her question as he watched them. On queue with the music that quickened, Aron and Wyatt danced on beat perfectly in sync. Eden's eyebrows rose in surprise while Rosalyn put her hands on her hips; Octavius put his elbow on Rosalyn's shoulder as the room watched the two. She heard Bastien and Lennox laugh from the couches as the two kicked in unison. The music soon ended and everyone gave an appreciative applause while Wyatt and Aron bowed.

"Right well the dance is pretty simple, it's four kicks with both left and right then a kick cross with the right then again with the left." Wyatt turned to the room slowly doing each step once more for them, "After that, it's a foot stomp right then left and turn oh and don't forget to clap while doing so, and then rinse and repeat."

"Where did you learn this?' Eden asked Wyatt who seemed happier than ever.

"I spent some time in Dallas Texas and happened to meet Aron in a honkey tonk bar." He explained. "What was it, a summer about five years ago?"

"That was five years ago? Man, time really flies doesn't it?" Aron laughed at some unspoken joke.

"Come on, let's try it!" Bastien spoke up and grabbed Eden by the arm, with no time to retaliate as the others started to dance the copperhead.

Eden stood at the end of the line of people next to Bastien who smirked at her attempts to keep up. Thankfully she still had her drink in her hand and decided she would need to be a little tipsy to deal with this, so she downed the rest of it and peered over. She watched the others and slowly attempted a few moves and found herself with two left feet. As she became too focused on her feet, she noticed a pair of shoes come up behind her which caused her to stumble. Hands caught her by the waist, she gasped sharply and froze as Wyatt's familiar voice sounded beside her ear.

"I'll always be here to catch you, Little Viper. If you let me inside those walls of yours."

"My trust doesn't come easily, Copperhead." She responded and turned her head to the right to look up at him, her body slowly relaxed in his arms. His hands hadn't moved from her waist.

His flirtatious demeanor changed as sparks seemed to dance in his electric eyes. "Copperhead? Is that a nickname bestowed upon me by the infamous Eden Miller?"

"I felt like it was fitting." *A dangerous snake that could lash out at any moment, alluring people with his charms. At least, that's what Eloise would say.* The issue was he was exactly that, charming with some sort of human side that made it seem like he genuinely cared. After they had their study session, she found that somehow he *had* actually started to break down her walls.

Sometimes, Eden found herself with the question if it all wasn't an act that somehow he had discovered who she was and wanted to play cat and mouse. So far, it didn't seem like it, however, as she looked into his eyes her thoughts seemed to melt away. For only a moment, she was consumed with the magnetic look in Wyatt's eyes. A soft smile on his face and a happy glimmer in his stormy eyes and when she didn't pull away from him, she felt him gently pull her a little closer. The motion sent a whiff of his cologne that was embedded into his clothes her way. Sandalwood and lavender with citrus filled the air between them the closer they got which pulled her deeper into her trance. His black leather jacket brushed against her arms, his hands still held her steady. The others still danced to their left with their backs to them, the moment they were sharing going unnoticed.

The two sides of her screamed inside her mind. One yelled at her to get his hands off, the other begged for the chance to see what it would be like to give into this forbidden pairing even if he had no clue just how big of a mistake he would make with her. *It's a good cover.* Bastien's words echoed in her mind as her gaze danced between the x's on his cheekbones to the spark in his irises. *He doesn't have to know the real me... It's all just an act here anyways.* Within a few moments she decided it may be time to start to give into this mysterious draw and placed her hands over his.

"Thank you for catching me." She finally spoke, completely engulfed by his gaze.

"No worries," his raspy voice was low in her ear. "So tell me, how does one win your trust?"

Eden thought for a moment, she couldn't tell him the real reason she could never trust a demon. Instead, she pulled at something buried within her, something real and she spoke as if he drew it out of her with a simple question.

"Show me that I can, that... You wouldn't walk away."

"If I walked away from you, it would be like a man in the desert turning away from his only source of water."

The group made their last round and turned to the side where Bastien knocked right into the two. The collision brought her back to reality and she shot him an annoyed glare as he gave them an apologetic look. Wyatt dropped his hands and took his spot beside her for the last thirty seconds of the dance.

Once the music stopped, everyone laughed and took their seats on the couch again. Silently, she hoped Bastien would come to sit beside her and found herself mistaken as Aron of all people decided to take a seat to her right. With a quick glance to the other Miller in the room, she pleaded with her eyes that he would take the seat next to her. However, Bastien smiled and took a seat directly across from her on the other couch where Lennox had returned to sit beside Rosalyn. Octavius had taken the armchair to the right of the couches and spread out which left the spot open for Wyatt who slid beside her. His arms stretched behind her on the back of the couch and he smiled.

"Anyone hungry?" He asked the room as they all started drinking again.

"Starving! What does the Omega's have in their fridge, Cade?" Bastien asked.

"I brought a demon favorite, deviled eggs!" Wyatt said excitedly and stood again. "I'll grab them!"

"No, I got it." Her uncle winked at the two of them before he got up and went into the kitchen. "I'll leave you two to get to know each other better."

Eden folded her arms, she caught the shit-eating smirk spread across Wyatt's face at his own joke and Bastien's encouragement. *I could slap that goofy smile right off, even if it is kinda cute.* She turned her attention towards the lesser of two awkward situations which for her was the two Heads of House locked in conversation. Aron ran a hand through his hair as he fixed the red bandana tied around his head as his attention darted occasionally toward Rosalyn. Eden knew when someone was uncomfortable around another and for some reason he seemed nervous around the brown-haired demon.

"I've heard you play guitar?" Lennox said as things went quiet. "Wyatt was telling me you keep your guitar in the common area cause people kept coming to your door to listen?"

"Guilty," He confirmed and turned to Wyatt who looked at him expectantly.

"Well then, let's hear it. Did you bring it?" Eden chimed in.

"I made him, he was going to leave it but I thought just in case the girls wanted a chance to listen in."

Aron stood and went behind the couch and pulled out a dark wood acoustic guitar with silver strings before he returned to his seat. He pulled the black velvet shoulder strap around himself and leaned over the edge of the instrument. "Any requests?" He asked, glancing around. "None? Alright, players' choice." With a quick adjustment of his hands, he started to let his fingers dance across the strings before anyone could answer. A string version of a classic rock song filled the quiet as Bastien returned with the plate of food and a friend. Immediately she recognized Corvus Bane, the fling on Bastien's phone with a heart next to his name. His brown hair contrasted with Bastien's black as they whispered to each other, the demon's hand on her uncle's back.

The music sent a sense of calm over Eden as he hummed along with the notes and ignored whatever he was up to. *Not my circus, not my monkeys... Well- he is my monkey but he's strong enough to keep himself in check.* Quickly, she convinced herself not to worry too much as she saw them sneak out the front door after he placed the food down. Without him there, she became a little awkward and found herself drift closer to Wyatt. Out of everyone in the room, he was the only one she had a sliver of trust with. He happily bobbed his head along with the others, reached into his pocket and pulled out his wallet. As the song came to an end he tossed dollar bills at Aron which made the room break out in laughter.

She laughed along with them, though it was all supposed to be an illusion of friendship for her, Eden found warmth fill her chest as she genuinely smiled for the first time this year.

The next day Eden's heels clicked on the tile floor as she walked down the halls toward the guidance office. It was time to keep an eye on the woman Bloodfang seemed so interested in. *I have to know more before I can prepare for any fight.* She turned a corner down an empty hall, with the hope she could get the trust of the Elder- To let her think she was another distressed student. Approaching the door, the name on a small silver plaque that read, 'Elder Andromeda Anderson' in long elegant letters. With a raised hand she knocked on the door and found it was already cracked.

With a light push it opened, Eden peered around the corner of the to find the Elder at her desk. Her long straight brown hair covered most of her face as she read over students' essays. The door let out a much louder creak than she wanted, in turn the sound alerted the woman to her entrance which caused her to glance up. Quickly, she moved to her feet and fixed her black pencil skirt, her cropped burnt orange satin blouse with balloon sleeves hung by her elbows, they swished as she moved around to the side of her desk. The shape of her sleeves a stark contrast to the deep V-shape and tight button-up corset around her waist. *Modern 1950 succubus, I can see why Bloodfang has a thing for her.*

Elder Anderson smiled brightly almost and seemed over excited someone had stopped in to see her. Eden had taken one of her classes the previous year and had gotten to know her as doating, kind, and at times protective. Andromeda treated her and every student as if they were her own children and was widely known among everyone in the school. After she had discovered her relation to Eloise, the Elder had invited her and a not-so-thrilled Elder Miller over for tea on multiple occasions. The memory of her mother's face when they got ready always made her laugh a little on the inside as the woman complained to herself about the need to keep up appearances. A high-pitched cheery voice bounced around the small office as she motioned to the set of chairs in front of her desk.

"Eden Miller, please come on in sweetheart. What can I do for you?" Andromeda asked and moved back behind her desk. Before she took a seat as she carefully pulled out a notepad and motioned for Eden to join her.

She took her own seat in front of the desk and paused as her eyes drifted to the notepad and pen. For a second she felt her throat tighten and Eloise's voice entered her mind. *Make sure to keep records of your time here to a minimum, school work only. When we leave it will be gathered and destroyed the week before.* She would have to remember to make this office a stop when they went to leave.

"Nothing you say leaves this office, hun, I only take notes for my, and your, personal records. They are locked up safe and tight, no one will ever see this. Okay? Not even Eloise." Eden looked back up to the woman who attempted to comfort her with a smile, bright blue eyes matched almost perfectly to the decade matching glasses she was wearing.

She nodded and spoke in a quiet voice and allowed a small tremble to lace her words. "Well, I know it's only my second year here but... it already feels like home and I keep staying up, worried about the hunters. For my housemates. I went into the bathroom with Rue, we were talking and when I walked out of the stall... Everything went black."

"Oh, my dear, I can understand feeling bad for surviving. For getting to continue your life while others leave us too early." her excited voice softened. "The security team has called in for more reinforcements already. As I understand, Lennox and Aron have plans for security at the houses already in motion. If I know anything, it's that your mother has everything handled at your place. Probably locked down tighter than anyone I've met. I promise you are safe. Can I get you some tea, maybe a snack?"

"No, I'm okay, thank you Elder Anderson." Eden shook her head, keeping her face concerned despite the new information. She almost released the smallest chuckle at the shared knowledge Eloise was a known paranoid person.

Silence fell between them for a moment as the succubus's gaze searched Eden's eyes. Her expression shifted slowly into concern as if she knew there was more going on. The woman placed her pen down and let the quiet hang before seemingly deciding to speak.

"Feel free to just call me Andy, no need for the Elder Anderson titles here. Forgive me if I'm being too forward but I believe there's more going on than just that. Is it just what happened at Club Crossroads?" She spoke matter-of-factly.

"Yes- No... I mean-." Eden spoke too quickly. Every word she said felt like a possible risk, but she had to gain trust. She chewed on her words before she decided it was possibly safe enough to get some advice on Lennox. "It's just- Eloise told me some things at the beginning of the year, and I'm not sure how to feel about it all."

"Nothing you say leaves this office," Andromeda repeated to her. She was able to hear the buzz of magic a succubus in her voice, the same emotional calm effect they had on their prey. "What did she tell you?"

"She told me that my birth mother is also attending the school. She told me who it was and I just... I see her every day and all I can think about is how she dumped me the first moment she could." As she spoke, she felt the words speed up and spill out faster than she could think.

Eden knew the magic wasn't malicious, however an underlying frustration brewed at the magics ability to so easily find itself behind one of her many walls. *Damn succubus powers.* The thought reminded her that the kind woman in front of her was one of the most powerful of the species and her powers were much stronger than her own.

"Are you excited that the woman who had you is here? What are your feelings about her?" She asked carefully, as she picked up her pen again.

"Well, I don't honestly know. I love my mom, she's the only person I know as a parent. There are so many...contradictory factors I don't know if I should even try to approach her. Besides, according to Eloise she's not the best person at times. Honestly, I don't even think she wanted a child- I want to know more, hear her side but I don't know if I'll ever get the answers I want or believe the ones I get."

"I see... Is Eloise the one telling you these things about your birth mother? Could she have personal reasons for not wanting you to meet her? Why do you think her opinion weighs so heavily for you?"

"Of course she is... But I think her reason is she wants to protect me from someone who she knows could hurt me..." Eden paused and considered the next question. "I mean she's my mom of course her opinion matters, she just cares. I would do anything for my family."

She didn't question Eloise's intentions on the subject. Honestly, it did just seem like she wanted to protect Eden from the hurt that she would probably experience if she and Lennox were to meet and have a normal conversation. Rejection had played on repeat since she even considered the thought.

"You have a pretty strong devotion to your family." Andromeda pointed out.

"I do, they welcomed me in when no one ever wanted me." She told her.

"I understand, more than you might think, my dear... Now you say your birth mother is a demon, which I can tell you're... at least part demon, and I know Eloise is not..." She stopped and seemed to consider her next words carefully. "Would your mom- Eloise... have any reason to feel the need to protect you from a... demon?"

Fuck, I slipped up. Her heart dropped into her stomach. She had already said too much. Eloise wouldn't be happy with the impression she was giving. Eden fidgeted with her hair a bit trying to recover. Her eyes showed the lost feeling she had felt since being told.

"I don't think it's against all demons- I think it's more against one specific one, and what she might say. Like before, she's just trying to protect me from getting hurt."

"How does this affect how you see yourself? This all comes down to what you want to do. You can do whatever you want to do about your birth mother whether you meet her and hear her out, or forget you ever knew about her. There could be an array of different reasons she had to give you up... you never know until you ask" She pointed out.

"I-" She thought on the first question, knowing as a posing demon she would have some feelings on that matter. To her surprise her next words were true. "I hate looking in the mirror."

Andromeda seemed to debate on her next action but moved slowly watching Eden's reaction close. She slid her glasses off, revealing her true blackened demon eyes. Eden had never seen the Elder do this, it was off-putting at first but she was giving her a comforting smile. *At least who she thinks I am.* Not letting herself have much of a visible reaction other than a quick blink of surprise. It wasn't a daily thing for Eden to witness, but Eloise had prepared her to be mostly numb just in case.

"It's okay to be who you are. The choice is all yours, not Eloise's," Andy said, placing her glasses back on her face, her eyes returning to the previous blue. "If you're curious about demons and your own lineage, meeting your birth mom could be very beneficial to knowing what type of demon you could be... even if she turned demon after having you, it's usually hereditary regardless."

"I actually don't know what I want," Eden admitted. "I don't think she'd have anything nice to say anyways. She didn't want me then, no reason she'd want to know me now.... I'm sorry, I'm wasting your time."

"Oh gosh honey not at all, this is exactly why I took this position, to help young demons, ghouls, and all sorts work through any issues they have. You have time to do what you need to for yourself. Until then, try to be more open to what you're feeling and take action."

Still conflicted from the emotions that arose, she pulled on the sleeve of her hoodie and made her way out of the office. With her head turned to the left she didn't notice someone walk around the corner straight into her path. The two almost collided but a set of hands stopped her, the touch caused Eden to jump and snap her head toward the person. Unexpectedly, she came face to face with Lennox, her bob-cut bright pink and white hair was the last thing she wanted to see right now.

"Hey there," she took her hands off her arms and smiled. "Sorry, you kinda appeared outta nowhere. Everything okay?"

"Yeah- fine." Eden told her awkwardly as the same dulled anger from the other day filled her ribcage. *Don't lose it.* "Are you doing okay?"

"Yeah, you know just having a session with Andy." Lennox admitted as she ran a hand through her hair.

Silver on Lennox's arms reflected the dull light in the hall and instantly caught Eden's attention. When her arm stopped, she saw the chain pattern coupled with strings of runes and sigils that weaved in and out of the links from her fingertips to her elbow. Completely distracted from her conversation with Elder Anderson, she couldn't stop herself as curiosity took over.

"What are those markings?" She asked a little quickly as the words fell out.

Lennox smiled lightly and peered down at her arms. "They are devotional markings, I am a devotee of the god, Xemos."

"Oh, I didn't know it had physical markings."

"It works kinda like the crosses on crossroad demons and sold-soul demons. Markings tell a demon's story in most cases. This one is just another story." Lennox paused and her eyebrows rose slightly. "I'm surprised you're not asking who he is, do you know of the mythology?"

"He's come up in some of my studies since I got here. I know the basics just not the minor details like the markings. How did you do it?" She asked as the information could be hard to come by later.

"Well, usually you study him, there's a ceremony to call upon him. Bring some candles, a feather, some books, pomegranate seeds, and a shell to an iron gate and call for him. Sometimes he just shows up when someone needs him and they end up becoming devotees." Lennox explained.

The demon motioned to the marking on the center of her forehead. A trident-looking shape with two strikes on the staff with three dots on either side of the three curved tips. She was surprised that Lennox, her real mother, was so forthcoming about something she would have considered personal. A warm sensation rose in her chest and made its way to the surface, comfort. As if just maybe someday they could actually talk about everything that had happened and just maybe she would have the answers she wanted, the true story.

"I'll have to look into him some time." Eden nodded and glanced over Lennox's shoulder.

"If you need help, shoot me a text. I'm more than happy to answer any questions you may have." She offered as she stepped aside for Eden and toward the office door. "I'll see you later, yeah?"

"Of course," she agreed with a small smile and continued away from the guidance office.

Suddenly, a voice came over the loudspeaker of the university. Vice Principal De Rosa bidded everyone a good afternoon and started off with a reminder of the curfew the school had set in place.

"Now students and Elders, I turn it over to the newest addition to the security team. Please everyone give an ear to Cleo Anderson." The siren's voice paused as the microphone was passed to this new person. Eden's heart stopped at the name. *Fuck... No-* The Millers and Cleo were complete opposites as far as supernatural creature hunters. Hunters like Cleo were a danger to the Millers, willing to also attempt to cut a brutal family down.

"Hello, staff, students, various creatures. My name is Cleo Anderson, and I'll get this out of the way, I am human, I am a hunter. That being said, I am here for one reason only. My sister Andromeda, to you Elder Anderson, has asked me to be here. Yes, we're twin sisters, yes she's a demon and I'm human, what's it to you? I am not here for any of you, this is a place of peace and I intend to restore it. As hard as it may be to believe, some hunters have morals and just want both sides to get along. If you believe you may have helpful information I can be found around the grounds and my cell number will be posted around with the others on the security team. Thank you and I hope I can be of some help to you all."

Finally, back down on the main floor. She had her phone out and her fingers already danced across her screen as she texted Bastien to see if he wanted to meet for lunch to talk about the announcement. As Eden made her way toward one of the side exits closest to Omega Alpha when the sound of a scuffle just around the corner caught her attention. Swiftly she put her phone in her pocket and her hand slipped up her sleeve for her knife. In one movement, she pressed her back to the wall and waited a few seconds before she turned her head around the corner, to see two familiar women having a very tense conversation.

"I'm not surprised you don't remember- but I remember you, and your mother... If I remember right, you told her to put this on me," Remi glared and motioned to herself where very visible scars covered every inch of visible skin. "Where's dear old mother? I'd love to have a talk with her if I'm being honest."

"Mother won't be available to talk, and frankly there wouldn't be much to be said, would there?" She tilted her head, almost in a challenge to the wolf.

"There wouldn't be- I think it would be more of a quick catch up followed by a funeral."

"I don't think that kind of threatening is necessary."

The next few seconds were a blur of movement as Remi reached out with long claws that extended from her fingers. Before the werewolf could catch the Matriarch, she gripped her wrist and pulled her into an open empty classroom. With silent steps, Eden followed them and stayed hidden from the corner of the doorframe. She leaned enough to see Eloise with squinted eyes, her gaze on the pure silver rings on her hand pressed into Remi Moon's neck. The skin exposed to the rings smoldered and Eden knew the smell of charred skin would soon follow.

"You're not going to keep getting away with any of it. I've heard through the grapevine that your daughter goes to school here as well. I'd imagine like mother like daughter? I assume you're in charge now, maybe I can cut off the seed before it becomes the next tree?" Remi growled in anger and pain.

"It would be hard to cut off anything from your proper home in hell." She hissed at the girl, Eden could see the rage in her mother's eyes. "You could have just walked away and we wouldn't have to be here, you wouldn't be in this situation but you had to go and threaten me, and now my daughter? Now you're not getting off so easily."

She slid her hand up to the wolf's jaw, clenched her cheeks between her finger and thumb and forced Remi to look her in the eyes. With her free hand, Eloise reached into her pocket and pulled out a silver knife. Eloise pressed the tip to the student's side and applied enough pressure to cut into her waist, her skin smoked at the site. Finally the smell of the burned skin found its way to Eden and filled the air around her. She went to the reserve of magic within her and pulled the blue string to open the flow of magic and quickly made the scent dissipate in case one of the wolves on the security team happened to be nearby.

"If you know what's good for you, you will keep our history from your newfound family." Eloise punctuated each word in her sentence with a tighter squeeze on the girl's face. "You will promise to never touch my daughter and if you break it- Your time in our basement all those years ago will look like a sunny day in the park. You'll leave with more than the word dog on your body if you live."

Eden could hear the sharp, pained intake of breath from Remi and had started to move further around the corner in case Eloise needed her. With the movement, her mother's eyes darted in her direction and widened before they returned back to the wolf. Silence followed Eloise's words and she saw the knife dig its way deeper into her side. The girl didn't seem to waver as if trying to fight through the pain.

"Don't be foolish, my little puppy." The hunter hissed to her prey.

"Fine-" Remi finally agreed.

"Say. It."

"I won't touch her!"

Eloise shoved her back toward the wall, pocketed her knife and stalked to where Eden was hidden. Her heels clicked on the tile and they grew closer until she grabbed her roughly and pulled her along. The two left Remi in the room as they made their way down the hall, Eloise's eyes darted to the cameras above them every few seconds.

"What the hell was that?" Eden asked, trying to pull her arm away, but the grip only tightened as if she was eight years old again.

"I had that under control." Her mother started angrily, her eyes flooded with something she couldn't quite place. "She could have seen you and tried to get revenge right there."

"I wasn't about to walk away, mother. What if she had shifted and attacked you? What kind of past do you two have?" The bell rang signaling classes letting out once more.

"I will explain later. Go home." Eloise let go of Eden's arm and turned into her empty classroom.

She rubbed her arm a bit and kept going down the hall as the emotional whiplash from the last two hours hit her all at once. Her conversation with Elder Andromeda and Lennox weighed heavy on her mind, especially now that she had Xemos's words to consider. The seed of doubt that had taken root inside her started to grow again and the sight of Eloise and Remi did nothing to improve that. This was something new; her mother was potentially already ready to lie and hide something from the past once more. With a frustrated sigh, she made her way back out of the school.

Quickly, Eden went around to the back of the house to go in through the side door to avoid her family. She reached out to pull open the door just as it suddenly swung open and was met with two men's laughs followed by a quick shush. Bastien and Corvus made their way out at the exact moment she was trying to sneak in which made her momentarily forget the day's events. Corvus moved a few steps down the stairs as her uncle closed the door quietly still with his eyes locked on Bastien. *Sneaking out like teenagers.* She rolled her eyes and laughed lightly. With an intentional clear of her throat, she caused the two to jump and turn to face her. Bastien let out a sigh of relief when his eyes found Eden there with her hands on her hips.

"Eden- It's just you." He smiled as the couple walked down the three steps toward her followed by the demon.

"Yup, just me Bas." She put on an obviously fake smile as Corvus approached her.

"Nice to see you again, Eden." He held out his hand to her, but took it back when she didn't move to shake it.

She nodded and tried to move past them as her irritation with the day grew. "And you, if you excuse me."

"Of course," He stepped aside as Basiten patted his shoulder.

"Don't worry, her bark is bigger than her bite." He whispered as she made her way to the door.

"Heard that! Suck it, Bastien!" Eden held up her middle finger at him, which he returned with a bright smile.

She made her way into the sitting room and rummaged through her bag for her notebook. She took a seat as she pulled it out and waited for the sound of the door latch. *What was he thinking bringing Corvus over here? If anyone else would have seen them-* Eden knew this was Bastien's secret routine he kept hidden from everyone in the family, fun between the mundane of waiting for the right moment to carry out Eloise's plan. Her eyes stayed glued to her unopened notebook as the consequences that could have followed if it had been Eloise or Richard that discovered them swirled in her mind. Footsteps broke her train of thought and she peered up to see Bastien make his way back toward his room.

Eden stood from her spot and took a few steps forward. "What the hell were you thinking, Bas? Bringing him here? You know it's too risky to bring your conquests here."

"I was thinking no one was supposed to be home." He stopped and told her defensively by the stairs.

"Yeah well, one of these days it might not be me who comes home unexpectedly. If Eloise, Richard, or for fucks sake Stacey were to be the one?" Her eyes grew wider as she spoke as she remembered Richard's reaction the night of Rue's death.

"Look- I know, okay? You don't have to worry about me." His voice raised, frustration plain on his face.

"Yes, I do Bastien. Of course, I do!" She raised hers in return and frowned. "I can't lose you, I need you with me when I become the matriarch."

"If you do-" His eyes widened as the words seemed to have fallen out.

The two locked eyes in the sudden heavy silence as the look on his face softened with a silent apology. His body seemed to relax and he stepped toward Eden whose face was still bright red with anger at his comment.

"You better explain what you mean by that."

With a sigh, he stopped a few feet from her. "I've been at almost all of your training sessions. When you first got here, you wanted nothing to do with the missions. It took two years for you to settle into your role, to stop questioning Eloise and Stacey every step of the way. I know what it looks like when you're questioning things, it's in your eyes. I'm surprised Eloise hasn't noticed."

"She's too busy making sure Stacey is happy with how the plans are going," the red on her face started to fade away. "Besides, you know I could never walk away from the family."

"But you could, if you're happy that's all that should matter."

"That's just it Bastien, it's not all that matters. Without Eloise I would have grown up in that orphanage and who knows where I would have been now if that was the case. I'm an Heiress and that is my duty to this family."

"It should matter, Eden. You're more than that." He told her softly. "You deserve to find happiness too."

Eden's eyes met Bastien's again, out of all the times they had this conversation there was finally an underlying sense of understanding between them. This time his words struck deeper than they ever had. It was clear how happy he was with the demon, he was different with Corvus and one day if everything kept going the way she saw it, he would be gone. A pang of sadness weighed her heart as the realization came to her though deep down she had already put the pieces together about a week ago. She looked at him gratefully, the sound of the door that squeaked open softly in the front entrance once more made her jump and quickly cut off the conversation.

Heels clicked on the floor which announced Eloise's arrival into the house. She turned to face her mother behind them, Eden could see the stress written in the Matriarch's eyes.

Bastien turned to her with stifled worry in his gaze as he seemed to realize how close he was to almost getting caught. "What's going on? Why is everyone home so early?"

"I could ask you the same thing," Eloise frowned.

"Mother- Would you please explain what I saw?" Eden coaxed impatiently.

"What did you see?" Bastien interrupted and looked pointedly at Eden. "You didn't tell me you saw Eloise doing something."

"I didn't have the chance, but since you must know I saw Mother here with a silver knife to Remi Moon's neck."

Eloise peered at Bastien and shot him a look to leave the room. "You mean I don't get to hear this?" He complained and crossed his arms over his chest. "You know Eden is just going to tell me later."

Eloise rubbed her temples as she walked over to the leather couches in the middle of the room. Eden followed her mother with Bastien close behind her, a look of concern now clear on his face. The two joined Eloise and took a seat in the two leather armchairs on the other side of the coffee table. Her face had fallen into her hands, elbows on her knees; she only met their eyes when they took their sets. She drew a deep breath in and Eden suddenly became aware of how tired her mother looked. *Is this my future?* The intrusive thought drew her attention away just before Eloise started to speak once more.

"When I was thirteen, we had just arrived at a house in Massachusetts and newly installed a setup in the basement. When Stacey and I went down together she had already brought a werewolf and locked it away. Remi who at the time was a loner anyways, had no one to come looking for her. For over a year she stayed with us as a training tool until she escaped. That was just before Stacey brought me here for the first time on a mission after she discovered the school's existence." Eloise explained briefly as she sat back against the cushions. "When I brought us all back five years ago, I found out that Coyote thought she was dead... And that's what I had hoped since that would have solved the current situation we find ourselves in."

She and Bastien starred as she told the story, Eden knew that her grandmother and mother had many arguments over using live training tools for years especially in the initial years of her in the family. *This must be the reason she won't use them.*

"Do you think she'll tell her brother?" Bastien asked.

"No, she won't risk losing the family she has found here. She knows what we are capable of. But as a precaution, I have a spell I can use to make sure she can't talk about it with anyone. I have to perform it tonight. She'll still remember but if she tries to talk about it, her words will start twisting." Eloise explained to the two.

"Good because I think we have an even bigger issue at hand." Eden told them.

"We do, Cleo Anderson has arrived at the school." Her mother told

Bastien who seemed confused.

"You mean the hunter with morals? Dammit, she's such a buzzkill." He leaned back into the chair.

"We have to tread lightly, make sure you aren't seen without your cover. Stay out of her sight, even with them you still are recognizable to her as she seems to know the family." Eloise rubbed her temples again. "I have to go do the spell before she finds the balls to go to anyone."

With a nod from both of them, she stood from her spot on the couch and made her way out of the room. It was quiet for a moment after the heavy conversations. It was only dinnertime, but she could have gone to bed as exhaustion tried to take over.

She caught Bastien's eyes and saw he also seemed just as tired, "Why don't we all go get some rest?"

"I will, I'm going to get dinner... Do you want me to bring you any-thing?"

"Well, maybe just a small thing." she let a grateful smile drift to her face. "I'll leave something by your door." He stood and put a hand on her shoulder before he squeezed it lightly and made his way out as well.

Night had fallen and Eden had found herself unable to find rest. Memories of the last few days replayed behind her eyelids every time she tried to sleep. To distract herself she started to read anything she could find on Xemos and had brought every relevant mythology book from their library up to her room. Books scattered across her desk, she flipped through the pages in search of his name. The image of his face in her mind's eye, she opened the next book in the pile. Finally, halfway through the seventh book she finally came across him among a pantheon of various gods and goddesses.

"In the beginning, there was Xemos, God of elemental magics, curses, academics, and necromancy along with 3 others. A twin sister Renas, Goddess of deals, destruction, and war. Themos, his brother, god of thieves, trickery, death, and law. Renas also became later known as a creation goddess due to her creation of man. Their brother, Themos would soon become jealous that she could create while everything around him seemed to die at his touch. Coming from his home under the earth, he cursed Renas so death came to any of her loved creations. This created the cycle of life and death.

Xemos would spend years studying and trying to break the curse on Renas. Eventually figuring out how to take the curse from her and put it into the world's first Death's Head Hawk Moth. marking them as a symbol that the curse was near.

When Themos discovered the curse was broken, he chained Xemos to an iron gate he created in a small woodland by a lake in Romania."

Eden paused when she saw the description of the place of the gate he was tied to. Her hair stood on end as she realized there was a good chance the place she met Xemos at training session was the gate he was tied to thousands of years ago. Though she still had trepidations, he hadn't lied about who he was. The mental image of the death head hawk moth that sat on his collar sent a shiver down her spine as she continued down the page.

"Renas eventually found him but was unable to free him from the chains wrapped around his arms. Going to Themos, she made a deal. If he freed Xemos, she would let Themos rule over the Gods.

Once the deal was struck, Xemos was released, meeting his wife in the small town. Each god would soon take a spouse and create a generation of demi-gods."

She stared at the wall in front of her and attention fell on the photos of various places she and Bastien had done missions in as it was tradition every time they went somewhere new. On the other side, a mirror reflected her image back at her. For the first time in a long time, she really took a look at herself. The dark circles that sat under her eyes seemed permanently set and her amethyst irises looked dull to her. She looked like the weight of the world was on her shoulders, and in that moment it felt like it.

Eden leaned closer to the mirror and started to see similar features to Lennox written across her face. Their noses were the same and she even saw the same face shape as her. Quickly, she reached out and turned her mirror around, and looked back at the photos of the family. *If I'm going to be a matriarch, I'm going to need to be able to protect them better. Do I even want to be the matriarch?* Wyatt's face came to mind and her heart sank. *If I don't they will kill him if they find out he's the reason. But would it even get to that point?* Right now he was interested in her but how could she trust that one day he wouldn't lose interest? *Even if he gets past the fact I'm human and I lied to him for months, one day I'll get old. A demon like him isn't going to want me when I'm old and gray. Either way, I may need to hear Xemos out.*

Eden stood from her seat and picked up the book she found him in. She searched her desk and found a shell Bastien had given her when they were young and stepped to her closet. Quickly, she grabbed a thick jacket and went to her spell tools and herbal collection. Eden bent down and searched her personal store of herbs for pomegranate seeds, candles, and a feather before she filled her pockets and left the house.

Determination filled her chest as she walked the same path she had the previous day. She had to see if the gate she read about and the one she came across were one and the same. She approached the edge of the lake, it was harder to retrace her steps to the gate in pitch black. Her gaze went up to the sky to find a crescent moon, Eden wished it was full for a little more light. She pulled on the blue thread of magic and lit a fire in the shape of an orb above her palm now that she was sure no one could see her from campus. *Where is that gate?*

Light illuminated the trees, she pressed forward into a clearing of pine. Eden walked for at least thirty minutes as the smell of pine found her followed by a cold breeze that drew goosebumps on her exposed wrists. Her eyes narrowed as the light from the fire in her hand fell on the cluster she had hid from Eloise in. Her heart skipped a beat and her pace picked up as her head turned in search of the gate. As she turned to the right of the trees, she saw it.

The mostly standing stone arch with precarious iron gates stood in the middle of the clearing. Eden approached the gate, pulled her jacket off, thankful she had worn a thermal long sleeve as she knelt down. Though the wind had died which made it much more bearable, it was still colder than she would have preferred and started to unpack the bag. *No wind this time, at least the candle will stay lit.* With quick hands, she placed the candles on either side of the gate and knelt in the center of the iron entrance. Eden tugged at the blue strand of her magic and with a snap, the tall white candles in front of the posts sprang to life. She then placed a feather, a dried pomegranate seed, and a shell in a circle in front of her herself and pulled out the book with Xemos's lore and placed it beside her.

A sudden wave of confusion made her freeze as she realized she had no idea how to actually call on the god. Lennox hadn't specified clear instructions, however she remembered his words from her encounter with the god. *"Eden, you have a choice and I can lead you toward where you want to be. When your mother made her promise to me, she received powers that were also passed to you. I can do the same for you, add to what you can already do, and assist you in your choices."* With a deep inhale, Eden gazed up to the moon and started to speak.

"Xemos, God of elemental magic, curses, academics, and necromancy. Twin to Renas, Goddess of deals, destruction, and war. Accept this offering as I have come to discuss your offer."

For a second, the clearing remained silent as she waited for him to appear. Her eyes drifted back down to the lit candle, she started to question if she had done it right. Her hand grazed the cover of the book which sat on her bag to keep it clean, under her fingertips the leather was cold. That was until the space around her seemed to warm and something unseen brushed her hand.

Eden turned and noticed a large moth fly toward her from behind in the night. She stayed still and watched it get closer until it flew overhead and landed on the gate above the right flame. Eden examined it closer as it settled, the brown and yellow spotted top wings fluttered to show the bottom portion of the wings, yellow with two brown stripes. A white patch in the shape of a skull looked back at her as the moth let out small high-pitched squeaks.

A hand rested on the gate on the other side beside the moth, the sudden appearance of the man caused her to jump. In the candlelight, the form of Xemos could be made out as the moth crawled to the collar of his shirt.

"I'm surprised to hear from you so soon, Miss. Miller." He came through the entrance of the ready to collapse gate and knelt on one knee in front of the circle she created. His expression held none of the surprise he spoke of, but a smile curved his lips.

"I met Lennox in the hallway and saw the marks on her arms," Eden admitted and motioned to the book beside her. "She gave me some more information, then I found your story."

"Ah you did. Tell me, what did you discover in the lore book?" He asked with a raised eyebrow.

"Actually, I do believe this is the very gate Themos chained you to."

"Very good, it is indeed." The god smiled softly with a spark in his eye that reminded her of Wyatt. "I value truth as much as I value knowledge. I will never lie to you, though I may not always tell you things directly."

"Why not?" The question fell from her mouth.

"Because, there are times when too much knowledge is dangerous. I will not put my devotees in harm's way unnecessarily."

"Why was Themos so jealous of Renas?"

"He was a grumpy god who couldn't keep a plant alive even if his immortal life depended on it. Renas breathed the very souls into her creations but was boastful about it when she drank. Humans fell in love with her creations and left her the best offerings of all of us. He became so jealous he decided the quickest way for our sister to know what it was like to know death was through the curse."

"The life cycle."

"Yes."

Eden stopped for a moment and watched the god's face shift into entertainment. Nothing in his demeanor showed annoyance of her questions like Eloise had when she tore apart everything her mother said.

"Why are you offering this to me?" She watched his gaze drift to his now extended hand.

She paused for a few seconds but stood with him without accepting his hand. "After only a few days you've managed to find one of the very few books with the truth inside. I am invested in you, Eden Miller. I think you will be great and I know you're looking for help."

"Have you been watching me?"

"Not on purpose, however your run in with Miss. Cade I did look in on."

"You are definitely honest." Her eyebrows rose slightly in surprise as he admitted to his attendance on that occasion.

"My deal still stands, Miss. Miller. I will help you gather facts and guide you forward. In exchange for the additional magic to protect the ones you love, you must accept my guidance. I will lead you to places you may not like so you can discover the truth. You will also learn from other devotees when I send them. Will you accept my terms?"

Eden nodded.

"I need you to say it out loud, Little Moth."

"I'm ready to accept your terms." Eden agreed after a small pause at the sudden nickname.

He stepped into the circle and held his hands out to her, their gazes locked. Her heart raced as she glanced at them, this was it and there was no way to turn back. "Take my hands if you're ready." His deep voice echoed in the clearing. Eden lifted her hands to his and placed them into his palms. His fingers closed around hers and chains started to form from his arms and crossed over her hands and twisted their way around to her elbows. Sigils started carving themselves into the metal links and the iron started to hum with magic.

"Eden Miller, will you adhere to the guidelines that you have been given by myself?" He asked as the sigils started to glow bright orange and started to heat up.

"I will," she confirmed through gritted teeth.

"Will you allow me to guide you in the protection of the path you choose?"

"I will."

"Then accept your power and put your trust in me, no matter where it will lead you."

The metal heated up to the point of burning her skin. She grimaced and fought back her reaction to the heat and only allowed herself one glance down to see the hot links. Panic rose in her chest and she felt her hands shake in his grip. Everything in her fought to pull away, to fight and pull out the weapon on her hip. *For my family,* she tried to remind herself why she was here.

"Hold on, Little Moth. It's almost over unless you wish to go back?" Xemos's velvet voice was calm, as if it didn't matter if she said yes even now. She was surprised she still had a choice as the metal left burns.

"No, I want to know the truth, and protect my family."

A strange sensation made its way from her arms and filled her body with warmth. The chains sunk into her skin and revealed the outline of healed silver scars in the shape of the chains and sigils had made around her arms. Xemos released her hands and dropped his own down to his sides. Eden's hands drifted to her arms where she found the matching marks to Lennox now branded silver into her skin. She swallowed past the lump in her throat and fought back the strange sadness that threatened to overtake her. *I'm not becoming her.* She attempted to fight off the feelings as she peered back at the god.

"Rest for a day before trying to overexert your magic. You will discover the elemental power you already lean into will become stronger. Your first lesson is to work with joining two elements into one for a better result. Start small and work your way up, okay?" Xemos instructed her. She nodded and he was already standing and took a few steps back. "I will see you in a few days, Miss. Miller. Go home before Eloise discovers you're not there."

Lennox

The evening sun peered through the curtains of Lennox's empty room which colored it a light yellow. The leaves on the vines around her room shifted to catch the last of the sun's rays and moved like a snake around her room. Music streamed from her laptop as her phone lay on the edge of her bed and chimed with the occasional notification. Black smoke started to appear in the center of the dorm and slowly became denser. In the center of the cloud, Lennox appeared. Her long ivy wings attempted to stretch, but the small room couldn't accommodate the ten-foot span as it brushed Ámpelos. With only about three feet of room on each side, they folded behind her. She adjusted the bottom of the emerald green ruffled dress she wore, the motion caused the smoke to dissipate.

Lennox moved towards her desk, she checked her phone for any missed calls, found none, and put her phone in her pocket. It was the first time since the semester had started she had been summoned by a witch in need. The ivy behind her slowly disappeared into her back as she went to her closet with a grimace as it did and was reminded of the cuts she'd created the previous night. Within moments she had pulled off her dress, she found herself a pair of black sweatpants with a green tank top and a pink knit cardigan. After she had pulled the new clothes on, Lennox looked at her shelf and noticed a small box sitting beside a shoebox.

A lump formed in her throat as she took a deep breath, reached up, and took it from its spot, and closed her closet. She allowed herself a few seconds before she lifted the top to reveal the citrine ring just as she remembered it. Her eyes locked on the deep amber color it held and it glistened in the amber light from outside. As if it were made of glass, she carefully took it from the slot and snapped the box closed in her left hand. The song from her laptop went on about how love was never really gone.

Tears blurred her vision which forced her to blink and now slid down her face as she turned to look out the window. Her next couple of breaths hitched in her chest as she looked at her hands. "I love you," her voice was drowned out by the music as she slid the ring on her right ring finger. Lennox gathered her sleeve into her palm and wiped the sadness away with it. She put the box on her desk and went over to the drawer in the desk, and pulled out an unopened bottle of bourbon. Grabbing a glass from inside it she broke the seal and poured enough to fill half the glass. "To you my love, and figuring out what the fuck happened." Lennox raised the glass toward the window and drank it two shots at a time.

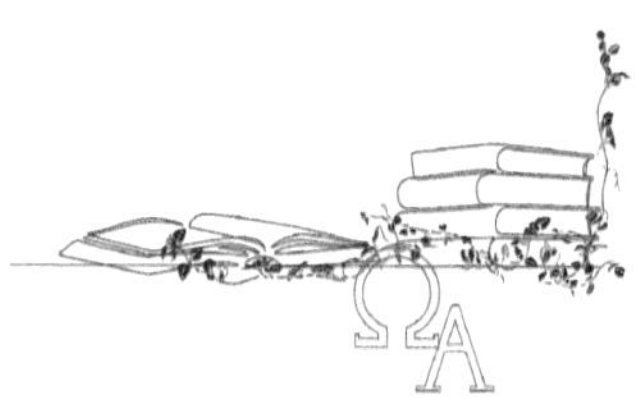

Her back was pressed against the cool wall as the room spun. Night had fallen and the room was only illuminated by candles and a purple desk light. She had turned on pop music to dance along to just as she and Rue did when they drank in their room. Grief had crashed its way with enough force she lost track of how much of the bottle she had drunk. Lennox peered down to find it was half-empty and was now aware of every drop as her emotions hid behind the alcohol. "I'll just put that down for a moment." She told herself out loud and placed the bottle down carefully beside her. She extended her arm and grabbed the cardigan she had discarded earlier, reached into the pocket, and pulled out her phone to see messages from Wyatt, Rosalyn, and Aron.

> Wyatt Steele-
> Mystery girl meeting soon? She's finally letting me take her out next weekend!
> Sent: 7:01 pm

> Rosalyn-
> Are you busy? Was hoping to drop by! I'm over at Kappa with Octavius at the moment but if you're up for a movie I'll stop by your room!
> Sent: 7:24 pm

Aron-
Got your headcount for the night? I'm about to put
the locks on the doors.
Sent: 8:55 pm

With a simple swipe she opened her phone, clicked the first message in her inbox and quickly typed a response without a glance at the name.

Lennox-
Not busy, just uhh- having my own little party?
Would love for you to join! I normally wouldn't ask
but when you get back would you be able to do the
headcount so Aron can do the lockdown? I don't
think I can, things aren't staying straight.
Sent: 8:56 pm

Lennox pressed send and moved to the next chat, her eyes going wide as she saw she was now in her chat with Rosalyn. She went back to the list of chats and clicked the one she had just responded to and found Aron's name right at the top. *Shit- FUCK- No no no no. I just wanted to be around familiar people.* Before she could type another message, her phone buzzed with a response as it appeared under Aron's name. *He's going to think I'm a hypocrite.*

Aron-
Your own little party, huh? Well, since you seem
pretty wasted I'll be right there to do your headcount and join you!
Sent: 8:56 pm

Lennox-
That wasn't meant for you, don't come.

Sent: 8:57 pm

Aron-
Oh I'm coming over and it seems you can't stop me.
Sent: 8:58 pm

With another slew of curse words, she texted Rosalyn back and shoved her phone away from her. The room continued to spin as her head tilted against the wall to glance at her door still covered with grown over vines from her grief. Lennox sighed and waved her hand to draw them back to the frame. Lennox weighed her options. She could run across the hall to Rosalyn's room for the night or she could stay here and pretend she didn't hear him knock. In her drunken state she decided the best way to avoid embarrassment was to turn up her music and refuse to answer. With a small struggle to stand, she stumbled over to her desk to turn up the music.

Without a single glance at her phone, she continued to drink from the bottle as memories of Rue and Felix threatened to surface. *This is so irresponsible, what the hell was I thinking? How long has it been? Maybe I got lucky and he just won't show up.* The room spun again as the music switched to one of her favorite dance songs, and pulled her away from her thoughts. Lost in the music and the alcohol Lennox started to dance once again completely unaware of the knock at her door. The sound of the doorknob was drowned out by the bass and the blond-haired demon poked his head around the frame of the door, unseen. With an entertained smile he reached into his pocket, pulled out his phone and started to record. His mischievous eyes lit up as he watched her dance with her back turned to him before he hid it away in his denim jacket once again.

"You know, it's not a good idea to have your door unlocked," he called as the song came to an end.

You know, it's not a good idea to have your door unlocked. She jumped and froze as air became trapped in her lungs. Her words were repeated back to her, and they stung like the day she saw him on the floor. A part of her thought Felix would be standing there, and when he wasn't her heart dropped. Without warning tears sprang to her eyes. Her hands shook and Lennox covered her face. *No, it's not him- but,* she turned to face Aron, much too drunk to shove any strong emotions down. Her feet carried her backwards until her hip met her desk, unable to muster words. *Leave oh gods please just leave,* the sober part of her begged.

"OH- oh fuck. Oh god," Aron stammered as he slipped the rest of the way into the room, carefully shut and locked the door behind him. "Lenny... Lennox... Hey, let's get you sat down, okay?"

Her vision was black as she forced her tears down with her eyes still closed. A set of hands came into contact with her shoulders which caused every muscle inside her to tense. Aron started to pull her forward but Lennox resisted as everything screamed for her to run, feet planted to the spot beside her desk. The vine-like thread of magic hummed inside her and begged for release as her grief took hold. *Yeah well, as long as I'm around someone will welcome you home,* Felix's voice echoed in her memory.

There was no control now as her mind flashed between the previous and current Head of House. It was all too much, magic forced adrenaline through her body and the rage of her loss caused her to lash out. Her arms came up and hit Aron square in the chest, twice. He grunted as her fists came into contact with his ribcage and surprise shifted to understanding. His forest eyes locked on her head as she lunged forward, her head bent down at his chest level. He released her shoulders and gently gripped her wrists, holding them between them.

"Whoa there, no need for that." Aron spoke in a calm but firm tone.

"What the hell are you doing here?" She yelled at him, her mistake completely forgotten.

"You texted me, and I figured I'd check on you." He explained as he bent down in an attempt to catch her eyes as she tried to pull her hands away.

Lennox opened her eyes for a brief moment but her vision was clouded in seconds as she struggled to breathe. "I- I'm fine, I didn't want anyone to see me like this. P- Please just go back to Kappa."

With a raised eyebrow he looked into her eyes. "You're clearly not fine, you need to sit down and drink some water. Can we get that done first, before you continue to beat me?"

Lennox blinked as she finally stilled, her eyes on his hands wrapped around her wrists, it didn't hurt but he wasn't about to let her move it seemed. She looked at him, her black demon eyes flashed for a moment as the last of her anger tried to scare him. His expression was calm which sent a chill down her spine as something deep within her stirred. A strange Deja Vu she couldn't put her finger on pulled at her already exhausted memory. In her mind's eye a flash of charcoal hands lit with fire as if it tried to remind her.

"I- yes- you're right. I'm so sorry you had to see that." the pink-haired demon agreed between short breaths still slurring a few words from the alcohol.

The two fell into silence as without a word Aron walked backward toward her bed, his eyes never moved from hers. Her mind tried to come to terms with the embarrassment of the situation and how he hadn't run. Instead, he had chosen to stay and help her through her grief even though she had been a complete ass to him. *Why?* Lennox asked herself as they reached the corner of her bed. Aron made sure she sat without issue before he motioned to the mini-fridge.

"You got water bottles in here? Ah- of course. Filtered lemon water, classic Lenny. Can you drink this yourself or do you need help?" He teased.

He pulled out the jug, found a clean cup on top of the fridge, poured a glass, and brought it over. *Probably partly relishing the moment of the perfect Head of House Lennox being so vulnerable.*

"Who doesn't like lemon water, huh?" She challenged but accepted the glass. "I'm still a big girl, I can drink it myself. It was just- you know, a free night and I just happened to have accidentally hit your name and not Rosalyn's."

Aron rolled his eyes at the lemon water comment but kept a cautionary hand under her cup until he was sure she had it. He peered over to the bottle on the ground, picked it up and took a seat beside her. He easily popped off the top and drank.

"If I'm gonna have to take care of you tonight I should get a couple of shots in myself. Seems like you really embodied the free spirit vibe tonight." He gestured to the empty room and smirked at her before he took another swig.

"You don't have to take care of me. I was doing fine until someone decided to stop my dance party. What you saw is just a tiny itsy hiccup. How about we just forget everything you saw and I can go back to my music? You can have the rest of the bottle if you want." She offered in hopes he would take the deal so she wouldn't be so mortified in the morning.

He glared at Lennox as she tried to lie to not only him but herself. He shook the bourbon around as he spoke. "I'm not going anywhere… one because if I bring this bottle outside this dorm, Fang will smell that shit in a second and hunt me the fuck down for being out this late. Second of all, you're clearly not fine and drinking for a reason and you need to own up to your feelings damn it."

Aron finished his reasoning with another swig of the bottle, he was the responsible one at the moment and she was mortified about that after decades of a good record. *He actually cares.* It was clear he at least did enough to stay, but she knew she would have done the same for him. It's what heads of house did for each other. A sense of calm washed over her as she realized she may have been wrong about him. *He's much more like Felix than the hair. This one has a heart too.* She opened her lips to speak but was cut off.

"So until then I will be here taking care of you in case any dildos come by while you're in this state. Do I make myself clear?" He started firmly but kept his voice gentle.

"Fine... But I think I could fend for myself pretty well." For the first time in her life, she didn't fear the void of death. Lennox held her finger up and the vines that climbed the wall seemed to shift around until they stopped a few moments later. The demon frowned as she struggled to keep hold of the vine of magic inside her.

"Maybe not- I guess it's a good idea you're here-"

She paused and glanced down as the chains on her arms lit with a dull silver glow. The fire in her chest burned as she felt the ivy attempt to extend from her shoulder blades once again and her legs threatened to carry her from the room.

"Besides, the only thing I need to own up to is why I haven't tracked down those fuckers. Oh- I guess I wasn't done being angry."

"Hey... You don't need to track down anyone, they have guys on that, like Coyote and Cathwulf, and now the big guy Fang. They'll be found." A hand drifted to her knee which she hadn't realized bounced as her thoughts raced. Her eyes drifted up to his and the glow dimmed ever so slowly.

"You've got the magic in you, that is definitely handy if you ever needed to fight. Just not when you can barely keep hold of the thread. Besides, you subconsciously wanted me here, that's why you sent me the message." He winked at Lennox as he took another swig.

She stood off the bed and walked a few steps to her desk. "I've told you, I meant to send that to Rosalyn."

"What are you doing?" He asked as she pulled a sweater over herself and went to pocket her phone.

"To talk to Coyote and the big guy."

"No, you're not." He stood and placed a hand over hers. Lennox stopped, glared up at him and gave him a rude gesture. "A middle finger, Lenny? I'll just let you stumble around campus in the middle of the night. Though I do have to say this side of you is more fun, very fiery. I didn't think demons that leaned toward earth had such rage."

"You haven't seen rage." A small smirk curved the edges of her lip and her purple eyes darkened.

"Now that I would pay good money to see."

He scoffed and pulled off her half on sweater and draped it on the back of the pink fluffy computer chair pushed under her desk. Lennox sighed and put her phone back onto her desk, begrudgingly aware that he was right. It wasn't safe to walk the grounds right now and a chat with the security team wouldn't do her any favors.

Out of the corner of her eyes she saw him peer at the label of the bourbon, his eyes went wide with shock. By the look on his face, the realization of the expensive imported bottle had hit him. Aron ran a hand through his hair and seemed to consider his next words as he motioned to it.

"This is good stuff. I can get rid of the evidence for sure. I see why you have this hidden away in your dorm." He smiled lightly.

"I'm glad you approve of the bourbon. It was to celebrate when I proposed to Rue." She said as the words slipped out before she could stop them. Aron's smile quickly faded as he gently placed the bottle on the desk. Lennox frowned and reached for it. "If you don't drink it, I will finish it off."

"I think you're done, missy. You've got good taste Leonard. It's a damn good bottle of bourbon. Although I'm sorry you're drinking it with me instead of her." He retorted and snatched the bottle from her hands.

"It's okay... Well- It's not all the time but I'd rather be drinking it with someone than finish it alone."

Silence drifted between them, the music she had danced to filled it. Lennox leaned against the wall as she had done earlier and Aron joined as they both sat on the floor. She rested her head against the wall and looked up at the ceiling. Surprisingly, the quiet wasn't as uncomfortable as she thought it would be alone with him. It took a second in her drunken state to realize this was the first time the two of them were completely alone now both with their eyes on the ceiling. *He's actually not being a complete ass.* A small smile found its way to her lip as she heard him take another drink.

"These vines... I have to know, are they like the ones you use to guard the houses?" He asked, the liquor sloshing as he motioned around the room.

"That's one of their functions. Ámpelos has somehow taken on his own personality over the years."

"I'm sure Ámpelos is handy during spicy times huh?" He asked with a smirk.

"I'm sure you'd like to know." She tilted her head toward him.

"There's a lot I'd like to know actually."

She paused for a second and her fingers drifted to the citrine ring. She turned it around on her finger as her eyes drifted to the bottle in his hand. Swiftly, she reached out once more and plucked it from his grasp, his hands attempted to take it back. *This could go fine or horribly.*

"Hey!" Aron protested. "You're cut off!"

"If you're going to ask me questions, I think I'm going to need a few more shots." Lennox took another drink before he could argue.

"Oh come on, it won't be that bad." He folded his arms over his chest.

"With mister spicy times, I never know what to expect."

He ran a hand through his hair and laughed, "Valid. Just save some for the rest of us."

She rolled her eyes and took another drink before she passed it back to him. "As much as I hate deals, if we go there we are going to make one."

"Luckily deals are my specialty." A mischievous smile drifted to his face

"The deal is a game of truth or dare. If you don't answer, you drink. If you're caught lying, you drink."

Aron leaned off the wall, crossed his legs and placed his elbows on his knees. He spun to face her with a renewed smile. The whole situation felt like a teenager's slumber party all of a sudden which helped her relax a bit more.

"So Lenny, tell me- Truth or dare?"

"I'll go with the truth."

"Alright then, how does one summon Lennox Cade?"

"With a phone call or a text," She laughed a little too hard.

"You know that's not what I mean," Aron scolded, his cheeks flushed from the liquor.

Lennox sighed and knew exactly why he asked. Over the last six weeks beside each other, it would be likely he would summon her at the worst times for the fun of it. She turned the water in her hand as the music continued in the background.

"Well, First you grab pink and black candles, tie them together, light them, and then you gotta call for me, usually just some version of "come to me" will suffice," she explained with a chuckle.

"Come to me? That's suggestive." He pointed out.

She shrugged. "I heard it one day and I followed it to a witch who needed help. Her Uncle was trying to have her exorcized because he thought she made a deal with the devil for power. It was the day I became known as a protector demon among witches instead of one that goes bump in the night."

"A protector demon? There's not that many around." Aron looked surprised as she peered at him proudly.

His expression softened toward her as he placed the bottle down again and pulled off his jean jacket. She noticed it was warm in the room, or maybe it was the bourbon.

"Truth or dare, bandanna boy."

"Bandanna boy? What doesn't it look good?" His hands reached for his head and hiccuped. "Usually it helps me get all the ladies."

"No, I just thought it's time you have a nickname since you've given me so many. Is the bandanna how you got Val home?" Lennox asked while deep down, she couldn't stand the thought of the two of them.

He paused for a moment, the look in his eyes darkening slightly at her name. "Let's not bring her up."

"No issues here, I'm not her biggest fan either." The face of Val Bane crossed her mind which caused her ears to turn red.

The memory of the two of them over twenty years ago standing at the crossroads that fateful night of her deal. The look in her eyes had mimicked a lion as it hunted its next meal. She could even remember the feeling of her long nails brushing against her hand as they sealed their pack. A curse broken for her soul.

As the room started to spin lightly once more as the added alcohol hit her system. By his reaction alone, something must have happened between the two of them to put a bad taste in his mouth. The feeling of relief washed over her, *at least he's probably not going to go running to her to tell her about all of this.* Out of the corner of her eye she saw Aron open his mouth to speak before he quickly shut it.

"What?" Lennox asked.

"Nothing, don't worry about it." he shook his head, picked up the bottle, and finished it off. His face twisted as the large shots went down.

She looked at him with a raised eyebrow and adjusted her position along the wall to face him. "What, are you afraid I'll punch you or something?"

"No, I just... Just when we were arguing she told me things about-Well..."

Lennox wasn't surprised but her heart raced in her chest as she imagined the possibilities of what Val had told him. "Of course she did. Why wouldn't she? You're new here and we work together... She has fun spilling anyone's past she can. What did she tell you...?"

Aron's expression shifted from his previous anger to concern. His eyes darted as he seemed to size her up as if the answer would be something she wouldn't like. She expected the worst but nodded to him to encourage him to tell her. She pulled her knees up, wrapped her arms around her legs, and rested her chin on her knees. Already he seemed to know more than she would have liked, Lennox guessed their housemates had told Aron every rumor. However, the familiar feeling of Xemos's presence unseen, washed over her. In her intuition quickly deciphered the message the god sent. Trust, he sent trust through her bond with the magic and as she came to understand she glanced back to him through her eyelashes.

He let a long breath out before she spoke. "She told me about your deal, not every detail but a good majority of. I know most Sold-Soul demons don't usually like their deals aired out."

"Not usually no... But in this case, I don't think I have a choice. We have to work together so you might as well know since she's here as well. When I was human, I was born into a family cursed by the head curse maker in hell. When I was old enough I tried to break the curse any way I could. I devoted myself to Xemos." She lifted her arm to show him the silver markings and motioned to her forehead. "I thought it was broken until my boyfriend at the time died. Thinking it was back I went to the crossroad and made a deal with Val to be sure I broke it. She didn't know I was pregnant at the time. A few months later I had my daughter and left for a month to make sure the curse was broken. The day I went to get Gemma, I died in a car accident and found out Val ended our deal early."

As she told her side of the story, his face shifted with various reactions. First there was understanding, then his eyes went wide in pure shock when he seemed to realize she meant Wyatt had been the one to curse the family. Finally, it ended with anger. Aron shifted closer to her as she spoke, held his hands up, and waved them to stop her.

"Wait wait wait, you're telling me you have a daughter and you were cursed by Wyatt?"

"I did. She's long grown now. Probably living a regular human life...

At least that's my hope for her." She corrected with a sigh. *Of course he put that one together.* "Well, more like he accidentally cursed my great great grandmother."

"We are- But Lennox... What Val did wasn't right even by demon standards. She broke your deal when she caused your death and took your soul eight years early." His anger at the break in Crossroad Demon Law flooded into his voice. His green eyes sparked to life with a small fire inside his pupils.

Though she had never attended the Crossroad Demon courses. This was something that went against the way they were taught. Lennox reached out a hand to him and rested it on his arm. Instantly she felt how warm his skin was and glanced down. To her surprise, there was a dull orange glow under his skin that followed the lines of his veins. *Fire, he's a fire based demon.* The most dangerous combination in battle paired together or opposed, earth and flame. The face of Armaros flashed in her memory. Lennox shoved the image down and gently squeezed his arm to get him to look at her despite how hot her hand became the longer she left it there.

"I guess it's my turn to calm down a drunk demon." She smiled softly as they met eyes.

"I guess so-" He chuckled nervously. 'Bandanna boy huh?"

"What? Don't like it?"

"That's my job Lenny-Boo. Leave it to the professional." He patted the top of her head as a smirk pulled at his lips.

"Let's get back to the game. Truth or dare?" She insisted and swatted his hand away as the room seemed to relax once more.

"Fine, I'll go with a truth as well."

"Alright, is there someone you have your eye on around here? And don't act like I haven't seen you check out every woman that you pass."

"Well, the semester is definitely young and there's lots of potential here," Aron admitted, his face contorted into thoughtfulness.

For a moment, a strange feeling rose in her chest. Maybe it was just a concern for who he was going to try and seduce next. *Or is it No.* She rejected the thought. So soon after Rue had passed she was too vulnerable. A wave of sleepiness washed over her which made her yawn.

"No, not yet. One more." he smiled at her, looking as tired as she suddenly felt.

'Fine, one more. Then I think it's bedtime for me."

"Truth or dare?" His eyes danced.

"Dare," she challenged.

Aron raised a brow at the decision and shifted stiffly. "Dare? Alright... I dare you... to be late- like pretty late- to your classes tomorrow... all of them. See how goody two shoes you really are."

"Late to class? How late are we talking? Like five minutes or-" Lennox paused.

"You absolute nerd, no... I mean like you're showing up halfway through class. My kind of late." Aron laughed loudly.

"But I have-"

"Doesn't matter."

"What if I?" She motioned to the empty bottle and frowned when she saw her escape route was empty.

Aron smirked. "No getting out of this one, Lenny."

"Fine. Just for tomorrow." Lennox shook her head as she yawned again.

Finally, she stood roughly from her spot on the floor and tripped over her foot as she attempted to find her balance. Once stable, she extended a hand to him. Without pause he accepted and rose to his feet, also struggling a bit as she peered around the room. It was then she realized he probably wouldn't be able to make it back to Kappa safely if he already could feel the strong drink. She moved over to her desk, shut off the music, and her heart leapt into her throat. It was her night off and Aron was here which left no one on patrol.

"WHO'S ON SECURITY!" Lennox panicked.

"Don't worry, I had Wyatt take over for the night once I got your text." He stretched and made his way over to her bed and flopped down on Rue's side. "You don't mind do ya Lenny? I don't know if I can trust you enough to not try to wander around the grounds in this state."

She paused and knew he tried to make his concern come off as a joke. Lennox weighed her options and came to the conclusion she probably didn't have much of a say in the matter nor did she have the energy to argue. "No funny business."

"Are you sure you can resist all this?" he motioned to himself as he pulled off his bandanna. She shot an annoyed glare and he raised his hands in surrender, then rested a palm over his heart. "No funny business, cross my unbeating heart and hope to die. We can even build a pillow fort in the middle if you want."

"I'll take your word for it."

They shifted beside each other in attempts to get comfortable under the covers. It was strange to have someone beside her again, though the movement of him beside her was strangely comforting. Once he settled, she noticed his eyes on her in the dull light from her desk lamp. Deep down she was grateful he showed up, *life continues on.* For the first time since Rue and Felix's deaths, the start of acceptance of life without them calmed her grief.

"Can I say something?" She asked, her stomach in nervous knots.

"You can always talk to me." His voice was quiet

"I wanted to tell you... I'm sorry for how I judged you when you first got here. I was grieving and I wasn't ready to accept the fact Felix had been replaced." The final shots from the bottle acted as a truth serum.

He rested his head in his palm as his tired eyes softened. "I know. I understand grief, Lennox and so you know. I don't hold it against you. It's just too much fun to press your buttons."

"Of course it is... I just- I won't let them get to you too you know... The hunters or anything else." She swore, not ready to admit to him some part of her still believed the curse was back. *I'm not about to lose anyone else.*

He grabbed her cheeks in one hand from under her chin and pulled her face towards him. "Hey, hey you listen here. I'm gonna keep you safe, alright? You call a dildo and I'll be right there to put the little plastic dick to an early grave you hear me?" He looked from one of her eyes to the other and back. "Oh my god, are your eyes purple?"

Her face flushed under his hands unseen in the dark, she didn't move surprised at the sudden action. By the look in his eyes, he was sincere. *If we have anything in common, we'd both go down for anyone here.* The realization gave her confidence they would work well together this semester.

She laughed as he slurred his words of comfort and followed his eyes. "Yes, they are purple."

"That's fuckin' dope." He complimented as he let his hands slip away and slid one under his pillow as he lay on his side faced in her direction once again. "Well bottom line I got your back, and you better have mine."

"I won't let anything happen to you, no matter what." She promised and held out her hand with only her pinky up once settled under her covers as her eyes started to close.

Aron gently intertwined his pinky with hers with a sleepy smile.

"There, now if you let me die I can break your pinky."

As the room darkened, the last thing Lennox saw was he had left his finger intertwined with hers as they both drifted off to sleep.

Her room was still in the night and Lennox lay peacefully asleep. The vines along her walls sleepily shifted around the room while she rolled under her sheets. The dorm room was still until black smoke filled through a small crack in the window. It collected on the floor spreading to cover the floor a few inches high. In the far corner of the room, the shadows rose and formed into a human shape. A demon in a black suit with tattered bat-like feathered wings stepped through the cloud. His silver hair slicked effortlessly away from his face as a smirk crossed his face. It only took a few steps for him to close the distance between himself and where she slept.

The man sat on the other side of the mattress, careful not to make it shift under him. His black eyes rested on her sleeping form and he reached out with his blackened hand to touch her shoulder. Lennox shifted again under the covers and pushed his hand away in her sleep. When it didn't move she tried again.

"My dear," His deep low voice made her eyes shoot open. "It's time to wake up."

She shot up and reached out to grab his hand from her shoulder. However he was faster than her, his fingers wrapped around her wrist. His grip tightened harshly as he peered down at her with the same venomous smile she remembered. Armaros shook his head as suddenly the sounds of chains caught her attention. Lennox's attention turned to the room around them and discovered what was once her room was now a cell in hell. Her heart started to race and she desperately tried to pull at her magic.

"No magic right now, Miss. Cade. I thought we'd have a little chat about that daughter of yours." He held a knife in his hand as he spoke.

The last time I saw him was before Xemos came to get me. The memory came to the forefront of her mind. "You leave her out of this."

"Oh but mommy dearest, don't you want to reunite with her lovely soul?"

"No! Not here, she will never follow in my footsteps!" Lennox yelled and went to attempt to stand.

Armaros bent down and shoved her backwards. Unable to stop her fall, she fell back. Her head hit the stone wall behind her which sent stars over her vision. He held the chains above her head to keep her suspended a few inches above the floor. His gaze was locked on hers as her body shook. In this moment she was reminded of just how strong he was. How easily she turned into a rag doll. Without complete access to her magic from Xemos during her transition from life to death, she was no match for the fallen angel. His free hand wound behind her head and his fingers twisted through the back of her hair. The demon pulled her closer, gripping her at the base of her head.

"My dear, I will get my way and there's nothing you can do to stop me. One day, who knows how many years from now, I will make a deal with her. She will follow in Mommy's footsteps. Now, I just need to know where precious little Gemma is. If you think about the answers, it will be a lot less painful. However, I don't mind doing it the hard way."

As she fought for control of the memories that forcibly came up, Lennox yelled out in pain. The hand that had held her chains had moved down, wrapped around her waist and pulled her to him. *Something is going on... This isn't how it went.*

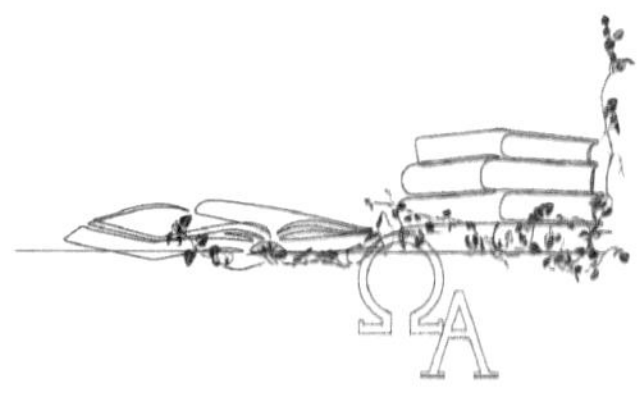

An arm held her waist tightly as she fought against the grip. *No... No no no, let me go.* Lennox couldn't speak. *No! You can't have her!* With a free arm she reached where another grip had appeared around her shoulders and clawed at the iron grasp around her. Her nails missed and dug right into the damaged skin between her shoulder blades which caused her to let out a louder scream than before.

"Len! It's time to wake up!" A combination of two familiar voices echoed as the face of Armaros smirked darkly down at her.

She couldn't pull her eyes from his black pits. "Please, anything else! I'll do anything, just don't touch her."

"Lennox, you're dreaming. Everyone is safe, come back to me." Armaros's low voice started to fade as the grip around her kept her in place as she thrashed.

Her eyes flew open ready to face the cruel gaze of Armaros above her. However, she found the face of Aron. Looking at her with a mix of fear and concern. He had an arm around her shoulders and the other wrapped around her waist. His grip was tight and she could feel her heart race and body shake as she tried to figure out what was going on. The light from her desk was dimmer than before and her gaze traveled to the barrier of foliage around herself with Aron bent over the edge.

The vines on the side he had slept on had been ripped apart which left enough of a hole for him to get to her. Her eyes drifted to the edges of the opening and noticed it had formed into poison ivy in defense of itself. Her eyes moved to his arm which had angry bumps that covered his exposed skin. *I... I did that.* She tried to speak but found a lump in her raw throat that wouldn't allow words right now as she finally met his eyes again.

"It's okay, breathe Lennox." Aron's voice instructed calmly. "We can talk in a minute."

He held her as her mind raced and her magic tried to continue the fight to be unleashed. *Why would the vines make a barrier? Was it just the nightmare causing this? What is he going to think of my ability to run this house?* Embarrassment filled her as they stayed in silence as Aron kept her close to his chest while her body shook with adrenaline.

"Breathe with me." His voice instructed softly as something wet dripped down her back suddenly hyper aware of herself it drew her attention momentarily. Her words refused to come and her breath hitched. "In and out."

Aron breathed more exaggerated than usual and waited patiently for her to match the moment. Slowly over the passing minutes, her body calmed and Aron slowly started to let go. At the same time the vines around them retracted to the walls once more. Lennox felt the hum of Ámpelos in the back of her mind, the sentient plant mistrusted the demon and he made no effort to hide it. She shoved the thought aside. *If he wanted to hurt me he would have.* She shook off the thought and turned her attention to his arms to distract herself from the looming sound of Armaros's voice.

"Let me fix that for you, please?" Lennox asked, the guilt for the poison ivy tugged at her.

He nodded as they sat up across from each other and held out his arms to her. His gaze didn't leave her face the entire time as she lifted her hand over his arm about an inch above his skin. With a tug at the green thread a dim green glow emanated from her palm and underneath it the rash faded away. Once done, they fell into silence once more. Aron ran his fingers through his hair, his expression fell into worry again.

"I have to ask, what happened?" He asked calmly.

"It was just a nightmare." She shook her head in an effort to get him to drop it.

"Don't you lie to me, Cade. That wasn't just a nightmare, you were clawing at your back. How long has this been going on?" He leaned toward her.

"I don't know, maybe since Rue died? If you would believe it, mostly it's the nights I do security. It's just old things from my past. I'm sorry you had to witness that, Aron." She turned her gaze toward her hands which did have a little blood on them. Unable to look at him, she drew in a shaky breath.

"Don't apologize, we all have pasts. Maybe you should take a few days from security?"

"Danger doesn't take a day off, besides I'll never sleep easily as long as *they* are out there."

"I think it's necessary, Len. What happens if you drain yourself and you can't fight if you have to?" He questioned and made a good point.

He reached toward her and rested a hand on her knee. With the embarrassment of the whole situation grew stronger by the second and Lennox wrung her hands for a moment before she stood from the bed. *I can't believe he's still here after all of this. He barely knows me and I'm pretty sure there are only a few people who would deal with this.* She made her way into the bathroom to wash her hands and found her reflection in the mirror, her eyes locked on the purple irises. Her pink hair was a mess and she noticed some red spots on the back of her shirt. Her back seared with pain as her eyes followed the blood to her back where she knew she had dug her nails in.

While she was lost in her thoughts, she hadn't noticed him move to the doorframe behind her. Lennox stayed within her own mind as he leaned against the frame with his arms crossed and concern in his eyes. Slowly, her eyes shifted from her reflection to the man who stood behind her. There was no hint of judgment in his eyes or body. He didn't tease her. It seemed as if he understood the darkest moments of life and for the first time in weeks she found herself beginning to trust him.

"I know you want to protect everyone, but thinking a few nights off will be good for you." Aron insisted.

"Fine, I'll take two nights off." She agreed as she dried her hands.

"You'll take four off."

"Three."

"Four, or it'll be a week. You don't have to worry, Wyatt and I have it." he smirked with amusement.

"Fine. you win this time. Next time you won't be so lucky."

Lennox walked past him and toward the bed, thankful for the fact she was no longer drunk. She strode over to the desk where her phone sat now dead and plugged it in beside her bed. With a turn she moved the blankets back up from the end of the bed and climbed back into bed with Aron close behind.

"You never told me what happened in your nightmare."

"Or… We could forget it ever happened." Lennox smiled sheepishly.

"I don't think so." He got comfortable once more. "Remember last night when we said we had each other's backs? I meant that you can trust me."

"I told you, it's just history that doesn't matter anymore."

"It seems to, I couldn't wake you up for ten minutes. What would we do if you couldn't wake up from one of these? What if it's because you're draining yourself? I know you probably don't view me as your friend, and that's fine but I do still care about everyone on this campus. Last I checked you were still a student here so you count in that. Though I won't force you to share."

Lennox sighed as she shifted the pillow under her head. "When I died and was taken to hell to meet with the crossroads demon I had made my deal with, she didn't show. Another demon took over the honor of her job for a few days. It- Was my time with him that haunts my nightmares."

"If I may ask, who was he?" His voice was flat, serious, and the concern in his eyes hid something darker she couldn't place.

She shook her head again, she felt the panic threaten to take over, scared if his name was spoken it would summon him. " I- I can't say his name."

"It's okay you don't have to say it right now." He quickly stopped her. "How about we just go back to sleep?"

"That would be nice actually," she pulled the covers under her chin.

"Aron?" She whispered before they closed their eyes.

"Yes?" He whispered back.

"Thank you for being here tonight, it's nice to feel safe here again."

"Don't sweat it, Lenny-Boo."

The next morning after everyone had left, Aron had reminded her she was supposed to be late to class, followed by a quiet argument about why he couldn't be seen leave her room. Lennox made her way down the stairs followed by an annoyed-looking Aron. They made it all the way to the front door without trouble and she opened the door for him to slip out. She closed the door gently and made her way into the kitchen needing some coffee for a hangover cure. As she turned the corner she was surprised to find Rosalyn with her hip against the counter and a cup of coffee of her own.

"Hey, don't you have class this morning?" Rosalyn asked.

"Decided to give myself the morning off. Sometimes you just gotta relax, you know?" Rosalyn paused as she eyed Lennox. "Well, maybe you do, sneaking out Aron like that."

"I wasn't sneaking him out." She denied as she poured a cup for herself.

"I've never heard that door shut so quietly. Nox, you know no one is going to judge you for how you grieve."

"Eww, Ros- Absolutely not!" She scrunched her nose at the implication.

Quickly, she explained everything that had happened the night before. From drunk texting Aron and discovering he had a much more caring side than she thought. Then to the rediscovery of Rue's ring, Lennox's eyes saddened as her eyes darted to her hand where the ring now lived. Rosalyn's eyes drifted to her hand where the citrine ring sat. The demon's usual cheerful demeanor softened. Something inside her sank at the look on her best friend's face. *I'm not that fragile... Am I?* Lennox questioned herself and how okay she actually was for the first time. *If I'm being honest with myself, I've never felt more unsteady.*

"Don't worry about it, what about you? How have you been handling everything? I know I threw those nightmares on you."

"Well, I can't lie and say I'm not worried. But, until we see any red flags or potential hunters, I guess we just keep moving forward. I just miss Felix and Rue." Rosalyn admitted.

"I do too." She peered at her mug for a second.

Rosalyn moved from her spot at the counter and motioned toward the small island in the middle of the kitchen. The two women pulled up bar stools and set their mugs down. There was a silent understanding in the air, which dissipated when Lennox spoke up once more.

"So, tell me what's new in the world of the lovely Rosalyn?"

"Well, I've actually been spending some time with Octavious! Girl, let me tell you, he is the absolute sweetest!" She smiled wistfully as she told her.

"Well, I could've told you that." Lennox laughed into her mug.

"I know, but we just never got to hang out like that, you know?"

"I think I have an idea." Lennox agreed and thought back to how fast she had dismissed Aron.

The two sat in the kitchen for a while as Lennox told her all of the Octavius stories she could. Happy that her friend was having fun, she took their mugs over to the dishwasher and placed them on the top rack as they laughed.

"You're telling me Felix and Wyatt took him out in the middle of the night and lit half the woodland on fire?" She asked incredulously.

"Not that they were trying, as they claim the fire got a little too tall while they were off by a tree." She framed the last words in air quotes.

Rosalyn tilted her head toward her and shook her head, "Boys."

"You know, you would think dating women is easier." she pointed out.

"Well, now you can say you really pulled an Aron, you missed a whole class." She pointed out as she laughed.

Lennox turned to face her friend and checked her watch. "Crap, you're right. I gotta go get ready to be late for the next one."

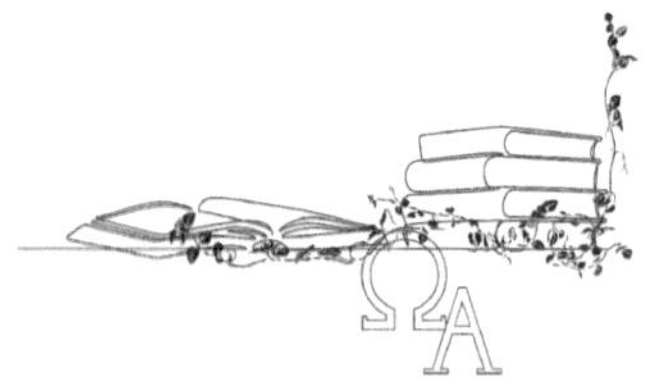

As classes ended for the day, Lennox made her way from the room and peered around the hall. To her left her eyes fell on Remi who waited for her, their daily walk back to Omega to make sure she got there without any trouble. *At least it's not Coyote or any of the security team insisting on walking with me.* She made her way over and smiled at the werewolf she had at least gotten to know.

"Hey! How was class?" She asked.

"You know, the usual- Aron walking in at the tail end and Celia giving him absolute hell the moment he walked in." An entertained smile crossed Remi's face.

The two walked down the halls each scanned the crowd for danger as students passed them. Lennox pulled her bag a little closer as her heart rate started to climb due to new found anxiety in large crowds. It was the first time she had ever been nervous within the gates of the school, but now it was almost as if there could be danger around any corner. Outside of the Armaros dreams, she had a recurring dream of walking around the school alone and turn the corner of the hall to find Rue and Felix dead followed by Rosalyn, Wyatt, Donnie, and the rest of the school.

Lennox forced herself out of her thoughts as they made their way through the front doors. Her eyes drifted to the water fountain in the middle of the courtyard. Other students quickly made their way in and out of the building and pulled their jackets closer in the cold breeze.

"How is Celia? Have you guys been on any fun dates recently?" Lennox asked in an attempt at conversation, calmer now out in the open.

"Really good actually, we were supposed to go into town for something she had planned. Things have been a bit- busy recently so we moved it to this weekend."

"Understandable, I hope you two have fun." Lennox nodded and glanced over at her.

Something seemed off about Remi, the usual determined spark in her gaze had faded and she seemed more on edge than usual. She waited for the two of them to make their way past the fountain and out of the u-shaped courtyard. Once they were on the cobblestone path to Omega, Lennox finally spoke up.

"You never have to tell me something you're not comfortable with, but is everything okay? You seem a bit off and I just want you to know you can talk to me if you need to."

"Yeah, I just..." Remi paused and chewed on her lip. Her brows furrowed as she seemed to consider her next words. "It's been a strange couple of days if I'm being honest."

"What's been going on?" Lennox asked as the wind blew her hair in her face.

With a sigh, she returned her gaze to Lennox, the werewolves face flushed bright pink in the cold. Guilt flashed in her eyes and it almost seemed she wouldn't want to share. Remi's eyes darted around them one last time for anyone who may hear them before she started to speak.

"Can I trust you to not tell anyone about this? If anyone ever knew... I don't want anyone getting hurt. Promise me if I tell you, you won't say anything."

Lennox frowned, worried. "If you're in danger, your brother and I need to know so we can keep you safe too."

"Can we talk about it somewhere private and warm?" She asked.

"Of course, my door is always open." Lennox agreed.

She nodded as she tucked the section of blonde hair behind her ear and Remi's brown eyes trailed off to the house as they approached. After they stepped inside, they went up the stairs straight to Lennox's dorm room where the Head of House closed the door behind them. She held her finger up to tell Remi to wait and moved over to her metaphysical supplies, pulled out a silver metal box with poppies carved into the surface and opened the latch. Lennox pulled out an incense stick, pinched the tip of it with her thumb and pointer finger and waited for smoke to rise from her fingers. She placed it on the table by her door as the trail of smoke rose into the air. As she turned to Remi, Lennox brought over her computer chair for Remi and motioned for her to sit.

The demon took a seat on her bed as Remi did and nodded. "As long as that is going you're okay to speak freely."

"Thank you. I just-" Remi paused and spoke carefully. "The other day I made the mistake of going somewhere alone. When I was on the run over the last few centuries from hunters, I got caught. I was held for over a year in their house to train the next generation. When I was walking down the halls, I came across-"

Remi's words were cut off by a cough and Lennox's eyebrows tilted down "Do you want some water?"

She cleared her throat and tried again. "No- I'm fine... I was walking down the halls and I came across..."

The name came out as gibberish each of the four times she attempted. After the words stumbled over themselves, she stood in frustration, Remi's irises shifted to bright yellow as she paced around the room. Lennox couldn't hear but the woman started to mutter to herself and looked out the window. *Why? Oh, oh no. They can use magic.* The realization hit her as the glimmer of magic caught her attention. It gave off notes of the ocean breeze but was easily recognizable as a type of concealment spell that had been used to guard the hunter's identity.

"It's okay, they put a spell on you so you can't tell anyone anything that could reveal them." She explained in hopes it would comfort her.

"Can you reverse it?" She asked desperately.

"I don't think I'm able to, no. But maybe your Uncle Fang or even

Elder Anderson's sister, Cleo can. From what I know of him, he's very skilled at magic. Maybe Cleo will be able to ask the right question to get information while he tries to break the spell." Lennox suggested and stood.

"Let's go then."

Without more than three words and a nod, Remi went to the door and opened it. Lennox quickly stood, grabbed her bag, and followed her out of the dorm again. She glanced over at the woman and swore she could see the rage burn in her eyes. *I should let one of them know we are coming.* Lennox brought out her phone as they walked the campus ground and dialed the security team's phone. Within a few rings, a deep voice answered the phone.

"Mathias Bloodfang, everything okay there Miss. Cade?"

"Yes and no, Remi has some information that could be helpful, however, there's a concealment spell." Lennox explained quickly.

There was a small pause on the other end before the man's voice came out even deeper, underlying anger in his voice as he spoke quickly. "Meet me in the security office. I'll get Coyote and Cleo."

"We'll see you in ten." She agreed.

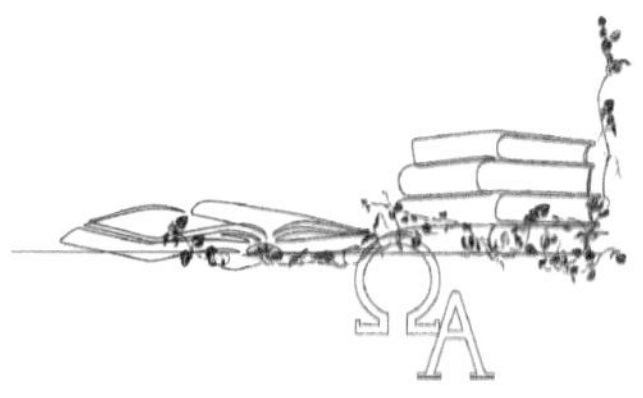

The security office was about the size of the average classroom in the building. In the far left corner sat about thirty monitors all with different views of campus and two chairs. In the right corner were three small desks and a closet which had a small clipboard next to it that had a list of weapons. When the two girls entered the office Lennox took notice of the seemingly broken door frame. Bloodfang shrugged off and muttered something about a false emergency when she had asked as they waited for Cleo, the immortal human hunter.

It took ten minutes for the woman to arrive from Elder Row, and once she did the room fell silent. Cleo behind one of the very few desks, her brown hair was pulled tight in a ponytail but still looked eerily like her sister, Elder Andromeda Anderson. *Andy was right, they would confuse people.* The Elder had told Lennox about her sister and how the two had become immortal. Cleo had gotten sick, so Andy's soul was sold off to Lucifer for a chance at a new life.

Coyote arrived a minute after Cleo, as he walked in the room and his gaze immediately settled on the wolf between herself and her Uncle. The man moved forward, worry in his eyes as they scanned her for any injuries.

"Is everything okay, Remi? Why didn't you come to us before?" Coyote asked as he gripped her by the shoulders and continued his inspection.

"You have us now, remember? Everything isn't all on you." Bloodfang added.

"I'm fine. I didn't want to worry you two. You've spent centuries worrying." Remi moved over to the left chair, her eyes still lit with frustration. "What matters is I have information that could help the school and I can't say it. So as soon as we fix that, I'll be able to explain everything. Can you break it, Uncle Fang?"

Coyote moved to sit in the other chair and took behind one of the other two desks by Cleo. Lennox kept her eyes on the woman as she took her seat, weary as she had never met a hunter with morals.

However, everyone trusted Elder Anderson so most seemed to be open-minded to her help which she tried to be as well. The seven-foot man moved behind his niece and placed a hand on her shoulder. "I'll do my best, kid." He closed his eyes and silence fell over the room. After only thirty seconds he sighed, cursed under his breath, and peered over to her.

"I can't, it's bound to an object. If we find whatever the spell is bound to then I can."

Remi growled and turned to Cleo. "Alright then, try to ask me something. Maybe we can work around this thing."

"I will do my best," she agreed.

Over the next several hours Remi obscurely explained what had happened in her past. Then the events that lead up to whatever occurred in the hall. Unfortunately even with the most basic or carefully worded questions, when she tried to give more details to identify the person the words came out as gibberish. Each time she started over, she became more desperate and frazzled.

As the words refused to come out Remi became increasingly angrier and Coyote insisted they take a break. However, she rejected the offer and insisted they keep going until an alarm on Lennox's phone pulled their attention away. With a quick glance down she saw it was already time to lock the houses down. *Right, I'm not allowed to do security tonight.* Quickly she shut it off, she looked apologetically at the group.

"It's okay, you all should get your rest and we can work on this tomorrow." Cleo instructed the room.

"No! We have to keep going! What if someone else gets hurt because of me?" A tear fell down Remi's face only to be quickly wiped away.

"I agree Rem, but we have to rest to be able to figure this out," Bloodfang stood. "Do you want to bunk with your brother and me tonight?"

"Actually, yes." She let a long breath of defeat out, and rubbed her already red eyes.

"Cleo, would you walk Miss. Cade to Omega Alpha?" Coyote asked, as he took his spot beside his sister. "Don't worry, she knows the way."

Lennox stood and nodded as they all made their way out of the room. *Cathwulf must be on night guard tonight. We are so close to getting them.* Lennox kept an eye on Remi as well, worried for her. She pushed down the small amount of hope that had drifted up and hid her own frustration from the others. After she had listened to the finer details of the woman's time with these hunters, she realized just how bad Remi's time with them had been. The way she had described their various training methods, stumbled over names as she pushed through the tongue tie, and showed them the word "Dog" that had been carved into the woman's left ribs.

When the group reached the grounds, they parted toward their separate homes. Remi and her family headed toward the Elder's homes, Lennox and Cleo toward the sorority. The woman held a polite conversation about her time at the school and gave her condolences to Felix and Rue. A false smile held to her face as they chatted about everything that had happened at the school up until today. The whole conversation started to feel like a small interrogation but knew Cleo meant well enough to gather as much as she could to help them.

Once they reached the doors of Omega, Wyatt popped out from his guard position. She felt the woman beside her grab her arm and pull her slightly behind her defensively. Wyatt's serious expression was replaced by a laugh when his eyes fell on the two.

"Lennox Cade, late to curfew? I better take a picture, this will never happen again!" He joked, and took out his phone.

"Mr. Steele, I know you and Aron are on guard tonight, but don't sneak up on people." Cleo scolded and shook her head with a hand on her weapons belt.

"My bad Miss Hunter Anderson, won't happen again." Wyatt teased.

"I'll leave you here Miss. Cade. I'll see you soon I hope." Cleo turned on her heels and made her way toward the Elder homes.

"I'll see you tomorrow, Wyatt." Lennox smiled softly, relieved the day was done.

"Night, Nox! Tomorrow I'll tell you about my study date with Eden Miller. Get some good rest." Wyatt smiled back and made his way down the stairs to make his rounds.

The week passed from Monday to Friday in the blink of an eye as Lennox and Remi attempted to figure out how to break the spell without the object. The two came up completely empty and left frustrated, both for different reasons as they each both chomped at the bit to be able to finally do something. When the two passed each other in the halls, she could see the look in Remi's eyes. The desire for revenge against the people who had left that brand. She could only imagine what it was like to have to stare her worst enemy in the eyes and be unable to do anything about it.

Lennox stood in the entrance hall of the main building, other students passed by her. Completely unaware of them as they passed, she had her eyes fixed on the photos of the three victims that had moved back to their original spots in the front of the vestibule. Rue's piano playlist sounded in her headphones as she became lost in memories of the two of them. Her laugh echoed from her memories of herself, Wyatt, Felix, Rue, and Rosalyn all together around the grounds.

Between the memories and music, she didn't hear Wyatt come up to her right. He opened his mouth to speak but stopped himself as he saw her stand there with her gaze locked on Rue. He turned toward the photos as well and stood beside her and waited. After a few minutes, she became aware of someone's presence and turned her head to see who had joined her and Remi.

"Shit, Wyatt! Sorry." She jumped, having completely forgotten they were meeting here.

"It's okay, I like to drop by too. Tell them what's new, you know?" He smiled softly down at her.

"I do actually… Thanks for meeting up with me here. Remi is a little preoccupied right now to go with me back to Omega."

"Of course, you know I got you." He beamed and wrapped an arm around her shoulder. "Let's go home."

The two made their way into the cold courtyard and chatted about the party he and Aron were planning for tomorrow night. Wyatt walked backward as he faced her and listed off everything they needed to pick up from town tonight.

"Oh! Some rum for the suitcase! What time will you come tomorrow? I know you like to get places early."

"I- I don't know if me showing up would be the best idea, Wyatt." She said quietly.

"Why- Oh, I understand," he stopped and peered over to Kappa. "Everyone should be at dinner, if you want to I'd be more than happy to go inside with you at your own pace. It's still safe, I swear."

She followed his gaze to the fraternity and pulled her bag strap closer to her. *It could be beneficial to be able to go in again... Just in case I need to.* A knot formed in her throat as she turned her attention to the stormy-eyed demon. Extending his hand to her, she took a hesitant step toward him. Taking his arm, they started walking down the path.

"I'll be right here the whole time," he reassured her. "If it gets too much we can turn around, but I would love to see my best friend at the party tomorrow night."

"I'll do my best." She agreed.

She kept a wary eye on the house as she approached though since she and Aron started the lock down she felt calmer than she had previously. However, every time she got too close to the door the images of the morning she found Fleix flooded her mind. *He's not going to walk out the door.* She had to remind herself things were different and the house was safe again. At about halfway there Lennox forced herself to peel her eyes away and to Wyatt.

"Distract me a bit, tell me about that date with you and Eden." She insisted as she recalled his words from the night she was walked home by Cleo.

"Well, I think it went well really. She seems to actually be into me despite not being my biggest fan the first day of classes." He smiled.

"She isn't the most... Cuddly person." Lennox returned his smile. "Are you sure about this one?"

"Len, I don't think I've been so sure of anyone in my life. When I see her I can almost feel my heart beating again. When she walks into the room something draws me to her, I want to be the reason she's smiling, even though it's rare." His voice turned wistful as he spoke of Eden.

"I don't see what you see, but I'm happy for you. You deserve to be happy." She told him genuinely.

"So do you." He whispered back as they approached the steps to the front door.

Her eyes fell on the gold doorknob as her feet came to a stop inches from it. *I need to be able to walk in there.* Silently, the memories threatened to overtake her mind and her body tensed. She fought to even her breath feeling her friend put a hand on her shoulder as if to remind her she wasn't alone this time. Her hand shook lightly as she reached toward the door knob but stopped and retracted when her gaze fell on her shaky hand.

"Behind this door is your second home. The place we became friends, where you forgave me for the past. Don't let them take away the future memories you could make here, then they win." Wyatt's deep voice came out softly beside her ear as he stared at the door with her.

Lennox nodded as she kept her attention. "You're right."

"I am, this is a safe place again. You're stronger than you think you are."

She took a step toward the door and rested her hand on the doorknob before she pulled it open. Her eyes darted around the entranceway as she let the door drift all the way open. Lennox drew a deep breath in while she stepped through the frame and into the house. Everything was just as she remembered it, the fraternity banner, the announcement board beside the door, followed by photos of past Heads of House framed down the hall. Her attention fell to the closest photo where Felix smiled brightly back at her. A knot formed in her throat as she heard Wyatt stop by her side. Lennox swallowed past the tightness and tore her eyes away from the man that was once her brother. Quickly, she scanned the room but found no signs of blood or Felix's misplaced items.

When her attention drifted to the demon beside her and found his gaze fixed on the photo just as hers had been. Within seconds she realized the usually electric eyed man was filled with his own grief. A pang fell into her chest as she remembered it was the same for Wyatt out of the five of them only three remained. Carefully, she reached out a hand and let her fingertips graze his pinky so as not to startle him. Wyatt's eyes didn't move but the rose decorated hand opened to allow the contact.

"He always wanted a brother like you." Her voice came out stronger than she felt which helped give her the strength to push the memories of his death away for now.

"He loved our little family." The demon smiled sadly.

"They both did... A part of me dreams that somehow they found each other wherever they ended up."

Wyatt paused and finally peered down to their hands. He turned her hand to glance at the citrine ring on Lennox's finger. "Rue was everything to you, Nox... I- I can't imagine losing someone like that."

Her eyes fell to Felix once more and she drew in another breath. "If I'm honest, I wished for a bit that they would have buried me with her. Imagined different ways I could find my way back to her but I could never leave you or Rosalyn like that."

"Good, cause we need you more than ever. I'm not going to lose you to a bunch of crazy hunters either. Besides, you gotta help me get some revenge." His gaze darkened.

Lennox did her best to let a smile find its way to her face but found it harder than expected. As the two looked at each other, something sparked to life once again within his iris. The grip on her hand tightened gently as he squeezed hers.

"Wyatt?" She asked quietly in a silent question.

"I'm fine, I promise. It's just- I may not be in those meetings with Fang and Coyote but I'm smart enough to know when someone is being targeted." She fell silent and flinched as she searched for the right words. "Just please, don't do anything that would make us lose you too, okay?"

"I won't." She promised and let go of his hand.

Wyatt smiled at her promise as he opened his mouth to speak but was cut off by the sound of a door upstairs close with a loud thud that echoed in the quiet house. Wyatt turned his attention toward the stairs and she did the same. Aron appeared from around the corridor and smiled when he saw the two of them.

"Well finally, Leonard! Took you long enough to join the party again! How about a coffee for you two? Maybe a round of Uno against the king?" He asked cheerfully as he made his way down.

"Sounds great! We have planned to chat about tomorrow night anyways," Wyatt agreed and motioned toward the kitchen. "Besides, it's time for that rematch you owe me."

"Why not," Lennox followed the two of them.

The previous embarrassment from the other night washed over her as Aron's eyes drifted to hers. His gaze hovered before he made his way over to the coffee pot. Wyatt pulled out her chair as he always did and sat beside her.

"So, Lenny. How was going to class Aron style, Monday?" He smirked and poured water in and pulled out mugs.

"It went well actually, I missed a whole class." She returned his smile.

"You missed class willingly?" Wyatt asked in surprise with raised eyebrows, his mouth hung slightly open.

"Not really, Mister over here dared me Sunday night." She explained.

"Ah yes- Sunday night. I'm glad someone was there to keep an eye on you. I told Aron I could go over but he didn't believe you were drunk."

"I was fine. I didn't need a babysitter… But I do appreciate not being alone that night." She admitted as she glanced over to Aron for a second.

Wyatt's eyes flicked between the two of them before it rested on Lennox as Aron had his back turned to pour the coffee. His eyebrows rose and he tilted his head toward the other demon with silent words. Lennox's eyes widened as her friend drew his own conclusions and quickly shook her head. *Him and his damn romance books.*

"The cards are in the cabinet if someone wants to grab them." Aron turned back to face them with two mugs in one hand and a third in the other.

Wyatt spoke before Lennox could move. "I got it!"

The black-haired demon got up and made his way into the other room. He shot Lennox one last look, *tell me everything later* face before he vanished around the corner. Her eyes fell on Aron as he made his way over and carefully took the two mugs from his hand, set one for Wyatt where he had been moments ago and the other in front of her. Relieved of all the hot drinks, he leaned against the island and took a sip.

"How's Remi doing?' He asked as his forest green eyes fell on her.

"She's angry- We can't trace the object the spell is bound to. Everything we do just goes in circles."

"I would be angry too, given what you told me. Not being able to say or do anything to help and to have your past in the school…" He trailed off for a moment before a serious look crossed his face. "How are you doing? Have the nightmares stopped? If not, Wyatt and I can keep doing guard."

"No, I'm okay. They've stopped for the most part, at least the worst of them." She told him. "I can go back to using the vines to guard the houses, you two need to catch a few nights of real sleep."

"Are you sure?" Aron asked, his eyes displayed his lack of sleep and proved he was as tired as she thought he was.

"Of course, you two have a party to host tomorrow night. If anything goes bump in the night, I'll call you."

Things clambered together as Wyatt rummaged through the other room for the game. A small smile formed on her face as she leaned to peer around the corner into the other room only to see him with his hands on his hips.

"Speaking of the party, Wyatt and I need to go into Millstone Grove to pick up the beer and liquor. Do you wanna come before curfew?" Aron asked her, his face bright with a smile.

She checked her watch and considered if they would be back in time. "Sure, why not."

"Yes, Let's go!" He put his mug down and walked around the corner to the other room where Wyatt stood in confusion. "Hey! Forget the Uno, we're going into town to get the stuff for the party now!"

"Well alright! Who wants to sign out the school car?" Wyatt asked as Lennox joined them.

"I will," Lennox agreed and followed them toward the door.

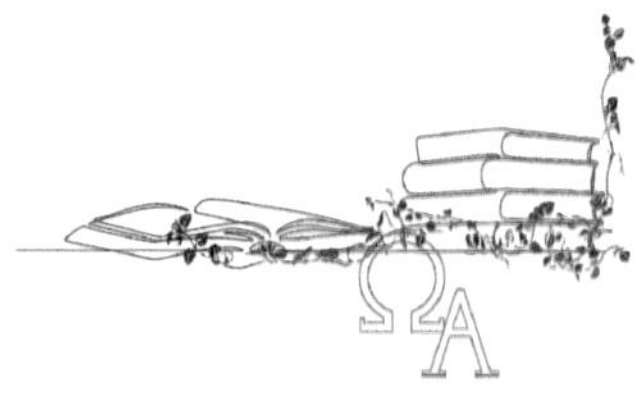

After they signed the school van out from the office they made their way back outside. Aron ran ahead and he yelled, "shotgun" as they approached. Once loaded up, the three of them pulled up to the open school gates and drove into their little town square. Lennox had re-mained within the gates since the night of Rue's death; it was like a breath of fresh air as they passed the small town beside the school. Millstone Grove was only about a twenty-minute drive from the school grounds through a small single-lane highway that wound around the surrounding woods.

The two boys started to list off all the things they planned to pick up from the small human town. As Lennox drove the curves in the road, she peered in the rearview mirror as Wyatt threw a crumpled piece of paper at Aron.

"If you think your handwriting is any better, you write the list." He laughed from the backseat.

"I will! Then I won't have to look at your chicken scratch." Aron stuck out his tongue.

"Okay kids, time for the spell. We are in Millstone. And for your information, neither of your handwriting is easy to read." She spoke up as they passed the welcome sign.

Lennox used her magic and let an image of her human self form in her mind as she pulled on the vine inside herself. She kept her eyes forward as she felt the warmth from the spell wash over her skin and glanced in the mirror once again. Her markings had faded from her face, her purple eyes shifted back to their original green, and her hair shifted from its usual all-over pink to the deep black she shared with Wyatt. This version of herself always reminded her that her human life had been a consequence of the Curse Creator behind her. It wasn't until she studied the effects of curses that she realized the victim would share physical characteristics of the demon.

At the same moment, Wyatt and Aron's markings also vanished and appeared human. Wyatt looked basically the same as he did at the school, full of tattoos, same hair, clothes without the demon markings. Accustomed to Wyatt's disguise she peered over to Aron out of curiosity. He still had his red bandanna on, holding his blonde hair out of his face but without the markings, she wouldn't have recognized him immediately. *He's kinda cute as a human.* The thought intruded which caused her to look forward once more.

She pulled onto the main street and turned right into the parking lot with the big sign that read Grove Liquor. After she came to a stop and parked the car, the three of them piled out and made their way to the door.

"You guys go ahead. I'll be out here, it's a nice evening." Lennox forced a smile as she took in the brisk air.

"Are you sure? You could always grab another bottle to keep hidden in your room." Aron smirked as his eyes scanned her face.

"Fine, I'll be there in a minute." She shook her head as Aron and Wyatt went to the counter to buy the barrels.

She turned her attention to the street which was mostly empty except for the few people at the grocery store across the way. Their voices carried toward her as they went about their days, unaware of the true nature of the suspicious school in the town over. An older couple made their way hand in hand to their car, until the wife peered over to where Lennox stood. The woman motioned toward the black van that seemed to be known among the humans. The two exchanged a nervous glance before they shuffled to their car. A little girl's voice drew her attention away from the judgy couple.

She turned to the left and saw a little girl with long black hair, no older than seven, run circles around her mother. In an instant a knot tied itself in her throat as it had done earlier, as it did every time she saw a little girl with black hair. The image of Gemma came to mind as she struggled to hold back the tears of guilt. Her daughter would be much older than the little girl, potentially with a family of her own. One of the tears fell from the corner of her eye and was quickly wiped away.

Lennox forced herself to look away and made her way back inside the store. She glanced around for the two she came with and found they had already seemed to disappear from the front. It only took an additional few seconds for her to hear them yell at each other from different aisles. She sighed and she followed the sound of Wyatt's voice over to the whiskey. Unable to stop the smile that crossed her face when she passed the bourbon, she stopped beside him.

"Hey, Len! No, we don't need twenty bottles of vodka. Just five of pineapple, two of orange, and three rums for the jungle juice." Wyatt called to Aron and shoved two handfuls of Jack Daniels toward her. "Hey look, tequila!"

"No!" Aron and Lennox spoke in unison.

"Wyatt, you're too emotionally unstable to have tequila at a public party." Aron turned the corner with a cart filled with two rows of various bottles.

"I'm sorry, I'm gonna have to agree with him on this one. Save that bottle for a private event." Lennox patted him on the back as she put the bottles in the cart and turned her attention to the shelves.

"It's just a house party, it's not like I'm going to fight someone." He shrugged and placed two more bottles in.

"Where there's a hoard of creatures of the night, there's always room for something to go wrong." Aron pushed the cart forward.

The two headed back to the front as Lennox looked up at the finer bottles of vodka. Her gaze traced along the options until they settled on a bottle blown into the shape of a sun. The glass was wrapped in intricate patterns of gold and on the label was a pair of white wings that read "Sol" in the middle.

"Hurry up, Nox! It's our turn!" Wyatt called.

"Coming!" She reached for the bottle and quickly made her way to the front.

"Whatcha got there, Leonard?" Aron leaned over as she placed the bottle on the counter. Something flashed in his eyes before he cracked a bright smile. "Good choice. Let's go home."

Eden

Eden stood in the doorframe of Eloise's classroom. Eloise had re-quested to meet here so they could walk home together. As the Matriarch packed her bag for the day, she muttered times and locations to herself. Once they were in a more secure area, Eloise would want to discuss the looming mission she was to send Bastien and herself to complete.

With her bag over her shoulder and her attention on her phone as it buzzed. She kept her expression neutral as another photo from Wyatt appeared on her screen. Wyatt stood a distance from a ladder with Aron on top as they set up Kappa for the party. The demon had a bright smile across his face while his friend attempted to grab a beer bong from the top of the cabinet with a thumb up. Her fingers dashed across the screen as she told him to focus on the task at hand. Seconds later her phone buzzed with a response.

Wyatt Steele-
It's hard to focus when it comes to my Little Viper.
-Sent 3:17 PM

Eden Miller-
I'm not *your* Little Viper.
-Sent 3:17 PM

Wyatt Steele-
You're right, not yet. One day you'll allow me in those walls of yours and I will stand beside you. You are your own woman and worth the wait.
-Sent 3:18 PM

Out of the corner of her eye she saw Eloise finally stand from her desk and start to pack books and papers to take home for the night. Eden quickly locked her phone and put it away to prevent The Matriarch from any accidental discovery. Her nail grazed her thumb as she watched Eloise approach, her heels clicked with each step and she adjusted her glasses.

"Learn anything useful today?" Eloise asked.

Eden shook her head and knew that she didn't mean in class. "Nothing of note, though I did see Elder Anderson and Elder Bloodfang in the hall. They were discussing the little spell on Remi Moon."

The two fell silent as they walked down the hall toward the exit that led to Elder Row. Their walks home were typically quiet as neither wanted much to be overheard by unwanted ears. As the two turned the corner to the exit, Eden opened her mouth to speak but was stopped when Cleo Anderson turned the corner at the same time.

"Elder Miller, I'm so glad I caught up with you." The woman smiled politely.

Eden came to a stop beside Eloise and her body immediately tensed as Eloise spoke. "How can I help you, Miss. Anderson?"

"I was hoping you would be able to assist in walking some of the students of Omega to their house tomorrow."

Cleo moved a stray piece of her black and streaked purple hair away from her face. Eden's eyes traced the thin scars across the woman's left eye and the few on her cheek. The Millers had run into the hunter on various occasions but never for long, which she was grateful for. However, she pulled on the thread of magic inside and added her own magic to the spell over their disguise to strengthen its barriers of detection. Under her sleeves, Eden felt the new chain sigils that trailed her skin heat as she channeled the new magic.

"Of course, whatever the security team needs." Eloise agreed while she kept an iron clad unreadable expression.

Cleo smiled and peered over to Eden. "It's very lucky such a large family has found its way back together. You don't see too many families of high elves left these days. My sister told me how hunters had separated you and all later arrived within the grounds within a few months of each other. It was lucky you all remembered Eloise had attended the school a few decades ago. All this business must be pretty difficult."

She nodded as Cleo repeated the cover story Eloise had created years ago to gain access to the school once more. "It hasn't been easy but we trust the Security Team."

"Good to hear." The woman looped her thumb into the weapons belt she wore around her waist, unlike Eden and Eloise whose were concealed. Cleo's expression shifted as her eyes drifted back to Eloise. "You two look familiar, have we all met?"

"Probably in passing, the supernatural world isn't that large compared to humans." Eloise mused.

"I've seen just over a thousand creatures enter these gates, however, even with five schools around the world, I'll agree ours is small." Elder Anderson walked up behind her sister followed by Elder Bloodfang.

"Isn't this just a regular double family reunion?" The large man smiled from beside the demon.

Eloise's eyes shot to the two behind Cleo and Eden's gaze fell to the two Elders. Bloodfang stood less than a step ahead of Andromeda as she watched the scene carefully. As the three Elder women chatted amongst themselves of tomorrow's plan for security measures, Eden kept her gaze on the man's expression. It wasn't until his eyes met hers did she start to worry her magic wasn't strong enough. *Can he see us?* The chains on her arms started to heat once more as she pulled harder on the string. However, the man didn't say anything and just sent a smile her way.

"Well, if you don't mind, I'd like to steal my sister." Andy smiled at Eloise.

"By all means. It's time I get home." Eloise agreed and nodded for Eden to follow her.

Eden walked slightly behind a group of her housemates and made her way toward Kappa Theta. Their laughs wafted from up ahead as she peered at the already lively house that had music that drifted in the cold air. She ignored the girls and reminisced on her talk with Bastien the other day, his words had hit her harder than she had expected. *If you do,* echoed in the back of her mind most of the day and as she lay in bed. With quick consideration of her options, she messed with her hair as she remembered Wyatt would most likely find her the moment she walked in the door.

The winter wind blew her hair as she approached the entrance and made her way in to find Bastien. When she crossed the threshold the music played loudly and she wove through the packed house. Eden made a beeline into the kitchen and found a large group of people in a large circle around the island. Bastien stood beside Corvus hand-in-hand as they talked with Rosalyn, Donnie, Leilani, and Octavius. Her eyes trailed to their hands and a pang of worry fell into her chest.

Lennox, Aron, Remi, and Celia seemed deep into their own conversation while Wyatt sat on the counter. The man swung his legs lightly and bounced his heels off of the drawers as he drank from his own red solo cup. Eden forced her gaze from him and eventually fell on Remi and her hair stood on end. With the knowledge of the past between the wolf and her mother, things were about to get awkward once she was noticed. As she made her way over to Bastien and Corvus she caught a hint of the discussion.

"I know Remi, I will help you all figure out how to break this," Aron told her with a smile and held up his drink toward her.

Celia looked over at him with an eye roll and sarcastic tone. "We're fucked then. You never attend classes."

"First of all, just because I don't have class... *Hiccup...* Doesn't mean I don't know how to be helpful. Second of all- I generally like werewolves, but you are a piece of work.”

“You just aren’t used to wolves like me,” she smirked as Eden went out of earshot, thankful she hadn’t been noticed as she passed behind the girl.

Eden kept Wyatt in the corner of her eye as he chatted and drank. He hadn’t noticed her quiet yet which typically would have been nothing to her. For the first time she considered a chance to sneak up on him as he always seemed to do but decided against it. She had never once flirted with any true intentions before, not since Holden years back. *Maybe it wasn’t time for that yet. Can’t be that easy to get to yet though it would help to have some experience in this area.* She moved to the left of Bastien and elbowed him as he laughed with the others.

“Eden!” Rosalyn spoke up as she joined the group. “You made it too!”

“I did, it’s good to see you.” She smiled, almost happy to be there. She had fun with them the other week despite it being a mission.

“It’s good to see you too,” Wyatt’s voice drifted from beside her.

“You found me quick.” Eden turned to the left as her eyes fell on him.

“I heard your name, that’s all I need to find you.” He winked and wrapped an arm around her waist in a side hug, without letting go.

This time she didn’t fight it and turned slightly within the crook of his arm toward the others and felt her nerves settle at his touch. Bastien turned to face the two, a giant ‘I told you so’ smile across his face. Her eyes narrowed at her uncle before she glanced around for the drink coolers.

“They are over on the other side of the island. What’s your drink of choice tonight Little Viper?” Wyatt leaned down, his lips beside her ear to be heard over the music.

“Whatever concoction you two have dreamed up, everyone seems to like it.” She noted to him as the music seemed to only get louder.

"One junk in the trunk coming up." he beamed and released her and went into the other room.

Octavius was deep in conversation with Rosalyn and Corvus about various Elders classes, Bastien slid jokes here and there, clearly in his social element. As opposed to Eden who stood there her nail traced over her fingertips and she listened with a polite attentive look. Her mind drifted to her earlier thoughts as he laughed about things Eloise had said to people in her classes. *I have to know if I'm capable of running the family... Or if maybe it is time to follow something that feels good.*

There was a choice to make, and her heart sank into her stomach as the realization came. In her mind there was no other way to test the theory out, she'd have to attempt to find a target that didn't need a dagger to terminate. Her eyes drifted to Octavius, *someone close to Lennox, check. Not a demon, check.* Thankfully, she had dealt with an Arachne before and knew it would be easy enough to overpower him.

As she watched the creature, she felt Rosalyn's eyes on her. The turn of her head toward Eden made her distant expression vanish and a smile formed on her face. The woman returned the gesture as Wyatt appeared beside her once more and handed her a red cup. His attention returned to the others; she tasted the drink out of curiosity. It reminded her of fruit punch, unable to even taste whatever they had put in, she knew another cup would be dangerous. *With what is going to happen tonight, I need just enough to shake the nerves.*

"How about a game of corn hole? We've got two sets outside." Wyatt suggested to the group.

"That sounds like a great idea!" Rosalyn exclaimed excitedly.

"Lennox, Aron, Celia, Remi! We're going outside! It's corn hole time!" He called the other group.

Shit, Eden peered over at them as she had wanted to avoid them at all costs.

As each of their names was called they peered over from their serious talk. Immediately Remi's eyes fell on her, her face drained of color before it went bright red. *I'm fucked if she's able to hint.* As her chest tightened and her jaw clenched, the two stared each other down. Eden raised an eyebrow as if daring her to try. The wolf's expression darkened and she stepped toward her. Eden crossed her arms and used the motion to unsnap the latch from the sheath that held her silver knife. She tilted her bottom arm down and she felt the cold metal against her inner wrist.

At that moment Wyatt said corn hole, Aron's face lit up and he bounced over with his own red solo cup in hand. As the demon swung around, he bumped straight into Rosalyn, his eyes widened in panic and he backed up straight into Eden. Unknowingly he broke the unnoticed tension between the two women as both of their gazes shot to him. She noted his reaction as he apologized quickly, grabbed Lennox's hand and pulled her along with him to the backyard. The others followed suit and Eden watched Celia whisper something to Remi as she checked the bands around her wrist.

"Come on then everyone, chop chop corn hole is waiting!" Wyatt chuckled from beside her.

"We are actually going to stay inside for a bit, We'll come out in a bit." Celia told Wyatt as she started to lead Remi toward the common room.

He offered her his arm and motioned in the direction everyone was going in.

The staggered group made their way into the open backyard that faced the entrance to the campus. Bastien, Corvus, Octavius, and Rosalyn all made their way to one set of the game, while Wyatt flagged over Aron and Lennox to play against them. Before she could attempt to protest the teams, everyone had settled at their boards. Wyatt stood across from her beside Aron, Lennox approached the opposite side of the board Eden stood on.

Her nerves shot a wave of anxiety over her which made her look for Bastien. Once her eyes found him, she noticed he was completely engrossed in the demon across the way.

"Don't listen to any of the trash talk the boys do," Lennox spoke up as they waited for them to throw first.

"Come on Daddy Long Legs! Get it in the hole!" Bastien's voice yelled over to Octavius from the neighboring board.

Octavius let out a loud laugh, along with everyone within earshot while Eden hid her discomfort as conflict arose once more in her mind. "I never do."

"Good, then you'll fit right in. How long have you and Wyatt been a thing?" Lennox questioned.

"Actually we aren't really together-together." Eden corrected but hesitated.

"Are you sure about that?" The demon eyed her knowingly. "You know, you're all that man talks about."

Her face shifted to surprise, though she should have known by the way he acted. The confirmation of Wyatt's feelings toward her sent the butterflies through her. *Could this be more than I thought?* For a moment a pang of guilt hit Eden as she was now face to face with the potential scope of Wyatt's feelings for her. Her gaze traveled back to the tattooed man who laughed beside one of his best friends. As she sipped her drink and her gaze fell to the face of each creature in attendance. For the first time, she saw the people around her as another group of students having a good time.

The game started and each pair took turns and took shots for every point they scored. Aron and Wyatt seemed to never miss the board and sunk each bean bag into the hole multiple times each. The girls laughed as they canceled out their scores time and time again while they taunted each other. Between turns, one would attempt to distract the other by making a lewd comment or loudly clear their throat.

At one point Aron seemed to say something to Wyatt which caused him to turn bright red and look away from the board toward Eden and made him miss completely. The man sent him an annoyed look and he peered over to her once again. A soft breeze blew a few pieces of hair into her face as she sent a very small smile in his direction. His expression softened slightly as their eyes met. Quickly, she decided it would be good to keep playing hard to get and turned to see how the other game was going. Bastien seemed to get every point in and when Eden looked at Rosalyn she saw surprise written across her face at how good he was.

In contrast, Lennox hit the board most of the time only occasionally one in. Where Eden hit the board more frequently than the head of house which made the game lean toward her and Wyatt. Aron threw the next one and made it just on the edge of the circle cut out and let out an exasperated sigh. Wyatt took his turn as he concentrated hard before he threw his corn sack and knocked both in the hole. Celebrating, Aron laughed and glanced over at him then elbowed him in the shoulder.

"Thanks for that one buddy! Couldn't have done it without you."

"Oh shut it, we are still tied and it's the girl's turn. We can still win this." Wyatt scolded him, confidently shouted to Eden. "Kick his ass!"

The genuine smile on her face widened as she watched the two push each other around and took sips of her drink here and there. By the end of the game she finished it already and already felt the slight buzz start.

In the last round, Aron missed the board on his last shot.

"Miss! Len, come on, we gotta win this one!" Aron called over.

"It's just a game!" She called back.

"Not with these two." Eden commented with a laugh.

"Most of the Kappa boys have always been competitive, these two just are a little louder about it." Lennox shook her head.

The score was tied nineteen to nineteen and it was back to Eden. She tossed each one and got one on the board, missed, and put another into the hole. When Wyatt saw it go in, he cheered and glanced at Aron with a bright smirk.

"My girls got it!" He said loudly and walked toward her.

"I'm not your girl and just out of curiosity how many of you two's concoctions have you had?" Eden asked and started to cross her arms over her chest as he wrapped an arm around her waist again. Aron complained under his breath as he joined the group.

"Enough to ask you if you'd consider it." His gray eyes bore into hers as he asked.

"How about you ask me when you're not intoxicated?" She let a smile drift onto her face as she felt a warmth within her chest at the suggestion.

Beside her, Lennox spoke with a chuckle as she held up her cup to the two of them, "Good game guys."

"Okay love birds, why don't we go wait for the others to finish their game?" Aron elbowed Wyatt and distracted him from Eden once again.

"Fine then, while we wait-"

He released her and turned around, Wyatt reached toward the Head of Kappa and grabbed him by the back of the jacket. Swiftly, he pulled his head into his chest in a headlock and messed up Aron's hair and bandanna with a fist. The two grappled for a few seconds before Remi and Celia walked up between Eden and Lennox. Remi watched her out of the corner of her eye, and stood as far as she could from the hunter. Thankfully she hadn't tried to say anything about the situation or gone after her, which was the last thing Eden wanted to deal with tonight as she plotted Octavius. All four women stood there watching the two of them all with various levels of entertainment.

"Who do you think is going to win?" Remi asked the group.

"My money is on Wyatt." Celia smirked.

"I don't know, they seem pretty evenly matched." Lennox opposed.

Aron reached up and pulled Wyatt down and away from himself. "You think that's enough to stop me?"

"No, but maybe I am!" Octavius had made his way over and joined in the tussle.

Eden took a moment while their eyes were on someone else to let out the breath she didn't know she held. Between her attempts to take Bastien's advice, her questions about the family, being around Lennox and Aron, and the other side of her path to Matriarch, Eden hadn't actually relaxed in weeks. Her muscles relaxed, she watched as Bastien joined in the pile of wrestling men.

No one stopped them, Rosalyn and Corvus joined the small group with the same entertained look at the others. Lennox and Rosalyn chatted among themselves for a second as the demon nodded toward Aron. Corvus casually asked Remi and Celia questions about themselves since they were new to the school. All the while, Eden's gaze followed Bastien's moves to make sure he would hold back so as to not draw unwanted attention. As he helped hold Wyatt from Octavius, his eye met hers. With a smirk, he swung his arm around his chest and pulled him down.

"More drinks, anyone?" Corvus asked them.

"I got it!" Wyatt popped his head out of the pile and made his way to his feet.

The pile was quickly broken up as the drunken men stumbled over to them. Wyatt took the empty cup from Eden gently and glanced at the others. Rosalyn held her cup out to him but it was quickly snatched away by Octavius.

His laugh boomed and Wyatt shook his head, "Anyone else?"

"I'll take one too," Lennox said, smiling as he handed her cup to him

"Alright, three new drinks coming up!" He turned and linked arms with Aron who had appeared behind him and started to head back inside, followed closely by Octavius and Bastien.

The evening turned into night, the area outside was illuminated by a large bonfire controlled by Aron to stave off the cold. Several of the others from Kappa and Omega sat around it and chatted amongst themselves. Eden sat in her lawn chair between Rosalyn and an empty one Wyatt had occupied. She watched the smoke rise into the sky, as the hum of chatter filled the air. She didn't mind being the quiet one in the group, it was easier to fit in this way as opposed to Bastien who made close friends with each one of them.

Her sightless gaze peered through the flames to the other side as she watched Bastien and Corvus smile and whisper to each other. *He does look happy...* The sight of them like this together started to shift her thoughts, her expression softened as she decided she would do what she had to in order to protect him. Eden turned her attention to the left, she found a now very drunk Lennox and Aron dance together with a small group of others by the speakers by the door. Her eyebrow rose as Aron seemed to have not only two left feet but a terrible rhythm. *It's almost sad I have to break them apart.* The daggers she had been instructed to make swam into her mind's eye.

Lost in her thoughts, she didn't notice Rosalyn attempt to get her attention until she felt someone tap on her arm. Eden jumped, turned toward her and attempted to laugh it off.

"Sorry, I didn't mean to scare you." The demon apologized.

"It's fine, what's up?"

"I know we didn't chat much last term, but I'm glad you're hanging out with us this semester, I've never seen Wyatt so bright-eyed." She smiled gently at Eden. *Why does everyone keep bringing him up?* In her tipsy state, she almost asked the very question out loud. "I don't mean to intrude on your personal business, but I have to know- How do you feel about him?"

Eden knew the answer she should give regardless of her true feelings toward the man, she took a moment to consider them. If she truly searched her heart, she knew something strong was quickly forcing its way up with every glance they shared. So strong in fact, she found herself question her family more everyday. No matter how much she didn't want to, she did care about him.

"As much as I hated him in the beginning... I can't imagine him not being around now." She admitted, the alcohol was enough to loosen her words. "I don't know how to handle that, until I figure out if we could keep that between us?"

"Of course, you have my word, girl!" Rosalyn bounced in her chair and bobbed her head to the music.

Eden's gaze fell back to the flames before she decided to go into the house to find another jacket. She stood from her chair and walked past the group and into Kappa. The music was muffled behind the walls of the mostly empty fraternity as she made her way through the halls. She made her way into the entranceway and found one of Bastien's jackets hung on a hook. With a smirk to herself as she slipped it on, she turned around to head back outside.

Within a few steps she was suddenly toe to toe with another member of Kappa Theta she had never met before. The frat member stood about five inches taller and from what she could see of him he was strong to go with it. He had short curly brown hair that sat on the top of his head in a ruffled mess. The sudden appearance and forced stop made her head spin again as her eyes trailed up to his face. The man had a drink in his hand, gazing back down at her with a look in his eyes that sent a shiver down her spine.

"I've never seen you at one of the house parties." He held out a hand to her and stepped toward her in another attempt to close the distance. "Nick's the name, and what may I ask, is yours sweet cheeks?"

Eden's eyes drifted over the man to size him up as she went toward the blue thread to her magic and the chains around her arms heated. *I can't attack him here, maybe if someone saw I might be able to claim self-defense. I don't want to draw attention to myself before I go for Octavius.* Her gaze darted to his feet as he took another step toward her. Every step he took, she retreated back until she felt her back touch the door. The cold wood sent another chill down her and fear started to cause her to grip the thread. Her hand slowly reached into her back pocket for her phone, her purple eyes brightened into a shade of blue. *If I can get any sort of message to Bastien I won't have to worry about hiding a body tonight.*

"I don't do parties, and I don't think you need to know who I am."

"Oh come on baby, don't play hard to get, I just want to talk." His voice dipped as he lifted the hand with the cup over her head and against the door and leaned even closer to her.

"I don't have anything to say to you." Her voice rose a little in an attempt to get it through his drunken head.

The demon was much too close for comfort. Eden slipped both of her arms behind her back to abandon her phone for the knife she had almost used on Remi earlier. It wouldn't be much help in actually killing him but it could make for a nice distraction. Her hair stood on end and her heart sped up in her chest, just as it did when on a hunt. Nick took his opportunity, his free hand moved to her arm, and gripped it tightly.

The next few seconds became a blur. As she moved to grab his wrist she pulled the thread and allowed her palm to be coated with ice. When it met his skin, his eyes widened and he jumped back as it transferred to his wrist. In seconds it started to spread up his hand. He started to panic until someone grabbed him by the frozen wrist. Eden's eyes fell to the familiar rose tattoo.

Her eyes moved to the familiar charcoal haired man now in front of Nick with his wrist held so tightly it started to lose color. His cup was now spilled on the floor a few feet from where she stood as he attempted to sputter out words. Wyatt's stormy eyes flashed with a crack of rage before it was replaced with a dark smile. He looked slightly down at his housemate then to his hand that had already started to thaw. The sound of the snap of electricity from his other hand caught Eden's attention and she stayed frozen on the spot.

"I know you're drunk, Nick. But you can't go around being a dick."

Nick sputtered in shock as his eyes darted between the hand Wyatt had on his and the one at his side. "I-It's not what it looks like, Wyatt. I was just getting to know the Omega girl."

"Omega girl's name is Eden." She spoke up and shifted the knife so

Wyatt wouldn't see it. "You couldn't take the fact that I wasn't interested."

"Eden, I'm sorry." Nick's wrist was released and he fixed the man's jacket before he placed both hands on either shoulder.

"You're how old and you don't know how to take a hint?" Another tug at the thread sent an overwhelming amount of energy down in reply. The air dropped a few more degrees but the chains and sigils on her arms were on fire.

"It won't happen again I swear." Nick watched her carefully and stumbled back into Wyatt.

"You, Aron, Lennox , and I will have a talk in the morning. If you dare so much as breathe in her direction again, you will deeply regret it." His deep voice growled as he let Nick go once more.

The drunken man stumbled away toward the backyard once more. Eden kept her eyes on him until he was out of sight. With the adrenaline and magic still mostly in control, her body moved instinctually. She swiftly sheathed her knife back in its holster so he wouldn't see it and avoided the gaze that was now on her. From the corner of her eyes, she could see his eyes scan her over and the anger seemed to fade as concern washed away the storm. Wyatt took a hesitant couple of steps toward her and extended a hand. The movement caused her attention to snap fully back to him, her eyes wide and her body tense.

"Are you okay?" He asked softly and broke the quiet between them.

"I'm fine- I don't need a bodyguard, I had it under control." Her voice raised slightly and her eyes drifted up and down to study his body language as he got closer.

"Eden-" He held his palms toward her.

"No, I am more than capable of handling myself."

"Eden-"

"Wyatt! I don't belong to you!" She told him, her body shook lightly as she pressed her back against the door once again.

"No, you don't, but I will always be there when you need me." He promised calmly and kept his expression even despite her raised voice.

Her eyes darted once again as she searched for an escape. Over the music she heard a loud crash from the other room which caused her to jump. He stopped a few feet from her as their gazes met once more. Wyatt kept both of his hands up in surrender and moved toward the wall so his right side was almost against it. Her eyes flashed to the exit route he offered if she chose to walk away.

"I promise, you're safe. What can I do to show you?" He softened his voice slightly.

Eden blinked up at him as she attempted to slow the thoughts that fought in her mind. Her body screamed for her to move, to walk away from what could turn into more danger. Except, this wasn't the normal type of danger hunters faced every day. Grave injuries, yes. Demons and creatures from people's nightmares, yes. The risk of death, yes, but this wasn't the same. Though she knew she should find Bastien, she found herself frozen as he proved to her she wasn't in danger anymore.

There was something in the way that Wyatt looked at her that seemed to calm her. Eden felt her muscles slowly start to relax as he seemed to understand more than she knew. When she didn't move, he took another step toward her, but this time she didn't flinch. He tilted his head down as he finally closed the distance between them. He reached out to place a hand on her shoulder but stopped his hand an inch above and lifted his eyebrows no more than a twitch as he waited for her permission to be touched. Eden took a small step toward him and allowed the contact. He smiled down at her and rested his hands on her shoulders. He held her there for a minute as her chest started to match the rise and fall of his. Eden blinked as she realized her chest ached from the struggle to breathe.

His hands slid down her arms to her hands, and in that moment he seemed completely wrapped up in her. *No one has ever looked at me like this before.* The heavy feeling of guilt for what she had to do tonight settled into the pit of her stomach. She tore her eyes from his burning gaze and peered over his left arm. *I can't tell him anything about how I feel real or fake until I know where I stand. It may be an act, but it doesn't feel like one anymore.*

It was then she heard his voice in almost a whisper, "You warned me the day we met to not waste my time on you. That I would regret meeting you. Eden, you are no waste of time and since our last few dates, I haven't regretted it once."

His words sent another, different kind of fear through her. He didn't attempt to hide the feelings she had heard so much about and it was plain as day in his eyes. The thought of what could happen if she shared his feelings, images of Stacey and Eloise came into her mind. The disappointed look in their eyes when Eden did something they didn't agree with. Her breath caught once more in her chest she peered up at him and shook her head unable to form words.

Wyatt stopped her. "It's okay, you don't have to say anything right now. I just needed you to know."

Eden walked into the common room of Kappa and took a seat on one of the black leather couches. She allowed her eyes to trail over to the lit fireplace and used each snap to bring her thoughts back down to reality. The scene played in her mind over and over. The way Wyatt had been so calm while a storm brewed underneath. The way the electricity had snapped into existence at his fingertips. How even Nick had seemed to be nervous to have upset Wyatt. Maybe it was because he was friends with Aron. Or maybe it was because there was something he knew that Eden didn't know about Wyatt and what he was capable of.

The demon's voice rang clearly in her mind. *You will deeply regret it.* The darkness in his tone told her he was a funeral pyre and she was a moth drawn in, unafraid to be burnt. The memory of him as he stepped aside to give her the option to walk away, he had known she felt cornered. He had helped her to calm down where normally the only person who could do the same was Bastien. Eden felt a slight nudge of energy shift inside her mind and peered around for the source. The energy was familiar to her and reminded her of her most recent encounter with the God, Xemos.

She waited for his appearance from around the doorway, but was confused when she saw Octavius meet her gaze. The sight of him made her stomach turn once more, now was a better time than any to get him away from the house. Her nerves sparked with anticipation as with a smile and cheer, he lifted his cup to her. He stumbled into the room and seemed to have no idea what had just occurred.

"Hey, Eden!" He yelled over excitedly. "Rosalyn and I were just wondering where you went! Everything okay?"

"Yeah, it's fine. Are you okay?" she asked with a raised eyebrow.

"I'm fantastic! This party is great, doncha think?"

"Yeah, Wyatt actually just asked me to see about some more bottles from Omega. Would you mind helping out? We aren't really supposed to be going places alone, you know?" Eden asked with an innocent smile.

"Sure! Wyatt's off hosting some sort of game with Aron by the fire. No one will mess with us!" He laughed and motioned for her to follow him out of the house.

The two walked into the night, under the occasional street lamps. Eden pulled the hood up on Bastien's jacket as the man rambled on about the latest gossip he had heard at the party. All the while she listened for anything useful she nodded and occasionally threw some fake enthusiasm. Her eyes scanned their surroundings as they approached the empty sorority house. *I can't do anything here... I have to get him at least into the tree line. At least I can put the same spell on him as Eloise did to Remi if I can't follow through…*

With a quick decision, she used her magic and levitated a small rock by the front door and sent it flying with a whoosh into the woods. In only a few seconds it collided with a tree with a loud crack. The sound caused Octavius to jump, all eight of his extra legs popped out from his back, Eden jumped and turned toward the sound. She let a nervous look replace the smile as the two glanced at each other.

"What was that?" He asked.

"I have no idea, we should make sure someone didn't wander over here and get lost in the woodlands." She started to move forward.

"Are you sure? Maybe we should call and wait for the security team?"

"By then they could have stumbled further in. It'll be fine." She shrugged and disappeared between the dark trees.

As the two moved through the forest Eden pushed aside low branches and Octavius peered around them as the night became darker. She could hear him beside her, his footsteps much heavier than hers. As they made their way deeper and deeper into the forest she waited for the familiar rush she would get when she was on a hunt. However, it never came. If anything she could feel the knot in her stomach tighten along with the lump in her throat. *You will make a fine Matriarch one day, Eden.* Eloise's voice echoed in her mind as the two of them came to a small opening in the darkness illuminated by moonlight. *Just prove it to yourself.*

"Hey, is anyone there?" He started to call out. "I don't think there's anyone out here, Eden. We should go back to the house." Octavius turned to her, sounding a little nervous.

"Why? We just got out here." She put on the mask of a darkened smile.

Before the man could react, Eden had her knife to his neck and her free hand on his back. With a quick tug on the threat, her magic sent a line of ice down his spine to prevent his extra legs from a second appearance. She shoved him toward the base of a tree just to the right of their path. His side struck the bark and produced a loud noise as it snapped off and his body slid down. Octavius's eyes shot up to her as she stood over him as he gasped for the air that was knocked from him. From under the charade, she felt a pang of guilt as his eyes filled with betrayal. He looked stone-cold sober as he started to stand. Quickly she put a foot on his hip and applied enough pressure to make him stop. The look in his eyes was enough to make her pause.

"You're one of them," He coughed as he struggled with the words. "You've been lying to everyone this whole time. Poor Wyatt…"

His words sent a stab of pain through her chest as the name dropped from his lips. Wyatt's eyes flashed in her mind, his voice, the way he would have looked at her as Octavius was, if he found out. The mere thought of betrayal on Wyatt's face instead of the way he had earlier was almost too much to bear. Suddenly, the familiar presence of Xemos entered her mind. *Follow where you want your life to go… Is this what you want? To keep living every day in a war with yourself?*

Her arm slowly dropped as her nerve faded and the mask fell. Xemos gently touched the blue thread from the source of her magic which sent images into her mind's eye. It was a strange room that reminded her of their family meeting room however the version of her that was there was a much older version of herself where Stacey currently stood. Eden was gray-haired, around her grandmother's age beside a man with gray and red short curly hair, bright eyes, and a confidence Eden would recognize anywhere. Heir Holden Holloway.

Three girls and two boys sat around with their spouses and children.

Though it was what she had always dreamed she noticed the look in her older self's eyes, *sadness*. Her gaze drifted to the man and felt her heart sink. There had been a time in her life when this was exactly what she wanted, however, as much as it had been at the time the same wasn't true anymore. Instead she saw the regret in the woman's face and felt herself long to see herself with Wyatt.

The feeling caught her off guard only having truly gotten to know him over the last few weeks they spent together. Somehow, he had wormed himself into her walls and now there was no way to get him back on the other side of them. As the god let go of the thread, the images faded away and the war in her mind seemed to come to a pause.

"Wait, show me what happens if I leave." Eden demanded softly.

"Not right now, Little Moth." Xemos's voice thrummed down the thread.

Her mind went quiet, her sightless gaze still fixed on her prey as he left. The two didn't move right away, he seemed confused and dared to move only to adjust how he sat on the ground. Eden shook her head and looked back at him. "I can't do this."

Her eyes snapped shut as the frustration at herself bubbled up. *He probably won't show me because it doesn't make sense.* Had she really thought Wyatt, a Crossroads Demon and herself a human trained to kill him could ever be possible? He would stay the same and she would grow old. No amount of love could keep her soul intact and allow her to truly live beside him. However, her memory forced one last round of images into her mind and the comfort she had found beside him. From the deepest part of her something drifted toward the surface and for the first time a light of hope flickered within her.

Within moments, she knew what she had to do. Quickly, she removed her foot from his body, and she bent beside him. Octavius pressed his back against the bark but she closed the distance easily. She placed her hand on his chest and gently moved him against the base of the tree with the silver markings on her arms. They illuminated as she pulled at the magic once more using the ice she had previously used it started to take the shape of chains. She extended them around the entire length of the tree and around the man to make sure he wouldn't go anywhere until morning and spoke as she did so.

"I am genuinely sorry for what I've done Octavius- You see I'm in a sticky situation... I owe a great amount to the family that took me in, but I care for Wyatt. For someone like me, that would turn me into a Heretic. It would mean losing everything I know to take a chance. I had to know if I am capable of running the family or if I should follow my heart like Bastien said." Eden explained.

"Miller, what the hell are you talking about? You're having family issues... So instead of seeing Andy, you kidnap someone to test a theory?!"

"If you knew who my family was you'd know this was pretty tame." She shook her head.

"Wait, no now it all makes sense... I wondered why the name sounded so familiar." His eyes bore his realization.

"I'm surprised more people didn't question us. Yet again, Miller is a common name. However, we *are* the hunters you're thinking of."

The man shrunk a little against the tree. His eyes didn't leave her for more than a second to dart around them. Octavius shook his head and spoke once more and seemed to gain nerve.

"It doesn't matter how you feel about Wyatt, he's going to be a wreck when he finds out you've been lying to him..." His eyes narrowed. "Besides, you're human, how would that even work? People like you hate us, I'm surprised you could ever see past that to even think of him with romantic potential."

Eden drew in a sharp breath. As much as she wanted to lash out at him for what he said he was right. Though now she was confronted with something she hadn't previously considered. If she was to truly be with him she would have to become the thing she despised the most. Her jaw clenched and she shifted her weight between both feet.

"That's for me to figure out... For now, what I needed to know is if I'm capable of upholding my family's beliefs."

"Why are you even telling me all this, Eden?" He questioned.

"Because you won't remember any of it."

She pushed everything aside and put her hand on the top of his head. The chains glowed dimly and joined a blue light that trailed from the top of her forearms. Slowly, it made its way to her fingertips and along the silver markings. The light found its way into the man's black hair and his eyelids dropped. Carefully, she erased her face from the memories over the last twenty minutes. With a strained tug at the thread, she created a sound within his memories that made him investigate the forest. One that ended in a drunken black out.

"Sleep now, all you will remember is you were drinking and you stumbled alone to Omega to get more alcohol. You heard a noise in the woods and you went to check it out. After that, the drinks took over. You don't remember how you were chained up or anything I've told you."

His head fell to the side and as she let go, he was out cold. Eden took a few steps back and she felt her shaky breath hitch in her chest. The weight of what her life had come to overtake her all at once. *What am I supposed to do? This life is all I know.* Though the choice was clear, she mourned as tears flowed from her eyes. Even in her desire to hurt Lennox, she couldn't kill one of her friends. If she did, it would tear Wyatt apart and she couldn't be the cause of his pain. Not after the way he proved his words tonight.

Eden walked in the front door of Kappa House once more and made her way into the kitchen where she saw mostly empty bottles of vodka lined up along the edge of the island. Her nerves were shot as she went and poured herself four separate glasses and downed them one after the other. With a grimace she turned around, leaned her back on the counter and gripped it on either side. Air returned to her lungs as the heat in her chest made its way down. She allowed herself a moment to draw in deeper breaths as the adrenaline coursed through her for the second time tonight. Once her body calmed, she pushed away, turned and had another four shots before she walked into the hall.

She had about five minutes before the world would spin and she was on the hunt for Bastien. The music still played from outside, people danced and sang along with the lyrics. She moved through the crowd almost desperate to find him. She weaved through the group until she caught a loud shout she recognized. Eden beelined for the source until he finally came into view. Bastien drunkenly sang along to the words with a drunk Corvus who looked at him with nothing but love for him.

She stopped in her tracks the moment tugged at her occasional hopeless romantic side. She suddenly wasn't all too willing to part the two at the moment so instead she turned around and made her way through the crowd once more. Roughly in the middle, she started to get bumped into as the world slowly started to turn again. All of a sudden, she felt someone fall into her right side. Eden stood firm for support and she saw a flash of bright pink hair. *Shit, it's her.* She recoiled slightly but allowed the woman to touch her forearm. *People are so touchy when they are drunk.*

"Hey sorry! Are you good Eden?" Lennox asked and frowned with concern.

"Yeah, I'm fine. I think the question is, are you?"

"Yeah yeah I'm fine- WAIT!"

Her hands gently grabbed Eden's arm, the silver marking seemed to catch the woman's attention. Her eyes widened after a quick look, the two locked gazes for a second with nearly identical eyes. She had to fight every urge to yank her arm away from the demon's grip, but somehow managed to stay still.

"Eden, when did you become a devotee?"

"Recently," She admitted.

There was a moment of quiet between the two as Lennox let go of her arm. "I'm sorry, I just didn't expect it. We just talked a few weeks ago, I'm guessing he came to you since then?"

"Actually he-"

Cut off by someone beside her she peered to her right to find Wyatt there. Her heart skipped a beat as the light of hope glowed brighter just in his presence. To her surprise she found herself with the desire to open up a little more to him, the thought caused the hair on her arm to stand on end. Maybe it was the multiple shots in less than five minutes, but she found a smile on her face.

"May I?" He looked back at her and held his arm open to her, his eyes fixed on her reactions carefully. She nodded and leaned into him and felt his arm encircle her shoulder. His sober eyes bore into hers and a smile grew on his lips as evidently he could see how drunk she was.

"I'm glad to see you're still here, My Little Viper… And apparently still partying?"

"Well I am here, might as well keep going," Eden told him as a smile drifted to his face.

"Nox, mind if I steal Eden away for the night?"

"Of course not, have fun you two." Lennox nodded to the pair with a soft smile and started to turn away.

"Tell Aron we snuck away to the town over, I'll call him when we are coming back so he doesn't try to set us on fire," Wyatt called after her.

"Wait, Wyatt, You two can't leave the grounds! We are in lockdown." She stopped and spun back around.

"Hunters won't follow us off campus. That is if Eden is willing to take a little adventure with me?"

Confused, Eden looked up at him after and felt her stomach twist a little at the mention of hunters. *We are leaving campus? Where does he think we are going at one am?* However much she wanted to go home, it was a great idea to get away from campus with him, if Octavius was found before they got back, she had the alibi of three of the most trusted within the school. Lennox had her arms folded over her chest and Wyatt looked at her with puppy dog eyes.

"That sounds fun if Lennox doesn't tell on us?" She raised her eyebrow and smirked at the irony and a way to piss off the demon.

"I know if I try to stop you, you're going to do it anyway. If you two get caught you better not bring Aron and I into it."

"Deal, come on Viper. I've got something to show you. His arm slid down to her hand and lightly pulled her through the crowd and into the night.

Wyatt led her by the hand to a small building by the front gates of the school with a bright smile plastered on his face. *He's like a kid on Christmas.* Deep down she knew they had to talk about what he said less than two hours ago. However, she wasn't going to be the one to start that conversation so she waited for him to bring it up. Initially, she thought he would be the moment they were alone, but he seemed to patiently wait for either the right moment or for her to, she couldn't decide. They walked quietly, excitement lingered in the air as they approached the garage.

The building looked much newer than the rest of the school with dark panels and multiple colored tan and brown bricks along the bottom. It was also long enough to hold about ten vehicles plus some odds and ends. Familiar with the place, she peered a few doors down to where Eloise's car was stored away. Before the door opened, Wyatt turned on his heel to face her and gently pulled her closer. Butterflies came alive inside of her as his eyes met hers again.

"Don't worry, I won't let any hunters get you." He winked.

Eden laughed a little at the irony, "The only person I'm worried about getting me is Eloise."

"She thinks you're at Omega and according to Lennox, you are." His tone shifted into velvet as he drew her closer until they were only inches apart.

There was another moment of silence as she ran her nail over her fingertips. His words in the entranceway crossed her mind again and caused her to question if this was something they needed to talk about before they left.

"Wyatt, about earlier…" She started before his hand squeezed hers.

"Not here, we can talk when we get there. Just enjoy yourself a little longer, there's no rush, Little Viper." He brushed a hair away from her face as the looming winter wind blew. "You have two more chances to back out, are you ready for an adventure?"

"I don't know… Is there any way this could end in death?" She asked, and quickly dropped the topic as he dropped her hand and turned toward the door.

"Well, that depends on your opinion of our mode of transportation."

As much as she hated to admit it, she found herself completely wrapped up in the moment of being with him. Now that she knew where she stood within herself, Bastein's advice was easier to implement. It was time to see if she could find happiness in another way of life. The door rolled up to reveal a blue Triumph Scrambler parked by the door.

Her eyes widened and she walked past him, over to the motorcycle. "I've seen this here, I always wondered whose it was."

"Well lucky you, you found him. Guess you don't need that last chance to back out?" He came up behind her.

"Lucky for you my family has had a few at various times, so no I don't."

"You realize you're trusting me with your life, right?" He asked as his eyebrow raised for a change.

"Are you not a good driver?" She questioned.

"I am, I just-"

"Well then, let's go." She motioned to the bike without issue.

With a mischievous smirk on her face, she swung her leg over the seat. Now she was thankful for the jackets and jeans she was wearing as she pulled her hair up and out of her face. Out of the corner of her eye, she saw Wyatt with his hands on his hips and he shook his head. He let out a deep chuckle as he walked over to the bench and picked up two black helmets. He extended one out to her as she tied her hair off.

"You're drunk, absolutely not. I'm driving." Wyatt said as he slid it over her head and lifted the visor so she could see.

"I wasn't- Well. I may have forgotten." She laughed a little at herself and moved back.

"Exactly." He put on his own helmet.

He swung his leg carefully over as he sat in front of her and started the engine which roared to life. Eden wrapped her arms around his torso and pushed the visor down and held tight to him as he pulled away quickly so they wouldn't be caught.

In the town over sat a late-night diner and an illuminated sign reading Lucky Lucy's Diner. With the motorcycle parked out front, Wyatt and Eden sat in a booth across from each other. Each had their own chocolate milkshake and a basket of fries sat between them.

"There's no way you haven't heard of fries and milkshakes!" Eden laughed as he watched her speechless.

"I haven't actually, I've spent most of my time around other demons." He reached out and picked up a fry to try it for himself. His eyes lit up as he went in for more.

"You know when you said adventure, I didn't exactly picture milkshakes."

"Adventure doesn't have to be life or death. It could just be a good time, which it always is when you're around."

Eden felt heat creep into her cheeks. "You're right, I'm glad you thought of it."

She was now mostly sober as they talked casually about the party. Wyatt told her all about him, Aron and Lennox who seemed rather close as they danced. He went on about how he planned to ask what was going on between them in the morning. They sat there, for how long she couldn't have told anyone. They laughed together and occasionally Eden cracked a joke here or there about Eloise.

As their laughs died down, Wyatt's face softened and he held his hand out to her from across the table. A knot formed in her throat as she knew the time had come to discuss what had happened in the entrance hall of Kappa. Eden took his extended hand and saw his eyes held seriousness that leaked into his voice as he spoke.

"Eden, I know it's probably too soon, but I need you to tell me what happened between you and Nick. When I talk with Aron in the morning I need to know how it all went down, I think you were the more sober one in the situation."

She drew in another long breath and recoiled a little as the memories entered her mind's eye. She kept her face even, there were bigger things on her mind. "It was all so fast, honestly, I was grabbing Bastien's coat. He came up behind me and started hitting on me. He got a little too close and I was about to kick his ass for it."

She motioned to the coat she still wore and attempted to keep herself casual. However, she noticed his expression hardened as she explained what happened and avoided his gaze for a second. Quickly she gave the summary of events, and glanced up at Wyatt. His face was now darker than she had ever seen before. He wore his emotions on his sleeve in front of her which made it easy to see if his words matched with his true intentions. In this case, he meant what he said.

"I have to be honest, I wanted to. I would tear anyone apart if a single hair was touched on your head without your approval."

Normally those words sent an instinctual chill down her spine, however, it didn't. Instead, it was eerily comforting to know he had her back maybe more than Bastien. She felt safe as she looked at their hands, his thumb gently drew circles there. Tension lingered in the air as he waited for her to speak again.

"I don't regret meeting you." Eden told him, continuing the conversation by the front door of Kappa. Unable to hold it back any longer they spilled out.

"You don't?" Wyatt asked his anger from before shifting as she spoke. "Are you sure you're ready to talk about this?"

"Wyatt, you made me question myself more than anyone I know. Yet somehow when you're in the room, all the questions stop. For the first time in a long time I feel like I don't have to look over my shoulder around someone other than Bastien. You knocked down walls and I have no idea how you accomplished it. There's so much I want to tell you, but I can't. You have wormed your way into my life. Now you've made me care about you and I'm scared."

"Why are you scared?" His voice dipped and a frown appeared.

"Because... For once in my life, I can't picture a day without someone. For once I'm terrified of the things I would do to keep you safe. Allowing myself to care about someone... I've never done that before."

Eden felt her face heat up as her stomach danced. Her eyes drifted back to his face to see his reaction. His eyes were alight with excitement, that giddy stupid smile she had come to appreciate seemed plastered to his lips.

"Eden Miller, am I your first boyfriend?" He asked teasingly.

"And if you are?"

"Then I will be your last, I don't plan on letting you go my Little Viper"

Lennox

The digital clock flashed in the corner of her desk in big numbers, two am. Lennox had just gotten back to her room from the party and she could feel the sleepiness start to overtake the spinning room. She pulled off her jacket but decided that the effort of changing clothes was too much effort, at this point. She climbed into bed for the night and let out a deep breath as she pulled the sheets up and closed her eyes. Just as she did, her phone rang demandingly from her bedside table.

Lennox shot upright, and fear gripped her chest as she threw the covers aside. *There's no reason for anyone to be calling.* Every muscle tensed as she rushed to her phone as she forced herself to sober up. She saw Aron's name and photo across her screen which sent a new wave of fear through her. Without hesitation, she answered and put the phone to her ear. Aron didn't wait for her to say anything before he started to talk worry plain in his voice.

"Len, it's Octavius. He isn't anywhere inside Kappa. Did you see him there when you did your headcount?"

"No, Rosalyn had asked if I'd seen him but we figured he had passed out somewhere upstairs." She started to throw on her jacket while she held the phone on her shoulder.

"Call the security team- Now. I'm on my way." The call ended.

Exhausted and still intoxicated she pulled her jacket on and speed dialed Coyote. With her fears confirmed she pushed her panic aside only to be replaced with a strong rage. *I will not lose anyone else. Not tonight.* As the phone rang, Lennox quickly made her way down the stairs and to the front entrance. She peered around the darkness to make sure there was no movement around her before she opened the door. As she stepped through the door frame, the vines used to lock the house down moved aside for her.

She stepped down the front three steps and turned back to the front door, her irises glowed a dull green. As adrenaline coursed through her, she pulled at the vine to her magic and sent more vines over the front door and windows of the Omega Alpha. The magic didn't stop until the barrier was so thick, no one could cut through.

Once she was satisfied she turned toward the main building. Vines started to grow from the freshly healed scratch marks over the large burn scars on her back. The ivy weaved into their familiar wing shape in seconds. The sigils along her chains sprang to life through the small holes she had cut into her shirts and jackets for cases like this. It was just then a deep groggy voice answered the phone. "Lennox, what's going on?" Coyote asked.

"Octavius is missing. Aron is on his way over to start looking for him."

"Don't leave Omega when he gets there, either of you. This could be a trap to lure you both out. I'm on my way. " He instructed as she heard a loud clatter in the background.

"It worked. I'm not burying anyone else... Trap or not, they are going to wish they hadn't come here."

The sound of footsteps behind her made her turn around, ready to fight if she had to. Aron was already halfway between the houses before he stopped and looked her up and down, surprise written all over his face. Lennox waited for him to make some comment and lifted her head a little as if in a challenge for him to. Instead, a smile drifted across his face as they looked at each other. His own eyes shifted pure black, the veins in his hand and up his arms now alight with something kin to lava. The energy shifted around them as both pulled at their reserves. With no questions asked, they were a team.

Lennox remembered Coyote was still on the other end when she heard his door shut through the phone. The sounds of him on his walkie talkie to inform the other members of the security team drifted through the speaker as well.

"Aron just got here, I'll share our location with you." She told him as her feet started to move toward the path to the main building.

"We aren't waiting for Coyote and the others?" Aron asked her and fell into step just behind her.

"No, every second counts... I learned that the hard way. You're welcome to stay here and wait, but I'm going to find him." She told him, her voice monotone as her eyes went midnight behind the dull green glow. She glanced around the dark grounds and listened to the sounds around them. The area was quiet as the cold hung in the air.

Coyote protested on the other end of the phone. "Don't do anything irrational Miss. Cade. We will be there in five minutes."

"I'm not waiting for anyone. " She hit the end button and slipped her phone into her pocket. He could still track them and this way was much quieter.

Lennox stopped in her tracks and peered into the treeline of the woodland. Her intuition pulled her toward the shadows and her feet followed. Behind her, Aron followed her into the forest without a single further question. This time he moved to walk beside her as they entered the treeline, he lifted his hand and small flames sparked to life from his fingertips. The light from the fire was enough to illuminate about five feet in front of them. As she peered over to him, Lennox saw the determination in his eyes. The orange glow played across his face and the flames danced in his eyes as he looked back at her. It was all the confirmation she needed to continue forward.

They walked for how long she didn't know, mostly in silence. Neither dared to call out, cautious since they didn't know what lingered just past the light. Their breath could be seen in the air as she moved more branches aside until suddenly, a whisper caught her attention. It was distant, almost like the whispers she heard when someone started to summon her. *Not now.* Lennox waited for the summoning to get stronger. However, the whispers grew as she turned to the right.

She motioned her head to the right and followed them as they grew louder. Slowly, they filled her mind so loudly that they consumed her thoughts entirely. After less than a minute or two, Aron's light illumi-nated someone's foot. The two stopped at the same time, their eyes fell on an unconscious Octavius. The twisted wings wound their way into her back once more. She trusted Aron to handle anything that could appear behind them. Her eyes went wide as she quickly bent down to him and put her hands on his shoulders. Lennox gently shook him in an attempt to wake him.

She frowned when she felt how cold he was. *He must have been out here for hours.* Her heart sank and her hands went to the zipper of her jacket as she peered at Aron. She was about to tell him to get the chain off of Octavius however he was already set to work as they melted away. Lennox turned back to their friend and took off her jacket, left in nothing but a tank top and jeans. As the ice-like chains melted away at Aron's touch he glanced over to Lennox. She placed her jacket around Octavius's shoulders and shivered slightly.

"It's okay, we've got you now." She told him, her eyes scanning for blood.

"Lennox, let me warm him up, you'll fr-" Aron walked toward them as he spoke and she felt his hand on her back. Right over the burn scars lined with fresh cuts as he bent down to them.

His words stopped and so did he, knelt down and motionless beside her. She looked back at him, worried and bent her head to him in an attempt to catch his attention. However, he didn't flinch. A statue.

"Aron? Hey, are you okay? Do I have to find a way to carry you both out of here?" She asked quietly and put a hand on his arm.

At the contact, he jumped and blinked back at her. His eyes were wide as if he saw her for the first time. "What? Ca- Lennox- I."

"Are you okay?"

The sound of heavy footsteps came from behind them. The two Heads of House snapped toward the sound ready to fight. From the shadows came two very tall men with disapproving looks. Coyote and Bloodfang peered down at them before they moved past them to Octavius. Bloodfang easily scooped up the man and started to wordlessly carry him away for medical attention. As he passed Lennox and Aron she noticed his face finally show his emotions. He had his hands balled into fists and his eyes dropped to the ground.

"I'll kill who did this to you…"

Coyote turned to the students in front of him and motioned for them to follow him out. Even in Aron's orange light, she could see the red in the man's face coupled with annoyed understanding. Lennox knew they were surely in trouble for not listening and she would take the brunt of that. *Besides- They know I wouldn't have done anything less.*

It was five in the morning by the time Coyote finished chewing them out for not waiting on them. Lennox knew that if there had been a hunter who set a trap for them they could have both been killed. However, Aron made it clear if he didn't think he could hold his own, he wouldn't have followed her. She insisted it was all due to her and she had no regrets, which made Coyote sigh in defeat. He released them to their houses for the night and instructed them to try and get some rest for the day before they would have a meeting with Principal Moon, the Security Team, and Cleo. As Aron had waited for her to leave with him, Lennox had turned to Coyote and met his gaze one last time.

"I'm not worried for myself, I'm on borrowed time anyways if they are trying to get me."

Lennox stepped from the room with Aron beside her as they left the lower level of the school. The morning light streamed through the hall windows when they went up the stairs to the main entrance. Neither demon spoke as they went through the doors into the courtyard. Lennox looked up at the sun which peaked over the horizon and let out a sigh.

"Borrowed time, huh?" The man broke the quiet.

A knot formed in her throat as she hoped he wouldn't ask. "I would have died around the same time I made my deal so yes, these last twenty two years have been borrowed."

"You're usually pretty optimistic Lenny."

"I just can't lose anyone else." She shook her head as she glanced at the two chapter houses. "I'd do anything to make sure everyone here was safe."

"I know you would... But the world needs people like you. So for us, don't do anything that could jeopardize that. Besides, I'm pretty sure Wyatt would take my ass down if I came back without you."

She smiled lightly and met his forest green eyes. "I won't make promises. Not this time."

"I knew you wouldn't. Just call me so we can assemble the team. We take on dildos together, agreed?"

"Agreed." She couldn't help the smile that drifted to her face as he held out his pinky which she twisted hers around.

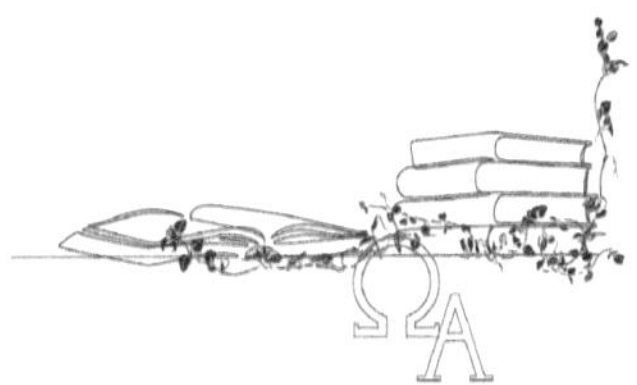

Lennox had returned to her room to attempt to get a semblance of sleep. She lay there for hours, stared at the ceiling, and went over the last few hours in her mind. Aron's pause came to mind as she remembered the way he froze when he touched her scar. *Maybe he just thought I'd get upset if he touched it?* She attempted to explain the strange event away.

Around eight she sat up in bed, unable to lay there anymore. She looked over to her phone for any messages but found nothing. She knew she had to tell Rosalyn what had happened last night and quickly texted to meet in an hour in her room. Lennox decided she had to check on Aron first and left the house once more and completely abandoned the walk in two's rule. She went directly to the front stairs, opened the door and made her way inside. She walked through the halls and went into the common room to text Aron she was downstairs.

When she looked up from her phone, she saw someone sat on the black leather couch by the fire. The very person she was here for was in front of her with a first aid kit in his lap. He was focused on his hand as he rolled gauze around it with his non-dominant side and seemed to struggle slightly. A pile of small shards of mirror sat in a bowl mixed with red. Blood dripped from cuts all over the top of his hand and knuckles onto his jeans. Lennox rushed forward and fear gripped at her chest.

"Aron? What happened?" She asked which caused him to jump.

"I- errr... Nothing, absolutely nothing!" He lied as she frowned at him.

"That isn't nothing. Did you punch a mirror or something?"

"I-" He stopped himself and turned away from her as she approached.

"I'm not judging you. Just let me help, okay? I won't ask any more questions." She told him and paused beside the couch.

He was quiet for a second before he nodded and let his injured hand drift toward her. Lennox's face softened as she sat beside him and hovered her hands over the bandages. He flinched a little as she picked up the gauze and watched her carefully as if she could break at any moment. *Does he think I'm not okay after what happened with Octavius? What is this about? It's like he thinks I'll shatter.* For a moment, she questioned whether or not his opinions of her had shifted since last night but she kept it to herself for now.

She made quick work of removing the bandages and sprayed the cleaning solution from inside the kit which caused him to grimace and draw in a sharp breath. As she worked in silence, the questions she dared not ask flew around her mind. Carefully She wrapped the bandages around the cuts and secured it with a careful tuck. As she worked, his eyes were trained on their hands and didn't move until she was done.

"There, I think I saved your hand. You can keep it for now." She teased lightly and started to put everything away.

"Thanks, doc." A small smile drifted to his face as his eyes met hers again as they both stood. "Would you mind if we kept this between us?"

"Of course, doctor patient confidentiality and all."

"I appreciate it, I guess you're cooler than I thought you were." He forced a smile.

"I am, you've just never noticed." She teased. "Well, if that's the only thing, I can let you get back to your day. I have to meet with Rosalyn soon, I don't want her to find out about what happened with Octavius from anyone else." She told him as he shifted side to side at Rosalyn's name.

"Actually, I was hoping you'd come over later to talk with Wyatt and Nick. Something happened last night at the party between Nick and Eden, Wyatt was a witness and will tell Eden's side. Can you come back over this afternoon around four?" He asked and seemed to slide back into his usual demeanor.

"Of course, I'll be there."

November

Eden

The knife hit the center of a paper with a dull thud. Eden and Bastien stood in the center of the basement toward a wooden board with photos of various targets pinned to it. Eden moved toward the board to retrieve Lennox's Dagger from her photo. She ignored the glint of the demon's name on the blade as she pulled it out and turned to face Bastien.

"The real person I want to throw this at is Nick." She told him venomously.

"Why *didn't* you cut his hand off?" Bastien crossed his arms over his chest and sank into a hip. She heard his phone hit a weapon inside the

Miller Peacock crest on the left side of his belt.

"Mr. Copperhead got in the way." She rolled her eyes as the memory of Wyatt popped into her mind and she felt a slight blush cross her face. "But this dagger definitely deserved to be shoved up Nick's-"

"Why did you make it?' He stopped her with his question and a raised eyebrow as his attention went to the dagger in her hand.

"Eloise had me make it and one for Aron, I'd imagine she's preparing to put the plan into motion."

"And how do you feel about that? Being the one to create Aron and Lennox's Daemonium Pugionem?" The question lingered for a second as Eden didn't respond.

She moved back to her original spot and faced the board once more. Her eyes fell to the photo of the pink haired Head of House and she searched within for an answer. As she held up her arm to aim the dagger once more, Bastien stepped in front of her.

"I saw you with Wyatt, Eden. The way you two look at each other. The way he treats you. I know you two took a little trip off campus to hide what you did to Octavius. He may not be able to tell anyone but I'm not dumb. When I heard Aron telling Wyatt what happened, it was easy enough to put together."

She froze, forced to look him in the eyes and admit every bitter word. "I had to know if I had it in me... Being able to handle both worlds... I don't Bas, you were right. I don't think I'll be able to do it as long as I care for him. So no- I'm not thrilled to kill Aron."

Bastien had been right, she had proved it to herself and now confirmed it to him. She averted her eyes to her left in hopes the weapons cabinet might appear to be more interesting than the conversation. Her eyes traced the intricate peacock designed into the metal. Just last year this admission would have caused him to give her a pep talk and extra training session. However, he now wrapped her up in an understanding hug. It clicked for Eden at that moment, they were in the same boat. *He's in love with a demon too.*

"Whatever you choose, you will be okay." He whispered by her ear before he let go.

"It will be years until I have to be a Matriarch, I will have time to figure out how Wyatt and I could work."

"That may be so, but your twenty-second birthday is next week Eden. The Hunters Arrangement." His statement hit her like a slap in the face as she remembered what that meant.

Her eyes drifted for a moment and she wrung her hands anxiously. She had been so busy with everything going on that the Hunter's Arrangement had slipped her mind from her sixteenth birthday when Eloise had come into her room and explained it to her. *Between sixteen and twenty-two every future Matriarch or Patriarch has the chance to discover their partner outside of The Salvamari. If they do not find one before their twenty-second birthday one will be selected for them by the current Matriarch.* The sound of Eloise's voice echoed in her mind as her heart and face fell. There was only a week to figure out what she wanted to do... Not years.

Wyatt's face returned to her mind as she realized the limited time they had. A pang of guilt sank into her stomach and she wanted nothing more than to go to him and tell him everything. Eden peered up to Bastein who had given her some space and turned back to the board as a wave of jealousy washed over her. *He has all the time he wants to figure out what he and Corvus are doing. He's a Baron.* With another flash of metal and a dull thud, Eden watched the knife hit Aron's photo.

"Have they already started searching for candidates?" She asked quietly.

"Stacey and Eloise have been calling around the other families."

A slight flush crept across her face, embarrassed. "Who are they?"

"As of right now, Baron's Chase and Brier Donovan, Heir Hunt Belmore, and Heir Holden Holloway."

Eden frowned at the names. "You can tell them I will reject Hunt. I'm pretty sure he wouldn't be able to look up from his pen and paper long enough to know I'm in the room."

"No record keepers, got it." Bastien smirked and tilted his head. "Anyone else?"

"How old is Brier now?" She wrinkled her nose in distaste as she remembered how small the carbon copy of his father had seemed.

"Turned nineteen a few months back, about four years younger than Chase."

"I can't marry someone younger than me."

"Understood, any other requests for a future husband? Maybe black hair, tattoos, and a Crossroads Demon." He teased.

"Funny- Just, please?"

"One Donovan Elephant and Holloway Lion coming up." He teased.

"You can't take anything serious, can you?" Eden sighed.

"You know I have your back."

The two continued their practice for a few more rounds before they decided to call it a night. Eden pocketed Lennox's dagger beside Aron's in her belt, as Basiten went over and cleaned up the knives laid out on the table by the weapons cabinet. *The Sullivan's would think our weapon stash is nothing.*

"How about we tell Eloise we are going to Hell Hound Pub tonight and you can go meet with Corvus?" She suggested it to him, surprised by her own words. She had never thought in a million years she would cover for him in a case like this. Now with so little time left she wanted to spend as much time as she could with Wyatt to help come to a decision.

"That sounds great actually, you should invite Wyatt." Bastien offered back.

"I'll consider it, maybe I'll enjoy a night out alone."

"Yeah, okay. Call him." He nudged her arm as he walked past her. "I'm gonna go get ready for our Miller night out."

Eden felt the heat return to her face as he went up the stairs. She walked over to the table and leaned against it. She pulled out her phone from a pocket she had added to her belt and pulled up Wyatt's contact. Eden stared at his photo for a moment and felt a smile drag her lips upward. The other night he had insisted on taking a photo of her with his phone and another together with her phone. Now as she looked at his smile and bright eyes, she was secretly happy they did as she hit the call button.

As she walked into the dark pub, Eden ran her hands down the black velvet dress she decided to wear. Though she couldn't hide more than her favorite knife on her thigh, she didn't feel the need for more than that. Wyatt had been almost over-excited when she called him to meet and even asked her to make it a real date night. She made her way over to a seat at the bar and the owner, Bryer came over with a large smile wide enough to show their fangs. Their bright silver hair was messy as if they had spent all day in the wind and their eyes were clear in the dim light. Bottles of various different alcohol were illuminated behind them on shelves and the dark wood walls kept the room mostly dark.

"What can I get you?" They asked as they stopped in front of her.

"Anything strong," she answered and peered at the door for a second.

"Are you meeting someone here, Miss. Miller?"

"Actually yes, but we are keeping it under wraps if you know what I mean." She let a small smile drift across her face.

"A good barkeep never tells their patrons secrets. It's safe with me."

Bryer smiled and turned away to make her drink as she pulled out her phone to check the time. Wyatt would be here any minute. She put her phone face up on the bar, Eden messed with her hair, annoyed with it in her face. After only a few minutes, Byrer brought a glass of a light red drink.

"Good luck tonight, I'll be around the corner if you need me once they get here. If you'll excuse me." They motioned to the back room.

She nodded and picked up the glass and ran it between her palms lost in thought. After a few seconds, she drank and picked up her phone to text Wyatt that she was there. The screen wavered as she typed. *What the hell... Vampire venom?* Eden's eyelids became heavy and she put down her drink and panic gripped at her chest.

"Bryer?" She called but they were already gone.

Eden willed her legs to move and found they felt much heavier than they should. *I only have seconds... Five.* The room started to spin and darken as she tried to stay awake. *Four.* She gripped the blue thread but found magic was unable to help her, she couldn't fight it for long. *Three.* She had to at least send something and hope Bastien would be asked about it. *Two.* She typed only a few words and hit send. *One.* All at once, she blacked out, her head fell onto the bar knocking over the drink and it shattered on the floor.

Eden Miller-
Wyatt I was here, tell Bas.
-Sent 7:14 pm

Lennox

The snow blew outside Lennox's dorm room window as she sat scrunched on her chair beside it. A cold afternoon breeze attempted to make its way inside as she studied for her next test. With her left leg crossed on the seat of the fuzzy chair, her right foot beside it and her arms which held her knee up as she read. Her tired eyes skimmed the page of an open book in front of her as she pulled the hair tie from her wrist. She gathered the top part of her hair in a bun at the back of her head and tied it out of the way. It had been a struggle to get any semblance of sleep over the last couple of nights. So she threw herself into her studies.

Her phone buzzed beside her and caused her to jump. Lennox didn't look at the screen right away. She had found every call and text sent a jolt of fear through her so she would give herself a minute before she checked. She let out a deep breath she peered over and saw Wyatt's name with a new message.

> Wyatt Steele-
> Hey Nox, can you give me a call when you have a moment? Nothing major just wanted to chat about something.
> -Sent: 6:46 pm

Quickly, she closed her book, unplugged her phone and unlocked it. A wave of relief calmed her nerves as he had at least reassured her before she hit the call button. It only rang twice before his raspy voice came from the other end.

"Hey, are you alone?" The question made her frown with concern.

"Yeah, what's wrong?"

"Nothing, well- Not entirely. Have you noticed something off with Aron? He seems jumpier than usual." He asked quickly and kept his voice low.

"I mean, I have…" She paused, Aron hadn't seemed to want anyone to know about his hand. Until he seemed like he was a danger to himself, she wasn't going to say anything.

"Do you have time to come over to talk more about this?"

"Yeah, I'll be right over." She agreed and ended the call.

Wyatt answered his door dressed in black sweatpants and one of the usual band t-shirts he wore. He smiled softly as their eyes met and he moved aside to invite her. Secretly, Lennox was grateful Aron was off in preparation for his guard night. She knew the two shared joining rooms as she walked in. Quickly, Wyatt ran ahead of her to grab the second door to his room as she glanced at the little living room they had made themselves beside the bathroom. She avoided the spot on the end of the blue couch Felix sat in just a few months ago.

Wyatt led her into his ever-so-familiar room, it was strangely comforting to see the motorcycle and band posters plastered everywhere. A collection of vinyl records lined the highest part of the walls all the way around the room and above the door. Even with the white walls, it felt darker with the black blankets on his bed and the dark furniture he had brought with him. On his desk sat one of his journals, a dirty romance book, and a small sprocket printer under a collage of photos of him and various friends he had made over the years. She smiled softly at the photo of Felix, Rue, Wyatt, and her. Before her eyes fell to a photo of him and Eden in the town over.

He cleared his throat, the sound caused her to return her attention back to the moment. He motioned for her to pick a spot and she sat on the edge of his bed and waited for him to start.

The demon let out a sigh as he took a seat in his desk chair. "I keep hearing him talking to someone. At first I thought it was just someone on the phone but last night I caught him talking in the bathroom and his phone was on the couch... What have you noticed?"

"Well at the meeting with us and Nick, Aron seemed on edge. Every time I got close he flinched a bit. I thought maybe it was because of what happened to Octavius- Maybe he's worried about the next time the hunters strike." Lennox rambled.

"We are all worried about when they will strike next. I don't think I could handle another phone call of a death or kidnapping." Wyatt shook his head as he peered down at the hourglass tattoo on his wrist. "But that doesn't explain why he's so jumpy around Rosalyn and you."

"Do you think he thinks he's next? Maybe Val told him about the curse and now he thinks it's back too." She avoided his eyes and picked at her fingers as an excuse.

The bed shifted as Wyatt turned to face her. Out of the corner of her eyes she could see sadness flutter across his face. A knot tied itself in her throat and she focused on the silver sigils and chains. A tattooed rose came into view as his hand covered both of hers.

"Nox." Wyatt exhaled the word. "You don't believe it's still around, do you?"

"Felix… Rue… Octavius." She listed every name as her eyes shot up to him.

"Ocatvius is safe."

"For now." Lennox stood and peered out the window. "I feel like it's been here this whole time, looming like a shadow just waiting."

"It's gone, I promise. Even if it's not, I will go down to hell and break into my office." Wyatt's voice deepened.

"If you go back down there it could be too hard to get you back. You left because you didn't want to be that person anymore, if you go down and Lucifer asks you to stay…"

"I wouldn't. I won't become that person again. Besides, I've got a family here and where else would I get the latest tea from? Aron always has the best stories."

"You two gossip like teenagers." Lennox rolled her eyes.

Lennox shook her head and returned to her seat as she considered what Wyatt had told her about Aron. The new information drew her eyebrows together in worry. Her gaze drifted for a second as different scenarios flooded her mind as she remembered the bowl of broken mirror pieces. He hadn't called anyone and if she hadn't walked in no one would have known. *What could be going on that Aron would act like this?*

"What should we do?" She asked finally.

"I think we should just watch and make sure he's okay. If you see anything else that's a red flag we should go to Andy." Wyatt shifted in his chair.

"Agreed," Lennox met his eyes again but held the secret for now.

A hush fell between them for a moment before Lennox rose an eyebrow at him to diffuse the tension. They hadn't had much time to talk about the interest he had taken in Eden so she motioned over to the photos on his wall and she decided it would be a good topic.

"So tell me about this adventure you two just had to take in the middle of the night." She coaxed.

"I'd say one of my favorite dates ever. We went to that shake shop and I think this was the first time she's ever shown me her true self." A wide smile drifted onto his face as he spoke of her.

"Well, that's a first. Eden is usually pretty closed off. You two must have something really good going on."

"Her walls don't break easily, but if she tells me something I want it to be because she wants to. I'm a patient man. I must admit, so far it's paid off."

"I'm genuinely happy for you, Wyatt. I always knew someone would come along for you." Lennox shifted to get a little more comfortable and leaned toward him. "Tell me about your first date, and how you two started chatting it up."

He laughed and crossed his legs in his chair as he started to tell her about the night he went over and they studied and drank. As the sun set through the window, Wyatt and Lennox talked about the last couple of months until the conversation switched around from him and Eden to the other night when they found Octavius. For once it felt like none of this semester had ever happened. They laughed together as the hours unknowingly passed. Wyatt had eventually joined her on his bed and the two lay beside each other as they took a turn sharing stories.

"Bastien told me her birthday is coming up, so I got her-" Wyatt scrolled through his phone when he stopped to peer at the top of the screen. "Shit, it's midnight, Nox."

"Midnight!" Lennox shot up from her spot in bed and her eyes darted to the window. It was pitch black outside which made her look at her own phone which confirmed the time. "Aron will give me absolute hell if he catches me trying to sneak home."

"You know what that means!" He said cheerfully and stood from his bed and moved to the open rack of outfits that held about ten almost identical black leather jackets. "It's a sleepover night! You can borrow a T-shirt and sweats. Pick a band."

"Thank you- Nirvana?" she asked as the shirt and pants were tossed to her.

"Of course, I'm not sending you out there late at night. I'll be in the other room for a few minutes so you can change."

Wyatt scooped up his phone and started to type as he left the room. After Lennox pulled off her day clothes and pulled on the borrowed ones, she decided to take a second look at the memories he had captured. Her eyes drifted to the photo of the first day she and Wyatt became friends. Her lips curved into a smile as she remembered the way he pulled out his camera with a confident, *"We're gonna want to remember this day. Our future selves wouldn't believe us."* The memory made her smile as she remembered the few summers she left the school to find him and take revenge for the curse he had created. She had been so angry after Xemos dropped her off at the school she had wanted the demon responsible dead, for the curse that prematurely took her life with Mason and Gemma.

Her eyes trailed the photos to one of Wyatt and Eden. His smile was different from the others in that one. His eyes which usually were bright and happy seemed to hold even brighter sparks as he sat beside her. Eden's expression was even a lot brighter than usual. For a moment she felt the grief of Rue's death weighing down on her. However, before she could let herself go down that path there was a knock at the door.

"You're good!" Lennox called and quickly turned back around as he reentered now dressed for bed as well.

They both went over, got comfortable on opposite sides of the bed and pulled up the covers. It was comforting to have someone beside her again and sleepiness took hold quickly as Wyatt's voice drifted over.

"Goodnight, Nox. I'll see you in the morning."

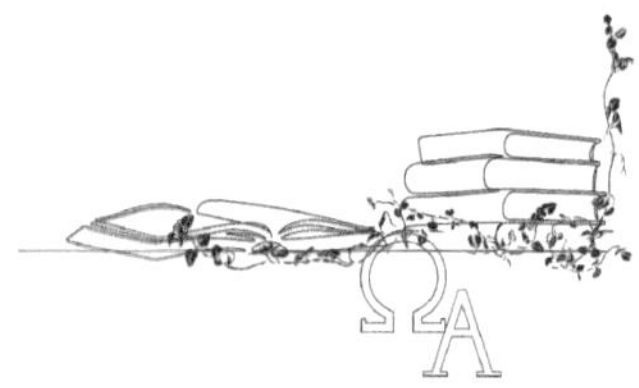

The next morning Lennox carefully shifted in the blankets and peered over to Wyatt who was still peacefully asleep. She moved carefully so as to not wake him up, got out of bed and tip-toed over to the door. Quietly, she snuck to the door and gently opened it. She slid through the frame and slowly latched it closed. The sound of the door behind her made her freeze with her hand still on the knob. *Please don't be who I think it is.* She squeezed her eyes shut for a second and let out a breath followed by a curse. Lennox turned her head to see Aron in the doorway with his mouth parted in surprise with his hand on the half closed door. Locked eyes, neither of them moved for a few seconds. She noticed him lean back a little and seemed to weigh his options before a mischievous smile crossed his lips.

"Well, this is something I definitely didn't expect to see at six in the morning- Not that I'm judging or anything, I thought you were into women?" He peered at her and crossed his arms over his chest with a glint in his eyes.

"Ew, no- He's dating Eden Miller and for your information, I'm into people." Lennox shook her head and latched Wyatt's door shut.

"Good to know, Lenoard." He closed the door and ran a hand through his hair and looked tired.

"I got tomorrow's guard, you should get some rest," Lennox told him as he walked over toward the small couch.

"You don't start your nights till Monday, I've got it. I have some free time this morning to catch up on sleep." Aron crash landed on the seat and pulled off his bandanna which left his hair a mess as he stretched his hands behind his head.

She rolled her eyes, followed him over and leaned over the back of the couch to look down at him. With a raised eyebrow and a smirk, she reached over and pulled the red fabric from his eyes.

"We've had a long couple of days, I can handle a switch in the schedule." She told him as he reached up and snatched it back from her.

"And I can handle my nights," He insisted and sat up mildly annoyed a few feet from her.

"I'm taking it tomorrow night. If you decide to join me I guess I can't stop you but there's no reason for both of us to pull guard."

"You couldn't stop me even if you tried, Lenny." Aron leaned in a little and peered up at her.

"I know I could take you." She narrowed her eyes playfully.

"Is that a challenge?"

"That's for you to decide. Now I'm going to make coffee, you get some rest."

Lennox turned away from him, and went over toward the door he had just come in from. She opened it just enough to get through so that she wouldn't wake Wyatt with the loud squeak it made when opened all the way.

"Leonard!" Aron's voice called over. "I gotta know, what kind of people are you into?"

"Well, mostly anyone that I don't work beside." She smirked.

"Ouch, a stab right in the gut." He flopped backward dramatically as she slipped out the door frame with a smile.

Lennox sat up front with books stacked up beside her in preparation for the lesson as she glanced around while students found their seats. The hum of the other students as they chatted among themselves filled the room. The Elder of Predator and Prey studies, Bloodfang stood at the front of the class beside Elder Andromeda Anderson who laughed about something he had whispered over to her. Watching as the barely over five-foot demon leaned toward him before she moved to the board at the front of the room. She started to write a large list of various types of magics and their subcategories. Lennox was so focused on the board as she wrote the list of elemental magics she almost missed Aron walk in at the last second.

She turned her attention to her supplies as if she hadn't noticed him yet. For the first time this year, she felt embarrassment wash over her from the other morning. She let her hair fall forward to obscure the heat creeping to her face and used it to look like her hunt for a pen was more important. Through the pink strands, she saw his shoes as he passed and threw himself into the desk behind her own with a thud. Lennox sat back up and the wood complained behind her as Aron got comfortable. Deep down she knew she should have kept to herself, but she couldn't resist as she turned in her seat.

"Look at you on time for once." "I'd never miss one of Fang's classes," Aron leaned toward her for a second.

"Yet this is the one you dared me to miss?" She questioned.

His smile grew into a smirk as his gaze circled the room. "I said *I* wouldn't miss it, you on the other hand it just happened to land that way. Where's Wyatt?"

"I was about to ask if you've seen him. Maybe he's visiting Eden since she's sick?"

"Sounds like him, love sick golden retriever. He really has it bad for her." Aron chuckled.

"Alright everyone, please turn your attention here." Bloodfang's deep voice echoed around the room.

Instantly the discussions around the room stopped. Lennox turned forward in her chair once more to face the two Elders as he turned to the list on the whiteboard Elder Anderson had just about finished with.

"Today we will be working on how dual combat can be applied by using your partner's strongest abilities to increase your own powers. In most cases, it is possible to defeat a target stronger than us when you have the option to combine your abilities with someone else. I have asked Elder Anderson here to help give a demonstration and then we will all practice in pairs."

He motioned to Andromeda who joined him beside a small table by his desk where a single black feather rested. As if on cue, she raised her hand and a soft breeze filled the room which pulled the feather into the air slowly. Lennox watched as it spun in circles and rose a few inches, mesmerized by the magic for a moment. Bloodfang then raised his hand, a light gray smoke colored the small vortex of air and a small spark sprang to life. The air ignited the feather and quickly engulfed it in flames until it was nothing but ash.

The two Elders turned to the class as some politely clapped while others seemed to look for the best pick for a partner. Elder Bloodfang gestured his hand to them to prompt their turn. The sounds of more creaking desks as students got up to find the best match to practice with. Lennox looked around in hopes to see Rosalyn in class today. *Her fire always works with mine.* Quickly, she discovered Octavius had already made his way over to her and asked to partner. Lennox peered around the room and searched for someone else who she knew had fire. It wasn't until the sound of an annoyed Aron from behind caught her attention since everyone had already paired. *Shit, he's the only other one.*

"If only Wyatt was here." He sighed dramatically as Rosalyn sat on the top of one of the desks.

"Lightning and fire don't really strengthen each other." She pointed out.

"Not at first but they work pretty good together in a real fight." Aron adjusted the red bandanna.

"The assignment isn't to burn down the school." Ceila chimed in from behind Octavius.

"Fine, fine. I'll just find someone else. Lenny-boo should do the trick, earth and fire." He turned his attention around the room after shooting a glare at the wolf.

He adjusted his jacket collar and made his way to her. A smile formed and eyes filled with determination and the hint of something she couldn't read. Something remained off about him as he stood beside her and his gaze stayed fixed on the front board where Andy and Blood-fang stood. *He won't even look at me... Maybe the other morning was too awkward.* For a few moments she tried to resolve the wave of anxiety that crashed into her. *No, he hasn't even made fun of me about the night. Something else is going on.*

"Are you ready to show them how it's done?" He finally spoke as the room filled with a low hum of chatter.

"Only if you use my name for once."

"Begin!" Elder Anderson's voice called to the room.

Lennox turned back toward the stack of books and quickly moved them to the seat. With only a glance to see if he was ready she started after he gave her a nod. She pulled at the inner thread of magic and pulled enough to allow a small trickle. Easily the magic obeyed as her sigils lit around her arms and lifted her hands in front of her. She quickly grew a multitude of vines that covered the top of the desk entirely. Slowly, they twisted their way up from a thick base about a foot tall, the top of the base draped over the sides which mimicked a willow tree.

It came to a halt as she held the magic and knew this should be enough to fuel a small fire. Lennox prepared to help control the flames if necessary and kept her right hand up as she glanced over at Aron. He had taken off his jean jacket while she prepared their display. Now with his forearms visible, she could see the same orange glow that traced his veins under his skin as the other night. As her eyes moved from his arms to his face as she noticed he watched her closer than usual. The look from earlier returned, worry coupled with something she couldn't recognize hidden under his usual demeanor. *Is he afraid I'm going to break?*

Before she could ask him anything, he turned to the small tree she had created. He held up his left hand, his usual forest green eyes glowed orange as he lightly touched one of the branches. Flames ignited into existence around his hand just above his skin and trailed their way onto the plant life before it traveled into the base. The flames grew much taller than expected and almost touched the ceiling.

Lennox grimaced as she had forgotten to cut off the right amount of magic to disconnect herself from the tree. Fire burned the thread as she held it and forced her to attempt to sever the flow. As she watched the fire travel and burn the vines her heart sank as she realized she couldn't let go. Every inch of her body started to heat almost unbearably. She couldn't pull her gaze away from the burning willow, and in her mind's eye, she was reminded of the time in Hell. Armaros had done the same to her wings. Her heart raced and every muscle tightened within her as she froze in her spot. A dull ring filled her ears as the demon's black and green ringed eyes took over her memories.

She couldn't move, her lungs rattled as she drew air in. *You're not there.* She tried to convince herself but the ringing was louder and blocked out the noise around her. Her magic pulled back on the thread as it started to drain her. Instinctively, she could feel the vines grow taller and reach for her though they were on fire, they aimed to protect and stop her from the dangers of overexertion. The heat in front of her grew so hot she could feel it on her cheeks.

"Clocks ticking... Those will reach your already scarred back before you know it... unless you tell me some stories." Armaros's voice echoed over the ringing.

"Len, enough demonstration." Aron's voice echoed and joined with Armaros's.

She shook her head and attempted to pull herself out of the memory and cut off the magic. The thread fell from her grasp and she lost control as the vines snaked toward her. Lennox suddenly yelled out as the fire inside her chest fought to come out and the vines from her back threatened to appear as Amraros's voice echoed again.

"Come back to me." The combination voices called to her.

Through all this her body had remained utterly motionless. Suddenly, a set of hands took her by the shoulders which caused her attention to finally shift away from the fire. The magic stopped and she came face-to-face with Aron. Her eyes met his except this time they were pitch black from his own magic as the smell of a quenched fire filled her nose. Worry was clearly written across his face as they looked at each other silently. She blinked at him and her eyebrows joined in confusion as his hands held her in place.

Elder Bloodfang had already extinguished the flames and the heat had died down. Elder Anderson was over with a group of people with their attention on another demonstration. However, Wyatt and Rosalyn all peered over at them with various reactions between fear and concern. Lennox swallowed the hard lump that had formed in her throat and returned her eyes to Aron who hadn't let her go yet, his eyes on her expressions.

"Are you back?"

"I- think so," she confirmed and moved to step away from him but swayed only to be held up by the demon. *Will I ever stop embarrassing myself in front of him?*

"Take a second, are you feeling dizzy?" Bloodfang asked as quietly as his deep voice could allow.

"I'm fine, just a fluke. It's no big deal."

"Lennox-" Aron moved his head to catch her eyes again.

"I'm fine Aron, let me go."

At her words, his hands dropped to his sides immediately and he took a step back. With enough space to breathe, Lennox forced air into her lungs until she noticed her hands were shaking. She returned her gaze to his and saw his glued to her trembling hands, his thoughts miles away it seemed. She took the opportunity to grab her bag before he could speak. With a quick turn to the Elders she opened her lips prepared to ask to leave early from class, but the Elders nodded before she could. Andy watched her with worry and moved to take a step out of the room.

Without a word she made her way to the front of the room and toward the door. Behind her, Lennox could hear Aron begin to argue with Rosalyn. Unable to catch the words between the two, she moved through the doorway and out into the hall.

"I told you I'm fine," Lennox called to whoever had followed her.

"You can't lie to me, I was there remember? It's been years, but I know what happens when *he* comes to mind." Rosalyn accentuated the reference to Armaros.

She turned to face her best friend as the memories threatened to force her magic through the thread. "It was just like that first day."

"I know." Rosalyn nodded and approached her carefully. "We are safe, he can't hurt us here."

"How are you handling all of this? Between Felix, Rue, and Octvaius? How are we ever supposed to feel safe? Now I can't stop having night-mares about Armaros when I can fall asleep."

"We are stronger than we were as fresh demons. We've studied and practiced for decades now. I'm not afraid of him anymore." A dark expression took over her face. "If I ever see him again, he would get everything coming to him... eighty years worth."

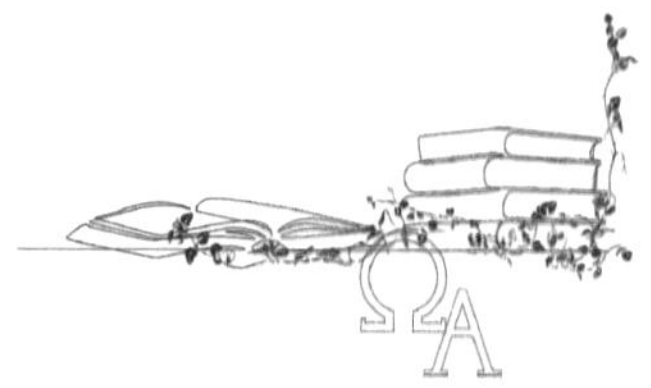

After class, Andy had searched for Lennox in the halls until she found her with Rosalyn in the students lounge. The Elder had offered to have a chat in her office down the hall, however she had turned it down much too tired to analyze every memory that had forced its way forward. Instead, Andy asked her to visit Elder Eloise Miller's room to deliver some papers and a security schedule. The two students made their way down the hall while they chatted about the next party Omega would host closer to the holidays. Lennox and Rosalyn turned left and came to a stop beside the door to the classroom with the Elder's name on the plaque.

"I'll be right back." Lennox said as she turned and walked through the doorway.

The room was as plain as the woman who taught within it. The walls were mostly bare except for posters the school had put up. The desks sat in short rows and the most exciting thing about it was the large collection of books under the long window. Eloise sat at her desk, her hair tied up in a messy bun and glasses that had slid half way down her nose. Eight books sat open across her desk and another dozen sat split into two piles on either corner of her desk.

"Elder Miller?" Lennox cleared her throat as the usually vigilant woman hadn't taken notice of her.

Eloise jumped and her eyes shot up. "Yes, Miss. Cade?"

"I'm here to give you papers from Andy." She stepped forward and went to place the papers down just as the woman took it from her before it could touch the books.

"Thank you, Miss. Cade."

Eloise shoved the papers into her bag and her attention quickly went back to the book she had been wrapped up in. Lennox frowned slightly as she scanned the spines of the books in the corner piles. Most were about herbs, hexes, curses, and poisons. *I've never seen her so untidy.*

"Is there something else I can do for you, Miss. Cade?"

"I- Well." She paused and tried to find a way to ask her question without being misunderstood. "Are you okay, Elder Miller?"

"Fine-" Her tone was harsh with an edge.

Lennox paused and remembered she was Eden's mom and she hadn't seen her housemate around in almost a week. "How's Eden?"

The woman's full attention was back on Lennox and her eyesbrow shot up. "She's still resting. I assume you received my email about her absence from Omega Alpha."

"I did."

"Then you'll know when she's ready to come back."

"I hope she gets well soon... If you need anything, I'd be happy to help." Lennox offered.

"I don't need help from you." Eloise snapped and returned to her book.

"I-I'm sorry." She stepped back and turned away to walk out the door.

Just before she left she heard the Elder speak one last time and it didn't seem intended to be heard. "Only a mother can understand."

Eden

Everything was dark, and Eden couldn't move her body. *Am I awake? Am I... am I dead?* She tried to make sense of what was going on as a small light illuminated a room off to her right from the endless dark. *What is this place?* She frowned and tried to recall her last memory. She had been at Club Crossroads with a drink in hand, nothing had seemed abnormal, except Bryer. They were usually a lot more chatty, but this time they didn't seem to want to talk very much. An uneasy feeling filled Eden as she thought about the possibilities. *Bryer is a vampire... would they? No.* She rejected the idea at first but considered what their motive could have been.

Confused, she stepped towards the doorway dimly lit by what seemed like a fire. Without hesitation, she walked into the room where she found Wyatt sat on a couch across from the fire. He turned to her with bright eyes and a wide smile on his face. For a moment, she was happy to see him and quickly approached him.

"I'm sure you have lots of questions, Little Miller."

"I do actually... What's going on? Why are you here?" She asked but came to an abrupt halt at the nickname he hadn't used since they had gotten closer.

"There's a lot I need to explain but first tell me, what do you know about a vampire's powers?"

"I think you have a question to answer before I give mine."

"And what would that be?" His eyebrows rose.

"Who are you?"

"I'm Wyatt Steele." He answered simply.

"No you're not." Eden shot back and went for her weapons belt but found it gone. "The Wyatt I know doesn't call me that much anymore. So I'm going to ask again, who are you?"

The man sighed and let the act drop. "I am a devotee of Xemos like you. You didn't seem like you trusted easily so I took the form of someone familiar. I'm here because Xemos wants me to show you the way on the right path as he promised."

Finally, a true answer in this complete darkness. Satisfied she thought back to her studies from the previous year and with Stacey. "A vampire has the ability to use their venom to knock out their prey. Not many people know what happens when they are asleep... Too many different testimonies from the ones who survive. Some say they had nightmares, others eye-opening experiences. Some never wake up-"

Her heart fell into her stomach as the words were spoken out loud.

She might not wake up. She moved around the couch and sat on the other end as her thoughts drifted back to why would Bryer do this. If she was here but not dead, that meant her physical body was more than likely fine. He slowly made his way over and a hand drifted to her shoulder.

When it made contact she didn't feel the same comfort feeling she usually got when he was around. Though this person had been sent by Xemos, whoever they were could never pass off for Wyatt. Her eyes drifted back up to his face, his expression serious and unWyatt-like. She placed her hand over the rose tattoo and pulled his hand down.

"Your body was delivered safely to your mother's doorstep." The Wyatt imposter confirmed and let her pull his hand down.

"How do you-"

"Because I am inside your mind." He explained as a knowing look appeared in his eyes. "Luckily this is a dream and you eventually will wake. Call me your dream man."

"So this isn't real?"

"It most definitely is."

"But why this way? If you know what's in my mind, you know things are complicated with him." she shot back at the fake Wyatt, crossing her arms.

"They are, however, you have to admit it, you don't find him so annoying anymore. Wyatt obviously cares for you. He is a key to unlocking what could be a good life if you're willing." He stated simply.

A key? Eden thought back on the future Xemos showed her. Holden, one of her current suitors, with a scar sat beside her several decades ahead. Wyatt had been nowhere in it. Her eyebrows knitted, there was no way a demon was the key to helping her not end up the same as the version of her in that vision.

"He's a demon and I'm a human. He has no idea who I am and even if I wanted to, it wouldn't work. I'm supposed to be helping rid the world of these terrible creatures."

"That's what you've been taught. Yes, some of them are as you say. However, you have stopped many times to wonder if there are some that aren't so bad. You've spent the last year questioning your mother's teachings internally. What is holding you back from accepting that the people you are around right now might actually be good?"

She turned to make him drop his hand and looked right into his eyes. "Duty."

It was true, she was raised to take Eloise's place in a family that held duty to the utmost degree. Family was more important than any bond created outside of The Salvamari. Her eyes turned to her hands in her lap and turned her wrist to glance at The Compass tattoo that had lived there the last 14 years.

"Eloise gave me a home... The least I can do is follow the Miller legacy."

He shook his head slowly. "You don't have to. You have a choice. That's what Xemos wants you to see. Your only obligations should be to yourself. If it were up to you, what would you do?"

Eden stopped, she had very occasionally considered what her life would be like if it wasn't filled with hunts and training sessions with Eloise or Stacey. She took a few minutes to consider the question and let the silence take over the room as the fire cracked. *I would have never killed Rue... I would have tried to get to know Lennox better before I told her who I was. I would listen to Bas and have fun discovering who I am and maybe have a chance to fall in love.* She was finally honest with herself for once.

"I would find balance... I would find a way to be happy, be an Heiress and pursue whatever this is." She answered finally.

"Does being a hunter bring you any happiness?"

"It used to... Right now it feels like a chore." She looked at her hands.

"Why don't you give yourself the chance to find out if it does? Your uncle is trying to show you that you can do anything. Give one of them a chance to show you what your future could be. I can show you someone's entire past if that's what you need to trust them."

She took in his words and considered who she would want to know more about. For a moment, she almost asked to see Lennox's past. However, that was something she wanted to hear directly from the source. Then, Eden looked at the strange version of Wyatt and conceded to her curiosity. *If he's going to be so persistent, I need to know who I'm dealing with. If he's who I'm supposed to be letting into my life.*

"I want to see Wyatt's biggest regret, I want to see what changed him into who he is."

With a nod he lifted his hand. The fire dimmed and along the wall behind it shadows danced. At first they were blurry images until the reflection shifted into an image of Wyatt at a crossroads in the midst of a deal with a brown haired, lanky man. The two voices were slightly distorted as they echoed around the room from every angle.

"It's my wife, she's dying of cancer. I need to save her. My soul for hers, please?" He begged Wyatt.

He smirked darkly and walked up to the man, "I can't stop death when it's their time. I require the soul of an innocent for that."

The man's face dropped before he quickly spoke again. "I'll give you my son's too."

"You would give me your child's too?"

"There will always be a chance for another if she lives." His voice shook.

The image in the mirror shifted and showed the face of Elder Iris

Winslow who looked back at her. Before Eden could speak, the image went hazy and shifted into a new scene. It was the inside of a house where a couple sat on the couch asleep while an infant rocked back and forth in a cradle. In a bright flash, Wyatt appeared in front of the couch with a dark smile. Without waking the man, he placed a hand on his chest and sent a small current of electricity through the man's heart.

Eden watched as it stopped and he turned to walk up the stairs. The baby's cries filled the air which caused her to cover her ears at the loudness. Wyatt's attention snapped to the bassinet and he froze in his spot as his eyes fell to the boy.

"What are you doing?" The woman's voice asked.

Wyatt didn't speak as he remained motionless. The view of his face shifted to the side as she saw regret cross his face. He didn't respond as he walked up to the bassinet and reached a hand in. Iris screamed as a spark left his finger, held over the infant's chest. The image faded and the fire grew once more.

Rage filled Eden, "He's exactly what he said he wasn't!"

"He was, however, that was the deal that broke and changed him. He was cruel, judgmental, and merciless just as you have been over the years. But I think it's time you see how it's possible to change and become better."

The words slapped her in the face. She was the same he was. They were more alike than she initially thought. With a long breath in, Eden turned to the imposter and tried to keep herself calm.

"I want to see everything he's done since."

"As you wish." He raised a hand and the shadows returned and a new scene formed.

Pink hair was the first thing that came into view, followed by a set of violet eyes. A beaten and burned Lennox Cade stood beside Xemos.

The two face to face with a darker version of Wyatt than she had ever seen. He was still the Wyatt she knew tattoos and all, however his eyes were made of midnight stars. The same color as the leather jacket and button-up he wore. Her eyes were immediately drawn to the black and blue-tipped horns that curved in spirals six inches up from his hair.

"You can't take a soul from Hell, Xemos." Wyatt growled as he stepped toward Lennox.

"I can, she is my ward. My claim on her soul was recognized before Lucifer's crows." The god stepped in front of her.

"Armaros still has questions."

"I thought Val was the demon who contested this?" Xemos started to walk forward while Wyatt stood in their way.

"Any demon may enter any cell and Armaros has decided to take interest." He shrugged. "Neither are contesting this, I am."

"Put your bruised ego aside Steele. You have done enough to the Cade family with your damn curse. If Lucifer wants to discuss this soul, he can call me back after I take her home." He directed a silent Lennox past Wyatt.

The demon grabbed the god's arm and the two locked eyes. Wyatt with a knowing smirk. "My ego is just fine, but I do appreciate the concern. Tell me, how did you unravel this one? That curse was some of my finest work."

"That curse's creation will bite you in the ass one day and you're going to wish you had never made it." Xemos's jaw tightened as he finally passed the horned demon.

The scene shifted once again as the story of Lennox and Wyatt played in front of her. Various times the two had come across each other over the course of thirteen years, their many arguments and full on fights flashed in quick succession. Finally the faces of various members of the chapter houses found their way forward. Wyatt as he slowly came to regret the people he had hurt. The nights he spent between Rosalyn's and Lennox's around the nights they struggled with their time in hell. Eden's heart dropped as Felix Toll looked back at her and laughed with Wyatt while he comforted him through the regret. The summer he had met Aron and every good thing he decided to do while they were among the humans over the last seven years.

Once it was all over, the shadows returned and she moved her gaze to where the imposter Wyatt was. However, he was no longer disguised. Now a man with dark skin, silver hair and lavender eyes looked back at her. A smile crossed his face as she took a seat beside him once more.

"It seems you have your own regrets." The man's voice shifted from Wyatt's rasp to clear.

"Doesn't everyone?" Eden questioned and wished she could return home.

"Have you learned everything you wanted to?"

"No, I still have more to find out."

His smile widened. "Good, you're truly one of us then."

Wyatt

Nothing made sense, the world seemed to fly by in fast colors. No picture could be made out to the human eye as voices and images came in and out of focus. Bright lights filled his vision and two blurs of bodies quickly took shape. One was of a woman he recognized as Eloise Miller but younger version, no older than thirty. The second was a child with midnight hair and bright purple eyes beside her while she pulled at her jacket's sleeve. They were outside, dusk ticked closer as the sun fell in the sky.

"Eden Miller, this is an order, you don't get to disappoint this family do you understand me?" The woman with a familiar voice rang out clearly and another voice could be heard but only a silhouette could be seen. "Give her a second."

Eloise's blurred figure turned around to the voice. "No. You and I both know in order to survive we must eliminate; we must act first before they do."

Who the blurry figure was, Wyatt didn't know at first, but his attention was brought back to a young and tear stained Eden. She couldn't have been much older than eleven-twelve but looked more mature and tired than an eleven-year-old should have been.

Eden's bottom lip trembled as she spoke and her voice was pleading, begging to get out of this situation to be anywhere but right here. "W-What if he is innocent? We don't know for sure that they are all bad, what if there is some good in him? I don't want to kill anyone."

As Eden attempted to calm herself, a cold nail on a chalkboard growl could be heard from the older woman. Her patience had been reached and now she was pissed. Eloise walked up to Eden, Eloise raised her hand and swung so quickly that the only thing that could be seen or heard was air and skin-on-skin contact. Eden's body hit the cold and damp ground.

"Do not test my patience again little girl, I am doing what is best for you, hell what is best for us! Why can't you just do what is asked of you?"

She rubbed her hands together to stop the sting from the slap as the child sat back up and brought her hand to her cheek. When Eden pulled her hand down, her amethyst eyes slowly fell to meet what looked to be blood from a busted lip.

"And please stop crying, emotions are a weakness we can't afford to possess." Eloise crooned

Smoke filled the air, while their bodies evaporated into thin air as his eyes flew open. He jerked out of bed and Wyatt's breath came out in heavy bursts as sweat fell from his collar bones. As the rise and fall of his chest slowed over the next few minutes, he ran a hand through his hair. His entire body was covered in sweat and he shivered from the coolness of his room and the memory of his nightmare. The demon slung his legs over the edge of the bed and firmly placed his feet on the cold hardwood. His heart sank as he realized that this wasn't a dream. It was a memory, her memory.

Five days. It had been five days since he had heard from or seen Eden in class. Every message sent was left on delivered which caused the knot in his chest to sink further and further with each day. *Even if she was sick, she'd have to wake up at some point?* He stared at his empty phone screen while music played over the speaker on his nightstand. Lost in thought, he peered over to the small, tightly wrapped box beside his speaker in waiting for Eden to open. His thoughts wandered which drowned out the bass from beside him as her violet eyes came to his mind. For only a few seconds he allowed himself to consider the possibility that she suddenly wanted nothing to do with him or even had skipped town for some reason. *She wouldn't have just up and left... Eden was there at the pub and she made sure I knew.*

Wyatt ran through the possibilities and opened the last text sent by her as he had done dozens of times over the last few days. *I was here. Tell Bas.* He had done exactly as she asked and tracked her cousin down and on the grounds that night. It had proven more difficult than he would have preferred at the moment. When he had finally found Corvus and

Bastien out at Club Crossroad he had been desperate to know if Eden was okay.

The memory replayed in his mind's eye. He had all but run to the two at the table and showed Bastien the text. The worried look on Bastien's face and his silence as he stared at the screen haunted his sleepless nights. He had quickly demanded to know what it had meant but the elf had tried to play it off. After a few choice words he was shut down by a very insistent Bastien.

Suddenly the music stopped and the room went eerily silent. As he returned from his memory. Wyatt frowned and tapped his phone to attempt to start it again but found the touch screen didn't work. He quickly sat up on his bed and jumped when he was met with a familiar man in a charcoal suit who now sat at his desk. His purple button-up stood out against the black fabric and silver tie he wore practically every time he had seen the god. The moth on his chest opened and closed its wings calmly as the man smiled at him.

"Damnit Xemos, haven't you ever heard of knocking?" Wyatt clenched his jaw, frustrated at the timing of the god's appearance.

"Why? You weren't doing anything." The tall man folded his hands in his lap.

"What do you want? I wasn't doing nothing, I have things to figure out and someone to find. Besides, last time I checked you and I should have stayed strangers."

"Do you really believe I want to be here right now? As I understand you've gotten involved with one of my devotees, Curse Bringer?"

He flinched at his old nickname, Wyatt's body tensed and his eyes widened as Xemos brought up Eden. His mind reeled and his jaw dropped as he pictured her in an attempt to remember if she had the same silver markings he had seen on Lennox over the years. His eyebrows came together as he realized since it was winter, she always wore long sleeves and he hadn't seen her bare arms. *Shit, if he's lying just to mess with me... But if she really is, he'll know she's missing.* He decided to keep her disappearance to himself for a moment and crossed his arms over his chest.

"What the hell did you just say?"

"You, Curse Bringer, have gotten yourself in with one of mine. Isn't that ironic? Haven't you noticed the silver markings on her arms? Though- maybe you didn't, they are relatively new. I thought you out of anyone would notice first. Though that would be pretty tough when she disappears for almost a week."

"I suggest you shut up now, or I will rip your throat out with my teeth Xemos. I don't have to play nice and you know I won't if it comes to it."

"What bothers you more? That she's missing and I know exactly where she is or that she said yes to me before you?" He asked and leaned forward in his chair.

Before his mind could process it, Wyatt's feet started to carry him forward. All he saw was red in the corners of his vision and it was as if he had been removed from his body which left him with absolutely no control over his actions while he was forced to watch. He crossed the short distance and in a stupid move gripped god's shoulder tightly. The smell of spearmint, leather, and sea salt filled the room.

Deep down he knew the man in front of him could take him down. They had only come to blows once over the centuries when Xemos had almost killed him for the curse on the Cade family. The two rivals glared daggers into each other's eyes as sparks formed in his. His anger and fear for Eden's life caused his magic to boil to the surface.

"You better tell me where she is right now or so help me Lucifer I will kill you. This better not be a joke."

"If I tell you immediately you will go running off- I have a deal for you. No jokes, no lies. Not today from either of us." Xemos gripped his wrist and forced his hand down while he moved to stand.

Quickly, Wyatt applied enough pressure to cause the man to sit back in the chair. A moment of pause fell between them as his eyes darted between his overzealous action and his trapped wrist. This time the dark-haired man rose once more and stood to meet Wyatt face-to-face at his full height now a few inches taller than him.

He lifted his chin up defiantly, Wyatt ripped his hand from his grip. With a breath he took a step back to prevent himself from any more drastic choices. *For Eden.* He gathered himself and narrowed his eyes back to Xemos.

"You have 30 minutes." He spoke calmly for the first time since his appearance.

"Fine then, right into it. Eden Miller's life changed course when Eloise adopted her. Since she's gotten darker falling into the trap of duty instilled in her. That is until this year. She's starting to question everything she knows and has come to me for guidance. You, unfortunately, are the key. In time, she will either have to open herself completely to you and your friends or continue down the path her family has put her on. In order to help her, I'd like to give you an advantage. No devotion, just a promise to keep her safe."

"Don't you think that's what I was already trying to do? Where were you when Nick was cornering her?" Wyatt challenged.

"I was there, you were also there." He pointed out. "There wasn't a need for me to make an appearance."

"Wait, I'm sorry I must stop you for a moment. I am a Crossroads Demon and Curse Maker am I not? How am I the key?"

"When you released that curse on the Cade line you bound yourself to them."

Wyatt paused and ran a hand through his hair as the words hit him. If his heart beat, it would have stopped then and there. *Eden is a Cade? Eden- Eden is Gemma. I'm dating my best friend's daughter?* Guilt found its way to his chest as he remembered the night Lennox had shared her past with him for the first time. When they finally became friends after years of anger at the other. She had said the curse was the entire reason she left Gemma to make the deal that eventually killed her.

He clenched his hands into fists, he felt his nails dig into his palms as he did his best to keep his composure. Everything in Wyatt froze as he blinked and stared at Xemos. Lennox had always spoken of Gemma but she had been human at the time. Neither of them had seemed to consider the possibility that somehow the girl would find her way here. The curse had never allowed more than one girl to be born at a time leaving no siblings. No other possibilities. This curse had haunted him almost as deeply as it had the family.

His eyes slammed shut, guilt grew in his stomach like lava. He often thought about the consequences of his drunken night, mothers lost loved ones, daughters lost mothers, and homes ripped apart from the seams. It had all stopped with Lennox but at a heavy price. How they managed to make it through after all that still to this day tugged at him.

He turned his gaze from Xemos and fixed his eyes on the wall of photos above his desk. He didn't understand how he didn't make the connection before as he looked at the photos from his and Eden's date and photos of Lennox he had taken over the years. The two had the same facial structure and bright purple eyes, the similarities had been distorted slightly but it was still there and now that he knew it was clear as day.

Lennox had always explained they had gone from a steel blue to purple after her devotion to the god in front of him and realized it must have passed with the magic Xemos offered. Wyatt crossed his arms, she had forgiven him a long time ago for his stupid mistake, and Aron... well he had helped Wyatt turn into the man he was today. He had shown him humanity, he had learned the ways of right and wrong, and how to ask for help and forgiveness. As hard as it was, he decided it was best to put this new information aside for the time being and finally moved to face Xemos once more. His face hardened as he asked the one question he needed an answer to.

"Where is she?"

"She's safe at the Miller Family home." Xemos answered.

Without another word, he turned and started to make his way to his door. However, before he got more than a few steps a hand grasped his shoulder and stopped him in his tracks. Wyatt's head snapped back in his direction and this time sparks snapped between his fingers as a warning. The look on Xemos's face hardened.

"You're forgetting my deal. I still have twenty-five minutes."

"You have as long as I stick around. I'm off to go bust down the Miller's door to make sure she's okay." Venom leaked into his voice.

"If you go you'll never know what I have to offer. Eloise is dangerous, Mr. Steele. I will strengthen your magic to help you get her back. You're going to need it." A smirk crossed Xemos's face.

"Anything to keep her safe."

The god let his hand slide from Wyatt's shoulder down to his shoulder blades the moment he agreed. His eyes turned the same purple as the girls as a sharp sensation dug against his back and into his skin. The feeling of electricity buzzed through his veins in retaliation as the glowing thread of magic within the demon was taken from him and stardust trailed its way the opposite direction and forced its way in.

Wyatt had no idea how much time had passed. Finally the fire in his back dimmed and the pressure of Xemos's hand slipped away.

A second of silence followed as the magic settled. Xemos took a few steps back and Wyatt straightened. It took an additional few minutes for him to catch his breath. His eyes met the man's gaze where there was a look of satisfaction. He said nothing as he stepped further away and extended his arm toward the door in dismissal. Wyatt followed his hand and peered over to the door. Quickly, he started to walk toward it again before he stopped with his hand on the doorknob.

"Something I never thought I'd say to you.... Thank you, Xemos."

"Don't mention it, Curse Bringer."

"Don't mention that... That's a part of me that I want to keep from the public eye Xemos, do you understand me? Eden Miller is to never know of the past. Only four people know and I tend to keep it that way. They respect my decision to forget that portion of my life." His eyes hardened, and his mind flashed back to a demon he had long forgotten and would often go out of his way to avoid.

With a nod of confirmation, Xemos faded away from his room in a swarm of moths that had disappeared in seconds. He turned the knob and swiftly made his way down and to the left of campus. Within a few minutes, he was pulling open the garage door and starting his motorcycle. With a loud roar, it thundered to life as he pulled away.

"Let's go Sydney, we've got a princess to save."

The curved back road to the Elder's homes circled him through the edge of the woodland and around to the last house on the street. Without hesitation, he pulled into the very small driveway that held a single black SUV. He put the kickstand down, took his helmet off, and made his way up to the Millers' front door. Nervously his hands went to his jacket and he adjusted it from the ride over.

He needed to remain calm, cool, and collected. However, a distracting burning sensation across his shoulder blades where the new markings of wings resided. He didn't need a mirror to see what the marking had taken the shape of, he had enough tattoos to catch the drift. The soreness reminded him of just how serious this whole situation between him and Eden had suddenly become and he had determined he wasn't going to walk away now. The last thing he needed was his emotions getting in the way. One hand formed a ball as it lifted to the wooden door, three hard knocks later Wyatt waited and ran the plan through his head

Get in.

Get to Eden.

Get out.

The door slowly opened as Wyatt sucked in a breath. Part of him had hoped that he would see Eden in front of him with an excuse for her silence. Instead, he was met by Elder Eloise Miller who peered at him with momentary surprise. Quickly it was exchanged for the neutral look she usually wore down the halls. With one hand behind the door and a keen eye on the slightly taller man, she looked like she hadn't slept in days. The smallest hint of whiskey emanated from her into the morning breeze.

"Wyatt, what a surprise to see you here… what is it you're after? I don't think you're in my classes…."

"Uh yeah, I am really sorry to bother you this early Elder Miller. I was actually here to check on Eden." His eyes moved just beyond her head and scanned as much of the room as he could see and started to strain his neck. "You see I haven't seen her in any of our classes we share, and she isn't picking up her phone."

"Eden went on a small road trip with her Uncle Alaric. They decided to go unplugged for a few days to clear their minds I suppose… Eden's idea. I'll have her call you when she's back?" She took a step to the door frame and brought the door closed. She moved to stand so only a sliver of space between the frame and the door showed while she kept a hand behind it.

He knew when he played with fire, especially after Eden's memory. Eloise had been proven to move to extremes fast however he wasn't going to be the one burning. In fact, he would burn this whole place to the ground if it meant seeing Eden safe. *I need to convince her to let me in.* Head tilted to the side as his eyes darkened and met those of the woman in the doorframe.

"You see Elder Miller, today is her birthday correct? The fourteenth? So I am sorry if I cannot wrap my head around the fact that she would leave on a day like today. One can't help but let the mind wander. I can't help but think something has happened to her."

"Of course, I know it's her birthday but this is what she wanted. I'm sorry Wyatt, but it was a last-minute decision for them to head out, they left behind all technology." She repeated herself, her voice mimicked the calm before the storm as she spat his name. A light tap sound behind the door filled the momentary silence.

He lifted his chin up but spoke again calmly but firmly. His words weren't completely true since she had just started to open up to him, however, they would sting. "With all due respect Eloise, I know your daughter maybe even better than you do."

"First, Mr. Steele. You may not be my student but you will address me as Elder Miller. Second, maybe you don't know my daughter as well as you thought you did. Sometimes she needs a little space from everyone, that would include you."

He paused for a moment and could feel his hands shake as his frustration turned to anger. Possible ways to get past Eloise and into the house flew through his mind again. He had already pissed the woman off and she was glaring daggers at him. *She probably thinks I have something to do with whatever happened. She's here. I know she's here.* There was only one option left.

"Oh, I know her quite well, Eloise." This was it, the next words had to make her drop her guard for only a moment. "I know how her eyes flutter when she is talking about something she loves."

Catch her attention.

Wyatt squared his shoulders and spoke again. "I know her love for plants because I have seen them myself. Specifically the bundle of lavender she had above her headboard."

Break her guard enough to slip through.

His eyes burned as the tension built in the back of his throat, "I know what she likes to wear to bed."

Breakthrough, get to Eden.

He took a few steps back and held his breath as the Elders' face went cherry red. Every muscle in his body tensed as he readied to move.

"I know her, it seems to me that it is you that has no idea what your daughter has been up to, that maybe it is you that truly has no idea who Eden is. But you're right Eloise, please forgive my assumptions. I'll look forward to that call from Eden."

Wyatt could feel the fire in Eloise's eyes as he shifted his weight from side to side. The Elder seemed to struggle to hold in her anger, both eyebrows rose and her visible hand shook. Her gaze darkened but she seemed to be in the middle of her own internal battle.

"Excuse me?" She demanded as her voice shook.

He didn't respond but fully turned his back to her. All he had to do was get her far enough away from the door. *Three.* The sound of her heels on the wooden porch grew louder as she stepped toward him and demanded an answer.

"Mister Steele!"

He took a few steps toward his motorcycle and still refused to answer as he stepped to the edge of the three steps. *Two.* The clicks stopped for a moment before the sound retreated toward the doorway again. *Shit, new tactic.* The door squeaked open as the angry Elder went back inside.

One.

Wyatt abandoned his previous plan and rushed back toward the entrance. Before the Elder could close the door he slapped a hand on the wood and pushed the door all the way open, Eloise aside with it. With a loud thud, it swung and hit the wall as he darted into the house. Metal clanged to the floor which caused him to turn to see a knife slide under the table beside the door. He swallowed the lump in his throat and returned to the task at hand. He stood in the middle of the foyer and he scanned the house for any sign of Eden. Besides the sound of the angry woman, not a single sound could be heard to give him any clues.

"Eden!" His voice came out cracked and hoarse as he called for her and stepped forward to go down a long hall of paintings of mysterious people.

"Who do you think you are?!" She screamed from where she lay on the floor where she started to frantically search for the knife.

"Where is she you monsters?" His eyes landed on the stairs.

"Us? Monsters!" She hollered as the blade scratched along the wooden floor when she found it.

Wyatt rushed for the stairs but barely had a hand on the rail before Eloise reached him. A wave of pain emanated from his head as she grasped a handful of his hair and pulled him backward into her. Without a center of balance she easily pushed him down onto his knees, his back against her thigh and a cold steel blade along his neck.

"Now where do you think you're going, demon?" Her voice came out shaken and thin, her mouth tight. She held him there and let the knife just press into his skin slightly, enough for him to feel the burn of the metal bite into his skin. "Don't you know running into someone's home is rude?"

He kept his gaze fixed on the stairs ahead. *She's there.. Get to Eden.* Wyatt tilted his chin down and leaned into the blade in challenge. "Do it, Eloise. Draw more suspicion to yourself and your family."

The blade suddenly slid out from under his chin. In a second, he felt the pressure on his back disappear only to be replaced by what felt like a foot shove him forward. The last thing he saw was the stairs in front of him rushing closer as the house blurred and faded into darkness.

There was nothing but darkness for what seemed like seconds as if he had merely blinked. The first thing he became aware of was the sound of objects as they were shuffled around followed by a soothing voice of Eden from what seemed right beside him. *You shouldn't have come.* His eyes flew open in excitement as he looked around for those mesmerizing gem-like eyes. Instead, he found himself in a darkened basement. Wyatt reached his hands up to rub his sore head until the sound of metal and an unusual heaviness on his wrists made him stop. His eyes darted over to find chains nailed into the base of the wall and floor which held him to the spot with only a foot of space to move.

The sound of a metal cabinet as it locked to his right caught his attention. Wyatt glanced over and saw Eloise Miller at a metal table over in the corner by the stairs with various tools and weapons laid out. His eyes fell on each, his chest tightened as he realized what was actually going on here as the woman had already rolled up her sleeves. As she talked on the phone with someone in what he assumed was an earpiece while his gaze fell on a familiar tattoo that traced the underside of her wrist. A compass with an "s" and dots within the curves. He had seen it over a few decades ago in a scuffle with hunters as he passed through Texas.

"No, Bastien, your housemate decided he needed to take matters into his own hands… No, he's not dead yet. Not unless I find out he had something to do with this. Go check on Eden and make sure he didn't bring anyone else to find her then come down here."

Wyatt watched as she started to pace, clearly lost in her thoughts. Eloise reached over, picked up a glass of whiskey on the rocks and quickly finished it off. He could see the stress written all over her face as she took out the ear piece and put her phone in a pocket on her weapons belt. The hunter pulled her glasses from her face momentarily and rubbed tired eyes and replaced them back on her face. *She's just as worried… What's happened to make Eloise so scared for her?*

For a second he had sympathy for her. They were both after the same thing, however, the chains around his wrists and images from his dream reminded him who she was. Who he just found out Eden was, though the memories had been enough to prove to him given the chance she wouldn't stay. He shook his head slightly as he rejected the thought that she was a willing part of this family. *She's not just a shit mother, the whole thing is a cult.*

"You are all Hunters." His statement hung in the air as Eloise turned to him.

"Very good, I'm glad you finally figured that out now that you're here. We are and now that we are all on the same page, I think it's time you and I have a chat."

With a sigh, the woman picked up a gun and knife from the table. A click reverberated along the walls and it was loaded. Wyatt watched her closely and followed her hand to a holster on her left hip. As she approached, her heels clicked with each purposeful step. Eloise stopped just out of reach of him and bent to his level where he could see the silent rage brew within her eyes as she peered over the top of her wire-rimmed glasses.

"Mr. Steele, you have made me do something I would have preferred not to. I don't know what you and my daughter have going on but I assure you I will get to the bottom of it. Though I am sure that it's an act, I can't have questions being asked." Her voice was calm, the same type of quiet before a battle broke out.

His eyes widened, narrowed and he smirked back at her. "You really don't know her then. I know an act when I see them. I've seen those walls you helped her build crumble slowly."

Before he could react her knife whisked right beside his ear. It hit the drywall behind him and stuck there. He didn't dare look away from the Elder as she stood once again and started to stalk toward him. Suddenly the sound of the door to the top of the stairs as it opened and shut made Wyatt panic. As footsteps made their way down seconds later he reached beside his head and he yanked the knife from the wall. As Bastien came into sight he threw it toward the new arrival before he had seen his friend. The man only stopped for a second to watch itself lodge into the wall again as he stood beside Eloise with a regretful look on his face and he avoided his friend's eyes.

"What the fuck, Wyatt?" Bastien gave him an incredulous look.

"Me? What the fuck yourself, Bas?" He asked as he shifted in his spot and filled the quiet with metal as it slid on the floor. "Look at me, you coward. You stand there, you face me like you have some real balls."

"This isn't the time you two." Eloise stopped them both and peered at who he thought was his friend. For the first time he took notice of how similar the two looked. "How is Eden?"

Wyatt leaned forward as this was something he wanted to know the answer to as well. Bastien shook his head to Eloise and ran a hand through his hair as he walked over to the large metal cabinet. The demon's stomach lurched as his thoughts ran wild with worry, until Bastien finally spoke again.

"Still asleep... The Mage left some potions to make sure she remained in good health until she wakes."

"Good, tell him to remain close by for when she does. There's no telling what happened and how she'll be."

The same frustration on Eloise's face earlier filled Wyatt. They also had no idea what happened to her and now he was trapped a few floors from her where he was utterly useless. His eyebrows came together as the two hunters continued to talk among each other as if he was nothing more than a decoration within the room.

"Where were you that night, Bastien? You and Eden were at the bar but she was delivered to our doorstep." She asked with frustration laced beneath her tone.

The man stopped for a moment but regained himself. "I was following someone suspicious outside."

"So suspicious that you left Eden alone long enough for her to be incapacitated and brought here?!" Eloise's voice boomed across the room.

"I know it's my fault, it's my job to keep her safe!"

"Yes it was, Barron... You better hope she wakes up soon, unharmed." Eloise took a step toward him with venom in her voice.

"She will."

"You know, I've kinda been around the block a few times. I might be able to help figure out what's going on."

Eloise's head snapped back to face him and her face twisted to mimic his. "You are not going anywhere near her."

"Don't you think maybe it's worth a shot?" Bastien countered.

"We have no idea who did this, for all we know he did and he's here to finish the job! It's not going to happen, brother."

"Brother? That's a pretty big age gap. I'm guessing Bastien was the oopsie?" Wyatt taunted them, unable to stop himself.

As he chuckled to himself Eloise turned on her heels and closed the distance in a matter of seconds. In quick succession, he saw her hand raise and felt a sting across his face. He was knocked sideways and saw stars. He looked up at her with an angry grimace, just in time to see the sickening darkness spread across Eloise's face.

"Eloise." Bastien stepped forward to intervene.

"No, if you can't deal with this, leave. If he's a threat to Eden, he's a threat to this family." She told him without a single glance away from Wyatt.

"I would never, I love her." The words he had never said to her slipped out before he could stop them.

"Love her? You're not capable of that." She told him as she walked over to the metal table and picked up a few things before she tucked them away in her belt. "I don't know why she has been spending so much time with a non-target but I assure you it is one-sided."

"I'm not so sure about that, the way she looks at me says different."

Wyatt attempted to use his new powers; he froze and suddenly found a block that prevented him from gripping the thread connected to his magic. His eyes widened as the danger of the situation became real. He was truly trapped. Most supernatural creatures who found themselves in The Salvamari chains wouldn't find their way out alive.

His thoughts drifted to the families of Hunters he was aware of. *Donovan, Belmore, Reyes, Holloway, Sullivan, Moore, and Miller. They hadn't even bothered to hide their last name, bold.* His heart sank as he remembered the dangerous reputation they had and were among the top families. Stories of their cruelty sent shivers down his spine each time he heard of them.

"Good, you know we are serious." Eloise's voice broke the quiet. "Now, tell me what did you do to Eden?"

Wyatt's mouth formed into a thin line and he spoke in a low voice. "Nothing. I'm trying to figure it out the same as you. I just want her to be okay."

"Lies. I know who you are, Steele. Your vanity is your downfall as you were easy enough to find information on... Tell me, Curse Bringer, why should I believe you had nothing to do with this given your binding to the Cade family?"

If he would have had a beating heart, it would have stopped then and there. The name of the old him he took so much pride in now felt like a ghost he couldn't banish. *She knows, fuck.* He frowned at the Elder, confused by her last statement and shifted slightly.

"I am not bound to anyone except Lucifer."

"You mean you don't know? I'm surprised to see you and Lennox are so close. It took most of the last few months to figure it out. Between the books you're featured in and the old grimoire of a witch that studied the curse with Lennox's grandmother. It put the puzzle together quite quickly. Every one of them had a marking, correct? The alchemy symbol for Steel?"

"As far as I was told, Eden doesn't have it. In any case, I still don't have a reason to hurt her. I would do anything to keep her safe."

"I. Don't. Believe. You." Eloise spat and turned away from him. Eloise continued a conversation with Bastien and the sound of a tea kettle calling from upstairs caught the attention of the two only momentarily.

"Look at me, damn it!" He growled.

They didn't. Left to his thoughts, he went over everything he could remember of the curse when he created it. *I was so drunk.* He cursed himself for his past self for being so stupid in the first place. A knot formed in his throat as he remembered when he tacked on the symbol at the end to mark the line's shoulder. At first he thought he had done it to make it easier to follow. Now, he realized he had bound himself to the victim as it was his personal sigil since his start as a curse creator. Lennox and Eden's faces filled his mind. Though she had no mark she was still a Cade. *If we are connected through this curse, are my feelings even real? Are hers? If they are even genuine.*

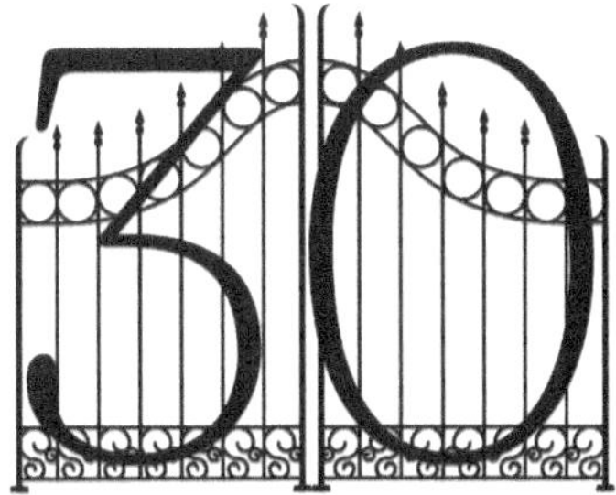

Eden

With a gasp for air, Eden sat upright and looked around even though most of the room was slightly fuzzy. She rubbed her eyes and strained them to try and focus on her surroundings. After her vision came into focus, she found herself in her bedroom at the Miller home. She gave herself a moment as each conversation and memory the devotee showed her replayed. Eden took in a deep breath as she stood roughly from the bed while her joints cracked slightly from the lack of use. The cold room sent a shiver through her body and she quickly grabbed a sweater and tugged it over her.

She glanced down to the bedside table where her phone sat on the charger which she figured Eloise had plugged. As the screen lit up she saw about five missed calls from Bastien, over ten from Wyatt followed by a long string of texts from him. Quickly, she slid the messages away as she planned out how she would explain her disappearance if her mother hadn't already.

She pulled up her conversation with Eloise, she hit the call button. However, there was no answer. With a frown, she decided to look around to see if anyone was home. *Someone has to be close by*. She pocketed her phone and going down the stairs she was met with a very still and quiet house. However, the lights were still on which signaled at least Bastien was here and found her way to the kitchen.

While she started some water for tea, Eden leaned against the counter. She ran a hand through her knotted hair and pulled it up and away from her neck to deal with later. *How am I going to explain this to Wyatt? Just when I thought I had all this figured out.* Her mind wandered to the look in his eyes as they sat in the late-night diner.

His eyes were lit up with excitement as he looked down at her. He stepped closer and wrapped an arm around her slowly and pulled her in. Her hands met with the coolness of the black leather jacket he seemed to always wear. "Don't worry, I won't let any hunters get you."

Lost in thought, she only broke from her daydreams when the loud scream of the kettle called. It quickly faded away as she removed it from the heat and the house fell into silence once more. That was until suddenly, the same voice from her memory drifted from somewhere in the house. She pushed off the counter and Eden looked around the kitchen worried her mind was now playing tricks on her due to the venom.

"Look at me, damn it!" His voice sounded more clear this time. Her eyes snapped to the basement door and her heart leapt into her throat.

For a second, every nerve in her body went numb. *He's here... No, no, no.* The pit in her stomach that had been there for weeks suddenly seemed to rip open wider than ever. The air in her lungs suspended for the next few seconds as the fear for his safety washed over her. A little voice in the back of her mind pushed through the realization that if he was here, he knew exactly who she and her family were. *He's not going to get out of there alive and you'll be a Heretic.* It taunted her as her hand drifted to her side for a weapon that wasn't there. *Could now be the time I have to truly make my choice?*

Fear gripped her which caused a lump to form in her throat. The image of Eloise stood in front of her with her hand wrapped around Eden's wrist filled her mind's eye. Her heart sped as she remembered the stories Bastien told her about the first Heretic. How after the Matriarch drew the magic from The Compass where a large letter 'H' appeared over it. Bastien also warned her the process wasn't exactly painless as the magic was forced out. Eden blinked the thoughts away as she heard more voices downstairs.

She dashed to the door and pulled it open. Eden took two steps at a time down the steep wooden stairs and found her worst nightmare looking back. Eloise and Bastien were by the table of weapons and tools while Wyatt was chained to the wall. All of them looked at her with various degrees of shock and relief across their faces. Her heart broke as her gaze fell to Wyatt for only a mere second, the very thing she warned Bastien of was now reality. *There's no way to hide now.* As she went down the last step she saw Wyatt smile at her in the classic fashion he always did.

"I'm here to save the princess!" He called to her, lightheartedly.

"Do you ever stop talking?" Eloise snapped at him and turned back to her. She walked over with her arms open. "Eden, my dear. I've been worried sick. How did you ever get in that state?”

Eden shook her head and took a step back from a now sur-prised-looking Eloise. The possibilities of how this could end ran through her head slowly and got worse with every scenario. If Eloise knew she had genuine feelings towards the man she knew he wouldn’t walk out of here. *Maybe Eloise doesn’t know we are seeing each other.* Eden procrastinated another glance at Wyatt as she positioned herself be-tween her family and the demon she had grown much too fond of. She couldn’t look at him. Not yet, she couldn’t see the look of betrayal he must be feeling after this discovery. She wouldn’t give her true feelings away, not yet.

“It was vampire venom.” She told them looking right at her uncle who looked back at her with relief and sympathy.

Her mother frowned at her as she stepped to block Wyatt. “Eden, why don’t you join us?”

“I’m okay right here,” she lifted her chin slightly and shifted her feet to stand her ground.

“That wasn’t a request. Come here, Eden.”

“Not until I know why you two have Wyatt Steele chained up in our basement.”

“Why would you care?” Her eyebrows rose over the rim of her glasses.

Eloise stood a little straighter and closed the distance between them. Her heels clicked on the floor and she stood just half a head taller as she peered down through her glasses darkly. It was now Eden could see the dark circles hidden behind the frames, she hadn’t slept. Her hair was tied into a braid that had half fallen out and she smelled of whiskey. *This is worse than I thought.* She cursed internally for not grabbing her knife from her room before she came down as she had no way to get to the cabinet.

"Your little friend," she accentuated the word. "Seemed a little more concerned for your safety than the others. All but busting down the front door."

"I didn't bust it down, I slipped by you," Wyatt interjected.

"I am going to cut out your tongue if you don't learn when to be quiet!" Eloise snapped.

Eden's throat tightened, of course, he wouldn't just sit there and wait to hear from her. From experience, she had learned he wasn't the type. Eden took another step back closer to Wyatt and Eloise followed now with a hand out to her unrelenting pull back to the family.

"This is your last chance to move past this with no questions asked." Her mother almost whispered to her with wide eyes. It was a threat.

"I can't do that." She told her in the same hushed voice. "I know he didn't go about this in the smartest way. I know Wyatt, he had good intentions."

"Are you defending this disgusting creature?"

"He may be a demon, but he has hurt no one."

"Hurt no one? Oh, dear Eden, this is my fault. I know you've been looking into Lennox but I didn't think you'd gotten sucked in. I saw your notebook on your desk when I brought you to your room. There are things I should have told you a few weeks ago when I connected the dots myself. Mister Steele here is the very reason you were left in that orphanage. Lennox left you because he was the one who created that curse that was supposed to pass to you next."

Slowly, Eden turned to face him. Her eyes drifted to the demon for a few seconds before she finally met his gaze. Wyatt's previous demeanor shifted, regret reflected in his eyes. The world stopped as Eloise's words weighed down the room. Eden felt her feet carry her a few steps toward him as emotions bubbled beneath the surface. The tips of her ears burned with the frustration of the thought she had been tricked by him. As she took notice of his busted lip as they parted as he started to speak.

"Eden, I- There's nothing I can say that changes what I did over a century ago. I will spend the rest of my time making up for it, I am not that person anymore. If I was, you would have never spoken to me past hello."

"How long have you known I was a Cade?" Her voice came out just barely more than a whisper.

"I just found out while I was down here."

"If I find out you're lying-"

"I'm not. The only thing I lied about was my past, as did you." He pointed out. "I told you I would show you that demons were different than what you thought. I intend to keep that promise if you'll let me. We just had to promise, no more lies."

A pang of guilt sank into the ever growing pit inside her. There was no way to deny he was being genuine. As hard as it was for her to believe in this moment, it was in his voice. Just as it always was, only this time all their secrets were out. As his voice revealed his honesty, she felt herself slowly calm and returned to the moment.

"Enough Eden, are you really going to let this creature convince you of this? I didn't raise you to be so naive." Eloise's voice drifted from behind her.

"At first he was a means to an end." She turned to face her mother. Strangely now that everything was out in the open she felt like a weight was lifted and the truth started to spill out. "A way to get close to Lennox and Aron... But then even after I pushed him away he kept coming back. Somehow, it's endearing. For once someone was on my side and for the most part I could depend on him."

"This isn't what the Miller family does. Do you want to end up like your great-great-grandfather?"

Eden opened her mouth to retort but quickly closed it as she realized she was about to follow right in the same path. She knew the story of the beautiful siren who had seduced him as easily as taking candy from a baby. Though Wyatt was no siren, he lured her in the same way. She moved to the ground, she saw Eloise's feet move past her. Her attention went to keep an eye on her mother, her eyes landed back on the one person she saw while she was in that dream world.

Wordlessly, his eyes pleaded with her. Though she had found out so many things about his past over the last few days, she couldn't let go of all the moments they had shared over the last few months. He had shown himself to be someone good, someone she could see herself happy beside. Her hand started to reach out to him before his eyes darted up at Eloise.

The woman bent down to him, her hand reached for the knife in her pocket. She pressed the metal to his cheek and peered up at Eden with a cruel smile. Eden knew the look and moved forward quickly, however wasn't fast enough to stop her from drawing a line across the side of his face with the blade. Wyatt sucked in a sharp breath as Eden swiftly bent down and grabbed Eloise's wrist. Carefully, she pulled it away from him and twisted her body once more between the two.

Eloise, who had been on the balls of her feet, was forced backward and stood as Eden pulled at her magic. Momentarily she had forgotten her powers would be stronger than what it had been. What was meant to be a tight grip with some ice behind it to make it harder for Eloise to lash out for a few seconds suddenly turned much colder. She forced her mother to take two steps back as her hand started to turn blue.

Eden watched as within a few moments it quickly shifted deeper and deeper purple. The air in the basement dropped a number of degrees and ice formed on her mothers' skin. Eloise let out a gasp followed by a small sound of pain The two women eyed their hands before their eyes locked. Her mother's eyes were narrowed at her and goosebumps formed on her arms as she paused.

"You've made your choice, don't back down now." Eloise's voice cracked ever so slightly.

In a fluid motion, her left hand shifted the knife around and away from Eden as she gripped her wrist tightly in return. The tips of her finger pressed into the center, Eden was forced to release. She used the force from her bottom arm and Eloise pushed their arms up which forced Eden to twist to face Bastien. Using her strength to push her forward, Eden stumbled and a pair of arms caught her which caused her eyes to shoot up to him.

"I'm sorry," He whispered as he helped her to stand.

"Hold her back! I won't have any more interference!" Eloise demanded.

Eden felt Bastien's hand on her arm and the sound of metal clanging together caught her attention. She looked over to Wyatt who looked at her with fear written in his face and as he attempted to stand. However, the metal sounded closer and now came from behind her. The grip on her arm vanished and something cold was clamped around both wrists behind her back. She craned her neck to see, she found one of the portable chains they kept around the basement.

She gritted her teeth and felt the magic-blocking properties they had charmed take hold. Her magic was beyond an invisible wall, just beyond reach of that blue thread. Eden glared at her Uncle and she took a step toward him and the weapon table. He shifted himself to block her path and shook his head and put both hands on either side of her. He bent down slightly, he caught her eyes seriously for the first time in years.

"This is for your own safety. If you want to help him you won't make this worse."

"That's easy for you to say," She hissed and spoke only loud enough for him to hear. "If it was Corvus in those chains you'd be just as scared as I am."

"I know…"

"You are the monsters and you can't even see it," Wyatt seethed from behind them which drew her eyes back to him. "You'd rather deal with me than make sure she's okay after what just happened!"

"I will have time once I deal with the intruder that seemed so anxious to get to her."

A loud smack followed his words which caused her to flinch and spin around. With a quick flash, the knife was sunk into his leg and dragged down an inch. A fire burned within her irises as Eloise did so and watched Wyatt's face contorted with pain. His whole body shook as he let out a loud scream. Eden's body quivered with anger, her mother was after information at any cost now and refused to listen to her. She stepped forward once more but was forced back when Bastien grabbed the chains and pulled.

"Do you truly believe that you are what's best for her? Not only are you a demon and she's raised to kill your kind but look at the pain you've already brought her. Though, I guess I have you to thank for bringing her to me." Eloise gripped his shoulder and pushed his back against the wall. "Even if I approve of this vile charade, how long will it be until you revert back to your natural ways? Demons. Don't. Change. Mister Steele. I think we show these two how easy that switch is, yes?"

Before he could attempt to move away, Eloise gripped the hilt of the knife and yanked it from his leg. Wyatt yelled out once more, body slumped forward as he gripped his leg. Blood started to pool around the chains, the sight sent a new wave of fear over her. *He can't die, he has no dagger available to us at least.* She had to remind herself as her eyes followed each tool in her mother's belt while she clung to the belief that she didn't have the time to make a Demon Dagger.

Wyatt pulled himself upright and locked eyes with her. Her breath caught in her chest for a second and her gaze softened for a second. In a moment of understanding, he didn't move as Eloise's grip closed around the chain on the right side and lifted it and his hand from the ground. *Fight back.* She begged him internally in hopes he could read her eyes. Eden's brows tilted down slightly to show her concern for him while Eloise was distracted. With another flash of silver, the blade was drawn across the top of his hand through the rose that resided there. He grimaced but never wavered and refused to give in to Eloise's wishes.

"A tough guy huh? Good to know." She reached down and twisted his now bloody hand until a snap was heard.

Wyatt yelled but didn't lash out. The demon forced his hand away from her, she let go and his eyes drifted to the side and he kept an even expression. Though the pain he felt was clear in his face this caused Eloise's jaw to clench. She became visibly annoyed and stabbed the knife back into him, this time his shoulder blade.

"Be useful and hold this, why don't you?" The Matriarch stood to her full height. Without turning to face Eden, she directed her next question behind her. "My dear daughter, how could you let yourself be fooled by this thing? Are you really going to throw yourself at the first sign of love?"

"I-" Eden stopped looking down to hide the hurt. The comment wasn't out of character for her mother but nevertheless it stung.

Eden could feel Wyatt's eyes on her as her mother berated her again.

The lump in her throat grew with every word. She started into her usual speech on how she always imagined her having this wonderful life as the top Matarich of the hunter families. Eden didn't dare look Eloise in the eyes and she felt the grip on her arm return as Bastien squeezed slightly. Embarrassment filled her as Wyatt heard everything, however his grip helped to keep her composure as the edges of her vision tainted itself red.

"This boy has made you soft. Weeks ago you were becoming a Matriarch this family could be proud of. Now look at you, all of this? I'm so disapp- Oh? I see how it is."

The sound of metal as it fell to the floor and heels click away made Eden finally peer up to her mother. Eloise closed the distance and came over to her and Bastien with a hand out. The Matriarch looked past Eden and spoke directly to Bastien.

"Give me the chains."

"Eloise- What are you doing?" He questioned as he pulled Eden closer to him.

"What I said earlier still stands... If you can't handle it- Get out. This is your last chance." She told him as her eyebrow rose.

He watched her closely but allowed her to take the other side of the chains. Eloise turned back to Wyatt and pulled Eden with her over to the hooks they installed along the bottom of the wall. As Eden realized where they were going, her eyes went wide. Never had another Miller been chained up in the basement, she knew Eloise was mad but this? Her nerves lit like wildfire as Eloise pulled the chains around the hook far enough she or Wyatt wouldn't be able to reach each other. Internally, she attempted to grip the blue thread but her hands slipped off. Eloise took a step back, her gaze unreadable as she looked between the two.

"You wanted to be beside him- You are." She continued to move back until she stood between them just out of reach. "Unless you want to remain where you belong."

"I am a Miller, but I don't agree with these old beliefs. There's more to these creatures than we know and it's time we open our minds."

"Open our minds!" Eloise took a step toward Eden so they were a few inches apart. "How many times has one of them almost killed one of us? How many lives do they have to destroy for you to see it, Eden? I've spent all these years trying to show you."

Wyatt spoke up, "There's no one on Earth that hasn't made a bad decision."

"A human's bad decision doesn't typically get people killed, or cursed." Eloise shot back as memories from her poisoned sleep flitted through Eden's mind.

"But it can." Eden challenged.

"Are you going to hunt down every murderer?" Wyatt asked.

"Once we rid this world of your kind, I will." Eloise hissed as her hand went to her weapons belt.

The room went silent as Eloise glared at them. Bastien stepped to the side and stood a few feet from where Eden was chained, ready to intervene. Her heart raced and her eyes shot to the dagger Eloise had her hand over. Her hands shook slightly in the cuffs as she returned her attention to her mother.

"Why can't you just let me make my own decisions?"

"Because, they have already been made. It is your twenty-second birthday today, you're due to meet the suitors over the next few weeks."

Her chest tightened at the reminder of The Hunter Arrangement. "Mother, I have no interest in any prospects you and Stacey have cho-sen."

"Eden, Holden is a wonderful option unlike Mister Steele here. I may be biased but he is my personal pick." Eloise's demeanor shifted as she became distracted by the new topic.

"Prospects?" Wyatt's question hung in the air.

"I'm not surprised she didn't tell you yet. I told you there was no way this would go anywhere past its little phase. She's going to be married this time next year."

"Little Viper, please tell me she's lying." His voice broke slightly.

The sound of his nickname for her caused her body to go rigid. She saw him look at her from the corner of her eyes. Guilt ate at her just as it did whenever the topic came up among the family. The sound of the chains as he shifted in his spot filled her ears as he attempted to catch her attention.

"Look at me, please." His tone turned desperate as he pleaded with her.

She couldn't speak as her mind raced to find the right way to explain.

"Eden, I need you to talk to me. No more of this second-hand bullshit. Are you engaged?"

"No, not yet..." She managed to choke out.

"Not yet? So you plan to be?" His voice came out harsher than she was used to. "I need to hear this from you."

"It's not really by choice... As next in line for the Matriarch position within the family, if I didn't find a suitable partner by my twenty-second birthday a marriage would be arranged so the families could continue."

"You're more than someone's prized mare, Eden." His voice broke again. "I'm right here, I'm never going anywhere." He interrupted.

"A suitable partner," Eloise reiterated to him.

"When I get out of these chains, I will watch the life leave your eyes."

His anger turned toward Eloise for a moment before he peered back to her.

"No, you won't... If Eloise dies I have to step up..." Eden breathed as her stomach lurched at the mental image of Wyatt over her dead mother. "I've wanted to tell you everything for weeks, Wyatt but could I have?"

His hardened expression shifted into a mix of defeat and pain as he let out a sigh. Wyatt shook his head at the ground before he lifted his eyes to her once more. He seemed to fight with himself as her eyes softened, his eyes traced every detail of her face.

"Yes, you could have. I would have stood beside you and helped you if you wanted to escape... Walk away from this. I've just seen firsthand how your mother treats you. Look at where you're at. Is this really the life you want to live?"

"She can't walk away, if she does the family line dies out. You owe that to the family after everything we've given you. After this little re-bellion." Eloise spoke up once more slowly and took a few steps toward her.

"Eden, you are more than a vessel for the next generation." He lifted an eyebrow, a different kind of desperation hidden in his voice now. "I've seen that for myself." "For once we can agree Mister Steele. She is much more and will be even while fulfilling the duties of the position."

The sound of Eloise's heels approached and Eden's gaze was pulled away from Wyatt. A hand brushed a strand of hair from her face as she looked into the earth brown pits of her mother's eyes. The previous rage had settled as she narrowed in on Eden.

"You can still move forward from this. You don't have to let this mistake haunt you. It will be a lot harder among The Salvamari if this gets out... You know your grandfather doesn't know how to keep his mouth shut."

"I still have a year until my duties are enacted. Until then you will let Wyatt and I go or I will fight my way out and stay out." Eden's tone darkened in response to her attempt at manipulation.

The threat hung in the air heavier than anything that had been said within the walls of the basement. Although it had come down to a choice sooner or later, she was desperate to keep both sides of her life for as long as she could. Unable to let go of either she glanced at Wyatt who let the smallest smile creep onto his face.

"You wouldn't walk away from this family." Eloise shook her head.

"Wouldn't I? Do you really want to test where I stand after you've just told him everything?"

Her mother paused for a moment and seemed to debate her question. She drew in a long breath and Eden continued to stare daggers between each other waiting for the other to break first. This was now a battle of wills and she was determined to win. Slowly, Eloise walked over and pulled out a key from her belt. With a click, the chains were unlocked.

"Your love for him will lead to your death, just as it did for Roy."

Eden opened the front door for Wyatt and let him step out first. For a moment she paused and looked over her shoulder to make sure they weren't followed. When she saw no one behind them she turned to face the grounds. The sun was on its way down as they stepped onto the grass outside the Miller home. They walked slowly down the street and Wyatt struggled a little with the cut on his leg. Eden pulled the jacket she wore off and used it to cover the blood that continued to stain his pants from the upper thigh of his jeans. Goosebumps formed as cool winter air danced across her arms followed by a small shiver.

She quickly tied the sleeves around his waist and felt his stormy eyes on her. As she knotted it she let a curtain of long hair hide her face until a hand gently placed itself on her arm. She froze for a second before she put her own hand over top and led his arm around her waist so they would look like they were on a date. His weight shifted against her ever so slightly and she started to move them forward.

"Eden."

The sound of her name sent a wave of guilt over her. She kept her eyes low, still attempting to muster the courage to meet his eyes. "Not here, we can talk when we get back to Kappa. It's almost curfew and we can get in much easier if we make it there in time."

"I'll be okay, I just need to be patched up... Are you okay?" His free hand reached over and tilted her head up to him as they walked.

She finally met his gaze which caused her to stop for a second. She had expected to see anger and frustration linger there, instead, she found confusion, concern, and guilt. The worry on her face faded and the tightness she had felt since she awoke unraveled. A strange laugh escaped her as she looked at him incredulously.

"You were used as a knife block today and you're worried about me?"

"Little Viper, you've been comatose the last five days and your mother had you chained up inside your home. I've been through worse."

"How do you always manage that?"

"Manage what?" He questioned and frowned slightly.

"Make everything seem like it's going to be okay."

"Because it will be," He promised.

Minutes before curfew the two of them made their way through the front door of Kappa Theta. She glanced around and breathed a sigh of relief at the empty room. Eden helped him to the stairs and they made it a few steps before a voice stopped them in their tracks. She shifted closer to him, gently pressed her leg against his and used it to cover any red stains. Her hand slid to the spot on his shoulder blade that now had a hole in the leather jacket.

"Well hey, there love birds! Spending the night Miller?" Aron asked as she craned her neck to see him standing in the entrance hall getting ready to go outside.

"Couldn't resist the invitation." She attempted to be casual.

"I'll see you in the morning, you two." He smirked and slipped out.

Finally, they walked into Wyatt's room where she helped him over to the bed. Eden gently lifted his arm back over her head and lowered him down. From the edge of the bed, she helped him pull off the jacket she had tied around his waist and the now ruined leather one. She swallowed the knot that tied itself in her throat as she caught a glimpse of each cut and stab wound and she turned away to find a place to put them.

"You're a hunter…" It was no question but a shocked statement now that they were finally safe.

"Yes, and you're the reason Lennox was cursed and I was left. Why I'm a Miller."

Silence fell between them for a few seconds before she turned to face him, still with the stained clothing. They were both hiding from their lives and now it slapped them both in the face at the same time. Nothing was left but bare bones to pick up. "I am and I have questions just as you probably do. Promise me, no more lies?"

"No more lies, from either of us," She agreed as he watched her face.

Wyatt patted the bed beside him to ask her to join him. With little hesitation, she approached and took a seat as his hand rested on her knee. As he spoke, he recounted a dream he had about a training session that had taken place over ten years ago. He described the scene as Eloise had hit a younger Eden and Bastien defended her.

"It was more than a dream… It was like a memory, have things always been like this? I know the Miller's have a cruel reputation but I didn't think it included family members."

"Eloise would never actually hurt me like a supernatural creature. But yes, training can get a little intense."

"I'm sorry that's how you grew up." His gaze drifted away from her and moved down. "That curse was never intended to leave my workroom."

"Then why did it?"

He sighed deeply before he looked back to her, regret clear on his face. "I was drunk and bored… To be honest I almost didn't send it away but then it got the better of me. I wanted to know who it would choose."

Eden fell silent once more as she took in his words. From her dreams this past week and this discovery it seemed she finally saw everything he was hiding. She let her hand fall on top of his, she held the other over the long cut on his leg. She pulled at the blue thread and allowed the magic to mend the injury and moved her hand to his shoulder blade before she repeated it. She let her eyes drift to him and scan him over, exhaustion clear in his face.

"I just need to know. Why does everyone around the victim die?" She asked almost not wanting to know the answer.

"It was a side effect of the ingredients I used, I've come to believe."

"Do you remember them? Maybe I could help figure out where it came from." She offered.

"I'm sorry, Little Viper. I don't remember them and the list is still locked away in my desk in hell." He yawned and turned her hand in his while he weaved his fingers through hers. "I have to know… Are you the one responsible for Felix and Rue?"

"No, that was Eloise-" Eden lied and internally cursed herself for it. As she looked into his eyes she knew if she told him the truth he would never forgive her. *One more lie.*

Wyatt nodded and squeezed her hand lightly. His eyes scanned her face and his lids drifted down. Though he was somehow still awake, he was pale from blood loss. Eden leaned her head down and she slowly placed it on his shoulder. Her gaze fixed on the wall of photos he had above his desk.

"I'm not interested in the arrangement my family has made." She started quietly.

"It's okay, that's tomorrow's conversation. That and any more questions can wait. You look exhausted."

"Me? Wyatt, I'm fine." *Lie number two.*

"You're not, but that's okay… We both need some rest, do you want to borrow a shirt and sweats?"

Wyatt stood after he released her hand, he pulled off the ruined shirt and walked over to his wardrobe. As he revealed once again an untouched torso, he looked at himself in the mirror for a moment at the dried blood on his skin. Mesmerized for a moment, she noticed the new-looking silver scars tracing into the shape of wings across his shoulder blades and a long black ink spine tattoo of the moon phases. Her eyes moved back to his reflection where she saw him smirk back at her. A hot blush crept into her face as she was caught staring. Quickly she looked away and down at her hands she heard a few drawers open and close.

"It's okay to look." His voice caused her to do just that. He had two sets of clothes and a small box wrapped in purple. "It's still your birth-day."

Her eyes widened for a moment, "You didn't have to get me any-thing."

"I wanted to Viper." He smiled softly at her as he placed a set of clothes and the box beside her.

Reaching down she picked it up and carefully undid his perfect wrap job. Eden pulled the paper away and she found a small blue velvet box. Confused, she opened the lid and was met with a thin bracelet with a single charm soldered to it.

"A Nazar bracelet," She breathed as she ran her fingertips along the blue sapphires and diamonds.

"To protect you when I can't be there. My time as a curse creator has made me believe in this stuff." He admitted as his jaw tightened at the title.

"Thank you, Copperhead. It's beautiful." She couldn't help the gen-uine smile that formed on her lips.

Wyatt knelt down in front of her and took the box while he pulled the bracelet out. Easily, he fastened it around her wrist, his touch was light as a feather across her skin. His head tilted up to her and for a moment, everything they had just been through was pushed to the side. Her heart skipped a beat as she realized he was only inches away. Before she could say anything he stood once again and handed her the box back.

"I'm glad you like it. I'm going to take a shower, if you want you can join?" He offered with a laugh.

"Nice try." Eden shook her head. "I'll go after you."

"Suit yourself. Don't get into too much trouble." He nodded and winked as he left the room.

"No promises," She called after him.

Once he was gone, she let out a long breath, relieved to have a moment alone. Eden fell backward on the bed and peered at the bracelet now on her wrist. A feeling of comfort washed over her as she realized the blankets smelled just like the cologne he wore.

The smell of old books filled the air as it did each time she was here. Eden had become so accustomed to it that she didn't take much notice of it anymore. With her back against the cool stone bay window, she had tucked herself away in the corner of the library. She tilted the book closer to her face as her reading glasses slowly slid down her nose unnoticed as the candle in front of her that flickered every time someone walked by. Frozen rain pattered against the window and echoed in the quiet library.

Eden read the same words over and over while her mind circled back to the events of yesterday. Every word her mother, who she had avoided since she entered the building this morning, had said. There was no way to go back, she knew everything and so did Wyatt. The morning had been filled with awkward questions and tender moments of forgiveness, though the lie she had told him continued to eat at her. *One lie doesn't eat away as fast as ten.*

It was for the best while they figured things out and if she truly left the family there wouldn't be a way for him to find out the truth. The chances of that were slim at the moment, giving her time to figure out how to tell him when it came down to it. Briefly, she wondered if any of The Salvamari knew what had happened already. Word always seemed to travel so fast around the families and this time would be no different. Would the suitors her mother and grandmother choose drop out now? Was she someone they would even want to be around after they heard about her fling with a demon? *Am I damaged goods now?*

The question reverberated around her brain. She had always felt some sort of damage compared to the others in the family, but now? Of course, she was. It had always been as if something about her didn't quite fit in the puzzle that was the Miller family. Eden had always wondered if it was because she was adopted the feeling only amplified by her now undeniable draw to him. *Do I love him because he's what Lennox became? No, it can't be. He's nothing like her. Respectful, kind, and aware. But If I choose him one day I will end up just like him... Like **her**.* She flinched at the thought she scolded herself internally. *Like a moth drawn to a flame*

Eden refused to believe she would ever end up like Lennox as her grip tightened on the book in her hands. Her phone vibrated in her pocket and quickly broke her from her thoughts. With a glance to her wrist, she looked at the message that popped up.

Bastien Miller-
Chase and Brier are here, Eloise would still like you
to stick with the schedule of the arrangement. I'm
so sorry, Eden. You were right, I would have done
anything to get him out of there. I hope you can
forgive me. No matter what happens, we are still
family, you and I.
-Sent 8:47 am

Eden Miller-
You can tell Eloise that I will still follow it as long as
she leaves Wyatt alone. You owe him an apology for
not letting me stop her. I don't like you much right
now, but I forgive you.
-Sent 8:49 am

That will take care of Eloise telling him anything.

Bastien Miller-
I'm already working on that- I'll see you at home for
the meeting. It'll be okay.
-Sent 8:53 am

Shit, of course, the election meeting today. Today was the day she would
be presented with all three approved suitors and be able to reject one
more. The sound of footsteps got closer which forced her to shove her
phone back in her pocket and lift the book to her face. She strained to
hear, Eden could make out two different paces as they stopped just on
the other side of her reading bench. She glanced over the top of her
book and she only saw the cast iron spiral staircase which went up to
the second floor that kept her hidden. Slowly, she shifted the book in
her hands and reached into her sleeve for the knife which resided there.

"Remi, you need to tell me what's been going on, you've been looking over your shoulder for a week now. Are you in some sort of trouble? Because if you are, Fang and I can figure it out with you. You aren't alone anymore." The voice of Coyote drifted over to Eden.

"I know I'm not... It has to deal with-" Her next words came out jumbled and incomprehensible.

There was a momentary pause between the siblings. "It's more than whatever that is. You did something, I can see it in your eyes. What did you do?"

"I didn't-"

"Don't lie to me. If you did and it affects our investigation people are going to start looking at you. I may know you have nothing to do with the murders but people are starting to point fingers in places they shouldn't. But you did something because you know something."

Eden heard Remi pause followed by a sigh. "I... I bribed Bryer at Crossroads to put Eden Miller under with his venom."

Every muscle within Eden screamed to move as the grip on the hilt of her knife tightened. With her heart thudding in her ears, her blood boiled as she sat straighter. She pressed her back into the wood behind her to force herself to remain in her spot.

"You could have killed her." He snapped in hushed shock. "Vampire venom reacts differently with everyone. I need you to promise me you won't make any more attempts on the Millers while we keep looking into them."

"You know I'm not the type to sit here and do nothing... I can't promise much more than that, I won't cause any more trouble that would interfere with what you are doing" She stopped as more words started to tumble out.

"Just try not to cause too much trouble whatever you do. I know better than to try and stop you completely." He let out a chuckle.

Suddenly the man came halfway into her view and leaned against the iron stairs. In the same moment Eden brought the book back up to her face and hid the knife inside the pages she was open to. *Don't look over.* As much as she wanted to, she could make this situation a lot worse. The desire to lash out crept ever closer to the surface as she stewed on the information. *She could have killed me...*

"Let's get back to Andy." She heard the iron creek a little at the tall werewolf's weight and his footsteps started to recede.

She stood in the kitchen with her hands wrapped around a mug. Eden could hear the footsteps of her family recede into the meeting room. Every hair on her body stood on edge as their low voices drifted into the room. Her stomach turned over and over and she knew Eloise had told Stacey by now which meant the rest of the family knew about yesterday's events.

She glanced over to the door of the basement where she had been chained up just over twenty-four hours ago. Her mother's words haunted her the night before and throughout the day. *She can't walk away, if she does the family line dies out. You owe that to the family after everything we've given you.* The sound of her name caused Eloise's voice to fade away.

When she looked up she was met with a more mature version of the Chase she had known growing up. With just over a year since she had seen him at the last annual Salvamarai Conclave. She noticed a few new scars across his arms. With angular, hollow cheekbones and a squared jaw, his clearwater eyes looked down at her from a few feet away.

"Baron Donovan, glad to see you arrived safely." Eden forced a smile and put down her untouched tea as he made his way over.

With a quick side hug, he looked down at her. "How is it possible you've found a way to look more stunning than usual?"

"Already trying to get on my good side?" She raised an eyebrow at him, only half joking.

"Depends, is it working?"

"You wish," She smirked up at him as he nudged her.

"I am hoping, but there is something I'd like to discuss with you about some recent events Stacey told me when I got here." His voice dropped slightly and a serious look appeared on his face. *Damnit...* "Something about you with a demon and needing to pull you away from him?"

He was always straight to the point, honest with her out of respect. She didn't move for a few seconds, Eden tried to find the best way to quickly brush off the question. There was no reason to tell a suitor anything about Wyatt. The thought of one of them with knowledge of his identity sent a wave of fear over her. *At least they have no idea who he is.*

"Are you coming?" Bastien appeared from around the corner at the perfect moment. "Oh, Chase, you found her. Do you mind if I take Eden for a bit?"

"Of course, Baron Miller. I'll be upstairs until the meeting begins."

He reached out and unexpectedly took her hand. Eden flinched a little and met his icy gaze but didn't pull away. A smile drifted to his lips just as he let go and made his way from the room. She sighed and peered at the mug she put down. Her eyes stayed on it for a second realizing she hadn't touched it.

"Do I have a choice?"

"You do, you're just not ready to make it." His hand found her shoulder and squeezed lightly. She took a step forward, she walked out from under his hand as her skin crawled slightly as Wyatt's screams played in her mind on repeat. *I wish people would stop touching me.*

With the motion, he turned and started to walk down the hall of portraits. She followed him into the meeting room, the last to join the table once again on the right of Eloise. Eden kept her line of sight ahead, she refused to meet the Matriarch's face. She could feel every eye on her, Richard especially as he glared disgustedly at her from beside Arthur, Alaric, and Bastien. Eloise cleared her throat and made everyone turn to her, all except Eden who continued to look forward.

"As we all know yesterday was Eden's twenty-second birthday... My dear, you do not have a suitable partner, and as is custom four suitors have been selected."

"A suitable partner... Though, her choice to go messing around with a demon should have made her a Heretic last night." Richard lifted a glass of whiskey to his lips.

"Richard," Stacey hissed disapprovingly.

"Do you want this family to die off? Bastien isn't having any kids any time soon." Eloise snapped at him.

"Why? You could just replace her with a new orphan."

Her hands shook as they balled into fists, narrowed eyes darted up to meet Richard's gaze. The repercussions of her actions now slapped her in the face in front of the whole family. Bastien reached toward his belt and looked just as upset as she felt. However, before either of them moved, a knife was stabbed into the wooden table. This caused her attention to be drawn to Eloise's now bright red face and Alaric to jump. Eloise stood from her chair, leaned forward and stared him down just as she had done the night before to Wyatt.

"I will not hear such things. Since you can't seem to keep your opinion to yourself, get out of my sight."

"Fine, don't come to me when she betrays us and we are left with nothing."

He picked up his whiskey glass and stormed out of the room without much more fuss. Eloise returned to her seat but remained on her feet as she scanned each face.

"Now then, as my choices for suitors, I have selected Heir Holden Holloway and Heir Hunt Belmore. As for Stacey, she has selected Baron's Chase and Brier Donovan. You had informed us through Baron Bastien Miller that you rejected Hunt Belmore, is that correct?" The Matriarch turned to her daughter and finally caught her eyes.

"Yes, I reject Heir Hunt Belmore."

"At this time you can eliminate one other if you so desire."

"I choose to reject Baron Brier Donovan." She kept her words short.

"Fine then, tomorrow you and Chase will spend the day getting to know each other, and later Holden."

Eden nodded and caught the gaze of Stacey who looked back at her with disappointment. However, she still spoke of her choice. "Chase is perfect. He is ineligible to become the head of his family since they are like us. He would stand beside you without trying to overshadow you."

"Holden comes from the top of the Patriarchal line within The Salvamari. It's the perfect way to bring us back to the top." Eloise shot a look at Stacey.

Tension within the room seemed to weigh heavier than ever before. She knew the two wanted to sell her a dream she didn't have anymore. As long as Eden sat in her seat beside Eloise, they seemed to hold out hope. However, desperation was in both of their voices, only to be heard by those truly listening.

"I have a month till I pick, until then I will remain neutral." Eden broke the silence.

"As you should. Now, onto the next order of business. With Daemonium Pugionem created by Eden, we are ready to go after our targets. Lennox Cade and Aron."

At the sound of their names, Eden felt her heart start to race. Her mind circled back to Wyatt who she knew would be crushed if she took any action against two of his remaining friends. *They can't die, not by my hands.* She was caught once again in the crossfire of her emotions but was reminded of where she was when she saw Eloise look at her expectantly, as if waiting for her to offer. When she didn't her mother turned away and looked around the room.

"Due to recent events, I believe it would be best for Alaric to make the first move." Eloise said.

"Me? Why me?" He sputtered in surprise.

"Because you won't look suspicious entering Omega in the middle of the night. You'll have heard a sound inside. Without her vines covering the entrance when her little sidekick is on patrol, it'll be easy to get in." Eloise explained and folded her arms over her chest.

Without argument, Alaric nodded.

The Matriarch's hands went to the belt she had strapped around her most times, and pulled out the dagger Eden had created for Lennox. She flipped the hilt toward the man and held it out where it was quickly accepted. The pit on Eden's stomach started to open once more as guilt found its way back to the surface, Wyatt's face once again the only thing on her mind.

The world was dark. For a moment, Eden stood alone in the center of the night. Slowly the room formed around her with several tall book-cases came into view. Unfamiliar, tall cathedral windows with dark wood trim which contrasted light walls caused her to frown. *Where am I?* The walls reflected the dull light in the mostly darkened space. The sound of a snap caused her to reach for her belt but found it empty. Her head snapped to her hip where she discovered the peacock that was always attached was missing. As she fumbled around her belt, her hand met cold metal on her left hip. There sat a royal purple and golden lion. *The Holloway crest... but where's mine?*

Eden turned slowly and found she was in some sort of meeting room. A long table and chairs were in the center and just to the right along the wall she found a dark stone fireplace with flames that roared inside. A man knelt down beside it with his gaze set on something inside them as he moved aside jars of dried ingredients and a pocket knife with fresh blood on the blade.

At first, all she could see was the back of his head. Her heart fell into her stomach as she eyed the red hair and connected the dots. Eden took a few careful steps toward him and looked into the flames. Between the flames was a dagger just like the one she had made for Lennox and Aron. The man turned to face her when she let out a small gasp.

The familiar face of Holden Holloway looked back at her, though he had a long scar that traced diagonally from his left eyebrow over the bridge of his nose and to his right cheekbone. Her hand covered her mouth as she realized this was a younger version of the man Xemos had shown her what felt like forever ago now. She let her eyes drift to her hand and saw a ring on her left hand beside the initials H.H. tattooed just to the bottom left of it.

There's no way... Holden doesn't have that scar... I don't have this tattoo...

This isn't real. "Holden? What are you doing?" She asked carefully.

"Like I promised Stacey I'm pulling you away from your little demon boy toy. He was lurking and that needs to be taken care of." Holden reached into the flames and pulled out the dagger with ease. "Don't worry, Little Bird. You'll be free of this annoyance soon."

"Eden." A familiar voice made her freeze.

The air inside her lungs caught, her eyes drifting to Wyatt Steele chained against the wall with his arms above his head once again. Eden's eyes darted from the dagger and Holden and back to Wyatt. Without hesitation, she started toward him but only made it a few steps before a hand was suddenly clamped around her throat. Her hands flew to Holden's but were stopped when he squeezed hard enough to cut off her air.

"I've told you before, Little Bird. Do not interfere with what I do. It is best for you in the long run, trust me."

Holden lifted the hand with the dagger and let the hot metal brush against her cheek. It burned for a second which caused her to flinch and stars started to fill her vision. His hand released her neck as his hands found their way into her hair as she coughed and gasped, her palm now where he had burned her. Holden tilted her head up and to the side, she was forced to meet his eyes as his lip twitched up. "I promise, I just want what's best for us." He whispered to her, his eyes locked on hers.

Within seconds, his hand slipped away as he closed the distance to Wyatt. All in one motion he lifted his arm while all Eden could do was scream when it was plunged into his chest. She pulled the blue thread of magic as hard as she could and her magic forced its way up, sparks snapped in the air around her as she ran at Holden. With a hand on his back she sent a wave of electricity through his body and she watched him fall in a heap to the floor. Her gaze shot up and tears formed as she saw Wyatt was already gone with the dagger through his unbeating heart.

With another scream, another shock through her body forced her to shoot up from her bed. Her hand flew to her neck but when she felt no pain, her eyes darted for her phone. A dim light illuminated the darkness of the night, she lunged over the side of her bed to where it had fallen and worked quickly to pull up Wyatt's contact. Eden's heart pounded so hard it felt like it was trying to escape its home. *I just need to hear his voice and know he's okay.*

She hit the call button, she held the phone to her ear. It rang a few times before it stopped and there was a half-asleep, confused voice on the other end.

"Eden? Is everything okay?"

She couldn't help but let a small smile across her face. "Yeah, I just— uhhh. Honestly... I had a nightmare and had to make sure you're okay."

"Little Viper," He chuckled on the other end which sent butterflies through her tired body. "I am more than okay, especially since it's you on the other end. Do you want me to come over and prove it?"

She felt her face turn bright red and was thankful he couldn't see it at the moment. "Yes."

"Your wish is my command. I'll see you soon my dear."

The call ended. There were no questions, no reasons he seemed to need other than she had called. Quickly, she went over to unlock her door for him and shot him a text to let him know to come right in. Afterwards, she went back to her bed, pulled her knees up to her chest and rested her chin down. Her mind rushed with images of Holden, his words wormed their way into the small pit of guilt that remained.

In what seemed like only a few minutes, her door was opening, squeaking lightly as he shut it again. Wyatt was dressed in plaid pajama pants and a band t-shirt, his tired eyes meeting hers. Approaching, he sat on the edge of the bed and put a hand on her arm.

"See, safe and sound." His thumb grazed her skin lightly.

"Good," Eden leaned toward him.

Wyatt's hand slipped around her and allowed her to rest her head on his chest. With a few scoots he slid himself closer toward the center of the bed. The two stayed like that for a while, and let the silence of the moment become comfortable. Slowly, he leaned his back against the headboard as her whole body relaxed in his arms.

"I thought you said you'd never let me in your bed." He teased

"Are you going to question it right now?"

"No, but I will tomorrow. Let's sleep for now." His thumb ran over her cheek. As she closed her eyes, Eden found it surprisingly easy to fall back into better dreams when he was there.

The next morning, Eden had gone downstairs to get coffee for the two of them while the rest of the house slept. A dull pain radiated from The Compass tattoo as it had since she invited Wyatt to her room. The sensation pricked at various parts of her hand and elbow and after hours of it, her muscles sore from the tension. With two steaming mugs, she pressed her back against her door to open it and kicked it closed gently with her foot. She repeated the action after she went through the mostly under-decorated common area attached to her roommate's door.

"Hope you're ready for the best coffee you've had?"

"It will be, I'm sure." He smiled from where he sat on the edge of the bed.

She handed him the cup and he quickly took a grateful sip. "Thank you for coming."

She sat beside him and let herself lean into his side. Her body relaxed as she let out a long breath before she took a drink of her own coffee. Wyatt didn't move an inch at the contact, aside from his eyes which she could feel on her. It was almost as if she could already hear his questions as she met his gaze.

"I will always be here when you want me." He promised as he had from the beginning.

"Then ask." She encouraged the topic she knew he wanted to ask.

"Not that I'm complaining, why did you call me last night, Little Viper?"

"I had a nightmare." Eden stated

It took ten minutes for her to explain every detail from down to the tattoo she had seen. This led into her explanation of what Xemos had shown her of a future for herself and Holden. The second half took another twenty minutes to explain as she let in to what had happened at the ceremony her family held. After this, silence hung in the air between them. Wyatt laced his fingers through Eden's free hand.

"You could walk away at any moment, I would be right here."

"You know I can't."

"Why not? I can grab a bag from my room and I will go and help you pack everything you need. You don't have to live this way, I want you by my side if you'll have me."

"I want that, but I can't just pack up and leave them."

"Yes, you can." He growled in frustration. "Eloise treats you like property. How is that right?"

"How would you prevent them from just taking me away? You can't come to every one of my classes"

"Watch me." His eyes darkened as he peered out her window, in direct view of Elder Row.

Eden's eyebrow rose. "How will you prevent them from killing you to get to me?"

"I'll kill them first- If that's okay with you."

"I'd rather you not kill my whole family."

"Noted, but I would if it came down to it." His grip tightened gently.

She took another drink from her cup as she mulled over her next words. "I know it's not what you want to hear, but I have to do this right... I can't be the reason you get killed."

Wyatt let out a sigh and took another drink. His eyes cracked with an emotion she couldn't register fast enough to decipher. He released her hand and wrapped his hand around her waist.

"I would do *anything* to make you happy, Eden. If this is how you want to do this, I'm behind you."

"It is how I want to do this, with you by my side." The second to last wall around her fell as he wormed his way further.

"Then I am yours."

December

Lennox

She stepped up the stairs to Kappa Theta, Lennox pulled her hood closer around her face to brace against the bitter wind. The phone rang in her headphones as she attempted to reach Wyatt for the third time since he suddenly went radio silent for two days. It was so unlike him and with everything that had happened, she had to make sure he wasn't also tied to a tree in the woods. She cursed to herself as the line cut to his voicemail once again, she opened the front door.

She quickly stomped the snow from her boots and peeled off the thick jacket as she listened for anyone around. Her eyes fell on a group of guys as they made their way from the kitchens and to the stairs, Nick at the front. He stopped when they saw her and he shifted on his feet for a few seconds at the sight of her.

"Hey, Cade. Everything okay?"

"Yes, don't worry I'm not here to tell you off this time. Have you guys seen Wyatt?" She asked with a slight smirk as the other boys oohed and taunted him.

"He's upstairs with Aron," Nick told her quickly before he turned on his heel and went toward the game room followed by his gang of cackling hyenas.

With an eye roll, Lennox hung up her jacket amidst the others and passed under the Fraternity banners. She made her way up two flights of stairs and to the right to the end of the long hall was a cracked door to Aron and Wyatt's conjoined rooms. The sounds of them laughing wafted down the hall to her as she approached.

"When's your birthday?" Wyatt's voice questioned.

"I don't know man, most demons don't! Do you know yours?"

"Of course I do! It's July thirteenth. I was told when I woke up after being created."

"Well shit, I guess I'll make mine.... December twenty-sixth. People will know me as the next antichrist." Aron laughed at his own joke.

"That's coming up soon," Lennox interjected, which made them both jump.

"Goddamnit, Nox! Why you gotta do that?" Wyatt scolded with his hand on his chest.

"I had to make sure you were still alive since you vanished for two days."

Lennox crossed her arms over her chest and raised an eyebrow at her best friend. Deep down she wanted to reach over and shake him for her worry. His demeanor shifted as he seemed to realize why she would be so worried and he hadn't been very responsive. Aron on the other hand eyed her closely just as he did that day in class, like she was breakable.

"I'm sorry, Len. I didn't mean to make you worry. I've just been a bit busy with Eden."

"Can't blame a man for forgetting the world exists for a few days," Aron commented. Lennox shot him a look and Aron cleared his throat. "Yeah, uhh a text could be good at least. Head counts and all."

"Yes, sir Head of House sir," Wyatt smirked.

"You two are going to be the death of me..." She started to turn toward the door but stopped when Wyatt asked about the one thing she was hoping he wouldn't.

"Speaking of that, how are you doing after predator and prey class?"

"Fine, has anyone been able to help Remi and Octavious be able to say what happened?" Lennox deflected and looked directly at Aron who ran a hand through his hair.

"No, not yet. Octavius is joining me on guard tonight though, he's hoping we can find something in a stack of books he got from Rosalyn."

"Aron, Head of Kappa House knows how to read?" She smirked as Aron threw a middle finger at her.

"Going already?" Wyatt frowned.

"Yes, unlike you two I have classes to attend."

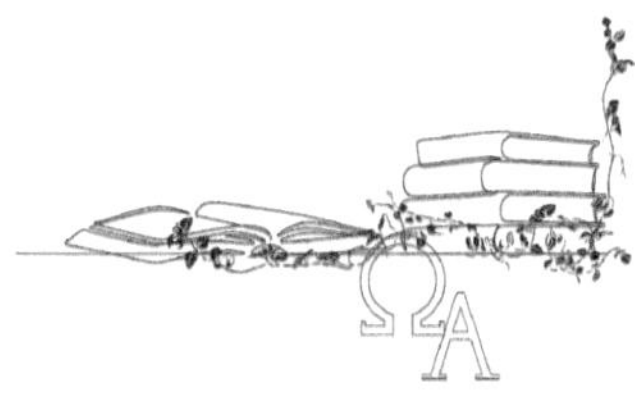

The clear night sky dimly illuminated the room as the full moon reached the top of the sky. With the windows tightly closed to brace against the freezing winds, the room was still as Lennox slept in her bed. It was almost as if the motionless vines covering the entrance were also asleep for the night. Omega Alpha was silent for the night except for the sounds of soft music as it drifted from under her door.

That was until the sound of soft click outside her room caused Ámpleos to quiver and start to weave itself tighter around the door. Above the headboard of her bed, more vines crept toward her. From inside her dream, the same click sounded at her door echoing among the darkness of a dreamless sleep. *Someone's trying to get in.* The feeling of leaves on the side of her face woke her fully but Lennox didn't have time to open her eyes let alone reach for her phone.

The doorknob twisted and the door opened a few inches as a deep voice whispered a string of curses at the sight. Lennox lay there motionless as she feigned sleep to have time to come up with a plan. *I have to find a way to alert Aron. If I do anything too brash they could move on to someone else. I'd rather be the target.* A sharp pain radiated through her body as the vines were cut and torn away from the door. She grimaced but remained still, the connection with the vines she used to guard her room and the houses would be helpful in a fight with whoever was about to come in.

Internally, she placed her hand on the thread to her magic and gently pulled. *Closer.* The sigils heated as she forced the light from them to remain hidden while footsteps slowly approached her bed. It was easy enough to track the intruder by his footsteps now only a few steps from her as her muscles tensed. *You will regret this.* Lennox opened her eyes, now a bright green as she sent the vines toward the intruder. They rushed forward to meet the person just two feet from her bed. In one motion she turned to her back to see who was above her and hoped to find Wyatt in the middle of a terrible prank.

Instead, her fears were confirmed. Above her was Elder Alaric Miller with his arm above his head, the glint of metal caught in the moonlight. In quick succession, they wrapped around his ankles and sent him to the ground with a thud. The weapon clattered to the floor and slid across the room. Lennox stood from the bed, she lifted her hand toward the candles at her altar. The flames sprung to life which gave her enough light to see him looking up at her.

She squinted as her tired eyes attempted to adjust to the light, her gaze followed the weapon now far out of reach. That was when her eyes found her name etched into the blade and caused her heart to drop into her stomach. *Daemonium Pugionem... He's a hunter.* With the distraction, she didn't realize how close he had fallen by her. A hand reached out and grabbed her by the ankle and pulled her down with him.

Lennox pulled at the thread and tried to use the vines to pull him away but felt herself pulled with him. She kicked out with her foot but was met with another pain as he used a new knife to cut the vine around his arm. Her back burned as the magic caused her wings to attempt to form and stretch. The vines that twisted out were forced sideways as she tried to turn and stand. *Damnit, not now.* She fought with the magic that forced through her body as Alaric pulled her closer. She lashed out at him again and her foot met his face followed by a crack as her heel caught him in the jaw.

The man growled in anger as he was forced to let go long enough for her to crawl a few inches. However, it was too late as he brought his elbow down on top of her shin. Another crack could be heard and a new, stronger wave of pain caused her to stop, the vines loosened slightly with a shudder. Lennox clenched her jaw and let out a yelp of pain as she gripped her leg. Alaric stumbled after the dagger and left her in the middle of the floor.

Her glowing eyes snapped toward him and the vines that had forced their way from her back extended in large wings in their full span. The chains glowed and she lifted her hand once more. Two more vines sprang to life from the back of her wings and flew forward as the Elder tried to grab for the weapon. However, she was too slow. The man quickly had it back in his possession and turned toward her with a dark smile.

He spit blood off to the side, looked over to the altar beside him and picked up one of the candles. Her eyes fell on the flame and she forced the attack to halt as her attention locked on the fire. A smirk appeared on the man's face as he took a step forward. *He'll burn the whole place down to take me down.* Her mind raced as she tried to plan her next move. The look in his eyes told her he wouldn't stop until one of them was dead. As he took another step, she slid back with her good leg and her wings met the back of the bed as she didn't have much space. In a final attempt to protect her, they wrapped themselves around her. Unable to see him for a few seconds, she heard him bend down just in front of her. For the first time in two decades, she was faced with the fear Armaros had brewed within her.

"It's over, Cade. This is for what you did." Alaric's harsh voice told her

A new but familiar sensation rushed through her as orange filled her vision. Her wings were on fire, a scream escaped her throat as the fire spread. Every nerve within her was on fire as the ivy couldn't retract and opened. His hand wrapped around her throat and cut off her air and pushed her against the side of the mattress. She couldn't move, he had all his weight on her as the fire grew on either side of them. Through the pain, she saw the flash of the dagger in the air above her once more. The world around her started to form black spots as finally the vines that had sprang to life before shot around him and pulled him back once more. This time they wrapped around his limbs and torso and dragged him up and against the wall. Ámpleos joined in the attack and held him against the wall which allowed her to retract the two from her back.

Like a snake, they squeezed ever tighter around him. The ones beside him covered the door once again and locked them both in. She stood roughly and forced the leaves to wither away to snuff out the fire on her wings. Slowly they vanished as she limped over to the man now caught like a fly in a spider web. Her adrenaline kept her body steady for the moment, but memories of Felix, Rue, and Armaros pooled just beneath as she realized the security team was right. They were after Heads of Houses.

"What's that you were saying about it being over?" Her hand shook slightly which gave her nerves away.

He said nothing and the vines tightened.

"Why are you after us?" Lennox questioned again.

No response.

"Damnit, just tell me! I don't want to kill you but I will."

"Then do it." Alaric challenged, his voice strained. "I'm not going to be telling you anything."

"Fine... I'll be the bad guy for once... This is for Rue and Felix. You won't hurt anyone else, ever again."

Lennox folded her arms over her chest, her eyes glowed green and she took a few steps back. Another vine slowly moved around his neck as the edges of her vision went red. Rage filled her as she looked at Alaric, potentially the person responsible for the two biggest losses of her life. The man slowly started to turn pale as he glared at her and his eyes closed.

Once he was as motionless as the night outside, everything shattered. The memories filled her vision. Felix on the floor of Kappa. Rue in her casket. The flowers she always tended to at their graves. Their laughs, her laugh. "NO!" She screamed as tears flooded her vision.

"Lennox, can you let us in? It's Coyote and the security team." A familiar voice caught her attention.

Panic filled her chest at the thought of the risk of opening the door. Though the red along the edges had gone blurry she eyed Alaric pinned against the wall still motionless. "No... no no no. I can't- He can't escape. He killed the others! If he gets out he could hurt someone again!"

"Lennox, who's in there with you?" She felt hands on the vines outside her door as if they brushed her arms. Coyote's voice sounded like a whisper in comparison to the screaming in her mind now overwhelmed with the feeling of invisible hands.

"NO! No- I have him contained but if he gets out he could kill the whole house!" *Denial.* Her voice broke as pain welled through her chest.

Nothing made sense. Images of Felix the day they met flashed in her mind followed by Alaric's body in front of her as she fought to compose herself to no avail. The conversation outside was barely audible but kept her attention.

"We need to get in there, cut the vines." Coyote's command sent a new wave of panic through her.

"No, the vines are connected to her at night, remember?" Elder Bloodfang quickly rebutted. "She has to let us in."

"We can't just stand here, but it does sound like she has it under control," Coyote argued after a moment of silence.

"We won't...Go drag Aron from his guard and Wyatt from bed so they can make themselves useful." Elder Bloodfang instructed.

Whether it was minutes or hours, Lennox couldn't tell. As their conversation faded away her gaze remained on Alaric against the wall. Music still played from her speaker and between the notes Lennox heard a small groan from the man. Her eyes went wide as she realized he was still alive, his shoulders moved slightly as he struggled to breathe. She took another step back and she felt her body start to shake as adrenaline filled her once more.

"You. Will. Not." She growled as they tightened around his neck.

Her foot met something other than ground and the sound of metal scratch on the wooden floor made her stop as she stumbled a bit. Quickly, she caught herself and her eyes drifted down. The glint of her name in the moonlight was the first thing she saw. Blood rushed from her face and the air was forced from her chest.

Lennox didn't move for a few seconds, her eyes unmoving from the weapon meant to kill her. *One cut... I'd be gone.* Her heart seemed to attempt to beat right out of her chest as she stared. That was until the connection between herself and Ámpleos sent another alert of danger through her. Several voices including Aron and Wyatt's outside the barricaded door sounded louder, amplified by the vines.

"Stay back until we know what's going on in there. I heard her say something." Bloodfang told someone.

"I'll talk to her if I damn well please. I heard her scream and if you think I'm not going in there then you've got another thing coming." Rosalyn's voice stopped

"We don't know if it's safe," Bloodfang reprimanded her.

"I don't give a fuck, that's my best friend. I can handle whatever is happening in that room and I can take you if I have to."

"I'll join you." Aron's voice caught her attention, the foliage around her room quivered at the sound. The same chill was sent down her spine.

The door squeaked as it was opened, however, the ivy was so thick light from the hall only peaked through a few tiny holes. Sparks cracked to life on the other side and sent a new wave of panic over her. Lennox could feel heat beside the vines and felt the magic direct them to lash out. Just in time, their footsteps stumbled back as Wyatt became the voice of reason.

"She's connected to Ámpleos at night, remember? You two burn them away, she'll feel it."

"Shit, you're right," Aron swore.

"If you two would have taken a second to listen." Elder Bloodfang told them.

"Not the time," Coyote whispered to him.

"I haven't heard anything since that scream, we gotta get in there." Rosalyn's footsteps paced outside.

Once again footsteps approached the tangled wall and she could feel a hand beside the spot the doorknob that was covered. Gently, someone started an attempt to guide the ivy away from itself. Light started to trickle in as they pushed away from the person's touch and a hand appeared through it.

"Call off your foliage, Lenoard." His request was soft but left no room for argument.

"Don't come in!" She called back as his hand found the knob.

"We can handle whatever you've got in there, let us in." The vines continued to pull away to let him in.

"Please Len, everyone will be safe." Rosalyn promised.

The door finally was free and slowly he pulled it open. Light from the hall illuminated her room and the scene within. In the hall stood everyone she had heard, Aron's eyes were already on her as they scanned her up and down for injuries. His gaze fell to the dagger at her feet and his expression quickly shifted from worry to fear. He took a few steps toward her before he glanced around the room. Aron came to a halt as his attention turned to Alaric pinned to the wall once again motionless.

"What... Lennox- Did you." His tone was suddenly cold.

Rosalyn barged through the doorframe and looked around the room. "What's taking so long? Is everything-"

Slowly, everyone in the hall peered around and entered the room. Lennox didn't move a muscle as each took in the obvious attempt on her life and the man who seemingly died in her room. Everyone but Aron made their way over to her, Wyatt and Rosalyn took her by the shoulders and pulled her to sit on the bed away from the dagger. With their help, she sat on the edge of the bed as the others moved around her room. The commotion around her started to feel like a sort of fever dream as she watched everyone. Elder Bloodfang went to pick up the weapon and Coyote went to check on Alaric.

"He's gone..." The words hung in the air, heavy as she realized he was dead.

"Are you okay? You didn't get knicked anywhere did you?" Rosalyn moved around her as she checked for cuts.

"No, I-I'm fine." Her words shook as they came out.

"Are you sure?" Wyatt knelt down in front of her and held out his hands. "Breathe, Nox. You're safe now. We are here."

The commotion around her was nothing more than a blur as she saw Aron who hadn't moved from his spot as he couldn't seem to pull his eyes from the dead hunter. He ran a hand through his hair and his head turned slightly as if to look at her, but returned forward. Silently, he stepped back through the doorframe and into the hall and vanished from sight.

Eden

Glasses clinked behind the bar as the woman behind it finished up the glasses for the evening. Music drifted from the speakers beside the register, the pub which was mostly empty would have been silent without it. Eden's fingers danced across the screen of her phone as she and Bastien talked about her date with Chase. He had taken her off-campus over to Crossroads Diner where they reminisced on childhood memories and his mission in Toronto, Canada where they invaded the Blue Jay Society. If she was honest with herself, she did enjoy his company however he didn't hold a candle to the attention she had on Wyatt. Chase would be her equal, but could he push her when she needed it? Since he was also from a Matrical family, he was almost too formal and treated her like a friend rather than a partner.

The glass beside her hand slowly dripped with condensation creating a ring on the napkin it had been placed on. Thoughts of Wyatt swirled in her mind almost as fast as her head spun. With a healthy buzz, she pulled up the chat they had going. A soft smile appeared on her face as she saw a new message. He had checked in with her over the last few days but Eden had made sure to allow him space to process everything he had discovered.

She blinked a few times at his photo before she locked her phone and placed it face down on the chestnut bar. As she scooped up her glass, she put the rim to her lips and downed the rest in one shot. Her eyes went to the Victorian-style wooden arches above her and she sucked air through her teeth. She hated how much whiskey now reminded her of events from the other week. The sound of the door behind her as it opened and closed caused her to perk up a little. Eden placed her glass beside the other three empty ones, she kept her head forward. Eden resisted the urge to see who joined the handful of people inside Hellhounds Pub as she didn't want to stick out.

"Can I get another double shot?" She asked the bartender.

"Make that two." A deep voice asked from beside her which caused her to jump slightly.

The woman nodded and went to the wall of bottles illuminated in cool blue light. Eden peered over and smiled as she noticed Wyatt already sat beside her. His green eyes sparked as he smirked and leaned closer. Wyatt slid his arm across the back of the bar chair and got comfortable, the action sent another round of sparks through her.

"How long have you been here, Miss Miller?" Wyatt motioned at the empty glasses being taken away as two fresh whiskeys on the rocks took their place.

"Well, I think I got here... After my second class? Maybe? What time is it now?" She asked, her face twisted momentarily in confusion.

"My Gods Eden," Wyatt's eyes widened in surprise as he took in her face to gauge how drunk she was. "You have been here all afternoon? How are you not under the table right now?"

"I didn't expect to see you here but I'm glad you are." She admitted, her hand slid next to his and rested beside the drink as she waited to see his reaction to her.

His hand slipped into hers, "You know you could have called me Viper, I believe you still have my number. Unless you deleted it?"

"You know I wouldn't have done that unless you were done with me."

When he accepted the touch, Eden felt her body relax and a long breath escape her. Her eyes drifted to their hands. His rose tattoo had the faintest scar from Eloise's knife. Her face fell as she noticed it and her hair fell forward as memories of him chained to the wall flashed in her mind's eye. The bracelet he gifted her stared back as she sensed his eyes on her. That was until she felt a finger under her chin and lifted her gaze back up. The two of them locked eyes, all words spoken without a single one said aloud. His stubbornness was plain in his eyes as his fingers traced their way up the side of her face and into her hair gently. The palm of his hand rested on her cheek, his gaze never wavered.

"This is your last chance to back out, Copperhead." She sighed and broke the silence. "I told you that day in the classroom you shouldn't have kept pursuing me."

He lowered his voice and frowned, "I wouldn't have wanted to do anything differently. Don't you understand Eden, I could hurt them. I could kill them all, but not you, never you. Hell if it were up to me, you would never see a single drop of your own blood again. Everything that happens next we can handle together and when you're ready I will help you leave... If that's what you want, still?"

"I do, it's just harder than I thought it would be... I still feel like I owe them."

"Listen to me. You do not owe them anything. You didn't ask for any of this and if memory serves me, you didn't want to." His words were heavy in her mind.

She leaned her head into his hand for a moment and Eden softened. For the first time she showed the truest side of her she could. There was no pressure to stand strong, no need to hide behind her walls. It was as if she saw him clearly for the first time; the truth hit her. *I'm in love and there's nothing I can do to change it now.* Wyatt lifted his right hand from hers and he brushed a piece of hair that had fallen into her face. Whether the alcohol or the man in front of her was to blame as the room spun once more she didn't care either way.

Slowly, he leaned closer to her and stopped about a foot from her face. His eyes followed his fingers as they trailed back down the side of her face, the right rested on the back of her chair once more. His thumb traced her bottom lip for a second which sent a shiver down her spine and breath caught in her lungs as his stormy eyes met hers again.

"Wanna play truth or dare?" Wyatt smirked.

"You know what you're doing..." Eden breathed as her heart raced.

"Do I?" His lips turned up into a half smile.

"You're just trying to kiss me."

Wyatt chuckled more to himself it seemed as he leaned closer, his face inches from hers. "Miss. Miller, I don't need a silly little game as an excuse to kiss you, I just need your willing permission."

"You have it." The words were barely audible.

His cologne filled her senses as he finally closed the last inches between them. At first, he was gentle as he pulled her into him, their lips met and his arms moved from their previous places and now wound around her. Eden's hand went to his shoulder and pulled herself a little closer and allowed herself to let go. Her eagerness at the moment seemed to encourage him. Within seconds his grip tightened with need and the kiss deepened in passion as sparks lit in her chest.

Finally, he pulled away and touched his forehead to hers. Eden peered at him and saw the usual storm within his eyes calm. She forced herself to pull away, the two adjusted themselves back into their seats and a blush crept into her face.

"Are you blushing, Viper?" He asked surprised as he took a sip from his drink.

"There's no need to point it out."

"On the contrary, it's cute." Wyatt winked. "I bet none of those suitors have seen this."

Eden shifted slightly and she adjusted her sweater and cleared her throat as the avoided topic came up. Her previously racing heart now almost came to a halt. Her thumbnail brushed against the tips of her fingers for a second before she distracted herself with her glass and shot down another mouthful. She could still feel his eyes on her as she shook her head.

"I don't want to." She started as nerves and drinks got the better of her.

"I know-"

"Until I can get away, this is something I have to do to make my family happy. It means nothing and won't happen." She couldn't stop herself.

His lips met hers again, this time only briefly and forced her to stop.

"Eden, I know, I promise you don't have to worry. I trust you. I want you to be safe when you're home and if it means going on a few dates so be it. I know where your heart lies, just know I'll be close by if you need me."

Her muscles relaxed once more at the thought of him being close by when she met with the last suitor. The whole thing was already awkward enough to know they were basically fighting to win her hand. Since she had grown up within the hunter families she had only imagined one of them as a potential partner. *Holden Holloway, the wild card of The Salvamari.* Over the years he had been so focused on his own training to take his father's place just as she was to take Eloise's. Things had never gone past a mild flirting. Eventually, they had become strangers again as he went to Phantom Academy and she to SCHUni.

"I'm supposed to take him on a tour of the grounds tomorrow."

"Well then, I'll just so happen to be by the garages working on my bike. Just in case you and him want to swing by." He smirked.

"As endearing as that is, the thought of bringing another hunter around my demon boyfriend sounds like a bad idea."

"He'll have no idea who I am, I'll just be another face on the grounds." His posture lifted confidently.

"Oh, Copperhead. You have no idea how these families work." Eden shook her head. "I have no doubts in my mind that Eloise and Stacey have both sent a photo of you to Chase and Holden. There's no way they are going to sit by and do nothing."

Her phone buzzed demandingly on the bar followed by a flash of large letters on her watch face. *Speak of the devil himself.* Holden's name vanished and showed the message just before she turned her wrist away. For a moment, guilt filled her chest. Though it was all in the plan and Wyatt was very aware of what was going on and choosing to stay by her side, it felt wrong. His eyes were on her again, his fingers lightly brushed her hand once more.

"I didn't expect them to in the slightest. In any case, I gotta make sure this kid is going to treat my girl with respect." Wyatt finished his drink.

The words my girl sent a rush through her and heat to return to her face. She shook her head also and also finished off the rest of her whiskey. "Holden is mostly harmless. He wouldn't do anything to hurt me."

"Ah, so mystery boy has a name. Good to know." He gave her a shoulder bump before he offered her a hand.

Her smile faded, Eden looked back to him and he nodded his head toward the door. She raised an eyebrow and opened her mouth to retaliate but was stopped when he pulled out some money for the drinks. Before she could make a case to stay a little longer, he held out the jacket she had hung on the back of her chair. Smoothly he helped her slip it on and pulled his black leather jacket closer around him before he slipped his hand into hers. With an arm on her back he led her out and the doors opened to the small single-road town, the sky colored shades of orange, pink, and red.

"The night is young, you don't want to spend it in a dark pub do you?"

"I can think of a few ways to spend the night."

"Aron is on guard tonight if you want to come over." He offered

Eden wrapped her arms around his waist, on the balls of her feet to get above his shoulders. When the world spun once again, she felt him pull her against him for balance. Completely enwrapped at the moment, it took her a few seconds to process what he said. *Aron's on guard for the night. Shit- Alaric will be going after Lennox tonight. If he thinks I have something to do with this, he's going to hate me.* Her mind circled a few times as Eden divided the best way to make it look like she wouldn't have known.

Do you really want to lie to your conscience? The familiar voice of Xemos reverberated in her mind.

"If I tell him now, he'll put himself at risk." She thought back to the god and intervened.

And he'll be angry if he finds out you knew and didn't help him stop it.

Once again, her phone distracted her. However, this time it was Eloise who called and caused her to sober up. Her face fell as she saw her mother's name on her watch. Eden looked up to Wyatt, he motioned for her to answer. She put her phone to her ear but wanted nothing more than to ignore her responsibilities.

"What, Mother?" She said a bit too harshly.

"I think the words you're looking for are, Yes, Matriarch." Eloise's voice scolded from the other end.

Pulling the phone away for a moment, an annoyed sigh escaped her before she returned it to her ear and spoke through clenched teeth. "Yes, Matriarch. What can I do for you?"

"You're being called for a mission with Bastien. Come to the house and prepare."

"But-"

"Now, Heiress Miller." The phone disconnected.

Eden turned to Wyatt with an apologetic look on her face. "Duty calls, unfortunately."

"You've been drinking, are you sure you're going to be okay with whatever they want you to do?"

"I'll have Bastien with me. I'll be fine."

"Call me when you get to Omega tonight. I don't care what time it is." He told her in a low voice.

Eden kissed his cheek and she dropped his hand and started off down a side path that led around the gates and to the home that didn't feel much like one anymore.

Shadows of trees flew by the window as Eden looked out into the winter night. From the passenger seat of the family SUV, she listened to Bastien drone on about Corvus and their night escapades off campus. As much as she tried to follow the conversation the blood on her silver arrow drew her full attention. Eden pulled out an old, stained rag from her go bag and wiped away the red with a pass of the fabric over the post of the arrow.

Her gaze stayed on the gray rag forever marked with years worth of blood on her hands. In the occasional light from street lamps, she noticed her hands were also colored red from the werewolf they took down. Her stomach twisted and her heart started to pound in her ears and progressively became louder. She ran the rag over the spots only helping a little as it was mostly dried already. With more force, she tried to clean the metal while her vision started to blur. All at once it was like she was seven again. New to the family. The lifestyle.

Her breath caught in her lungs and a constricted sob unwillingly left her. Bastien's hand suddenly covered hers which made her stop. Her eyes shot over to him, seeing a much older version of the Bastien from her memories. The sight brought her back to the moment, she in fact was an adult she cleared her throat and forced herself to regain composure.

"You don't have to pretend right now."

"Yes, I do, If Eloise or Stacey saw that... I can't unravel now."

"Nothing has changed, Squeaks. You can unravel around me." Bastien squeezed her hand.

"Can I? Your father is already plotting how to kill me and don't act like he's not."

"Whatever Richard tries, I will keep you safe just as I always have."

"He won't stop until I'm dead and you know that." Eden countered.

"Then it will end with him dead. I'm not going to let anything happen to you." Bastien promised.

Eden peered out the window and lost herself in her thoughts as the town outside the ground passed by. For a few moments she allowed herself to think of Wyatt and his offer to protect her if she left the family. A sad smile crossed her face as Bastein rolled up to the entrance of SCHUni. *Home sweet home, for now.* The metal complained as it opened for the car. Once there was enough room, the car pulled behind the iron gates.

As he parked in the school's garage, she put the rag and arrow into her bag before she got out. The only light inside the place was a small overhead lamp that came on when they pulled in. It was just enough light to see Wyatt's motorcycle on the other end and the memory of their date. A pained smile to her lips as Bastien came around the other side. He nudged her shoulder and motioned for her to follow.

It was ten minutes later when the two walked back into the Miller Home. Inside the lights were still on in the entranceway. They pulled off their jackets and put their bags in the front closet. Eden took careful steps forward. *There's no reason for anyone to still be awake, it's well after four in the morning.* As she glanced around her eyes met Eloise and Stacey in the front living room. Her mother paced while her grandmother sat stoic, between them one of the daggers she had made on the coffee table. Immediately she knew something had gone wrong and for a second she was almost happy about it. As strong as her distaste for Lennox was, she didn't want to see the look on Wyatt's face if Alaric had succeeded.

"What's happened?" Bastien asked from behind her.

"Eden, Bastien," Eloise turned at the question. "The mission on Miss. Cade failed. Alaric almost lost the dagger but we got it back before it was taken to the principal. Unfortunately, the demon knows of the dagger's existence now."

"So what's next?" He asked and moved to place a hand on her shoulder.

She stepped forward and into the room. "It's up to Eden."

"As it should have been in the first place," Stacey interjected. "We know she would have taken care of it."

"Yes Mother, I know exactly what your opinion is." Eloise snapped and turned back to Eden, her gaze pierced through her. "Take it, Eden. You can use it how you see fit... I believe you still have revenge and questions for Miss. Cade?"

The words caught her off guard. Eden blinked and her eyes fell to the weapon on the table. The truth in her mother's words rang like alarm bells in her mind. The pink-haired demon's face formed in her mind's eye. Yes, she wanted her questions answered. Yes, a part of her still wanted her dead for abandoning her even though deep down she had seen firsthand how demons can change. Where forgiveness for even the darkest parts of someone can lead.

When Eden didn't move, Eloise stepped over and swiped the dagger from the table. In a matter of seconds, they were standing inches from each other. The woman glared darkly down at her daughter and pressed the handle of the dagger into Eden's diaphragm. Her hand automatically went to Eloise's wrist where the two stayed for a moment in a standoff. All three generations of Miller women stood motionless as Bastien's hand shifted to his weapons belt. His fingers wrapped around the handle of his gun, housed beside the peacock on his left hip.

"You will be a part of this family, so help me."

"And if I refuse, Matriarch?" Eden hissed.

"Holden is upstairs and is ready to join the family at any moment shall you not behave. Your choice will be gone and I can make it happen tonight. By morning you will be gone to the Holloway household until you're ready to continue your duties." Eloise's words were a threat, they all knew it.

"Sounds like your mind is already made up."

"It is, though I'd prefer you were more willing."

"I'd be more willing if you could accept my feelings for Wyatt."

Eloise sighed and shook her head. "All I'm doing is keeping you safe.... Now, we can do this the easy or hard way... What will it be?"

Her eyes darkened as her grip on her mother's hand tightened. Anger darted toward the surface and threatened to boil over. Eden slid the blade from her hands, she took it and put it in her weapon belt. She dropped her hand to her side and took a step back. With her chin tilted up slightly, she noticed Stacey still had her head forward and now refused to look at her.

"When I am Matriarch, The Salvamari will never be the same."

As her hands shook, she made her way from the room and back into the entrance hall. Bastien called from behind her and she heard him take a few steps to follow, however, Eloise's voice made him stop. Quickly, she pulled her jacket back on and without another word left the house, this time for Kappa Theta. *I can't do this anymore.*

In the shared space between Wyatt and Aron's room, Eden sat on the couch. Silently, she pulled the blanket from Wyatt's bed he had given her closer. Her blank gaze stayed on the window where she didn't truly see the snow that was slowly building on the edge. With her chin resting on her hands on the back of the cushion the last hour rewound itself in the back of her mind. The look on Wyatt's face when she showed up with blood still on her hands and tears in her eyes filled her mind. Wordlessly, he had helped her get her jacket and stained shirt off.

Wyatt had been respectful for someone who seemed to want nothing more than to take her to bed. She was left with a tank top as he stood behind her in the mirror. Through the reflection his eyes caught hers as his hands gently held her shoulders. He still didn't speak as he reached beside her to turn on the water and picked up a washcloth from a drawer to her left. His movements were slow. His eyes never left hers as the full weight of everything finally fell. The tears spilled over as a sob escaped her and her vision blurred. Her hands went to the sinks edge where red imprints marked the counter as she gripped it, knuckles white. Eden forced her eyes closed.

"It's okay." Wyatt's deep voice hummed as his hands brushed against her forearm.

More sobs wracked her chest as he wrapped his arms tightly around her. When he did hear head leaned forward as midnight hair covered her face. Pain that had a vise-like grip on her heart for years suddenly poured out. The faces of every victim of her family played behind her lids ending with Wyatt chained at the mercy of Eloise.

"I'm sorry." The words fell out between tears.

"It's okay." There was no judgment in his voice.

"I'm so sorry." *You have no idea what I've done.*

"Viper," he sighed as she felt an arm release her. Another sob shook her body. "Shhh..."

The sound of running water caught her attention. Between the strands of her hair she saw Wyatt's hand wringing out a washcloth. As he moved, her gaze focused on the now cut rose tattoo. A wave of guilt fell over her as he ran the cloth down her arm. With every stroke, the tears started to fade. Eventually, he whipped away every speck of red off her hands and arms. Once it was gone, the tears stopped.

"I'm sorry, I just-" Eden started to apologize.

He shook his head. "We both have blood on our hands... I've seen the darkest parts of you and I haven't run. I told you I'm here, allow me to help bring that glow back."

"I don't think moisturizer is going to bring it back at this point." A small laugh escaped her as they went back to the couches.

"Funny, Viper." A smile returned to her face as relief filled his eyes.

The sound of the door as it opened and closed behind her caused her to turn. Wyatt walked through the door with two steaming mugs in hand. A bright smile was plastered on his face as he approached and joined her on the couch.

"Lavender and Mugwort tea for the lady, regular coffee for me."

"Thank you." Eden gratefully took the mug.

"Are you sure you're ready to do this?" He asked, his left hand met hers.

"I can't keep going on missions and coming back like this... If they knew, I would be done anyway. Eloise is already willing to ship me away."

The color in Wyatt's face drained. "Where would they send you?"

"They would use The Arrangement to send me with Holden. One of the many emergency clauses of The Slavamari. If I walk away now they won't be able to."

"Are you sure about that?"

"I would do my best to make sure it didn't happen," Eden told him, her eyes hardening as her mother's words echoed in her mind

The two finished their drinks and talked casually about what they would do after they got her things. Quickly, she went back into his room and found a set of washed clothes she had accidentally left the night before. Eden pulled them on and opened the door once more to ask if he was ready; she noticed he must have changed before he went downstairs.

"Good, you found them. You can keep the t-shirt and sweats you stole if you want." He offered with a smirk.

"Well then, I guess it's good you offered. I wasn't planning on bringing them back." She teased and went to the door.

Before she could touch the doorknob, he grabbed it and pulled it open. She shot him a half-annoyed look before the two of them went to the entrance hall and put on winter coats. As she zipped up her jacket, the weight of what they were about to do started to settle. *He's so good at being distracting.* Eden glanced at him as he pulled on a black beanie.

"You okay?"

"Fine... Just never thought this was something I'd do." She admitted as he stepped toward her.

"Is it something you're still ready to do? Last chance to back out." He quoted her words back to him as his hands gripped either side of her arms gently.

"It either happens on my terms or theirs, I'd rather it be on mine."

With a suitcase open on her bed, Eden rustled through her drawers for everything she would need. Wyatt helped fold and put things in the bag as she tossed it over to him, occasionally he peaked out the cracked door. She packed her laptop, twenty books on creatures the family had collected, as much of her apothecary as she could take, the books on Xemos, and extra weapons stashed around her room. Quickly, she put them into a seperate bag. Within twenty minutes she had most of everything she deemed necessary, the rest Bastien could steal back for her.

"Do you have the note?" Wyatt asked.

"What note?" A voice asked from behind him.

Eden turned to see who had appeared only to find Stacey in the doorframe. A storm of rage filled her eyes as she glared at Wyatt though her demeanor stayed calm. *The most dangerous version of Stacey.* With the suitcase in his hand Wyatt took careful steps back toward Eden and positioned himself so his shoulder covered her left side. The action sent a momentary recognition through her, it was just how the Miller men were trained to do the same. If it wasn't for Stacey in front of them, she would have found it much more endearing.

"Where are you going, my dear?"

"I'm done with The Salvamari, Matron." She told her, proud her voice came out evenly.

The woman shook her head with an entertained scoff. "No, you're not..."

"You don't get a say in the matter." She took a step and moved past Wyatt.

Her gaze never wavered from Stacey as she closed the distance with him close behind. The Matron didn't move from the doorway. Eden saw the dark look in her eyes as she got closer. Just as the two women were shoulder to shoulder Stacey's hand shot out and grabbed Eden's wrist. With a swift grip on the thread, magic forced its way forward. She felt it flow out and into the other hunter. Electricity sparked around her wrist which caused the Matron to let go with a look of surprise that Eden would use her powers against her.

Within seconds, Wyatt was between them his back to Eden. In the next moment she watched as Stacey grabbed him by the shoulders. With the bags, he was easily thrown off balance and off to the side out the door. Stacey raised her hands and a barrier of shimmering shadows barred him from entering the room.

"I hope he wiped his fitly paws before coming into this house." Stacey said, turning to Eden. "Tell your little hell hound to go wait outside like a good little demon."

Sparks cracked from his hands. "I'm not going anywhere."

"This is a family matter." Stacey demanded to Wyatt.

"I'll be fine. I'll be right there." She insisted for his safety.

Wyatt watched her face for a moment before he disappeared down the hall. Once they were alone, Eden drew in a long breath before she turned to face her Grandmother. All the years of her being the favorite now long forgotten as they stood in silence for a few seconds.

"Are you sure you want to do this? Follow down the same path as that Cade? Become a Heretic?"

The question threw her off. "You're not giving me much of a choice, Stacey."

"You're not giving me much of a choice either, Eden. I know you know how this is going to end. This is not what you were meant for." The woman took a step toward her, but she took another back. Pain filled Eden's eyes. "Why can't you let me try? I know it's not ideal for the family but-" "The family, Eden, how will you ever have children and continue the family line if you're with a demon? Are you willing to give up this family and your future for him? Give up the chance to have a happy human life like you always dreamed of? I will not stand by and let him destroy you. Destroy everything you've worked so hard for. You're not in your right mind. Maybe you need to spend a few months with the Donovan's." "Destroy everything you've worked for you mean?"

The accusation hung in the air and caused the woman's calm demeanor to fade away. Stacey gritted her teeth and grabbed her right hand once more only this time there was no magic behind it. Her fingers pulled at her sleeve and roughly rolled it up to reveal the Compass and her new addition. Stacey's eyes went wide as the silver chain and sigils that trailed up her arm and over the tattoo. She turned Eden's arm over in her hands and examined them closely but quickly dropped her arm in frustration. *Does she know what these are?* Her purple eyes stayed on the woman's face for any clues.

"Did you do this for him?" She snapped accusatively, this was confirmation enough.

"No… I did it to protect the family… Cleo had just come to the school. Though she hasn't tried anything I was worried."

Stacey's face fell and she started to pace beside Eden's bed. "You could have been a great Matriarch, better than Gwen ever was…"

Pain reverberated in her ribcage and she tightened her grip on the bag. Stacey had been the top Matriarch of The Salvamari before the title passed to the Donovan family after the escape of the angel Lumina and Nikoli a Heretic. Greer took her and Stacey had been angry ever since.

"You'll become Lennox if you stay with him. You're already on her path." She motioned to the silver markings. "Is that what you want? To become selfish? Heartless? A murderer?"

"You have no proof that Lennox has killed a human. You're going off your assumptions. Yes she is guilty of a lot but she hasn't killed any humans I'm aware of." Eden turned and tried to step through the barrier but was unable.

"I decide who comes and goes from this room now… You know she killed Alaric while he was on his mission."

Eden froze but kept her back to Stacey to hide the slowly saddening look in her eyes knowing this was more than just a ploy to use her anger at Lennox. She hadn't been very close to him however he was a part of the family and as such she had a responsibility to him.

"You didn't say anything last night... You just said he failed, not dead."

"You left before I could tell you."

"It makes no difference. I am not going to remain here and continue to add more blood to my name. I'm done with all of this death, the blind devotion The Salvamari expects. Now let me out of here."

Sudden movement on the other side of the barrier caught her attention. Quickly she reached for her belt but froze once more as her eyes locked on Holden Holloway. He looked exactly as he had in the nightmare, including the new scar. A knot formed in her throat as her eyes went to the gold and royal purple lion carved into the family crest that sat on his right hip. A wave of mixed emotions washed over her as he smiled and stepped through the barrier. All at once the nightmare felt a lot more real. For the first time she was weary of Holden as he approached her.

"My my, Heiress Miller. Still as beautiful as I remember."

Eden straightened as her body tensed, memories of their last meeting flashed in her mind. Holden had pulled her up to the study at the Holloway home for a private conversation which ended with a mutual agreement to focus on taking their places before any romantic endeavors could be explored. Coming within a foot of her, Holden brought his hand up, moving a piece of hair from her face just as he had done three years ago before he left her in the study.

For a moment, the older version of Holden Xemos had shown her was on the young man's face in front of her. Their gazes locked, and she forced herself to stay collected as his eyes searched hers, for her feelings toward him. He was close enough to see the small details on his face and in his eyes. Every freckle on his cheeks including the ones hidden under a short, well-kept beard that accentuated his diamond shaped face. Hidden among the gray in his irises a hint of blue could be found when looking long enough.

"Heir Holloway, good to see you've made it." Her body shifted into the formalities she had learned over the years and extended a hand toward him.

His hand met hers as he put his lips next to her ear and spoke in a soft whisper. "There's no need for that, Little Bird. Everyone knows why we are here and honestly, I was excited to hear you were still single despite this whole demon situation. My hope is to catch your attention... Again."

"I think you and Holden here should have a chat. He will be able to take the barrier away when he deems fit. I'll be back in an hour to check on you two."

Stacey's voice caught her attention as she moved around the two and toward the door. Eden's first instinct was to follow in case she decided it was a good time to drag Wyatt back down to the basement. However, Holden stopped her easily with a hand on her shoulder as Stacey walked into the hall. With no other way out, she decided to keep quiet for Wyatt's safety. If he heard her yelling at Holden, he may try to do something risky.

"Let me out-"

"No," He said simply and dropped his hand.

"So you're actually going to participate in this nonsense?"

"Only because I recently have seen what happens when someone of our rank steps out of line and is given a chance to come to their senses. Eden, you are the Miller's only Heiress and you're out there falling for what that demon has made you think is love?"

Her ears turned bright red as anger and a hint of unwanted embarrassment fell over her. Eden wasn't embarrassed of Wyatt, but now stood in front of Holden and being scolded for it she couldn't help the shame it brought to the surface.

"It's not an act, Holden. These creatures are more than what they seem. At least the ones I've seen- They aren't all out just to hurt humans."

"So this demon has never hurt a human? He is innocent?" He questioned with a raised eyebrow and motioned for her to sit. Eden fell silent, knowing the answer wouldn't clear his name. "Lennox Cade?"

"How-" The name coming from his lips sent her hair on edge.

"Eloise told me everything about what's going on here the night you woke up. She felt we could relate." Holden motioned to the long scar obvious on his face.

"I wasn't going to ask."

His voice went soft for a moment as the old feelings she shoved away in a box tried to open once more. Once open, she feared it would indeed pull her back in just as her family wanted. Holden motioned toward the chair at her desk as he went to sit on the chest at the end of her bed.

"When I started my mission at Phantom Academy I was also tricked into thinking these creatures could be more than what our families taught us. Hell, I even did the same thing you did, only she was a werewolf, Marabell."

Holden continued the story about how the pair had met but her heart dropped at the name, the very one Eloise had given Bastien and her the night before. *The wolf we killed.* Once again the emotions from last night flew to the surface. She recalled Eloise's demeanor when she was briefing them on the mission. It hit her why her mother had watched her so closely, she had known something she didn't. Until now. *Blood on my hands.* Her gaze fell to her hands unsure whether or not Holden was aware of events of the day before.

"When my father found out he showed me everything she had done just the prior year, everyone she had killed. Then ran his favorite pocket knife over my face as a reminder. I'm sure by now he's had her taken care of, as Stacey should be doing right now with yours." Eden's gaze snapped back up to Holden's, every nerve lit up as she pulled on the thread. Outwardly, she flinched ever so slightly and watched him adjust in his seat. "Calm down, I said should be. Fortunately for you, Eloise has made her promise not to touch him. You're a bit more of a wild card than me."

She scoffed, partially relieved, half entertained by the thought of her being a wild card. "I'll calm down when I'm good and ready. Funny coming from you seeing as that's what all the Heirs call you."

"And if they find out you've done the same as I, they are going to call us the perfect pair. Though I don't think it's going to be a secret much longer, you know how word travels. In any case, we can fix that at our wedding."

"That's presumptuous. You're banking on the fact I'm staying as an Heir." She folded her arms over her chest.

"You're banking on the fact I won't tell Eloise I saw Bastien kissing a demon last night."

This time she couldn't hold back from the reaction to his words as her face fell. In one swift motion Eden stood from her chair and pulled her knife from her sleeve. Anger was clear in her eyes as she crossed to him, her knee on the chest between his legs and hand on the bedpost beside him. The hand with the blade went under his chin as she glared down at him and her hair fell into her face slightly.

Holden didn't move or even react to her. Instead his hand came up and his fingers slowly weaved into her hair tucking it behind her ear as he tilted his head up. The movement made her hand shift as the metal grazed his skin.

"Do you want to start that war, Little Bird?" A smug smirk crossed his face.

With an irritated growl she didn't waver from her stance. "You dare tell anyone and I will."

"I won't if you finish one last mission. Then we revisit your status as an Heiress? If you still think it's worth becoming a heretic after that I will let you walk away from me."

Yet again here she was about to pick between what she wanted and what the family wanted her to do. The difference was this time it involved someone she deeply cared for within the family. *Wyatt isn't going to be happy about this.* Eden had a distinct feeling that this would have something to do with Aron and Lennox's daggers. She pulled her knife away and placed it back into its sheath, she took some steps back to put space between them once more.

"Finish your hunt on Cade. Take your revenge and Bastien will be in the clear from me, I promise."

Eden took a moment to consider however each path boiled down to disaster if she didn't agree. This was the best route, she knew Holden would keep his word. "This is my last hunt... After this, I'm done."

"Oh Little Bird, I don't think so but we'll see in time." Holden brought his arm up and released the barrier. "I'll see you for my tour of campus tomorrow after lunch."

The moment it was dropped she picked up her bag and walked out. She took every other step, she went out the front door where Wyatt was standing with the bag he had left with. When the door opened he looked up, his look of worry fell away as a smile crossed his face.

However, after he met her eyes, it dropped and he met her at the bottom of the small set of steps. Wordlessly, he pulled her into his arms.

"Someone caught Bastien and Corvus, if I don't complete my last mission they'll make him a Heretic and kill Corvus... I can't let that happen." Her voice was barely audible.

Wyatt didn't speak for a moment, the sense of disappointment lingered in the air. He held her shoulders and looked down at her. "Is this the last one?"

"Yes, I'm done after this. He won't tell anyone about them if I do this."

"What's the mission?" He asked the one question she was hoping he wouldn't.

"I can't tell you... But you wouldn't like it."

"I'm not going to beg you to tell me, Viper. All my darkest parts are yours as yours are mine. Tell me when you're ready," His hands slid down her arms and took her hands as he kissed her gently. He released one and turned toward Omega Alpha as he went back to the Chapter House.

Eden and Holden walked across the ground of the school, her small ball of fire followed them as they stayed on the sidewalk. Ice salt crunched under their feet and the sun was particularly warm for a winter day. Grateful for it, she pointed out various buildings and areas in the school where she took classes. As they walked past the woodland's edge his head turned toward the three tall gravestones tucked between the trees.

"These are marked this year. Are they yours?"

"Two out of three." She admitted and avoided the sight of them as they continued.

"Usually you don't hold back this much. Where's the Eden that liked to brag?"

"I was under vampire venom for a week." She retorted as they made their way toward the school garage.

"And that caused the great Heiress Miller to crumble?"

"No, the realization that The Salvamari wasn't what I thought it was."

She brought her hands closer to the fire as a cold breeze sent a shiver through her, Eden peered over to Holden. The person she was three years ago would have been ecstatic at the situation however that version of her was too far gone to be excited. The sound of music played from about sixty feet away from the garage. The doors were open and she instantly knew Wyatt had remembered his offer and was around if she needed him. Internally she breathed a sigh of relief knowing he was close by.

"Is there a reason you insisted on an outdoor tour in the middle of winter?" The question fell out.

"What's the first step when you enter new surroundings?" Holden shot back.

As if automatically, she recited the line they were all taught. "Scout and route. Scout the situation and plan your route to the target... Who's your target?"

"You." He smirked.

A hand gripped hers suddenly and pulled her back. The force made her turn back toward him and away from the garage. With a tug she forced her hand out of his grasp and placed her hands on his chest to stop the momentum of his actions. However, the smile on his face told her that this was still the end result he wanted.

"You know I have no real interest in this arrangement. Not anymore." His arms wound around Eden and kept her in place as she spoke.

"Not anymore? Are you saying you did at one point?" He asked.

"You shut us down three years ago, Holden. You're the one who suggested we couldn't have any distractions." Eden's eyebrow rose and she went to turn away.

"I was wrong." He admitted and his hands shot to her wrists. "Stay... Hear me out"

He peered at her through his eyelashes before he looked up quickly to scan their surroundings as a smirk flashed on his lips. The small ball of fire sent sparks into the air as it snapped loudly and slowly rose above their heads. Slowly, he stepped forward and led her back toward a tree sticking just outside of the woodline out of sight from the garage. It was clear he had also heard the music in the area and now wanted to be completely alone.

"I thought I was supposed to be hearing you out."

"Not in the middle of the grounds." He whispered in her ear.

Eden felt her back press against the rough bark, the sensation sent her nerves a light once more. The feeling of being cornered overwhelmed her as it brought her back to the night of the party in the entranceway. Adrenaline coursed through her and her heart skipped as the man looked down at her. Eden's body shivered and she turned her head in the direction of the garage where the music had seemed to get fainter. Abruptly, one of her hands was released but she was too focused on the quieted song.

Holden's fingertip pushed her chin and directed her eyes back to him. Forced to meet his gaze she went to reach for the dagger hidden under her jacket. However, he pressed his body into her and blocked the path to any of her other hidden weapons. She watched as his once alluring eyes now darkened. Everything shifted suddenly from a walk around campus to what felt like a trap.

"Get off me, Heir Holloway." She attempted to break his weight held firm on her.

"You and I make sense, so why is it you seem so determined to deny it?" His grip on her other wrist tightened. "I am what is right for you and I will make you see it. Even if I have to clip your wings. Is that what you want, Little Bird?"

"Don't you know, a Viper will strike when threatened." Wyatt's voice growled from behind Holden.

The sound sent ice into her veins as she saw Holden's eyes light up. Eden had seen it before, he was ready for the hunt and seemed to know exactly who was behind him. His right hand went toward her gun tucked in a chest holster under her jacket and he turned only slightly to face Wyatt but kept his weight on her body. As he did so she was finally able to see Wyatt who was feet from them and stood five inches taller than Holden. Electricity cracked in lines between his fingers as the storm raged in his eyes.

"Is that a threat, Steele?"

"No, it's a promise. A Copperhead's bite isn't as venomous as a Viper's. I wouldn't dare stand in the way of a Viper's revenge. Now, I believe she said to get off of her. I'd hate to see you get bit." Wyatt taunted and peered over Holden's shoulder and locked eyes with her.

Eden's body didn't move from the tree, the fear she hid when her fellow hunter suddenly trapped her played in her eyes for both of them to see. Holden brought up the stolen gun and pointed it at Wyatt with a smile as she struggled under him.

"She won't do it, not to me. You see, Heiress Miller here knows she's not the top of the food chain when it comes to our families. Eloise picked a Holloway for a reason and it seems I found it. To think, I didn't even need to hunt you down."

"I don't give a fuck who you are," The sparks cracked brighter and he grabbed Holden by the arm. "I'll teach you some respect for women."

Wyatt pulled on Holden's arm and forced him off of Eden. With all his strength he turned them so the two traded places and brought his arm down overtop of the hunter's hand in an attempt to disarm him. This was quickly followed by a jolt of electricity up Holden's arm, however, the shock caused his finger to pull the trigger. The dulled sound made all of them freeze and both men looked in her direction. Her gaze followed theirs to her left shoulder she saw there was a small hole in the tree behind her. When she turned back to Wyatt she saw a mixture of shock, anger, and fear as he looked back at her with revelation in his eyes.

Without a single word, he turned toward Holden and grabbed him by the collar of his shirt. He drew his right arm back and drove it into the man's eye before he let him drop to the snow. Eden flinched but didn't stop him, something was different about Holden from a few years ago and it scared her. Wyatt took a few steps back to stand between the two, his body blocked her view and she noticed his fists shake.

"You could have killed her! Is that what you want?" He spat.

"Maybe if you weren't so reckless when you fought my finger wouldn't have slipped." Holden snapped back.

Wyatt lifted his hand as the sparks snapped around his fingers once more ready to lash out. Eden moved away from the tree quickly and stood beside him. Gently, she placed her hand on his arm and guided it back down before sliding her hand into his.

"Are you okay?" He whispered

"Fine, it didn't hit me." She looked past him, her attention on Holden while he returned to his feet.

Holden stood to his full height, his eye now bright red and glaring daggers at the two. He adjusted his clothes and pocketed Eden's gun into his own weapons belt before he held a hand out to her with the same look in his eyes before Wyatt had appeared.

"Come with me, Little Bird."

"No..." She could hear Wyatt's huff of irritation at the nickname.

"We had a deal, you need to come home. Or I tell Eloise of Bastien and his pet."

"Our deal had nothing to do with us." Eden said through gritted teeth. "Just the mission."

Holden's hand balled into a fist as he looked down at their hands. "You chose me first, Eden. Remember that when you choose between Donovan and I."

He turned and started to make his way back toward Elder row where she knew he would lurk for the next month as well as Chase. Eden drew in a slow, shaky breath and avoided the gaze she could feel on her. A set of familiar hands slowly came into view and her eyes fell on the scarred rose tattoo. She forced her eyes shut to hide the amount of emotions and adrenaline still coursing through her body.

"I think it's time for a drink." Wyatt offered quietly.

"Please," her voice broke as he wound an arm around her waist and led her toward Kappa Theta House.

Lennox

The white halls were quiet as everyone in the school had gone to the cafeteria for dinner. It was a bad time to be alone and she knew that. However, after the events of the last few days, anxiety of staying still too long took over. *I've made this walk for years.* Quickly, Lennox made her way down a hardly used side hall to get to the closest exit by Omega Alpha. Her eyes fixed on the posters that had been hung above the dark wood wainscoting over the last couple of weeks. Pictured was a silhouette of a person with words over their head. *See something suspicious? Call The Security Team.* A scoff escaped her as she tore her eyes from the words.

Her footsteps were quiet as she passed by closed classroom doors. Lennox pulled her green knit sweater closer around her in preparation to go outside. Suddenly, the announcement speaker echoed down the halls and declared everyone to head back to their rooms in two hours. While she walked down the hall, she felt the buzz of her phone in her pocket followed by one on her wrist. Lennox's hand slipped into her pocket as she passed the last corner to the exit. Her eyes went to her phone and found a message from Rosalyn with an invitation out. Before she could finish reading, she noticed a figure just over the top of her phone. With a quick glance up she was met with Eden Miller.

She jumped but relaxed when she saw it was her housemate. Eden leaned against the doorframe of an empty room with her arms folded over her chest. Lennox couldn't read her face but laughed at herself when she jumped. She shook her head and took a few steps toward the elf. Slowly, her amethyst eyes darkened with every step. When she was a few feet from her, Eden pushed off the doorframe and took a few steps to the right.

"Sorry, I didn't expect anyone to be here." She apologized while her heart sank into her stomach as she realized she was blocking the exit. "Is- Everything okay?"

"No, it's not. I have been waiting all year to talk to you about this, Lennox." The girl said in an even, dark tone making her hair stand on end. There was anger in her eyes and venom leaked into her voice.

"You can always talk to me-"

"No, I couldn't. Why would you want to listen to the girl you left at an orphanage?" Eden shot back with a raised eyebrow.

Her violet eyes went wide as her gaze shot back to Eden's amethyst iris, frozen to the spot. *She... She's Gemma?* Goosebumps trailed up her arms. For the first time since she came to the school, Lennox saw who

Eden was. Every inch of her felt like static as her nerves lit like wildfire. Her gaze darted over her every feature and finally she saw the small face of the daughter she had given up to protect so long ago. Their eyes were so close she should have put it together. What Eden didn't know was she looked just like most Cade women did. Black hair, narrow face, and high cheekbones. *How did I never see it?*

Lennox's gaze softened slightly as the two stood there in silence. She had spent years praying to Xemos to somehow allow her to find out what had happened to her daughter. Though this wasn't what she had imagined, she wanted nothing more than to hug her. However, the look on Eden's face sent a strange shiver down her spine. Internally, she gripped the vine and felt her arms heat. With every passing moment, the woman's face brightened redder with anger. *I don't blame her, she never knew why I had to leave her there.*

"Gemma? Let me just-"

"No, I'm a Miller, and you... You're the gum on the bottom of my shoe." Eden snapped.

"You have every reason to hate me," Lennox told her calmly. However, something wasn't right. "Please let me just explain."

"No, Lennox. We are doing this my way... I am going to ask the questions and if I don't like the answer, I will kill you right away. If I do, you live for a few extra minutes." She took a few steps towards Lennox and dropped her crossed arms. A flash of metal in the daylight caught her attention. Every nerve in her body lit like wildfire. The demon took a few steps back when she recognized what it was. *Mors Pugio, Death Dagger.*

Eden closed the distance with the weapon poised for the attack. With a tug on the vine of magic it sprang to life. The dim green glow sparked behind her eyes. Lennox had put two and two together the night of the attack. She wasn't here to talk about what had happened or why she had left her. Eden was here to kill her for revenge. Eden was a hunter. She had spent last semester getting to know everyone and this semester carrying out her plans. A surge of betrayal shot through her as she faced Eden.

Eden had killed Felix and the Elder.

Eden had killed Rue in the bathroom.

Eden had vanished from the party multiple times the night Octavious went missing.

"It was you, this whole time?" The words came out broken as her heart shattered.

"I couldn't go for you right away. Mother said it was better to slowly take what you loved. She was right, it was much sweeter than going straight for you but then you slipped through Alaric's fingers... Now it's my turn and I won't miss Lenny-Boo." Almost a few feet away, Eden raised the dagger and aimed right for her throat.

"You're a hunter..." The statement lingered in the air.

The weight of the situation overshadowed any thoughts of a peaceful mother-daughter reunion. This was life and death. *I don't want to do this-* With another tug, Lennox opened the floodgate of her powers with her hands in front of her. Glass shattered behind the hunter as vines broke through the door and shot through the frame to grab her. The plant life wound its way around her wrists and knees and stopped Eden in her tracks. With a motion of her fingers, she directed them to pull her back a few feet as she reached with her other hand to her phone to call Aron.

A frustrated yell echoed along the halls as Eden failed to dodge them. In their grip she struggled to cut them from her limbs which only caused them to tighten. Lennox's phone caught in her pocket and forced her to glance away from the hunter. With the momentary lapse, she felt her pull and cut the vines on her left arm. Piercing pain shot through the demon and she returned her attention to her attacker. Eden forced a hand free and silver glowed along her arms. Her eyes now illuminated bright blue while between her hands an orb of water formed and went right for her. Just before it hit, the water turned to ice as it collided with her hand.

Lennox cursed as her hand was crushed, the magic was cut off. The vines dropped and she continued to back away. She only stopped to try and read the name carved onto the metal but noticed something was different from the dagger Alaric had been armed with. As she attempted to get a better look, Eden grabbed ahold of the plant with her free hand and froze it. The frost snaked and slowly extended to the base outside which rendered them useless.

With a pause, she locked eyes with the girl once more and stood her ground. *No one else will be harmed today.* She tugged on her magic once more and stepped toward Eden. However, before she could even put her foot down, the floor beneath turned to ice. She placed her foot down but was taken to the ground. Lennox's head bounced off the floor. The hunter closed the distance easily and kicked her in the ribs. Lennox curled her knees in after the audible snap as her foot met bone. She groaned and yelled out in pain. Before she could attempt to stand she felt the cold metal of the dagger against her neck, her daughter knelt beside her.

"Now- Mommy dearest. Did you really not want me? Or was there something more going on?"

"Of course I wanted you! It was only till I was sure the curse was broken." Lennox coughed with the strain and felt a few ribs were at least fractured, one definitely broken. *She's a lot stronger than she looks.*

"Don't lie to me!" Eden's eyes bore into hers, it almost seemed she was fighting tears. She seemed conflicted and unsure of what she would do next. "You never had to make that crossroads deal! Look what happened because of what you did!"

"I'm not. Eden- You don't have to do this. I will tell you everything."

The dagger was removed from her neck. For only a moment, she thought that maybe it was enough to get her to listen to sense. However, something seemed to snap in Eden as Lennox spoke. Her eyes went wild with anger and her face went bright red as the tears spilled over.

"I- I wish I could believe you cared... I just don't. You lie, you made that deal when Xemos told you the curse was broken. You didn't have to do that! You could have just kept living happily... You could have- We could have. Instead, you're here still trying to save your own ass. I knew Eloise was right, deep down." Eden's voice broke.

She knew what was about to happen. *If I go down, everyone will know who did it.* She had to find some way to get Aron's attention. With one last pull at her already weakened magic she closed her eyes. In her mind's eye she imagined an ivy leaf with the code word, dildo on it. With every ounce she had left she willed it to grow out of Aron's bright red headband. In the same moment with a flash of silver, the dagger was driven up into her ribcage.

The area burned hotter than any fire Lennox had felt before. An ear-piercing scream escaped her and was quickly muffled by Eden's hand over her face. As the burning intensified Lennox locked eyes and struggled against the woman's grip. This was it. This would be how she would die. The others would have to find a way to stop Eden. The faces of everyone she loved filled her vision. As the fire spread, she listed off their names in her mind in goodbye. *Andy, Celia, Remi, Wyatt, Rosalyn, Aron, Felix, Rue.* With the final two faces, Lennox leaned into the fire and pain. *I'm on my way to find you two, wait for me.*

She waited for the darkness to overtake her and in that moment she hoped it would. Every bone in her body was exhausted, and at night her dreams had become darker. The loneliness that filled her had finally dragged her down. She had missed Rue every day since her death and some nights she waited for someone to reunite them. *We need you.* Wyatt's voice interrupted her as the fire stopped moving within her.

"Fight damnit!" Eden yelled. "Fight or I'll take out as many people I can before I leave."

Lennox didn't move as suddenly the heat in her chest moved to her spin where it was white hot. She kicked and screamed against Eden who held her down with a grimace. An overwhelming amount of fear crushed her as the grounds of the school filled her vision. *She may never see you again if not like this.* A deep voice rumbled within her mind and shattered past her mental shields. The voice made her hair stand on end as she struggled to breathe and the corners of her vision started to blur slightly. The world started to fall quiet.

In the distance, a familiar raw pained scream broke through the silence of her demise. Lennox's attention shot toward the sound and she fought against her grip to stand once more. Her face went pale as the sound of his echoing scream took her breath away. *Aron.* The primal sound twisted her stomach, they had gotten to him too and now he would be just like the others. Gone, another hole in her heart. Another person to mourn every day. Another name on the headstones she visited almost daily. Her vision blurred as tears sprang to her eyes. She would never see him bounce up to the chapter house. His bright red bandanna would be laid on his casket as they buried him too.

Every muscle coiled and readied for a fight as she took her hand off the dagger. In her rage, Lennox gripped Eden's wrist and forced it away from her mouth. For a moment, she could see the flash of confusion cross the woman's face at the sound of the faraway scream. *This is my fault, I didn't warn him fast enough.*

"ARON!" She lifted her head from the ground and let out a scream, her body still shaking with the pain of the fire in her back.

As she fought harder to get free she could feel the metal sink deeper into her side. *No... I have to get to him. He can't die alone.* Something deep within her stirred at the thought of his last view of the world being his killer. A stranger. Just as she had.

Lennox blinked away her tears and she looked back to Eden as she grabbed the rose bud hilt and pushed it deeper into the demon's chest. She didn't see her daughter, instead a woman who had killed three people she cared for. She wanted revenge almost as much as she wanted to beg for her forgiveness. With as much strength as she could muster she clawed at Eden. When her hands met her shoulders, she shoved back as far as she could. The hunter stumbled back and Lennox stood and tried to run. However, Eden was still faster as she was grabbed and forced back against the wall as the hunter put all of her strength into keeping her there.

The girl had made the mistake leaving Lennox's hands free; she still had a chance. She grimaced from the pain of movement as she turned under her. As she reached around her side, her eyes fell to the hidden weapons belt and saw a second dagger that stuck out of the side. In a last attempt to win, she reached for it and a spark of hope lit when her hand found the handle. Lennox swiftly pulled it from her sheath and held it directly under Eden's jaw above her.

"You've done what you needed to do, now it's my turn." She gripped the thread of magic but her hand slipped, a wall blocked her and her face shifted in pained confusion.

Eden smiled, "Not while that's doing its job you won't. You're as fragile as me right now."

A sharp pain flared as Eden reached and twisted the dagger. At the same time the wind was knocked out of her an elbow was slammed into her stomach and then again into her ribs where two shattered. With a soundless scream, Lennox's grip loosened on the dagger in her hands where the hunter took the chance to snatch it back from her. As she coughed, a hand grabbed her collar and pulled her to her feet.

"Why won't you die!" Eden gritted her teeth and looked at the blade in her hand.

Suddenly, Lennox felt her grip loosen and vanish as bright orange flames erupted on both sides of her. Without the support of Eden, she started to fall back as her leg gave out. While stumbling back she saw her daughter's gaze fixed over her head with true fear in her eyes. She could feel the heat of the fire behind her but within a matter of seconds, the orange glow dimmed when a large set of tattered black wings sheltered her. Familiar arms pulled her into their body as she fell, a shot of pain wracked her body when the dagger brushed against a black suit jacket. An arm slid under her knees and another gripped her by the shoulder as they eased the momentum of her fall as if she was nothing more than a rag doll.

She hadn't looked up to see who had saved her, but through a small gap in the wings in front of her she could see Eden's face. She sat against the opposite wall and stared at the person in shock. The second dagger had clattered to the floor a few feet away from her and there was a small trail of blood dripping down the side of her head. She dropped her gaze to the weapon where she saw her own name flash in the light. *If that's mine, whose is this?* The hunter held up her hands and attempted to sputter words out but couldn't seem to find them.

"I- Ar-" Her eyes darted between Lennox and the fallen dagger, seeming to debate going back to get the weapon.

"If you don't get out of here in the next three seconds I will make sure you don't walk out alive." A combination of two very familiar voices echoed from above her head which sent a shiver down her spine.

Her attention shifted to the wings that shielded her. The relief she had felt vanished as her gaze traced the edges of the massive shadows. Long charcoal black feathers were perfectly full at the shoulders but toward the tips they had started to thin out and fall off to reveal a more bat-like bottom edge. Her heart stopped at the sight of the very wings she had seen in her nightmares. Lennox forced her eyes away from her daughter and peered to the side to see who had rescued her. Her breath caught in her throat as a knot formed, as she saw who the wings belonged to.

She let out an audible gasp as her eyes moved up to his face. The person who looked back at her looked like Aron but with the wings and clothes of Armaros. His face had remained the same however his once green eyes were now the same pitch black with a ring of green in the center that haunted her. His expression softened under his red bandanna as their eyes met. Lennox's eyes drifted away from his face as her hand found its way to his jacket. She hadn't noticed until now that it wasn't the usual denim material and instead found a black suit jacket and midnight button-up.

She felt her magic pull at her in an attempt to defend herself against a new enemy as the smell of smoke on his body completely filled her senses. A loud scream reverberated in her mind as everything inside her told her to run. The memories from her nightmares had become so vivid, it was as if she was still there at times and now she had two people who didn't like her in the same place. Panic filled her chest and caused her heart to race but her body wouldn't move. Yet, she didn't fight against him as the realization he was protecting her settled her desire to run.

Lennox recoiled as their eyes met once more, she had expected to see the same merciless glare from Hell. However, it wasn't the same as when he did in her nightmares. This time she found worry and fear written all over his face. His eyes fell on the dagger that was still in her chest and understanding flashed as sparks sprang to life inside them.

"Aron?" His name came out as no more than a whisper of disbelief. He wasn't dead but he also wasn't just Aron.

"Len...I-I can explain... Just..." The voices softened before the sound of metal scratching on the floor caught his attention. He roared in anger as his body heated up around her. "WHY ARE YOU STILL HERE?!"

By the time Lennox shot a glance over Eden had already picked up the dagger and was gone before he could finish his sentence. The demon turned his attention back to her with a grimace as his demeanor and voice shifted slightly.

"Lennox, dear. It's been so long you look good-" Armaros's deep voice came from his lips which caused her to flinch. His demeanor shifted drastically again as Aron's regular voice came out once more. "HEY- I'm still in control here."

She couldn't look away from him as she shook slightly from the fear and pain in her side. Once she was sure Eden was gone, Lennox let go of his suit jacket as her eyes trailed to his clothes. *It's all just how I remembered.* The hall was utterly silent as she took everything in, still encircled by his grip. She attempted to pull herself together once more and tried to find words but failed. Lennox focused on his red bandanna and used it to slow her heart rate. *I'm still in control here.* His words sent a small wave of comfort over her despite how upset she was. Not realizing in the silence she was just staring at him, she attempted to mask the lingering fear in her eyes as he spoke.

"You saw that dagger had her name on it, right?" Aron's voice questioned.

"I see everything you see- So yes I did. If that was her Death Dagger... Where is ours?" Armaros asked with their combined voices.

"I think I know..." Aron replied.

Gently, he shifted her in his arms as he moved from his knees to his feet. She winced a little as every movement caused the dagger to shift and dig deeper. Lennox saw him flinch and guilt fill his eyes as he walked them away from the broken glass on the floor to a small set of stairs about ten feet away. She watched as he scanned the area with every step and only glanced down when her body tensed and the fire burned from within.

The pain kindled rage as she looked into the face of the man she had come to trust. *I was right to hate him at the beginning of the year? Does Aron still exist, or was that just a front to get into the school?Is he here for Rosalyn?* The faded edges of her vision turned red hot as she tried again and again to pull at the thread of magic but failed. Gently, he placed her on the stairs and his hands drifted over the rose bud handle. However, when she was released Lennox shrunk away from him and her eyes flashed green in a silent threat.

"Len... I promise, it's me, Aron... I have a lot to explain but that dagger needs to come out now, I don't know what that will do to you but it can't stay there." Aron's voice wavered as he seemed to try to keep it more prominent over his counterpart.

"I can do it." Lennox argued.

"Yes you can, but you don't have to."

"Why are you even here?"

"I promise, I'll tell you everything. You can hate me after this but please, I can't lose you because this stayed in too long." His words came rushed as he eyed the hilt.

She drew in a deep breath and nodded in agreement as his hand reached for the dagger. Her gaze followed the same charred black hand that caused the scars on her back, the one that reached for her throat in her nightmares. The man moved slowly and watched her body closely, just as he had since the night Octavius had been stolen. His fingers wrapped around it which caused her to suck air through her teeth as it moved ever so slightly.

"This'll only hurt a moment dear, I promise." Armaros's voice snuck out soft, almost calming.

In one swift motion, the dagger was plucked from her ribcage. Lennox yelled out as the fire burned and vanished. She leaned forward as a rush of magic and unfamiliar emotions raged inside of her. At the same time something long dormant snapped back into place in the back of her magical connections. *I can't believe it, only three times in history... It's mine.* A deep voice echoed in her mind though as she caught her breath she could hear Armaros mutter to himself. A strange underlying sensation of curiosity, dismay, and sadness entered her mind.

"Oh... oh this is interesting. This will be very interesting indeed."

Her gaze dropped to his hand as it moved the dagger around in the light. Her body tensed as the name magically carved into the blade shone brightly. *Armaros, Eden knew exactly who Aron was.* Lennox had never heard anything about a demon getting stabbed by a Demon Dagger meant for someone else. She pulled on the thread to test herself and found everything had returned to normal minus the still bleeding wound.

"It was meant for you... What does this mean?" She motioned to the blood still in shock at the situation they found themselves in.

"I don't know what it means... it seems he does though." He looked back to her with Aron's voice.

"It means an interesting road for the two... or I suppose three of us now..." Armaros hinted at the knowledge of something.

"What does that even mean?" Aron muttered to no avail. "Of course now you shut up."

He held the dagger closer to himself, as the two stayed in silence for a few seconds. Internally she struggled to reconcile that the demon knelt in front of her was not only the person she had been working beside for months, but the one who tortured her and Rosalyn.

"Len... I promise I'm still me, but this... This is also me." His voice filled with sorrow, still doubling with Armaros. He flipped the dagger and pointed the hilt gently to Lennox. "You keep this... It's the only way you'll feel safe around me now."

Within her mind, a war started to rage. It overshadowed the fear now that Armaros was quiet. As she took the dagger into the palm of her hand, she didn't move from the stairs. The memories of hell took over again, only broken up by images of herself and Aron in her room as they discussed her nightmares.

Suddenly, it all made sense. Why after he brushed up against her he suddenly was almost nervous to be around her. The times she had confided in him. *Did he know who I was talking about? How could he not, he's the one who did it.* The day she fixed his hand after the mirror accident. All the while her eyes stayed on the name on the dagger. Finally, her anger overpowered her to move and she shifted roughly a little further from him.

"How could you?" Was all that mustered out as her face started turning red and her blood boiled underneath while her voice began to raise.

"I- I trusted you. I told you everything from my nightmares and you just let me tell you. As if you didn't already know? Or was I just someone you forgot about? So insignificant that only twenty-one years later you can't remember my face? How long were you planning on hiding this from me? Letting me be the fool you string along just as you used to."

"How could I forget you, Dear? Aron had me packed away and hidden, all it took was a little jogging of the memory..." Armaros made a new appearance, a hand brushed her shoulder which caused her to recoil a little. He pulled his hand away and ran it through his hair forcing it to slick back a little.

She paused. "You remembered the night you touched my back... Saw the scars."

"Yes, it was that moment we remembered. You even fixed Aron up from our little fight with each other... dreadful we didn't tell you sooner-"

It was as if he had read her mind, but then she remembered the old mind link Armaros had created between them in Hell to discover her entire human past. *Can he still?* A smile crossed his lips briefly as Armaros was cut off by Aron wrapping his hands around his head and doubling over to fight for control.

"STOP- Stop, you're making it so much worse." He looked back up at Lennox, his eyes normal green again. "Lennox. I'm so sorry there's no way to make this all up to you... I just- I- fuck I don't even know what to say...."

"Of course I did, You're- He's my friend... Was my friend. I don't know what to believe anymore. You've been behind my nightmares all along. Ámpelos knew you were the bigger danger compared to Eden. You've spent weeks looking Rosalyn in the face or did you forget her too? Or is eight years not long enough to not need a refresh? If you're here to drag her to hell, you're going to have to go through me." She accused while her eyes lit green as the magic drained her last bit of energy.

"I promise he- We're not here for any of that... I could tell you the whole story but I feel like you're not ready to talk about all that... Rosalyn's story is something we both regret being a part of." He added simply, Aramros's voice layered evenly, showing they both felt the same way about it.

"Don't say anything... I don't want to hear it, Aron... A- Armaros." The name came out rough. "I- I can't do this."

He bit his lip as she snapped at him and did exactly as she asked. Watching him she could see the hurt in his eyes though bound by her rage but in the moment she didn't care. Lennox stood from where he had left her, and gasped since the wound hadn't closed. She wanted nothing more than to get back to Omega Alpha. She wavered on one leg and her vision blurred for a moment. When she took a step forward, pain shot through her leg causing her to fall forward.

Lennox ended up back on all fours and from the corner of her eyes, she saw Aron had jumped up and reached out to try and catch her as she fell but hesitated to touch her. Her heart pounded in her ears as she gasped for breath. She heard him take a few steps toward her and carefully knelt beside her once again. His appearance slowly shifted back to Aron's, first with the wings as they folded away into his back with a grunt of pain. The suit shifted back to his regular clothes and he was back to regular Aron as he offered a hand.

"That should make you more comfortable, dear." Armaros's voice and eyes flashed back.

"Dude- seriously not helping anytime you talk," Aron shushed. "Let me help you get cleaned up and... And then you can never talk to either of us again."

The final flash of black set her off once again and she flinched from his hand. "I don't want your help- Please, don't touch me."

He stayed perfectly still and kneeling next to Lennox but simply bore his palms to her in a surrendering position. Their voices came out simultaneously again. "As you wish."

She struggled to her feet holding the dagger to her chest with a final tug on the magic she forced the shattered bones to snap into place enough to walk. She left him where he was knelt and with her back to him as she made her way towards the broken glass to go home. Lennox stepped over it and she heard the crunch beneath her feet, thankful for the noise as her breath hitched in her chest. Her vision blurring with angry tears she kept hidden from him. *You will not see me break again.* She wanted to promise herself but knew that wasn't possible.

"I would never want to see you break. A part of me did not enjoy seeing it the first time, admittedly... " Armaros's voice came out crystal clear and gestured to the dagger that could take his life. "Just take care of yourself... Take care of that."

The two of them spoke in unison and separated once again. However, when Armaros came alone she found her feet came to a halt in the doorway, gaze glued to the broken glass. She felt two tears spill over as she turned to face him. A knot had tied itself in her throat and made words hard to form. She drew a strangled deep breath in and her eyes filled with the betrayal she felt inside.

"Really? Because the look in your eyes all those years ago told me otherwise. I've spent the last few weeks seeing the joy it brought you to hurt Rosalyn and me." Her voice was low, angry. She paused before her next words came out. "I don't know who you are anymore, Aron. Come to me when you've figured it out."

She turned as she felt her chest tremble, unable to look at him at the moment. She took one last pause and looked down at the dagger in her hands, the name of the man she hated most flashed in the daylight. The threat over their lives was much more real now and she could either take care of it or protect the weapon that could kill the demon she hated all because he was inside of one she cared about. She turned it around as her thoughts raced before her eyes returned to the grounds. *I can't- I don't think I could hurt him, even if he is Armaros.*

"No one will be able to use this against you. Not even me..." She turned and made her way to the broken door frame as the two bickered again.

"I thought she'd be more grateful for us saving her life." Armaros slipped through Aron's mouth.

"Shut the fuck up, this is your... our fault... this is our fault she doesn't trust us anymore... we put that scar on her back and her soul."

The other's laughter from the room below wafted up the stairs in waves that rose and fell. Lennox stood with her hand on the knob of Rosalyn's room, where she had slept the last three nights after Alaric and Eden almost killed her only to be saved by Aron. Her breath suspended as she mentally shoved the betrayal into a box and shoved it into a corner to be opened later. *Just get through this and you can go to sleep for the night.* Not that sleep helped, the nightmares were worse than ever last night and she had woken Rosalyn up every few hours. She had been so understanding each time Lennox woke her up, though it didn't stop her from the guilt.

From the top of the stairs, she watched as Wyatt pulled off his jacket and ruffled the snow out of his hair as it fell on the carpet. All in a span of seconds, the memory of Eden played in her mind like a broken movie projector. Lennox's eyes went wide as she realized he probably had no idea who she really was. *Oh my gods, Wyatt is dating my daughter. I have to tell him.*

She seized the opportunity to pull his attention and put a hand on the banister. With a simple tug of the thread she sent a vine down at lightning speed toward the hook by the front door. It swiftly scooped up the jacket by the collar straight out of Wyatt's hands and let it hang just above his head. Wyatt jumped and looked around in confusion before a smile formed on his face when he saw the plant life. He tugged it down from the leaves and put it on the hook before he turned to face the stairs. As Lennox walked down, she saw the dark circles under his eyes the closer she got. Greeting him with a hug she found the forced smile seemed to come slightly easier than upstairs.

"Well hey there stranger."

"How are you doing? It's been a few days since-" He paused and cleared his throat.

"I'm okay, I'm rooming with Rosalyn for a few more days while she helps me get things cleaned up."

"Good, I'm glad you're not alone or I'd be offering up my room." He smiled and turned to the common area as voices continued to drift in.

"I appreciate it, but I'm sure you'd much rather have Eden over." Lennox brought up the name to see his reaction mostly but knew she wouldn't be able to sleep so close to Armaros.

"I've got time for everyone." His attention turned toward the common area and she saw the tips of his ears go red. "Are you ready to join the party?"

"I do but we really need to talk."

"How about over some drinks?" He smiled and peered over to her.

Lennox scanned as much of his face she could see. Wyatt avoided her eyes for a second and it was all she needed as their gaze met and his usual smile masked. He knew *something*. With a nod she started to follow behind him, her view mostly blocked due to the top of her head level with his shoulders. From the bottom of his short-sleeved black t-shirt, her eyes fell to bits of silver on the back of his arm. Only able to see an inch of a few silver lines, her brows furrowed as they distracted her from trying to figure out how to warn him. *Those look like my chains... No, he would never.*

"Did you make a deal with Xemos?" The words of disbelief came out with no filter and no way to retract them as a hand reached out for a second before she pulled back.

Wyatt's feet stopped and his whole body seemed to turn to rock. "Yes."

"You hate him why would you-""Because I need to be stronger to keep everyone safe. I can't do that if I can't fight the hunters." He snapped as his eyes filled with a storm that hid something else within.

Taken aback, Lennox took a small step back to give the demon some room. She forced herself to hide the pang she felt at his raised voice and let the others chatter fill the silence. It had been a long time since she had seen him this stressed which only helped her push her own issues aside for the moment.

"You aren't alone in keeping everyone safe, Wyatt, you know that."

"I know, there's just so much going on right now... We almost lost you that night."

You almost lost me twice thanks to your girlfriend... My daughter. She shuttered internally. "Does it have anything to do with Eden?"

Wyatt's jaw clenched as his eyes shifted to the left. "It's complicated."

"It's much more complicated than I think you know... Wyatt, she's-"

As Lennox went to give him the warning, his expression shifted from happiness to fear. With a swift step toward her, he reached out and took her by the shoulders. The movement sent a wave of shock through her, surprised at the action that told her everything she needed to know. Lennox took a step away from him to put her at arm's length, a light tinge of green filled her vision as her eyes reflected the advancing magic. Held in a stand-off, they didn't move for a few seconds before the burn of betrayal in her chest caused her vision to shift red.

"You're dating my daughter... And you already knew that. How long were you going to wait to tell me?"

"Excuse me? Nox, I don't know what you're talking about." He shook his head as a spark snapped behind his head.

"You've never lied to me before Wyatt, I wouldn't start now... You know exactly who she is don't you?" Her heart dropped at the look in his eyes.

"Are you two making out in here or something?" A new voice echoed down the hall at them.

Lennox peered over his shoulder and saw two of their friends with their heads around the corner. Octavius with a devious smirk on his face and Rosalyn with a raised eyebrow and cheerful tone. Immediately, the heaviness in the air faded away like it was never there. A fire burned deep within Lennox as she wanted to demand answers. How long had he protected a hunter, probably the very one who killed two of the most important people in her life?

"Ew, Ros, No." Her tone came out harsher than she intended.

"Hey, it wasn't that bad that one night." Wyatt folded his arms over his chest and seemed relieved someone interrupted them.

"I'm not saying it was bad. You and I looked at each other, even drunk off our asses, and couldn't take any of it seriously."

"Still, I wasn't that bad. Come on, Len. I got a reputation to uphold."

"I just can't see you as anything more than a brother."

"Eden seems perfectly fine with your reputation. Come on you two, we have to start planning for the party!" Rosalyn said lighthearted and pulled Octavius back into the room.

Lennox shook her head and followed her down the hall before she spun on her heel to face Wyatt when Rosalyn turned the corner. "Don't think we won't talk about this later."

The two entered the room one after the other, and took the two remaining seats on the couch in front of the coffee table. She sank into her seat and tried to appear as normal as possible while the conversation turned to the topic at hand. Rosalyn opened her planner and set it in her lap with a pen in hand as she looked between the three of them.

"Alright, so Wyatt has already agreed to keep him distracted in the town over until about lunch. I was thinking then Lennox if you could have him help with something in Omega while the rest of us set up inside Kappa."

Her nerves flared, "I think I might be better at setting up. If I'm distracting him he'll know something's up."

"You two are always hanging out, why would that be suspicious?" Rosalyn's eyebrow rose at her and she shrunk ever so slightly.

"Yeah, Len's not really great at secrets at times." Wyatt agreed and took the attention off of her. "Octavious could drag him somewhere?"

"Whoever, I just need someone to keep him out of Kappa until seven." Rosalyn waved her hands as she wrote something down. "You guys figure that out then."

The next hour was filled with job assignments and things they needed to get for the party. Wyatt had agreed to call the brewery in Millstone Grove to supply them with a keg of his favorite beer. Octavius would make the playlist and Rosalyn would gather the decorations. As the others talked between each other, Lennox found herself slowly fade into her memories as if she were only a ghost. Armaros's black eyes haunted her in the sunlight even with the new mixture of the red bandanna. It had made it almost impossible to connect two such different people as one. Aron had never once acted like Armaros and if he really didn't remember her or Rosalyn until recently how was she supposed to stay mad at him? *It doesn't change anything... He's always been Armaros even if he didn't remember us... He knew who he was and chose to hide it.*

Wyatt's voice echoed from far off and a lump twisted itself into her throat as she recalled the look in Eden's eyes. The frustrated, *why won't you die,* played in the back of her mind followed by the sound of glass as it shattered behind her. As she relived the moment over and over, she realized he had used a single wing to push Eden away. Her heart skipped a beat and she clasped her shaking hands together. Possibilities of how much he knew were listed in her mind like a checklist. *Is there a possibility he knew she was just a hunter and not Gemma? No, the look on his face wasn't shocked at the information. Has he been protecting her this whole time? Or is that why we found Octavious alive? I need answers.*

Lennox kept her gaze on her hands and continued to let the others converse with each other as the water dissipated from her eyes. Betrayal settled into her stomach and made her feel queasy. Aron was Armaros, Eden was Gemma, and Wyatt knew exactly who had killed their loved ones. *How could he protect her?*

"Love makes people do strange things, Miss. Cade." A familiar presence washed over her and the voice of Xemos sounded clear.

Love makes people blind. She told him with a huff as another pang of betrayal fell into the pit of her stomach. *How much of this did you know?*

There was a pause as Xemos sent a wave of discontentment over her.

"You've questioned me more this year than you did the year you made the deal. In eighteen years, have I not proven that you can trust me? I have always kept you safe, have I not?"

You have but-

"You needed to discover this on your own. Trust my judgment. I will not let harm befall you and in time you will understand, Little Phoenix."

The nickname Xemos had called her occasionally over the years always caught her attention. She could sense in his voice that this wasn't a matter he would be going into an explanation about. He only used it when she questioned him about this plan he told her he had for her the day she walked through the gates of SCHUni. When it came to her devotion over the years, she knew there was more to come that would indeed make sense later.

"Alright guys, I think we are all good. Lennox? Did you have any other ideas?" Rosalyn's voice pulled her back into the moment.

"No, I think that's good."

"Alright people, let's make it happen!"

She watched as Octavius stood and approached Rosalyn while out of the corner of her eye, she noticed Wyatt watching her closely. Her attention drifted toward Wyatt as she struggled to find anything to say to him. This may be a part of Xemos's plan for her but that didn't mean the feeling of betrayal was going away any time soon.

"Lennox," His voice was hardly a whisper. "I promise, I had no idea about what Alaric did."

"Stop... Not here."

He drew in a sharp breath and nodded as she stood from her spot. With a step around him she passed the laughing couple, the sight sent another wave of irritation over her. She walked right out of the room, her chest tight as she stepped into the hall. With every intention to go upstairs since it was almost curfew, her feet started to carry her toward the front door. Before she left, she grabbed her green and cream-lined winter jacket from its hook and left Omega house.

Footsteps followed behind her as Wyatt stayed close behind her. With every exhale, she saw her breath drift away on the wind. The moment the winter air touched her face her lungs expanded; an audible gasp sprang forward. Lennox continued down the steps, she lifted her hand and a small flame sparked into existence. The dull warmth brushed against her face and she kept her eyes locked on the closed gate in the front of the school about a two-minute walk away.

"Nox, please talk to me." Wyatt's voice made her stop.

Lennox spun on her heel. "What am I supposed to say? You knew she was one of them and never bothered to warn us?"

"Like you called the moment you found out?" He shot back.

"She stabbed me!" Her eyes widened.

"Her mother locked me in their basement!" He stepped closer to her. "Neither of us are handling this right. We both want to protect the people we love."

"We do but there's a hunter on your list." Lennox lowered her voice.

"She's on yours too. No matter if you want to admit it or not, you want to protect her too. You're the Protector of Witches. Eden is a Witch. You can't hurt her."

"I don't want to, but I am done with funerals. She has a family, and they do not belong here."

"She belongs with us. That family is terrible. If you care about her at all, you'll show her there's more to life than anger." Wyatt's gaze hardened before he went back to the house.

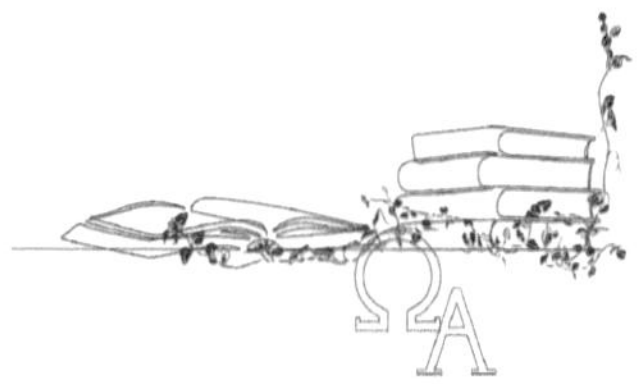

The grounds of the school were eerily quiet as she followed the small path to the front. She let her gaze drift to the stone pillars that held up the tall, curved, and spiked gate, she spotted the mostly burned candles she had left over the years as they poked just an inch above the snow. Quickly, she knelt down and used the flames she carried with her to carefully melt the snow around them. Being careful to not let it get too close to the wax she revealed two purple and one black pillar-shaped candle. Each stood about seven inches tall and had many hardened drips over the edges.

As she guided the flame over the wicks she let them spring to life, each tall and strong. Lennox closed her eyes and let the silence of the evening clear her mind. She kept the orb of light above her head now as she placed the palms of her hands down on the exposed ground beside the candles. The image of purple asters filled her mind's eye and slowly she tugged on the thread of magic and allowed it to flow into the ground.

Leaves and stems grew from the wet soil and sprouted buds. Within seconds purple asters surrounded the candles and grew slightly up the stone and brought some color to the winter. A small smile pulled at her lips though frustrated, she leaned into her devotion.

"The Greeks believed this flower gave them wisdom and faith... I'll trust you, but I don't know if I can handle what you're putting me through."

No response came, in fact the only sound was the soft flapping of wings. Paranoia filled her mind as she thought Armaros was trying to sneak up behind her. Her eyes flew open and scanned the grounds behind her but found nothing. A sudden loud caw sent her attention to the lower part of the gate almost at her eye level.

A black raven sat perched above Lennox, twisting its head to the side a few times and letting out another more mellow coo. Her eyebrows met as she watched it, utterly confused. *Xemos never sends ravens.* Another caw sounded loudly as it peered back toward Omega Alpha House before it turned to her again. She rose to her feet and took a step back, as the hair rose on the back of her neck. The raven opened its wings and cawed again.

Lennox's head tilted as something inside her intuition told her to head back to the house. However, curiosity at this black bird and why it was determined she went back held her in place. The two didn't move as it occasionally looked around the grounds behind her and let out another demanding caw. Inside her mental barriers, something brushed against the shield as if it instructed her home. The touch made her spin around and look around the empty grounds. Her eyes drifted from Omega to Kappa and back before a final caw made her jump. She turned her head just in time to watch the raven start to disappear into the sky.

With a swipe of her hand she sent a small rush of wind to extinguish the candles before turning back for the house. With her arms wrapped around herself she peered up to confirm it was gone and found it circled over her while she walked. The raven followed her until she made it to the stairs of the house, once there it vanished from view. *What the hell is going on?*

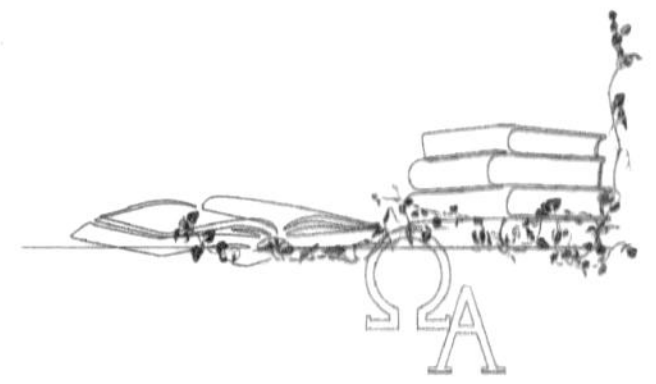

As she pulled a sweatshirt over her head, Lennox couldn't let go of the image of the raven as it watched her. Her thoughts raced as she considered Eden had somehow watched her through the bird and waited for the right time to corner her again. *But I've never seen a raven around before. If it was Eden, it would have been around a lot more.* Eventually she chalked it up to the curious nature of the creatures and brushed it off as Rosalyn walked through the door. The door shut with a soft thud as she started to get ready for bed.

A heavy silence settled into the room as Lennox ran a makeup wipe over her face, erasing the pink eyeshadow she wore everyday. She brushed it over the permanent dots along her eye sockets and symbol of Xemos over her forehead. As she looked in the mirror, she attempted to find a semblance of familiarity in her features.

"You know, Nox you're really shitty at hiding when something is going on. I think that's the quietest I've seen you at any meeting... Like ever."

Shit. Lennox sighed as she turned to face her best friend as guilt bubbled up and she met her eyes. "I know... It's just that a lot has happened these last few days."

A smile found its way to Rosalyn's heart shaped face and she came over. The kindness sent her stomach into knots as she knew it had come time to tell her. She had no idea that Armaros was not only on earth for the first time since they left hell, he was their friend.

"Well then, pop a squat and tell me what's up." She motioned to the two small maroon vintage arm chairs in the foyer opposite from her desk.

The two sat and Lennox bit the inside of her cheek before deciding to speak. "After the night when Alaric broke into my room isn't the only thing that's been going on. Yesterday, I was on my way back here and Eden Miller cornered me."

A gasp from Rosalyn made her pause. "Eden? But why-"

"Because she's a hunter... She's... Also Gemma." She let the words hang so they could sink in. "She's mad that I left her at the orphanage and didn't believe me when I told her that I was coming to get her the day I died. She had a Death Dagger. I would have been dead if Aron hadn't shown up in time."

"Well that's a good thing right?"

"Yes, but there's more to the story than just that." Lennox prepared herself.

"What, like he knew when it was going to happen? How come you haven't told Coyote or Fang... We need to-"

The demon shook her head and shifted in her seat. Slowly, she lifted the bottom of her school sweatshirt and revealed the still healing stab wound. Around the soon to be scar, deep red colored her veins like darkened spider webs. Rosalyn reached out but retracted her hand as her brown speckled eyes went to the injury in utter shock.

"How are you still alive?" Rosalyn breathed.

"Eden stabbed me with someone else's dagger and by the look on her face, it was meant for Aron- But it didn't have his name on it" She accentuated the fact.

"Stop beating around the bush, Len. Whose name was on the dagger?"

The question was unavoidable and she deserved to know. "Armaros-"

Rosalyn tensed at the name and looked at her with disbelief. "Why would Eden create a dagger for him if he's still in Hell?"

"Because he's not in Hell anymore. He's here, Ros… He's residing inside Aron. I don't understand how or why he's here but-"

Lennox's words faded as she watched her friends' eyes widen as they darted from the door and back to her. For a millisecond she seemed to fade away which caused Lennox to hold her breath, she knew she was reliving every second of the decades she was trapped. She didn't move for the longest time until suddenly Rosalyn's hands flew to her head as she let out a scream she figured would echo across the campus. She slammed her eyes shut and when they opened again they were filled with purple light while lavender flames danced around her body.

Lennox raised her palm up and sent a barrier around the room so her fire wouldn't catch on anything and burn the house down. She watched carefully as Rosalyn pulled at her magic and the fire grew steadily. Over the years she knew there wasn't anything she could do to help the situation other than be there at the end. She knew Rosalyn had been training in case they ever ran into Armaros again. It was showing now as the heat turned the room into a sauna. The barrier prevented any more of her screams from being heard from the outside.

Her own memories of the screams inside Hell attempted to push their way forward remembering every one of the demons she had been chained beside. As the flames continued to shoot in various directions, Lennox went over to each entry point in the room and held her palm aiming above it. Slowly a protection sigil drew itself on each in green fire in the shape of a triangle with a single, longer line through the center followed by a smaller horizontal line at the point of the shape.

It took just over a half hour for the flames to slowly die down. Meanwhile, Lennox busied herself with the extension of newly created vines over the door and windows and left the sigils out for her to see. The room slowly darkened; the only source of light was from two lamps by the bed. Lennox turned and peered over to her with a calm expression, she stood under the sigil and tried to appear as unthreatening as possible. Rosalyn's chest heaved as she attempted to catch her breath, her still widened eyes on Lennox.

"I've made it so no one, not even them, can get in." Her eyes darted above Lennox's head but she didn't move. "Why don't we go to bed and talk more tomorrow?"

Rosalyn moved as if in slow motion, pure exhaustion in her face. With a small nod, she stepped toward the bed. Lennox followed and went to the other side of the bed while she watched Rosalyn out of the corner of her eye. Once under the blankets, both rolled opposite ways as her eyes fell onto the ivy-covered window. The last thing she saw before she attempted to sleep.

That was until the sound of music drifted in from outside, just loud enough to cause the ivy to shake. Ámpleos sent an alert to her that someone untrusted was nearby. Her violet eyes shot open and Lennox carefully sat up and moved the blankets off of her. As she glanced in the darkness she heard the music drift in from the window closest to her. With a glance to make sure Rosalyn was still asleep, she shifted her feet to the floor and crossed her arms as a shiver wracked her body. With a simple wave of her hand, the plant life retracted and enabled her to see. In the shadows of the night traced along the snow banks stood a familiar man, as he held up a speaker and a nervous look on his face.

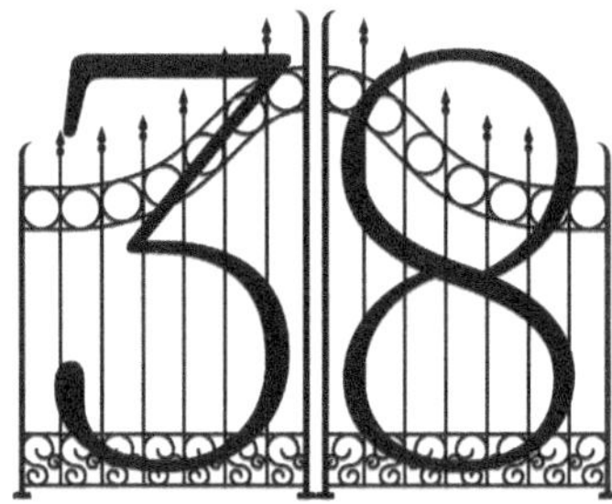

The red bandanna was all Lennox needed to see under the street-light to know exactly who it was, *Aron*. A wave of fear washed over her as she watched him draw attention to himself and the house at midnight. The familiar song that played with lyrics about forgiveness and taking a moment to forget the world. She watched him for a few seconds while she decided if she should tell him to leave or talk to him. Since yesterday afternoon she wanted nothing more than to interrogate him, yell everything that had been running through her mind. She shook her head and reinforced the barrier she had put around the room to keep out external sounds.

With a swipe of her hand, she brought the ivy back over the window and turned away from it. Though just as she stepped toward the bed, her phone buzzed on its charger and flashed a photo of the demon standing outside. With a frown she tapped the ignore button and quickly typed out a message.

> Lennox-
> You're going to wake up everyone in my house. Shut off the music.
> -Sent 12:02 am

> Aron-
> Come down and I will. I just want to talk and I promise he will not make an appearance. It's just me tonight, please Lennox, let me explain.
> -Sent 12:03 am

> Lennox-
> You realize I barely trust just you right now, right?
> -Sent 12:03 am

> Aron-
> Fair, I don't expect you to. Just give me one hour and I will tell you anything you want to know. No more lies, bring the dagger- You can take me out if you decide.
> -Sent 12:05 am

Her eyes didn't move from the message on her phone. As much as she wanted to trust Aron, she didn't trust Armaros and now they were one in the same. Lennox had spent hours with her nose in her demon studies book on possession in an attempt to begin to understand this Doctor Jekyll and Mister Hyde situation. Xemos's words from earlier reverberated within her as she moved her gaze to the sigil above the door. *Trust my judgment. I will not let harm befall you and in time you will understand, Little Phoenix.*

With a glance over to her friend sound asleep in bed, Lennox tip-toed over to the bag of things Rosalyn had grabbed from her room the night of the attack. Silently she rummaged through it and dug all the way to the bottom where a copy of last year's advanced magics course book resided. She flipped open the cover and a few pages to reveal the very dagger that had been in her side just over twenty-four hours ago. Quickly, she pulled it out and closed the book before she put it back at the bottom of the bag. Ever so carefully she slid it into her pajama pants pocket but paused when she felt something brush against her mental barriers followed by a soft coo. She quickly turned her attention to the window and found the raven perched on the vines outside through the window.

Lennox watched the bird silently as confusion crossed her face. *Is this the same raven?* It peered behind itself and looked back at her before it suddenly took off. With no time to question the bird's presence, she went to the door and the vines retracted when she reached for the knob. As quietly as she could, she opened and shut the door only far enough to get through without waking Rosalyn. With success, she covered the doors once more and sent extra magic into them so Rosalyn could get out if she woke up before she got back.

She grabbed her green jacket once more and shifted the dagger to the inner pocket before she made her way out the front door. When she lifted her palm up an orb of flames ignited just above her skin and floated eye level to her right. In the light of the lamps, Lennox could see Aron about ten feet from the front door as he pushed his speaker back into a bag and swung it on. A flame like hers was lit beside him and kept the bitter cold air at bay. When she shut the door he jumped and peered up to her with mild surprise. He ran his hand through his hair and took a visible breath before he started to walk to her.

Even in the darkness, there was enough light from the full moon above for her to see his emerald eyes gauge her reaction. She refused to look away since when he had seen her last she held back tears they both knew were there. Her eyes scanned every move he made as he closed the distance and that's when she saw it. The look she had seen on various faces throughout the school after Felix and Rue's murder. As if she might lose it at any moment, like she was fragile.

When he stopped he bore both of his palms face up. "You have every right to be mad. After tonight if you want me to leave you alone I will. You have the right to know everything I can tell you."

"You felt like now was the best time? A day later? You know, normally people usually wait for the pissed off party to come to them." She snapped and hid the recoil she felt on the inside. It was easy to be mad at Aron, however, the back of her mind reminded her who he was as last night's nightmare had reminded her how dangerous he was.

"I guess I'm bad at waiting when I know I can do something to help you understand. You're as smart as a whip and stronger than a lot of demons I've met, Len. You and Rosalyn will know everything, I owe you that."

"So you decided that blasting music in the middle of the night was the best way to get my attention? You really don't care about rules, do you?"

"It got you out here didn't it?" He came to a stop at the bottom of the stairs. "I thought you already knew I was a rule breaker, Lenny-Boo?"

The two watched each other for a moment before she nodded and walked down the three stairs and onto the path. Lennox only hesitated for a second when she came within arms reach of him as a small shadow of a hopeful smile twinged at his lips.

"You're right, I'm here and ready to hear it all." She folded her arms over her chest.

"We shouldn't talk here, too many ears." He glanced at the few rooms whose lights had turned on.

"If you cared about that, I wouldn't have woken up half of Omega."

"If we are caught out here and not in one of the houses by the security team they are going to think something's up."

"What about the gazebo by the lake? They wouldn't have too many reasons to go that way and maybe they won't think anything of our scents around the grounds since they know I patrol." Aron suggested.

With another nod, she turned a little to the right to start to head toward the back of campus. As she walked she saw Aron out of the corner of her eyes, he kept some distance between them as the quiet of night took over. Lennox forced herself to keep her eyes ahead and forced herself to trust him no matter how scared she was of the demon that lay beneath. *He's been there for weeks, he would have hurt us if he wanted to.* She reminded herself quickly but still didn't find much comfort in the thought as they crossed the campus in ten minutes.

The moonlight shone off the frozen lake and reflected like a mirror. The pine trees that surrounded the stone gazebo were covered in a dusting of snow. Her eyes traced the white columns that lead up to a silver dome roof with a tall point on the top. On the edge of the roof was a ring of iron spikes that mimicked the front gate. The trees that circled the small structure prevented a large amount of snow from piling on the inside.

As she walked under the dome, she glanced up and sent her flames halfway to the top. She kept her attention on the rising fire and saw Aron's flame also drift into view where it met hers and joined together. Suddenly the night around the gazebo fluttered momentarily as a shield developed around each column, a barrier she knew would prevent any passersby from the sight of their fires. With a deep breath, she pushed off any malicious intentions on his end that invaded her mind and shoved the trapped feeling that washed over her down deeper. Occasional gusts sent a trail of warmth down that Lennox could feel on her cheeks and at the same time a pair of eyes. Finally, she dropped her gaze and met those familiar green eyes.

"How?" Was all she could muster herself to ask after a pause.

"How is Armaros within me? Or how could I not tell you?" His voice was even, calm.

"Both."

"Well, I'm still just a bit hazy on all the details but from what I've discovered he possessed a human body to start a new life. It sounded like he was running from something but he won't share what it was. He- We then became one and after that he laid dormant for so long that I kinda just forgot he was there."

She looked at him incredulously. "You forgot he was there?"

"Someone doesn't talk to you for two decades, you kinda forget they exist, Len." The fire snapped above them and a few embers fell out and faded within seconds. The sound caused her to blink in surprise as he continued. "As for the second, how could I have told you after we just became friends? When was the right time to tell you I suddenly remembered I have the one person who tortured two people I consider friends? I needed time to process and figure out what the hell was happening in my head."

"So the night with the mirror..."

"We were fighting, it was hard to come to terms with what I discovered of our past."

Lennox's heart ached a little as she remembered the cuts all over his hand. She had held true to her word and didn't bring it up again. Suddenly, it all made sense of why over the last few weeks since he brushed her old burn scars he had acted so strange. She had been too distracted to notice he was going through something. As empathy willed itself up, regret that wasn't hers found its way beneath the surface and caused her brows to furrow slightly.

She tried to fit the two together and passed it off as her forgiveness for second chances even when she shouldn't. Possibly, it was the way he seemed almost as tormented by the past as she was that caused her change of heart. She shifted her weight and finally unlocked her gaze from his as he motioned toward a stone bench on the edge of the gazebo. They both took a seat on opposite ends and she considered her next question.

"So he wanted to start over and you, Aron, I'm imagining a human at the time, agreed to let him possess you?"

"I think so, but the human me, I don't really remember much of and eventually I just called myself Aron. I know he liked rock and roll-Maybe that's why I do." For a second his words trailed off as he seemed to fade before he came back. "His name was Darren- Fuck, Derek! Sorry, Derek."

Her eyes softened ever so slightly as he stumbled over his words and watched him rake his hand through his hair and look at her cautiously. "It's okay, I'm not going to use the dagger because of a wrong name. I'm mad, but I'm not that mad."

For a second he stood frozen before he let out a laugh and his demeanor loosened. "Well, I guess you could say I'm Derek and Armaros's love child."

She couldn't stop the laugh that followed as the tension between them faded into more of a haze than a looming cloud. The force sent a stab of pain through her side from her still sore wound. After she had seen the wound surrounded with darkened veins that spanned at most three inches from the center, something nagged at her. The same way different waves of emotions occasionally washed over her. *Oh... oh this is interesting. This will be very interesting indeed.* Armaros's words echoed as they had been which brought goosebumps to her skin.

"Are you okay?" He suddenly asked and motioned to her hand over the spot. "I can try to heal you if you'd like."

"It's okay, I've been trying and I don't think it's able to be... I do have something I do want to ask though. When you- Armaros- well both of you saved me and saw the dagger he said something about this being interesting... I couldn't help to notice he went pretty quiet after that and I had this strange wave of emotions hit that didn't seem to make sense for what was happening."

Aron flinched and paused for a second as his brows furrowed. It was a few seconds before he blinked and shook his head. "I asked him after you walked away, he locked up his thoughts and he still won't tell me even though the information could be useful right now."

"I thought we all agreed on no more lies."

His jaw clenched before his expression softened once more. "I guess it's more of a secret."

"So he can hide things from you, can you do the same?" She questioned as curiosity got the better of her.

"It pisses me off but no I can't. It's hard to block him out for extended periods of time but even when I do it seems he can still see the memories."

She considered the statements for a moment, they made sense given the power imbalance between one of the strongest demons from Hell and a human body turned demon. Images of the ten foot long tattered black wings flashed briefly and brought with it a new question.

"What was that scream I heard before you arrived? I thought- I thought you were dead." She tried her best to hide the old emotions from the moment that threatened to well up.

"I was so far away, you were in the halls and I was in my room when the dildo leaf appeared. As fast as I ran, I knew there was no way I was going to make it to you in time on my own. Armaros-" He paused at the name and watched her reaction, with none he continued. " He convinced me to let him out so we could help you, hence the wings and suit."

"He's not him without the suit." She fiddled with the edge of her sleeve.

A lingering question dangled between them, one she didn't want to be the one to ask. She attempted to picture Kappa with another new head of house within six months of each other which sent a new type of grief over her as she remembered Felix. For some reason it didn't feel right if Aron didn't walk into the kitchen at random hours to challenge her to Uno or with some movie in hand she had never heard of, yelling about her living under a rock. Ultimately, the possibility of the presence of the demon from her nightmares around in any capacity made her want him gone, however she cared about the person in front of her, now one of her closest friends.

"Are you going to stay?"

For a second he was silent and his eyes fell to his hands. Lennox stayed silent while he seemed to debate his answer either with Armaros or himself she wasn't sure. Slowly he shifted in his seat, faced her and slid a bit closer. A light touch on her hands made her look down as Aron's covered hers to steady them, she hadn't even been aware they began to shake.

"I came here to have fun and get away from my duties as a crossroad demon. This is your home and Rosalyn made it hers too. If it makes things more comfortable to have me gone, I'll leave."

"I- No." She looked away as she spoke too fast; with a quick inhale she felt the heat in her ears.

His eyebrows rose in surprise followed by the smallest smile. "That's not what I was expecting. Are you sure you still want me around? Even with him on board?"

"With Eden knowing so much, we need you here... Then I think we should talk about it together once there's less danger. What if she goes after someone else to get you to come back?"

Aron nodded in agreement and kept his eyes on hers. "You'd miss me too much anyways. Besides, what if the next Head of House wasn't as cool?"

Lennox let out another laugh, "Who else is going to annoy me for actually going to class or doing my work? Since we're being honest, I think we make a good team, and I can't lose anyone else. Not right now."

"I knew it, you'd miss me." He teased.

His hands slipped away as finally her body seemed to settle, even with the knowledge of who he was, he was still Aron. Once again, she found forgiveness for a second chance but knew Rosalyn wouldn't be able to. She would want him to leave, not that she blamed her in the slightest. However, she decided she'd find a way to make it work. After the discovery that her own daughter was actively trying to kill her, she felt as if she'd snap if anyone else vanished from her life.

"Rosalyn is going to kill me when she finds out." Aron pointed out.

Her heart fell into her stomach. "Oh, absolutely."

"Comforting, Leonard. Did you say anything?" Lennox fell silent. "Shit, I'm surprised I'm still breathing."

"She's been my best friend since I died. She deserved to know, I was only with him for less than a month, she was with him for decades. ”

“It's okay, I'll find a way to talk to her... Maybe all three of us?”

“Only if she wants me there.” She agreed.

At the same time, the two turned their attention to the frozen lake, the quiet of the night doing nothing to help fill the silence. That was until his stomach rumbled loudly. With another laugh, Lennox looked over and rested her arm on the gate.

“Skipped dinner?”

“Haven't really been hungry.” He admitted and rubbed the back of his head.

With a quick grip on the internal thread, she stood and went to the edge of the gazebo where there was an empty spot between two pine trees. With a gentle tug she allowed the image of a tall tree to fill her mind. It was hard to see in the shadows, it wasn't until the tree stood about three feet that it started to be visible. Within minutes a pomegranate tree formed with two of the fruits within arms reach. Once done, she reached up and plucked them from their spots before she turned back toward Aron. When their eyes met again, his jaw had dropped ever so slightly as more unheard conversation seemed to go on within his mind. She took her previous seat and passed him the one in her left hand.

“That was kick ass, Lennyboo! You gotta show me how to do that.”

“Maybe if you came to class you'd know.” She retorted as they broke open the shells.

The two pulled the seeds out and Lennox's mind began to wonder again. *How could I hate and protect two different people who are really one at the same time?* The whole situation was ludicrous and something she had never seen before even in her studies of demon possession for her Magical Arts class. No matter how much she wanted to tell Armaros to leave and go back to where he came from, she couldn't without the loss of Aron. If he was going to stay she had to accept him, all of him, including the darkness.

She fixed the messenger bag strap on her shoulder and made her walk down the halls to the front entrance. Lennox's eyes scanned the area before she turned each corner as the memory of the anger in Eden's eyes haunted her once again. The hair on the back of her neck stood on end with the memory of the dagger as it found its way into her side. As she turned the final corner the demon came face to face with the very photos of Rue and Felix she spent so much time in front of. After weeks of chaos it felt as if it has been years since she saw their faces even in this form.

She came to a brief halt in front of them, grief struck her though it wasn't as strong as it had once been. Instead, it was replaced with a deep anger that fueled her from the core. *My own daughter killed them.* The concept was almost too wild to be reality, but it was. Eden resembled Lennox in so many ways it was surprising she hadn't noticed it before. All the Cade women had pin straight black hair and sharp features. Within her mind a new thought sparked to life and pulled itself forward. *The purple eyes should have been a dead give away,* the thought scolded.

"Tragic what happened." A new voice sounded from beside her.

Lennox jumped, turning on her heels to face the person who stood almost a whole foot taller than her. Her eyebrows met as she looked up at him, trying to place him from any classes over the years yet she couldn't. She eyed his ginger hair and distinct scar over his eye. She would have remembered seeing him before. *How did I not hear you coming?*

"It was…" She responded quietly and returned her eyes to their photos after the man did as well.

"I regret not getting the chance to know them- Is there anything you regret?"

The question sent up red flags instantly as her body tensed. "I've never seen you around before, are you a part of Kappa Theta?"

"I'm just passing through the grounds for a few weeks, I'm a friend of Eden's."

At the very moment the man spoke her name, her feet carried her a few steps back from him when Aron's voice clearly echoed within her mind. A new connection forced its way through the barriers in her mind and to the forefront of her mind's eye. Images swam in her vision as emotions that didn't belong to her mixed with her own nerves from the man next to her. The connection was strong, dark and precise as it demanded her attention. An image of where Aron was layered over the unknown man sending a chill down her spine. *How did you-* There wasn't time to finish her question as she attempted to use the foreign connection to ask him.

Motionless, she watched Rosalyn who stood about ten feet away, her hands and blackened eyes alight with purple fire. Pure anger resided in every burning flame visible by the pure brightness of them. It had been twenty years since she had seen her friend this angry.

"You took everything from me… You. Took. It. All." A strained scream from the woman pierced her mind and deep within Lennox an overwhelming fear for her life took hold. The fear wasn't hers, it was his.

Come to me!

Within seconds every nerve was alight with energy, the strange man was completely forgotten as the vines sprang from her back and twisted into wings. She let her feet carry her once more, this time for the doors. She whipped it open and took to the air as fast as she could her now also blackened demon eyes scanned the grounds. She forced the thread as close as she could and allowed the magic to drive her faster, silver sigils and green eyes alight. Finally, she saw a large purple ball of fire formed in the space between the back of the grounds and lake. She dived toward it and pulled up just as the wings unfurled to land heavily between the two of them.

Crouched down, her hand touched the earth, branches from the trees behind them rushed forward and tangled into a barrier in front of Rosalyn and the fire. Before it could finish, purple light rushed over the wood, heat blew through the small openings when it blew over her face. Her wings opened wider and blocked the heat from Aron. As the fire attempted to burn the branches, she pushed more magic in to reinforce them. However, the magic didn't block out the same scream the woman had let out the other night. Once the color faded from the branches she moved them to the sides to look at her best friend.

"I know you want him dead, but we should talk about this before you do anything." She attempted to reason with her.

"Talk! Lennox, are you fucking serious? That's Armaros!" Rosalyn pointed behind her, fingertips still alight. "You know the demon who killed my husband. The demon I lost my child because of! He used me as a pincushion for fun and played his little mind games on both of us and look at you, falling for it- How can you stand between me and my revenge? You should be beside me."

Still glued to the spot, Rosalyn's words slapped her in the face. She knew she would confront him, however, Lennox had hoped that after their chat by the lake she would get to her before that happened. The last sentences sent guilt through her and sank into her chest. *From her perspective she's right but... I can't hurt him, not while he's still inside Aron. Not without a good enough reason.*

She turned her head to the side, her eyes darted to the man she was protecting. Aron's red bandanna was falling off revealing several deep cuts coupled with mostly severe burns. He had himself propped up as he watched her, their eyes met for the first time since she arrived. Fear plain in his drooping eyes as he fought to stay awake.

"Len, come on we can finish this and rid the world of a monster like him."

Lennox returned her attention ahead and saw Rosalyn had her hand out to her. "This is so much more complicated than I originally thought. He explained everything to me and he's not like Armaros. If he was, he would have gone after you when he realized you were here."

"I'm not worried about him coming after me, I can hold my own- But he doesn't deserve to draw another breath." Lennox fell quiet as Rosalyn extended her hand once more. "Why are you not next to me in this?"

"Because he saved my life when Eden tried to kill me the other day.

The Armaros we knew would have never helped Aron to save anyone."

"Saving you once doesn't mean he's instantly not the Armaros we knew."

The demon scanned her face as the conflicted thoughts inside her mind reflected in her eyes. The fire around the woman's fingertips grew in strength as her eyes hardened and her hand dropped back to her side.

"You care about him." Her voice broke at the refusal to join her.

"I care about Aron, not Armaros- I would love to see him burn too but you do that and you're killing our friend- We've lost too many already, Ros."

"He's no friend of ours and as long as you protect him you can leave me out of the equation."

"Rosalyn-"

"I'm not ready to talk and as much as I want to go through you to get to him... I won't this time. But Cade, next time you try to stop me I won't let you."

Lennox shifted toward her as she turned away, the fire faded into smoke and left the clearing silent. Finally she got a good look around as she guided the branches back to their trees and the snow was mostly melted thirty feet in all directions around them. Her gaze drifted to Aron who sat up in the charred grass breathing heavily, Lennox swiftly made her way over to him. Her wings folded back as she reached him and knelt down. She scanned him for the most severe injuries and her face dropped as she realized the extent of the damage. It was much more than she could heal with magic alone. Her gaze trailed up to his face which had bruises already forming by several deep cuts.

"Hey there Lenoard, right on time a second later and I would have been literal toast."

"I'm sorry," The knot in her throat blocked the questions she wanted to ask as her eyes returned to their usual purple irises. *Did you even fight back?* Rosalyn hadn't had a scratch on her and she assumed from his state, he didn't.

"Don't be, it's okay. Not letting her kill me definitely makes up for it."

His eyelids slowly started to close as he seemed to be unable to stay awake. "You're in good hands, I promise."

Aron smiled gently as he held up a hand to her as he lifted his pinky with raised eyebrows. "Got each other's backs, right?"

Lennox looped her pinky into his for a second, he blacked out and went limp. Carefully she slid her hands under his legs and shoulders and slowly lifted him from the ground. She unfurled her wings once more and used the energy from the summoning he did to fuel the strength she needed to carry him. As she flew she looked around the grounds for the red-haired man, the memory of Eden's new friend sent a new wave of fear for their lives over her. *I'll have to call Fang when I get back.*

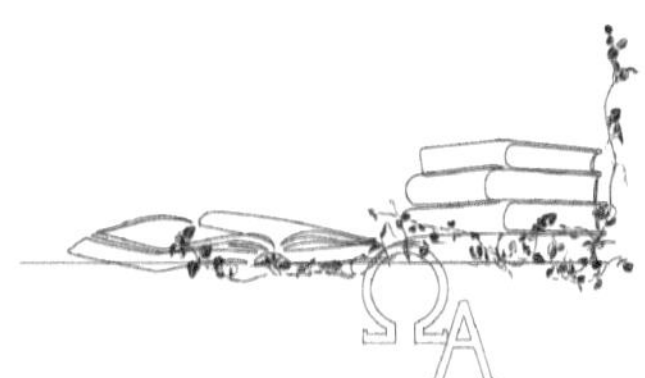

With a quick tug on the thread, the balcony doors to her room opened as she approached. A few feet before she landed, Lennox pulled her wings in tight. They vanished into her back the moment her feet touched the ground. Gently, she placed him on the bed before she turned to the vines surrounding the walls. With a simple motion, she directed them as she did so many times before, they covered the door and the window. Once she felt they would both be safe she turned to her alter and worked as fast as her hands allowed. She snapped her fingers and brought the candles on the sacred space to life. She drew in a deep breath and turned back toward Aron, standing beside the bed.

Fear clutched her chest as she went to pull out her phone. Quickly, she went to text Wyatt to tell him about the strange man and what had happened. However, she paused as her mind raced. *Can I trust him? He knew about Eden... Did he know about what she was going to do to me? Does he know this strange man?* She stared at the screen as the cursor blinked. *How can I tell him about Aron without telling him about Armaros?* Her fingers danced across the screen.

Lennox Cade-
I need you to keep an eye on Kappa. Aron is with me, we are planning some more defenses. You and I still need to talk.
-Sent 4:13 PM

Wyatt Steele-
You got it boss, Kappa is safe with me. We will when we are both ready.
-Sent 4:14 PM

As light as she could, she pulled the bandanna from his hair and placed it on the side table. Her eyes drifted to the burns that covered forty percent of his body, clearly seen under the singed clothes caused her to grimace with sympathy. Lennox lifted her hands just above his chest and pulled at her magic for the final time that night with the help of the energy that hovered by the altar. Slowly the silver glow brightened when it illuminated the slowly darkening room as she directed the magic toward his burns and cuts. As her hand traced over him it left healed skin behind it. The magic pulled at her already lowered energy from the summoning but finally petered out once it was done.

The strain caused her body to heat and her face flushed bright red as she took a heavy seat in her pink computer chair. Lennox gave herself a moment to breathe as approval washed over her from the familiar source of Xemos's presence. She peered to the side through the small breaks in the vines and saw the sun was already making its way down the horizon. With a glance down at her smart watch she realized it was almost curfew which brought forward a string of curses. Completely drained she had no way to bring the vines around both houses and Aron was incapacitated.

Fear tugged at her as she realized it was the perfect chance for the hunters. As for how many were on campus she was unsure now, to go after more students. Picking up her phone once more she was met again with Wyatt's messages.

"Can I trust him?" She asked out loud to Xemos who for the first time in a while formed in front of her with an amused smirk on his face.

"Yes, but I can understand if you didn't want to trust the Curse Bringer. I don't always either."

"How long were you going to wait to tell me about her? Did you truly have to hide it?" She questioned as her voice broke with the realization they were both now devoted to the god.

"Little Phoenix-" His tone dipped and he tilted his chin down slightly. "These are not questions to be asked yet. Right now I will assist you again to protect your friends from her newest friend if you so choose not to trust Wyatt."

Lennox nodded and didn't push the subject too tired to insist. "Thank you, Xemos. For everything."

"I admired the asters you left. Your faith has never gone unnoticed." He told her kindly before he faded from the room.

The demon turned to the notepad on her desk and quickly wrote a note for Aron.

"Aron, I went to Kappa to put up the vines. No one will be able to get into my room while I'm gone. Here's a shirt of Wyatt's, I noticed yours is a bit damaged. I found your phone in your pocket and if you need me before I get back you know how to reach me. ~Lennox."

She placed it on the side table by his bandanna and moved the vines and left the room to go to Kappa Theta. With her phone to her ear it rang to Elder Bloodfang as she made her way down the stairs When she walked into the main entrance, she was met with Bastien and the same red-haired man from the hallway in some deep discussion. For a second they looked at each other before Bastien motioned toward the door behind her and started to move closer.

"What are you two doing here? It's curfew." Her hair stood on end as his eyes bore into her, but she didn't back off.

"We are going to spend the night at Eloise's and wanted to see if Eden was coming." Basiten said, quickly and stepped between the two.

"Was she there?" The question tumbled out and her eyes widened slightly.

"No, We were going to check around campus." Bastien explained.

Lennox eyed both men up for a second while her stomach turned. Her attention moved to Bastien, her friend for the last few years. *He's one of them... This whole time.* The bitter taste of betrayal had already started to become overly familiar. This last week had shown her she didn't know the people around her like she thought. *He cried beside the rest of us at their funerals.*

"Just don't get caught on the grounds-" Lennox put a hand up and her eyes hardened. It took everything in her to maintain her composure until it was time to confront him. She still had to tell Coyote everything that had happened. "I didn't catch your friend's name though."

The red-haired man smirked a bit and held a hand to her. "Holden Holloway, and I'm guessing you're Miss. Cade, Head of Omega?"

"I'm impressed. When you walked in you didn't seem to be the type of person who could dig far enough to find anything."

Holden held up a hand. "And just what is that supposed to mean, Pinky Pie?"

"It means, you look like you have everyone else doing the hard work for you."

"I'll see you later, Lennox!" Bastien interjected and started to push Holden through the door with a nervous laugh.

"Bastien," she stopped them just before they left.

"Yeah, Len?"

"Make sure that next time you or Holden come to Omega make sure you call me first. These are very dangerous times, wouldn't you agree?" She raised an eyebrow.

Bastien came to a brief halt and peered over to her. He seemed un-surprised but sad as he nodded. "They are, I'll call next time."

She watched as they two turned and closed the front door. Happy that two of the people she was worried about wouldn't be inside the house for the night, she quickly took a head count and sent it to the security team. After, she entered her room quietly once she moved the barrier out of her way. She slipped through the door and allowed it to form again, thankful it ran on its own magic source. Lennox peered around to the bed where sat Aron now awake and upright with no shirt and his back to her. It seemed he had just woken up as he unfurled the note she had left for him. Frozen with the door mostly closed, her eyes scanned multiple scars all across his back all of various lengths, depth, and layered one over next. The sleepiness she had felt previously was replaced with a barrage of new emotions.

"What happened?" She breathed before she could stop the words.

The man jumped and whipped his head around to meet her eyes before he quickly shoved the new shirt over his head. "I fought off a dragon when I was in the hills of Scotland a few years back."

As he covered his back once more, Lennox made her way over to the bed. She shook her head at him and sat next to him and put a hand on his knee. She waited for him to look at her first and hoped he would open up a little. *With everything I've learned over the last couple days, I still feel like he's a huge question mark.*

"I know what you're doing, Aron. What really happened?"

For a moment he was silent as his gaze darted to his hands. "They're Armaros's- From what he's told me-"

Aron's voice was cut off as a deeper one replaced his, one of his eyes went pure charochol. "I think you might trust it more if it came from me, my dear."

Lennox's body tensed at his appearance. Quickly, she removed her hand from his knee with her head held a bit higher to disguise the nerves. "I would have believed Aron just fine, but I don't think either of us have a say in what you do."

"I guess you don't, though none of us really do have a say in what happens to us do they?"

"No, we don't but we can control ourselves from destroying other people's lives."

"You wanted the truth, did you not?" He challenged with a half smile.

"Yes, but you didn't have to interrupt." She folded her arms over her chest just as Aron spoke up.

"Yeah, I had the whole thing covered, Armpit."

"It's not your story to tell. Let us speak." The deeper voice seemed to win the internal fight and he took a deep breath. Armaros's single black eye bore into Lennox's violet ones. "Before the creation of humanity I was an angel, the left hand of God. After the discovery of things gone awry, I fell from my position as a Throne Angel. After I arrived here and saw Rosalyn, it reminded me of my time in hell. Reminded me how much I hated myself."

"These are lash marks, they're recent..."

"They are." He admitted, almost too quiet for her to hear.

She didn't speak immediately as she took in the new information. The secrets he seemed to hold so closely had paid off since she could mostly only find a sentence or two about his fall in a few books. A knot tied itself in her stomach as she realized who she thought was a monster for all these years had a heart deep within the darkness. Lennox went to speak but stopped, speechless at the unexpected humanity of the demon. She was still angry, but for the first time a strange pull tugged at her chest as she met both Aron and Armaros's gaze. Her hand returned to his shoulder, surprising even herself as she tried to comfort her friend. *This is definitely going to take some getting used to.* Their eyes moved to his shoulder and his body seemed to relax a little. Finally, she seemed to find her voice again.

"Thank you for sticking to our promise."

"See, you do know how to use your words. Are you gonna finally tell us what the hell you know?" Aron's voice cut Armaros's off as he took an opportunity to get answers as well.

"No," His deep, irritated voice answered.

With the single word, Aron's midnight eye returned to its normal green iris which flooded with annoyance. He shook his head and rubbed the spot above his temple with a sigh as he turned back to her.

"I guess that's on his time." Lennox slid her hand off his shoulder.

Aron stood roughly and picked up the bandanna from the nightstand.

"How are you feeling? You should get some more rest."

"A bit sore and a headache but I think I'll live. Thank you, Lennox." He gave her a genuine smile.

"Call it even, ass saving for ass saving." She smiled in return as he let out a laugh while he tied the red fabric into his hair. "Besides, I gotta go check on everyone in Kappa, I called Wyatt to walk with me back to the house since he was here with Eden last night."

At the sound of her daughter's name, she was swiftly on her feet. Lennox's blood ran cold as she moved the vines from the windows and doors. All at once she realized she had locked everyone in with Eden last night. As her heart raced, she wrung her hands and she made a metal note to figure out a way to lock everyone's rooms. She would have to make it so only each member of Omega could get through like she did for Rosalyn. Her breathing quickened as panic rose in her chest.

"What's wrong?" He asked and peered down at Lennox while he put on his half destroyed jacket.

"You're not going to believe me... The other night when I was talking with Wyatt I tried to warn him about Eden but it seemed like he already knew and was trying to help her hide it."

Aron stopped and looked shocked at her. "No, that's impossible. Wyatt may be blind in love sometimes but he would never help anyone who wanted to hurt any of his friends."

"That's what I thought too but he stopped me from saying out loud she was a hunter."

Aron and Lennox looked between each other neither knowing what truly to believe as there was a knock at her door. His eyes widened as he whispered. "Is he on their side?"

"If I'm being honest, I have no idea. I'll be on standby if you need me, Eden has a new friend named Holden. I saw him here last night with Bastien Miller looking for her." She told him before the door was opened to Wyatt who smiled as if nothing was going on.

"Hey there love birds! Ready to- Is that my shirt?" Wyatt asked and eyed Lennox with an arched eyebrow.

"Not love birds, bro. Just drop it for now." He told him as the two left Omega and Lennox was left to wonder how many friends she had left and if her once enemy was now the only one left.

Eden

She closed the door to Eloise's office with a messenger bag slung over her shoulder. Eden went over to her desk and unpiled a stack of books from the back corner. Her most recent assignment had been to go over everything her mother had discovered over the last few months. Study the Fallen Angel held within the body of Aron and get him into the basement once they had his dagger back. If she was honest with herself there wasn't much to go off of. Most of it seemed like rumors, however that could be solved soon enough. Her attention briefly turned to the dagger that sat to her right, the name of the demon who kept slipping through their fingers causing her jaw to clench.

The true question was how to get a demon with an angel lurking underneath into the basement without drawing too much attention. Eden leaned back in her chair as her thoughts drifted to the other day and the way he swooped in to help her. If there was anything she knew about each Head of House since being at SCHUni, it was they both liked to play heroes. *I can play into that.* Eden picked up her phone and went to pull up Aron's contact before a knock on her door stopped her. Quickly, she placed it back down and pulled open the door to see Holden standing in the door frame with an arm on the side, his eyes already on hers.

"Can I help you with something, Heir Holloway?" She asked and folded her arms, bitterness filling her mouth.

"Oh come on, Eden. I know you don't have the dagger back yet, let me help you."

"Heiress Miller," She corrected him as she refused to back down despite his higher ranking. "Niceties still apply here since you almost shot me and on that particular note I think you can see why I don't want help from you."

"If it wasn't for that demon I would never have had to steal your gun."

"If you all would just accept the fact I just don't have a place in this family anymore, maybe we'd all be happier."

Silence filled the space between them for a moment before she went to close the door. *Always saying too damn much.* It was much more than she wanted him to know. She thought back to all the larger family meetings with the other Heirs and Heiresses and remembered the comments. *She'll be nothing useful to this family, Matriarch Miller couldn't produce any Heirs before her husband's death so what makes her think an orphan would be able to run the family?* A hand stopped her before she could try to push the door closed.

"Little Bird, you do have a place among The Salavamari. Beside me."

Holden took a step toward Eden as he pushed on the door to keep it open. He slid his hand down from the door and reached out for Eden who moved to step back just before his hand found its way tracing down her arm to her hand.

"I told you I'm not interested in the arrangement, I'm doing all of this to protect Bastien and that's it. I don't feel anything for you anymore."

"That's a shame, you and I would make a great team. The two enforcer families joining together for the first time. We'd be a force to be reckoned with." Holden leaned in before someone behind him cleared their throat.

"If she chooses you, that is, Heir Holloway." Chase's voice was polite but with a sharp edge. "Mission assignment and research may not be as exciting but it's the most vital part of our jobs."

"Baron Donovan," Holden's hand dropped from her as he turned fully to face the blond-haired Baron. "I'd say too much time in the library makes it harder when it comes time to fight."

"There's strength in balance, Heir Holloway. Brawn doesn't always win." His ice-like eyes pierced into Holden's.

"I just believe I have the best chances, given our past." He smirked as if he had won already.

"I think both of you have very even chances. Now if you excuse me, I have a demon to trap and a dagger to get back."

"Catch you later, Heiress." Chase sent a smile as Holden stepped toward her.

She swiftly made her way back into her room, closed the door and locked it with a click. Now wasn't the time to get distracted with the arrangement though Eden could hear them fight outside her door. She ignored it, went back to her phone and the task at hand. Quickly, she typed a message to Aron she felt the familiar pang of her heart as it dropped into her stomach as Wyatt came to mind. They had spent last night drinking their stress away where he tried to find out what things she had to do that he wouldn't like. *For Bastien and Corvus to be able to have their chance.*

> Eden Miller-
> If you surrender yourself to us and bring your dagger to Elder Row, I will destroy her dagger and leave her be.
> -Sent 4:56 pm

Over an hour passed as she waited for him to respond during which Eloise had attempted to drop in on her but she hadn't answered her door. Eden was busy as she waded through her pool of guilt as she thought of Lennox and everything she had told her in the hallway. *Of course I wanted you! It was only till I was sure the curse was broken.* The very curse Wyatt had put on her blood family. The one Xemos had helped Lennox break. However, the memory of her deal with a Crossroad Demon caused the anger to rise once more. A loud chime on her phone drew her attention as a single letter appeared on her screen.

> Aron-
> K.
> -Sent 6:04 pm

More hours passed...

7 pm... Eloise attempted to talk to Eden about the arrangement.

8 pm... Eden warned the house of her plans, everyone would stay out of her way once he got here.

9 pm... A crack of lightning, had Wyatt figured out what she was doing?

Aron-
I'm here
-Sent 9:39 pm

She slid Lennox's dagger into her weapons belt. As she waited, she allowed her fingertips to trace the outline of the crest on her right hip. Her skin crawled as she peered down at the peacock. *For Bastien.* Within a few minutes she saw a shadow lurking outside the front door looking around nervously. *It worked.* Eden opened the door and met the demon's eyes, her hair stood on end as she remembered Armaros glaring at her. The image of the rage she saw that day had turned up a few times in her dreams since she attacked Lennox the first time. A murderous fire burned white hot within the pitch black that covered his irises which bore into her very soul. However, he was Aron again as if none of it had ever happened, disdain in his gaze. She peered around behind him for a second for any footprints that didn't belong to him before his voice caught her attention once more.

"Yes, I'm alone. Are you going to kill me here or do I get to come in?"

"Out here leaves too many witnesses, duh." Eden sneered and stepped aside for him to follow her inside.

Aron walked into the house, his attention captured by the dark victorian style Stacey and Eloise had decorated the interior with. Her gaze followed his to an old photo of the entire Salvamari from over sixty years ago. She moved to stand beside him and looked for a clue of where he had his dagger stashed away. As if he knew, his hand reached into a side pocket within his jean jacket and produced the weapon. He held out the rosebud hilt and nodded his head toward it. Slowly, she reached out to take it and found he wasn't going to let go of it right away. "I just need to know why."

Her eyes darkened, "We protect humanity from creatures who want to use them as play toys. You don't get to play God without it coming to bite you in the ass."

The dagger suddenly slipped from her hands as Aron retracted it from her grip. Eden's eyes snapped up to his face to see one of his eyes had gone black. "How dare you."

The same distorted version of two voices as they spoke at once filled the entrance way. In the light there was a flash and the color red as he swiped at her. Without a second thought she had her gun out in a second and shot it at his leg. He roared as it ripped through his thigh and at the same time a searing pain across her collarbone now radiated as something cut into her chest.

Eden launched herself toward him as he stumbled slightly. She raised the butt of the gun above her head with both hands and brought it down at an angle to hit beside his temple. With a loud thud, Aron dropped to the ground motionless. She allowed herself a minute to catch her breath as the adrenaline of the moment faded, the sound of footsteps made her turn on her heel to the left.

"That was hot, Heiress Miller. I'm impressed." Holden smiled from the doorway of the kitchen.

"Is there not a corner of this house you're not fucking lurking in?" She spat at him as Bastien appeared beside him.

"I told you she could handle it," Her Uncle smiled before he approached her with the dagger that had been tossed to the side.

"You want me to patch you up?" Holden offered with a mischievous glint in his eyes that reminded her of Wyatt.

"I'd rather sew it back together myself without lidocaine."

Eden walked past the two, knowing Bastien would take their new prisoner to the basement while she stopped the bleeding on the still stinging cut. Her hand went to the spot still fresh and bleeding as she walked back to her room. Her eyes fell on the disturbing familiar sight of blood on her hands, this time it was her own. An unsettled feeling replaced itself in her chest. *He was aiming for the throat.*

The stale basement air filled Eden's lungs as she stood beside the metal table, waiting for their newest captee to wake. The sounds of Basiten going through their weapons cabinet was the only thing that filled the quiet as she silently plotted how to lure her true target here. Remembering the other night where Wyatt had begged her to tell him what she was doing to keep Bastien safe however it had turned into an argument about the duties she was being forced to uphold to keep her uncle safe. She had to swallow the guilt that had formed in her throat as she shook her head and stopped speaking for the evening.

"This would be easier if we had that summoning spell," Bastien complained.

"Don't you think I know that? I went into her room the other day and found nothing in her personal journals. Chase and Holden are still reading through hundreds of old grimoires." Eden shook her head in irritation.

"You don't even want to be doing this." He pointed out. "So why are you?"

"I'm doing it to protect you, Bas. Holden saw you and Corvus. You're the only family who cared about what I truly wanted and I wanted to return the favor."

His eyes filled with sorrow as he looked at her. "Eden, you didn't have to. I know how happy you are with Wyatt, you don't have to stay to protect me, you deserve to leave if you don't want to stay. You didn't have to stay just so I wouldn't become a Heretic, I am a Baron and easily am already on my way there."

"It's easier said than done and you know that. It doesn't matter what's done is done and right now I want my revenge on that peppy bitch. If I'm going to do this, I'm going to do it the Miller way."

On one hand she didn't want to return to who she was before she had met Wyatt. He had changed her forever, but on the other hand the grudge toward Lennox still remained. The anger Eloise had put there and helped to fester over the semester. Though Xemos seemed to think they could move past their differences, Eden continued forward despite the sudden quiet from the god. She glanced over to Aron for a second to make sure he was still asleep and moved to the weapons cabinet and started to pull out enchanted knives. Her eyes fell on the shine in the dim light and could feel the magic as it buzzed through the handle tipped with a poison that would prevent any demon from healing the wounds it creates for days.

"He's Armaros too, we have to be careful. Even with those chains we don't know if they will hold him the same as other demons."

"I'll be right behind you and everyone else is nearby just in case." Bastien promised as he helped prepare the other tools she pulled and passed to him.

After about ten minutes the sound of the chains moving across the floor drew her eye to the right. As he did, she picked up the dagger with his name and hooked it to the back right hip of her weapons belt. Quickly, she added three more spelled knives each with its own kickback. Her eyes moved to the man who now sat against the wall with the cuffs around his wrists. The chains only allowed him to move a few inches in any given direction. Once he realized this, his attention turned to her as he glared at her with a dark smirk and black eyes.

"Well if it isn't Wednesday and Pugsley from the Adams Family!" The demonic voice echoed.

"I resent the Pugsley comment," Basiten added as he added a spelled weapon to his own belt before joining Eden.

"If you don't wanna be Pugsley, stop acting like him."

Eden rolled her eyes at the two. "Would you stop feeding into him for a second? We actually have things to get done."

"Ah yes, just like her, but missing the braids and the bangs. Nothing I couldn't fix."

"If you ever touch me I will cut off your fingers one at a time." Eden threatened with narrowed eyes.

"Oh, Lenny's daughter has some bark to her! This is going to be fun isn't it? But I am curious while you're doing all this, does Wyatt know you're trying to kill more of his friends?"

She gritted her teeth and her eyes went a dull blue as his smirk widened at her reaction. Anger bubbled up in her chest and she pulled on the blue thread. Eden brought both of her hands up vertically in front of her and brought up the first two fingers of each hand.With a swipe across each other and turned the chains to ice so she could get close to him. Aron struggled for a moment as she stalked toward him, her hand going for her belt. For a second there was something that shifted in his eyes as if he wasn't fully present for two seconds before seeming to return to the moment. It was so fast she almost questioned if it had happened. With one of the daggers she had equipped herself with was drawn in seconds. She pressed the cold blade in the space between his collarbone and throat. Her right hand was on his left shoulder as she leaned down beside his ear.

"Wyatt will never know," She breathed. "Because we both know you're not leaving here alive."

"I will and you will beg me to leave after I kill one of you." He growled the threat.

Slowly she applied pressure so the blade cut into his skin which drew the deepest color of red blood she had ever seen. Once she was happy with the depth she dragged it as slow as possible all the way to the top of his shoulder. His body shook under her hand as he let out a strained gunt of pain she pulled away and stepped out of reach. She watched as the skin around the cut turned black as if frostbite had set in. Red covered her hands and soon an image of Lennox entered her mind, unable to see past the anger. She only debated for a few moments on how much she was going to allow him to know. *He probably has heard her side, why not share mine.*

"You want to know why? Lennox and I have unfinished business. As I've discovered over the semester, Val was the one she met at the Crossroads, a place she should have never gone. She let her paranoia get in the way and look at what she is now. She's not who she appears to be, hell look at how easily she killed Alaric."

"I don't agree with what she did, but you all were threatening her life, she did what she had to." Eden paused and remembered something Rosalyn had let spill while the two were drinking with Bastien and Octavious. "All she did was lie and you saved her. From what I know of your true nature, you're not one for liars, are you?"

"Honesty is the golden rule... just like sharing and using our words. We all learned that in preschool, right Pugsley? You were just there last year, congrats on your graduation to big boy school by the way!" He continued his demeaning jokes as he scanned the room.

"Sharing, like how you shared your double life with the group? That went over really well didn't it? I saw the look on her face when she saw you. It seems as if the golden rule doesn't apply to you either?"

Aron suddenly seemed to have no retorts which caused a smile to cross her face. She turned her attention to Bastien. "You know, when I was told who I was making the dagger for, I almost didn't believe it. I mean, the head of the frat boys, a fallen angel? I wondered why I had been assigned so many books about angel lore by Eloise two years ago."

Eden pocketed the knife once more and turned to glance at the stairs. She could hear the footsteps of the others above them as they milled around the kitchen by the door. Eden paced but stayed a few feet from him as she went over the few things she had discovered.

"Let me see what the books got right and wrong." She locked eyes on him and scanned his features for reactions as she spoke. "So you fell, right? Smashed into hell and became a demon at God's will? Brought magic to the witches of Earth. Then after decades or centuries records of your deals seemed to fade off. Your need for privacy has seemed to pay off. I am curious as to how you obtained a new body? Possession I'm guessing."

"Look at her everyone, she does know how to connect the dots. Might be a Miller but your Cade is showing. Always looking for answers in books, such a nerd like your mom."

Eden glared and quickly drove down the knife she had just used and let it sink into the shoulder she had cut into. Another patch of black froze his skin right at the joint, a second grunt of pain echoed on the walls as she bent down to his level a few inches from him. It was better to ignore her strong desire to pull out the one with his name for now.

"Enough with the shit, Aron. I know you know how to summon her."

"There it is, the real reason you haven't just killed me already. I'm the bait." His eyes hardly showed the fear and only widened for a second beneath the anger burning in his pupils. "You're scared of me."

She scoffed, "Absolutely not."

"You are of *him*." Aron accentuated the last word.

Eden watched as the whites of his eyes filled with darkness and only left the green ring in the center. The sound of the chains suddenly as they broke from the ice sent panic through her as his hands grabbed her hips, the still attached chains now giving him a small amount of movement,and forced her away. She stumbled and slid back. On her feet in seconds, she felt her heart trying to beat out of her chest as his twisted smile formed across his lips once more.

"Girl, your knives do nothing more than give me a new piercing, I don't give a fuck what you do to me, I'm not going to tell you how to summon her here. You think you're so much better than us? We aren't the only ones with a torture chamber." Aron's voice went deeper but not as deep as Armaros's.

"We will stop when you're all back where you belong. The world doesn't need someone like her or you running around." She repeated Eloise's words from the other night. "I still think two demons with the ability to take someone's soul so easily are the biggest threat to humanity despite my personal vendettas. With the daggers tucked in my belt at least I have the solutions."

She pulled out the one belonging to Lennox and held it up so her name shone for both of them to see. Her eyes examined the sharpness for a second before she glanced back to Aron. His eyes were now locked on the weapon as well, desire in his eyes as he pulled against the chains. *He did this to his victims for fun, there's no way I'm going to get to him this way- I have to play his game better than him... Sheer will of the mind.*

"Nature always finds a way to bring back balance doesn't it? I almost didn't believe the great Armaros would leave hell but then Arthur and Richard tracked down two demons, Silas and Lumina from what I hear, and then it started to make sense once you saved your little girlfriend."

She watched his face shift from anger to rage at the name of the demons. He slammed his eyes shut and shook his head as if suddenly fighting within himself. His body shifted forward as his hands clutched at his head as it seemed to become overbearing, Aron shouted out loud.

"STOP-" His eyes opened up wide to reveal flames that danced across his skin blackening his protruding arm veins.

"You'd better believe me now!" Armaros replied, in that combined voice of his and Aron's. "Lumina? She's here?! Why!"

Armaros tried to lunge at Eden but was stopped by chains. He propped up on his knees and pulled his arms into his chest in an attempt to break them but thankfully they held him to the spot no matter how hard he pulled. He hunched forward, a pair of black charred wings with feathers hanging from the top but not all the way down jutted from his back, sparks of fire spit across the room as he did. As they flew around the room, Eden held up her hand with a quick tug and put up a shield in front of herself just in time for one to miss her head.

"Why would I know the true answer to that?"

Eden twisted her fingers into a fist and pulled the moisture from the air to quickly extinguish them. The silver chain markings flashed in the last seconds of the orange glow. In one motion she had Lennox's dagger poised for a fight behind the shield slightly distorting Armaros in front of her. The two didn't move as she heard Bastien move to the left of Eden once more.

"You're supposed to destroy the dagger of Lennox Cade... You reek of lies, you were right. I don't like liars."Armaros snarled, his eyes blazed stronger and his voice boomed along the walls.

"I don't like demons so I'd say we are on the same page." She did her best to hide the deep fear the sight of him instilled. "I wonder what would happen if I stick her dagger into your heart? Though I believe you know since magic is your thing."

"I'd tell you but I don't think your narrow minded human mind could handle it. Besides, you've caused enough trouble in my life"

Eden's teeth gnashed. "The only way Lennox's dagger will be destroyed is when it's lodged in her chest and I promise you will be there to see me do it."

She turned and went to the table and took out the enchanted knives. From the corner she could see Bastien look at her with confusion. With a nod for him to join her, she refused to say anything else as each was laid back on the metal table.

"You better hope these chains continue to hold me. If I get out, one of you is going to die. To think, she worked so hard to keep your fragile soul safe." Eden said nothing. "You're in over your head, Little Cade. Xemos can't keep you safe from me."

"Go upstairs and tell Chase to come down, will you Bas? I'm done for now." She continued to ignore the raging demon's threats.

"I can't leave you down here alone." He frowned back.

"I'll be fine, please get Baron Donovan. I don't think there's much else to do here now. He can sit here until the little miss hero gets here or we find a way to summon her."

Bastien looked conflicted before going to the stairs and made his way up two at a time. Eden picked up the familiar stained cloth from her bag and wiped off the blood from the blade she had used on Aron. The only sound in the basement now was of the chains as they moved when he shifted. Out of the corner of her eye she saw him struggle to pull his wings into a better position as he was too close to the wall. Neither broke the silence as Armaros glared as if she was the worst person he had ever seen. It was five minutes before something seemed to shift in him as his voice caused her to turn toward him.

"She refused to tell me where you were, who you were. She spent every ounce of energy keeping you safe from me until I took the memories for myself, but now- Your soul is mine."

"I would never make a deal with a demon, let alone you." She snarled back before the door at the top of the stairs opened and shut.

Before Eden made her way to her room, Chase had informed her that Armaros had soon faded after she walked away even after he had tried to prompt the demon out himself. Aron had gone mostly silent minus a few choice words for the Baron. She had spent the remainder of her night awake thinking of the possibilities of why he seemed to be so enraged at the names of Silas and Lumina. Roars of frustration echoed through the halls of the house every so often through the night which didn't help her find sleep any easier. Each time sent a memory forward, every snarky comparison to Lennox. The look on Wyatt's face when he would eventually realize her lies, the mere thought of it sent up a wave of tears as she lay in bed.

Her phone had lit up beside her a few times but she hadn't dared to look at the messages she knew were from Wyatt as she pulled the covers closer. Only after the third time did she text him back with some explanation that Eloise had kept her busy all evening and ended it with a black heart before sleep pulled her under for a mere two hours.

Her alarm went off beside her ear which caused her to jump from her dreamless sleep and look around. She knew it was time for her shift soon and quickly pulled off the clothes she had forgotten to change out of and replaced them with tight black pants, a long sleeve black turtleneck and finished it off with her weapons belt. With the daggers into their holsters, she tied her long hair back into a tight ponytail. Chase, Holden, Bastien and she took turns in five hour shifts to make sure the demon didn't sleep in hopes that the lack of rest would eventually cause him to slip.

Earlier that morning she had walked out her bedroom door and found Holden stood a few feet away with an irritated look on his face. Her own tired eyes mirrored his expression, it seemed no matter how much she pushed him away he kept coming back, unlike Chase who seemed to let her come to him. Neither helped their cases even if Wyatt wasn't in the picture. *For however long that is now.* She had gone to ask him what he wanted so bad that he had to wait outside her room but he cut her off.

"You called for Donovan over me? I find that quite insulting, Little Bird." He crossed his arms over his chest.

"I thought Mister top Patriarch would be too busy to guard him, don't you usually say things like that are above you?"

She took a few steps to move past him and bumped his shoulder as she did. A hand gripped her left wrist tightly which forced her to turn around. "Little Bird, where do you think you're flying off to this time? I'm not done with our chat."

"I am, besides I have a prisoner to talk to and that's a bit higher on my list of priorities right now."

Eden wrenched herself free and made her way down the stairs, Holden about four feet behind her. She could feel his gaze burn into her back while she walked into the front entrance. She went into the kitchen when Holden cut her off just after the end of the stairs. *Damnit, I forgot how fast he can be.* Slowly, he leaned closer to her on the step just below hers. He still stood taller, his hand extending much slower and took hers gently.

"I said, my dear, I'm not done with our conversation. I hate being this person, but I need you to trust me and that means you call for me, not

Donovan." There was a glint of something in his eyes she couldn't read.

"Last I checked you were aware I'm uninterested in either option, meaning I don't trust you."

"Come on, Eden. Be realistic. If you were going to leave the family for that demon you wouldn't have stayed to protect Bastien, your Baron. But how is he going to do anything for your family, since he's ineligible to take over the Millers? Instead, here we are and for some reason you haven't sent me away.... Having second thoughts?"

She felt her face turn almost as bright red as his hair as the frustration, guilt, and anger flooded over. Adrenaline built in her arms wanting nothing more than to let her fist meet his face. Instead, she let a smile drift to her lips as her eyes from his gaze, lips, and up once more just as she had done so many years before when they were flirting. His eyes softened as he seemed to connect the dots. Eden placed her left hand on his chest and slid it up his shoulder; she led him backward toward the wall with the generations of Matriarchs.

She made sure his eyes were locked on hers and moved her right hand to her belt. Silently pulled out the Glock on her right hip and kept it low, out of his sight. When his back touched the wall she slid her knee between his thighs since he was at least six inches taller than her it would keep him from moving. Moving the gun up she kept the safety on as she pressed it to his side.

"If I had a choice I would chain you beside Aron."

"Using names still? Those things are monsters and you need to remember that you are an Heiress and you and I have duties to our families. You would be a part of the strongest families, the other Heiresses would kill for that chance. Instead, you really want to follow in Roy Miller's footsteps?"

"My duty is to myself... Let them then, because I'm done with this family once these two are dead."

"We will see about that, my dear. You will come to realize I am the only one who could possibly begin to understand you."

Suddenly, the sound of the front door opening and closing from behind caused her to look over, her heart leapt into her throat. Immediately she saw the scarred rose tattoo of Wyatt and let her eyes drift to his face which seemed torn between confusion and irritation. His stormy eyes lit a little as he took notice of the gun she had pressed into the man's side.

"Don't let me interrupt you two," He raised his eyebrow at them and folded his arms over his chest. "Unless this is about more stuff you won't tell me? That's something I'd like to interrupt..."

Eden released Holden and took a few steps back from him as she put her weapon away. "This is more about how he can't seem to figure out when to not poke and prod at my emotions."

"Well, as hot as it was to see you with a gun, it seems to me you two have a deeper history than I thought when you told me about the arrangement... Took months to get you that close to me." Wyatt rocked on his feet and approached her with slow caution.

Eden slid the gun back into her belt and met him half way knowing she would have to look him in the eye and lie. *As if Aron isn't right below our feet.* She let a soft smile find its way to her face and took his hand, even though they weren't on the best of terms she could still feel the pull she knew they both felt.

"I thought you weren't supposed to talk about ex's for the first few months of a relationship?" She tried to curb the tension she felt that radiated from him.

"Usually yes, but it would be nice to know if your ex is one of the people trying to steal away what's mine. Though admittedly he's doing a poor job by the looks of things."

"You think you've won, demon but have you forgotten where you're standing?" Holden's expression darkened as he stalked forward to stand to Eden's left. "And it seems like she doesn't tell you very much, that's a shame."

"I don't need to know more until later, I trust her."

"That's cute, Heiress Miller has someone's trust."

Eden felt Holden's voice get closer and it sent her hair on end. She glanced up and saw the defensive look in Wyatt's eyes as his hand slid from her arm to her waist and pulled her closer. She knew the action was exclusively to get her further from Holden; she felt their bodies meet which caused her to relax slightly.

"Why don't you and I blow this popsicle stand for a bit? I'm sure whatever they have you doing can wait." Wyatt offered and peered down to her.

"I can't, I'm sorry… More stuff I can't talk about just yet."

Wyatt sighed, obviously disappointed. "Why?"

"She's protecting her allegiances." Holden interrupted and looked Wyatt dead in the eyes.

"She's trying to get away from your cult and a crazy marriage she doesn't want." Wyatt snapped back.

"She can talk for herself." Eden interjected, her voice rose above both of theirs.

Both men glanced at her and momentarily went quiet as each glared daggers at the other. For only those few seconds, Eden could see the representation of two possible futures before her. One with a window that was closing ever so quickly. The other wide open and waiting for her to take the first step. She could feel Wyatt's hand gently guide her to face him, a serious look written across his face as he pretended Holden wasn't there.

"Well good, because I need to know if your crazy mother took Aron."

Eden frowned and looked at him confused. "Aron? I thought him and Lennox were off somewhere together as usual."

"No, Lennox came to me this morning asking if Aron was in his room."

"Seems like you're down a demon, unfortunately for you we usually don't allow such filth to enter this house." Holden spoke up.

"Not unless they're in the basement." Wyatt glared at him and gently let Eden go before he took a few steps toward the Holloway Heir.

The two were now less than four feet apart, each digging into the other in any way they could. As the bickering became louder, she heard footsteps echoing from various parts of the house. The two men were so distracted by one another they didn't notice Chase, Stacey, Eloise, and Bastien all stood behind Holden and her.

"The Curse Bringer thinks he deserves someone to love him, and out of probably hundreds of thousands of options you decide to go for not only a powerful hunter, but a descendant from the very line you cursed!" Holden's face was now flushed with an anger she had only seen a few times.

Eden watched as Wyatt's face shifted at the name, the anger faded into a calm storm that she knew would come later. The lightning flashed in his pupils before he scanned each new arrival before he turned back to her.

"Fine, I'll go but I need to know if Aron is here." He looked at Eden as if she was the only one in the room.

"No, I haven't seen him around- I'm sorry, Wyatt." She took a step forward and took his hand in hers, her thumb traced the top of his hand. At that moment she didn't care if her family was around to judge her. "I'll see you later tonight? Kappa let's say about seven?"

"That's a good idea, with a few glasses I think." He shook his head and took a step toward her, closing the distance and placed a kiss on her cheek. Before he pulled away he whispered something so quiet she almost didn't catch it. "I'm trusting you this time, but if I find out you're lying you know I won't be able to trust you again. Don't let your family change you back into their pawn."

Wyatt turned without another word and went back out the front door, only giving her one last glance before the other family members went about their business. All except for Chase and Holden who were now eyeing each other up. *Men and their testosterone.* Eden shook her head and went past them to the basement mulling over everything that had just happened. No matter what she did at this point, she had lied and Wyatt was going to find out. Now it was time to decide if it would be tonight and from her own lips, or if he would have to discover her betrayal himself.

With the stained cloth in hand, Eden wiped the same knife for about five minutes while she was lost in thought. She had gone to spend the night in Kappa after she decided it would be her last chance to have a good night with Wyatt before everything eventually exploded in her face. He had been his usual self when she arrived and turned on his favorite songs to show her on his record player. With each song she had felt the weight of her lies and became lost inside her mind in wishful thinking. Eventually he had pulled her out of it as he pulled her into his arms where Eden wished she didn't have to leave.

"Earth to Eden," Bastien waved his hand in front of her face.

She jumped and dropped the weapon to the floor. She quickly scooped it up before she spoke. "What Bas?"

"Are you sure you still want to do this? You know once he finds out-"

"I will worry about Wyatt once you and Corvus are safe from our family. Even if he is mad, maybe one day he'd understand. We've both done some pretty fucked up things."

"If you do this, Eden, I don't know if you'll ever get the chance to walk away again."

She stayed quiet as his words took root, if Wyatt walked away from her as he said he would, she wouldn't leave. She would remain with The Salvamari and marry Holden or Chase. Her eyes drifted away from him and to the two Demon Daggers on the table as she took one final chance to deliberate. *It would be helpful if you'd weigh in, Xemos.* She waited for his voice to enter her mind through the chain-like connection in her mind.

When nothing came, she sighed defeated and scooped them back up. Quickly, she settled them into their homes inside her belt she looked at Aron who was half awake, his eyes on the floor beneath him. Her eyes scanned over the various ways Chase and Holden had tried to get him to talk. Each wound sent a new and heavier pang of guilt into her stomach as each had sealed her decision to protect Bastien.

"It's too late, we have the dagger and his best friend. Lennox will join him soon and I'm the very pawn he told me not to become... Once again."

Her mother had somehow won again, she had convinced her to follow along in her missions and had even enlisted Holden to help keep her there. It had worked, Eloise had let her keep Wyatt even if it was only for a short period of time while Holden did what he did best. Observed her weaknesses and trapped her with her own soft heart. Anger and radical acceptance filled her chest as she knew her choice had been made for her and she had already sealed her fate. The realization sent something dark and clouded over her mind as red filled the edges of her vision. The bracelet Wyatt had given her now sent light pulses of electricity which felt like flutters that she decided to ignore, however, it swiftly grounded her back to the moment.

She hated Eloise at this moment as much as she hated Lennox. Now a new decision had to be made- Who to take revenge on first? Before she could decide, someone seemed to have made it for her and it was time to push forward. *If I'm a pawn, I'll show them what a pawn can do.* The door above them opened and shut followed by slow, deliberate footsteps that didn't match any of the Miller's. There was no question about who it was since everyone else hadn't left the house since Aron's arrival.

"Someone came to play hero, just like I thought." She took a few steps toward the chained demon and bent down slightly with a smirk across her face. "Hey, good news for you two. We don't need that summoning anymore, she came to save you."

Aron's eyes shot up to meet Eden's showing his hatred for her, an angry growl escaped his chest as she stood. "You better hope you don't miss when you try to kill me."

"Oh, I promise I won't."

Eden went up the stairs and followed silently behind Lennox whose bright pink hair made it easy to see from a good distance. She climbed the stairs decorated with fake pine branches and lights to the second floor and peered around the doors and seemed lost on where to go next. Eden pressed her back into the shadows of the stairs where she knew she wouldn't be seen if the demon turned around grateful for the wreath of holly for extra cover.

It was a few minutes before she heard the demon's footsteps recede down the hallway and continued to follow her. The house was so silent she could have heard a pin drop as she rounded the corner to see

Lennox opening the door to Eloise's office. The demon wore her true demonic form, large wings made of twisted vines which took up a good portion of the hall. Her eyes illuminated green and the silver chains on her arms glowed in the dimly lit hall while the buzz of magic filled the air. Seconds after Lennox crossed the threshold of the office she was pushed back out by the throat. Eloise appeared from her office as she forced the demon back out, easily since she stood a few inches taller than her.

"Now just where do you think you're going?" Eloise hissed as she pressed the demon against the wall which almost knocked into a tall nutcracker standing in the hallway.

"I know your crazy family took Aron!"

Lennox snapped and gripped at the woman's wrists. She was able to take hold of one and with a flash of light Eloise shook it off while she yelled in pain. When her hand moved it left behind angry bumps much like poison ivy. The slender woman used her strength and slammed Lennox by the throat into the wall harder than before. Her head bounced off the drywall which made the photos hanging above shift and threaten to fall on top of them.

"Actually, just my daughter. She knew you'd play the good guy so don't worry, she has a spot for you right next to your little friend." The disgust in her eyes as she stared at Lennox was so clear Eden could see it from down the hall. "You've made it all so much easier for me by delivering yourself here. Once you two are gone, Mr. Steele will soon follow and I get to be the good guy to Eden once again."

Lennox was holding her head and seemed too dizzy to fight back though she grabbed at Eloise once more, kicking a foot out. The hunter dodged her foot and moved her foot between the demon's legs and forced it out to the side. As she turned her body, Eloise used the force of Lennox's fall to shove her toward the ground. Her head bounced off the hardwood floor where she remained motionless, wings limply encased her form. From the doorframe of the office Holden appeared and stepped right on the edge of the ivy which caused it to retract back into her body the glow from her chains still dimly lit.

"So who's this bubblegum bitch?" He asked as he followed the Matriarch's gaze, neither of them had noticed Eden.

Eden's eyebrows met as she watched the two closely. It wasn't uncommon for a suitor to have meetings with the Matriarch who selected them, however, she had seen them chatting at least once a day since Aron arrived. Holden's threat of telling Eloise about Bastien and Corvus made her question if this had been their plan all along. *We are just trying to get you back on the right path Eden, I love you and I only want what's best.* Eloise's voice chimed in behind him from the other night as she had prepared to go to Kappa. In the moment she thought she had been referring to the other Miller family members, *had she meant Holden and her?* There was no time for questions, they had both demons now and the timer was ticking on when Wyatt and the school would realize both are now missing.

"Unfortunately, the one who gave birth to me." Eden had already made her way to them and acted as if she had just walked up to the scene.

Both hunters turned to face her, Eloise looking at her in surprise before she wiped it from her face with a proud smile. "Eden, you were right, and in two days."

"I knew she wouldn't be able to resist saving him. He told Chase that she had the dagger hidden and he didn't even tell Lennox he was taking it back. It was only a matter of time."

She shoved her anger at the two aside as she moved to take Lennox downstairs herself. Holden stepped forward and lifted their victim from the floor and put her over his shoulder. Eden frowned but didn't say anything to oppose him. He turned away from them as they started to make her way down the hall with Holden close behind her. *Has Eloise really turned me into this again?* She looked to Holden. *Or is it because of him?*

When the two entered the basement Bastien was already stationed by the table with a pair of cuffs like the ones they had on Aron. He stepped forward as Holden went to the hook on the floor five feet from Aron, quickly secured the chains to her wrists and hooked it to the bolt. Beside them the Head of House pulled against his own theaters in an attempt to get closer.

"Len?! What did you do to her?" He demanded but was ignored by the two men. His eyes shot to Eden who crossed her arms over her chest.

Aron raised his eyebrows at her and scanned her face for what she didn't know. "I did nothing, it was more of an Eloise thing."

"You've done all this, don't act innocent." The deeper voice of Armaros growled. "You say you're here to protect Humanity, say you don't like demons, probably not Angels either for that matter. You put yourself at such a superior level to all of us immortal beings, yet here you stand the only one destroying lives for the hell of it."

Eden felt the knot in her throat pull even tighter as only last week she would have never made a move against the two. The Fallen Angel's words tugged at the side of her Wyatt had created. She kept her eyes on Holden as they finished with the chains and stepped beside her. Something snapped within her as anger seeped into the edges of her vision again. Here it was, her revenge was staring her in the face, yet it was bittered by the distaste for Eloise and Holden and the impending downfall of the best thing she ever had.

"Don't worry, you two will be the last lives I take."

From the corner of her eye she saw Bastien give her a small smile and nod. Eden stepped toward the still sleeping demon and turned her head slightly to keep Aron in her sight. He pulled at his chains in attempts to stop her and his veins started to glow orange as the heat beneath tried to escape. He was held to his spot only able to use strong short bursts of powers due to the chains which made her feel slightly less weary of being so close.

"Hey, time to wake up." She kicked Lennox's foot and frowned. She bent down to her level and patted her with an open hand a bit rougher than needed. "Come on now, it's time to have some fun and maybe a chat before you die- Mother."

When the demon still didn't move she pulled out one of the enchanted daggers from her belt. Eden turned it in her palm and rose it above her shoulder before she plunged it right into Lennox's left thigh. When it made contact the silver blade started turning orange and a blood curdling scream was released from her victim. A smirk followed as she looked over to an angry Aron who still pulled at his restraints with a clenched jaw as his own grunts echoed behind her screams.

Lennox leaned forward and tried to grab for the burning metal in her leg as she let out shorter screams and groans of pain. Between the screams she took in her surroundings and froze when her eyes fell on Aron beside her. Eden watched her eyes widen in satisfying fear as dots seemed to connect in her mind. Quickly, Eden pushed her back into the wall, grabbed her face and forced her to look directly at her. Her heart raced as she stared into the purple eyes she and Lennox shared.

"I've been waiting to use that one, your lover boy here wouldn't find it effective so I saved it for you. You know, fire doesn't really hurt fire." She told her barely heard over the woman's pain.

With her left hand she retrieved it, stood and moved out of range once more as Lennox caught her breath before she spoke. "You seem to like to save the best for last."

"You've put that together, already? I mean they told me you were smart but it took a bit longer than I thought it would. I thought you'd put it together on the day wings here saved you and hunt me down yourself."

"That's definitely still on the table," Aron interjected.

"The girls are talking now, you've had two days to make your threats, and honestly Mister Hyde is a bit more threatening than a frat boy." Eden snapped before she returned her attention to Lennox.

"I knew they weren't really your targets." She glared through gritted teeth.

"Felix was actually, Rue well- She was for fun. Revenge."

Anger flared up within the demon and quickly faded into frustration as her eyes went a dull green and faded back to purple. "Let him go and you can do whatever you want to me, Aron isn't part of the reason you're angry."

Eden let out a laugh before shaking her head, "It's funny how you think you're the one in the position to make any more deals with any-one. That's what put you here in the first place."

She turned to Bastien who quietly watched behind her and nodded for him to leave. He gave her a concerned look which Eden ignored and tilted her head and motioned with her eyes to the door. Without a question he turned and went up the stairs.

"I was doing what I had to- What I thought would keep you safe."

Lennox's voice wafted over to Eden making her turn back to them.

"You don't have to explain yourself to her, she's not going to see it for what it was." Aron spoke up.

"Like how you don't have to explain what that dagger meant?" Eden snapped back. "You know she's just going to figure it out whether you want her to or not. That you two are now bo-"

"That is none of your business, Child." Armaros's deep voice replaced Aron's followed by black eyes.

"It's something I'd like to know too." Lennox interjected as the chains rattled when she turned to face the demon. "Preferably before I die."

The black eyes faded back to green and Aron looked apologetically at her. "He seems to think now isn't the right time."

"There may be no other time," Lennox rolled her eyes.

"Do you two ever not bicker? I mean, hell I'm the one with the daggers." Eden put her hands on her hips, already tired of the two. "If you don't find a way to keep yourself contained, I will."

"Do it," He challenged.

Her gaze fell on the two sided demon and decided now was the time to test the extent of her magic. Her eyes shifted back to blue as she stalked forward and got within an inch of his reach. The orange in his veins slowly faded as in the space between his chest and her hand formed an orb of clear liquid formed as she drained the water from his muscles. She kept her gaze on him close; he seemed to weaken just enough to make him non lethal until his body found a way to cope with the loss.

"Since we were so rudely interrupted, I'd like to know how you thought a deal with a Crossroads Demon was going to keep your child safe?" She turned her attention back to Lennox who watched with fear plain in her eyes.

Lennox let out a shutter as Eden stepped over to her. "When your father died… I thought Wyatt's curse had come back. Xemos told me it was a coincidence- People die- I didn't believe him and I had to make sure it would never come for you."

"You devoted yourself to him and he told me himself he doesn't lie to his devotees. So I ask again, why?"

"I couldn't believe him because it had taken so much already. I couldn't let you take on the curse too. It wasn't your burden to bear."

Eden paused as she listened, and considered Lennox's words, however she had only known Eloise as a mother figure. No matter how hard Eden had fought against the family values at first Eloise had never abandoned her. Never dropped her at a doorstep as someone else's problem.

"You didn't have to leave your child. Family is a bond, a promise and you broke it."

With the orb of water still floating between the chained up demons, she guided over the metal chains where it formed into thick ice around the chains attached to Lennox completely immobilizing her. Once again she pulled out the fire dagger and held it over the same spot she had cut Aron. She sent a smirk over to the man before pressing the blade deeply into her skin. The two locked eyes as Lennox screamed louder when she dragged the smoking metal across her skin.

Eden turned her attention back to Lennox as she pulled the knife away. Out of the corner of her eyes she saw a black feathered wing shoot in front of her victim. It suddenly went forward and caught Eden roughly in the stomach knocking the wind out of her as she was forced a few feet away. Her eyes darted to Aron whose eyes had returned to black and smiled as fire lit up inside them. Under her anger she felt the instinctual human fear

As she slid on the floor she grabbed at the wing and pulled his dagger from her belt. He seemed to have spotted this and retracted away from her once more and used it to shield Lennox. Armaros let out a low deep laugh.

"You're afraid… Pulling out your sure weapon right away- Look how easily you want to kill me! It's so weak." His eyes darkened as he forced himself forward in an effort to get closer. "From all the time spent torturing in hell I can practically taste the fear in someone's actions, and the fear in you is strong and sweet. You don't deserve someone like Mister Steele, whore."

The red returned to Eden's vision and her grip tightened on the hilt of the weapon still in her hand. She stalked forward, and raised the dagger with the full intent of burying it in his chest every thought in her mind dissipated. The only thing in her line of vision was the demon's wide smirk and she could have sworn he still welcomed the attack. Until a set of arms wrapped around her waist and pulled her back a few steps.

"It's what he wants, don't give in just yet, Little Bird- Savor it."

"Let me go, Holden!" She snapped and pushed at his hands in attempts to get him to do what she demanded. "You and Eloise wanted this! Just let me finish it!"

"Not yet, not when you can use her against him. We need to know what he's not telling us." Holden's voice dipped low beside her ear as she continued to fight him.

She stopped as he squeezed her side hard enough to make her grimace. He didn't even deny her accusations. "I knew it."

"You knew what?" He roughly turned her to face him.

"I knew you and Eloise were working together to make it so I'd have no choice but to come back!"

"Of course we were, Eden. Eloise would never allow you to destroy yourself. We knew you would protect Bastien."

His voice was irritatingly calm as he looked down on her. "I was happy! I've told you, I don't belong in this family."

"I think you do," Armaros's deep chuckle drifted over. "Because if you cared about Wyatt, you wouldn't have brought us down here."

"Eden, you still have that chance. You can still destroy the daggers and we will defend you to Wyatt." Lennox spoke quickly and met Eden's eyes.

Silence filled the room as she looked between two of Wyatt's best friends and Holden who still held her in place. Air caught in her lungs as she forced the man's hands off of her finally. *I can't do this... There can't still be a chance.* Eden settled the dagger back into her belt and let her feet carry her towards the stairs as the feeling of being trapped flooded and sent her heart racing.

"Little Bird-"

She heard footsteps behind her. "Stop me and you'll be the next one with a dagger in their body."

Among the darkness inside of her there was a small beacon of light that begged for her to follow it out the door only twenty feet from her. She could go to Wyatt and explain everything, help Aron and Lennox escape. However, it was then that more questions burdened her of their future. Where would they be in five years? Ten years? Twenty? Where would they be, she still human and him immortal? No, she would die and he would continue, unless she became like him. The thought sent her skin crawling as she moved toward her room. *Is love worth the sacrifice of my humanity?*

Her skin crawled as Eden stood in front of the basement door. Every word Armaros had said swirled inside her mind like a broken record. The dark circles under her eyes showed her lack of sleep as various scenarios played in her mind's eye of Wyatt finding out she had killed them. Her eyes fell on the mahogany stain as behind it she could hear the two voices of her captees as they bickered about something she couldn't make out. A set of hands found their way to her shoulders in the stillness of the house. She drew in a shaky breath and felt the muscles in her legs already begging her to turn and walk out and never look back.

"You're so close, Eden. You've been so patient and now is the time to do what we came here to do." Eloise's monotone voice hinted at excitement as the grip on her shoulders tightened.

You can still go to him. Lennox's voice fought with her mothers. "You mean you're so close... To get what you wanted."

"What we both wanted. Did you not want to show Richard you are exactly what this family needs?"

"I told you what I wanted Mother, instead you let me believe I could just maybe-" Her voice caught in her throat as Eloise turned her around.

"Maybe what? Have the family and the demon?" She raised an eyebrow, her lips turned into a thin line. "You are a Miller, are you not? You go with him, you'll be a Cade. Is he really someone you would give your humanity up for? Become everything *she* did?"

Eloise bent slightly to be at Eden's levels, her chestnut eyes locked on her. The same question she had been asking herself all night was now thrown at her and stabbed like the knife she shoved into the demons below.

"He could be..."

Instantly rage filled the woman's eyes as she took a step back. "If you want to be his little pet, go ahead. I won't stop you this time. You want to be done with The Salavamari? Step out the door and see what that will really be like but don't come back here when he doesn't want you anymore. Look at what you've done already. You've killed his best friends and you have two more of them downstairs. Do you think he's going to forgive you for all of that? Or did you already start lying to him again about the deaths of Felix and Rue?"

In a matter of moments the light Lennox had opened to her, extinguished. Eloise's words struck her right where they needed to as her vision blurred slightly. Quickly Eden forced the emotions down and remained locked eyes with her mother.

"You've made your choices and it's time to follow through." She motioned to the door. "I promise no matter what comes next you will always have us and soon you'll have Holden or Chase. I think if you gave them a chance you could be happier than with some demon. You're worth so much more than what he can offer you in a Matriarchal family."

Eloise stepped forward and cupped Eden's face gently, her hardened features softened as she spoke. She was right, her path had officially come to a crossroads and as she looked down both one was full of uncertainty. The other was something she was brought up to know like the back of her hand, however, the vision of an older, unfulfilled version of herself Xemos had shown her still lingered in the back of her mind.

He hadn't shown her what her life could be with Wyatt, if they made it past this point, if she ever got away. *Maybe he didn't show me because it would have led to his death? Eloise would never let me go; she's proved that over and over again. She'd kill him if I ran off-*

"What do you decide, Eden?"

She glanced down at her wrist, the bracelet Wyatt had given her once again felt heavy. *I'll just lead to his demise... Maybe this is how it's supposed to be. This way he can live.* Once again, Eden fell into the world Eloise laid out to her. She turned to face the door once more and put a hand on the knob with a pause before opening it.

"Good girl, I'll be right behind you." Eloise followed her down the stairs.

The daggers in her belt felt heavy as both Lennox and Aron looked up at her. Holden stood between them with a sickle in one hand and a gun in the other pointed at Aron, his attention on the pink haired demon as he tilted the blade under her chin around around the opposite side of her face using the flat part to direct her attention to him.

"It's been fun, what did I hear him call you? Lenny-boo." His next words were directed to the Matriarch and Heiress by the stairs. "Unfortunately the two headed one still wouldn't talk."

Holden dragged the tip along Lennox's jaw which left the thinnest line, almost like a papercut. A low growl came from Aron as he did which caused a muffled shot to be discharged from Holden's gun right into the demon's hip, the sound dulled by the silencer he had fitted to the weapon. The demon let out a deep grunt of pain and gritted his teeth as the hunter stepped away. He turned and as usual locked eyes with Eden who didn't react as he returned the gun to his right hip. He ambled over to the two women and as Holden stepped closer to her, his eyes searched her for something.

As he passed her right side she felt his hand brush against her hip. He paused and looked down as the two kept their eyes on the other. Wyatt's face filled her minds eye and she stepped away from his hand and broke eye contact first. Quietly, there was a smug sound of confirmation as he found what he was looking for. Eden ignored him for now and turned to Lennox and Aron who watched the exchange closely. Eloise and Holden stepped away over to the weapons table and started to talk quietly, their words a low hum in the background as she brought out the fire enchanted dagger.

With every slow step she took forward, Eden could feel the adrenaline filling every muscle in her body. A switch flipped inside her mind, the one she had formed when she was new to the family. The images of Wyatt faded as all the years of training took over as she stalked her prey. Her eyes traced over the cuts and bruises Holden had left on them during the night, most of them half healed and had dried over the hours.

"I think it's time to find out what demon boy won't tell us."

Eden smirked as she stopped just in front of the pink haired demon.

Lennox tried to move herself back but Eden grabbed her foot. With her left hand she pinned it to the floor by the ankle and leaned toward her. When she caught her gaze she could see the terror in her eyes and relished in the fact Lennox was scared of her. She returned her eyes to Aron, she bent her elbow and with all her strength pressed down and heard the crack of bones. Curiosity sparked inside of her as the other demon flinched.

Lennox's scream echoed on the stone walls of the basement as her chains rattled. Her gaze snapped back to her as she tried to pull away again. As she shook her head, Eden raised the hand with the spelled dagger and forced it into her inner thigh. Again she could hear Aron suppress another grunt as the smell of burning skin filled her nose.

Between the sounds of Lennox's screams the voice of Chase and Bastien as they yelled upstairs drew her attention. Within seconds the door at the top of the stairs flew open and someone came running down the stairs. Eden stood and spun on her heels to face whoever had come down so abruptly. Wyatt stood frozen at the bottom of the stairs staring directly at her. His electric eyes were alight with anger as they darted around and assessed the situation.

At the sight of him, the cloud of anger seemed to break up ever so slightly. No one in the basement moved for what felt like an eternity as he looked between Aron and Lennox chained up. To Eden with a dagger in her hand and the very two that would end their lives strapped to her and finally to Holden and Eloise in the corner. His gaze finally rested back onto Eden who saw the disappointment in his face which almost made her heart stop. *He'll never forgive me...*

"Eden, what have you done?" His voice cracked a bit as he looked at her. He took a step toward her and only stopped once he stood between her and Lennox.

"I told you... I was protecting Bastien and Corvus." She managed to choke out, the pain of what was about to happen hit her in a devastating blow.

"By hurting them! Eloise already killed Felix and Rue and you- You're helping her kill them!"

"Wyatt-"

"No, Eden! If you told me I would have taken you and Bastien as far as we could have gotten but instead this is what you do?" He motioned behind him. "I can understand protecting your family but this is mine. I thought you wanted to be part of it."

"She'll never be one of you, I made sure of that." Eloise interjected.

"Clearly..." He turned to Eden with betrayal in his eyes. "I tried to help you get out, all you would have had to do was bring that bag to Kappa and we could have been gone with a single word. I loved you, Eden with everything I am... I would have done anything for you even after everything." He turned his back on Eden and moved toward his friends.

"I didn't ask for you to try to save me that day. I warned you from the very beginning that you didn't want to pursue me." She reminded and started toward him.

He turned back to her and took two long steps to stop right in her face. "I guess I should have listened but as I told you, I'm a stubborn man."

His eyes darkened down at her. The sight made her want to scream, to throw all the daggers down and fall to her knees for his forgiveness. However, the hope that would have caused her to do so had been squashed so tightly that she didn't dare. She stared into his eyes as if trying to memorize them, she would never see the way he looked at her as if she was the only person who existed again. He would never wrap her into his arms and help return the air to her lungs. That was all gone, replaced by rage and pain that reflected in its place.

"Fuck!" He turned away once more and bent down to the base of the chains. "I can't look at you right now."

"What are you doing?" Eden stepped forward with the fire dagger still in her hand, though she knew she would never use it on him.

"You chose your family, I'm choosing mine."

"I can't let you do that, Wyatt. I'm sorry."

The man swiftly turned back to face her as sparks lit his eyes as they stared each other down. For a moment she saw the side of Wyatt her mother had warned her about and for once she didn't know if Wyatt wouldn't lash out at her. Both were squatted down, Lennox's chains in one of his hands.

"Are you going to stop me, Viper?" He spat out the nickname.

"Only if you make me."

They stayed frozen for a moment to see who would make the first move. Wyatt's hand slowly went to the base where the chains were hooked but stopped when he saw the tip of a raised dagger pointed right at him. Internally, Eden begged him to stop, not to make her do what she was about to. As his fingers went to undo the base she launched herself forward, her left hand pulled behind her. His arm came up and blocked the knife as he let go of the chains. With his right hand he reached in front of her but her left hand grabbed his wrist.

Suddenly, both of his hands held hers tightly and he pulled her onto her back. Eden used the momentum to return to her knees and forced his arms to cross. As their hands collided the knife slipped from her grip. She reached up and grabbed it from the air and caught it in her right hand that forced it forward about an inch from his stomach. Wyatt grabbed her shoulders at the same time which made both of them stop as they locked eyes for a final time.

"I'm sorry." She whispered to him in hopes that in the two words she could convey the entirety of her guilt. " I'm their pawn and there's no way out of this game."

"Me too, we could have won but you decided to let *them* win instead."

His eyes lit up and she felt a pulse of electricity flow through her causing her muscles to lock up where she was knelt down. She could only move her eyes as he moved around her to Aron and quickly undid the chains from their base. Eden tried to make herself move but watched as Eloise stormed past her. Without hesitation The Matriarch pulled the demon up by the shoulder and pushed him face first into the wall. Her fingers gripped his hair and she shoved his head as hard as she could, just as she had done to Lennox the day before, Wyatt fell to the ground motionless. Her eyes followed his body down and Eden watched in horror as Eloise with her left hand already had Holden's sickle poised under his chin.

"You will not terrorize my family any more, Steele."

She tried to yell out, but her jaw wouldn't move. She could do nothing to stop what was about to happen, no matter what she did she would be the one to lead him to his death. At least that's what she thought until Aron whipped his chains under Eloise's chin and pulled her off Wyatt. The demon dragged the woman back toward the weapons table, his wings unfurled fully behind him as Holden attempted to step in. With a single motion one of the wings sent the man back into the opposite wall and he fell on the stairs a fair distance away with a thud and grunt.

The tingle in her muscles that held her there slowly faded, however not enough. Her body still refused to move more than her head.

Aron pulled Eloise all the way over to the metal table still littered with various weapons and reached at random to pick up a saí. The man turned his whole body and pulled Eloise up so she stood and struggled to breathe. Eden watched her mother kick behind herself as annoyed anger drifted across his face. He simply moved and shifted the light woman around. The sounds of the chains echoed as they fell to the floor was followed by a gasp of air quickly cut off once more by his hand as he pulled her to him.

Eden struggled against the spell that had rendered her motionless, her gaze drifted to Eloise's hand which had stopped reaching toward Armaros. Instead, the two women met each other's eyes as she slipped off the Matriarch ring with acceptance in her eyes. Eden's heart dropped as her mothers hand clutched the ring, *Eloise knew*. Just as she felt her legs start to move again she watched the flash of silver as the saí was plunged into the center of Eloise's torso and pulled down. A scream of pain ripped from her throat as he dropped her to let the woman land uncontrolled with a thud, her head bounced on the floor. Eden's own screams filled the basement as the spell was released. She ran to her mothers side and completely ignored the demon that loomed over them.

The life of the Matriarch faded fast as the two women looked into each other's eyes. Eden's vision blurred as she watched her mother fight to stay awake. Something shifted in her eyes as blood dripped from her nose. The rigid mask the woman held constantly suddenly dropped and she looked at Eden in a way she had never seen before. Pure pride and sadness.

"I always knew how amazing you would be, Eden. From... From the moment I saw you sitting by yourself in that orphanage I knew you were... Extraordinary."

"Don't do that, You're going to be okay." Eden's voice choked out and broke as she called for the others. "Bastien! Chase! Stacey!"

"They can't hear you," Aron's demonic voice combined with Armaros echoed in the silence as he pointed to the shield around the stairs that blocked Holden from getting to them. Eden looked up and saw one eye was black and the other was Aron's usual green eye. "You wanted the monsters you thought we were- You got them because you trapped us like animals."

Every word stabbed like the ones she inflicted on him. The knot in her throat tightened as Eloise struggled to breathe and she pulled her mother into her lap as she moved her hair from her face. A tear fell and she saw her hands shake as life continued to fade from her mother's eyes. Blood stained hers and Eden's clothes, the red covered her hands as she tried to keep pressure somewhere, anywhere she could.

"You will make one hell of a Matriarch, Eden. I pass my... Responsibilities to you Eden Olivia Miller, may you guide us into a better world."

Those words crushed Eden's very soul. It was only said when a Matriarch passed the title to their heir. As a long breath was released the light from her eyes dulled and Eden's eyes slammed shut as her whole world changed in an instant. No longer an Heiress, but in a matter of seconds, the youngest Matriarch in four generations. Softly, she reached into Eloise's palm and took the ring from her hand, her gaze locked on the empty eyes of her mother.

Her heart sank into her stomach as she tried to imagine a life without her. Sure, they had their bad times with the good moments. However as often as she had tried to, she couldn't imagine her world without Eloise, she couldn't do it. Her head snapped up to the two men in one body, who still seemed to be trying to decide if she was next. Eden's next words spilled out as she remembered he was still a Crossroad

Demon.

"I- I want to make a deal."

"Excuse me, Child?" Armaros's voice returned, now a growl as she spoke.

"Hell no!" Lennox yelled from her spot against the wall which caused him to peer at her momentarily. A look of regret filled the green eye of Aron, but Armaros held steady as he looked at Eden like she was nothing more than a thorn in his side.

"Bring her back and I'll never hurt you or Lennox again... Take my soul if I ever do." She reached into her belt and held both Lennox and his daggers towards him, hilts first.

His eyebrow rose as he considered her proposal silently. Her hand shook as she kept them extended to him. "She wouldn't be human, are you sure it's worth it?"

"Yes, I can't lead the family without her. Please Aron... Armaros, bring her back. I'll give you anything. I already lost Wyatt, I just want her back."

"Eden, don't you dare!" Holden yelled from the stairs still trapped while he banged on the wards that kept him locked in place.

"Aron- Armaros." Lennox pleaded with him, her voice strained.

The demon smirked, like he had won the game they had played all along. Confidence radiated from him as if he knew this is where they would have ended up. As if she had walked right into some sort of trap, however, at this very moment she didn't care. He reached out and took both daggers from her hands and pocketed them. It was another ten seconds while the man allowed the loudest silence Eden had ever heard to fill the room. He moved toward her cold and calculated until they were less than three feet apart. Fear attempted to bubble to the surface, but Eden swallowed it back down her hands now empty- She was utterly defenseless and her life was in his hands.

"Kneel and beg."

"What?" Eden blinked, she had thought he would take her down for even daring to ask.

"I told you… On your knees and ask me." It wasn't a suggestion. "If I let you live you will never harm Lennox, Wyatt, Rosalyn, or myself again. Anyone within the grounds of this school, you make a move to kill us. You're mine."

Kneeling isn't necessary for deals. Eden quickly went over her studies of Crossroad Deals.

"It's not necessary, Child." His voice deepened with anger. "However, you will kneel."

Eden's mouth dropped a little, she had never heard of his abilities for mind reading. She regained herself before she spoke, his night sky eye glared daggers into her. "If I don't?"

"I'll house the very dagger you were going to kill me with in your chest."

Eden's gaze drifted to Eloise's body then to Wyatt who was still motionless. Her heart fell further into her stomach as regret filled every part of her being. *It's too late… Maybe one day if I become one of them I'll be able to apologize.* To the left of Wyatt was Lennox who looked between herself and Aron in horror. For the first time she saw the guilt and something that reminded her of the way Eloise watched her when she was scared she would be hurt. *I… I never thought she actually cared.*

Movement from the man in front of her caught her attention once more as he extended his hand and lowered it in a silent command. Eden's jaw tightened and red flushed her face as she ever so slowly knelt down in front of him. Armaros crouched and his elbows rested on his knees as he met her eyes for a final time.

"Take this deal and you're mine if you break it, you fully understand this, correct?"

"I do."

Armaros held out a hand to her which she took. A spark sprang to life inside their palms and she could feel the heat form. "Your mothers life... To keep the lives of the people on these grounds safe. Any attacks spearheaded by you will break our covenant, do you agree to these terms?"

"I do."

His grip was tight and burned hot as his veins were orange under his skin. Smoke rose from their hands and for a few seconds she felt her palm burn which caused her to wince and lock her jaw. When he let go there was a small 'x' at the base of her thumb as if branded into her skin.

"Step back." He commanded as he placed his hand over the wound.

Eden did so and watched him closely as a silver dim light appeared under his hands. The light slowly flowed into Eloise's body and she seemed to fade from the room. Eden went to speak but Aron shook his head as her body dissipated in a glow of light.

"Where-"

"She'll wake up in her room in a few days. She'll be confined to Romania for five years. As to what she is now, I believe a discussion with Mort about her new personal hell would be recommended."

Eden stood there for a moment now unsure of what to say to them as she looked between Aron, Lennox and a still motionless Wyatt. She knew there was no apology that could make up for any of this. There was no way Lennox or Aron were going to help her fix things between her and Wyatt. *I'm a Matarach now... I can't leave.* Sadness welled up in her chest.

"I know you probably won't but... Tell him I've never cared about anyone the way I cared about him... And in another life I hope we can start again... In five minutes you all will have the evening to leave without anyone stopping you."

Eden stood to her full height and turned her back to the demons inside the basement and made her way over to the stairs. The shield that was holding Holden back was finally dropped as she reached it. Within seconds she was wrapped into his arms and swiftly pulled up the stairs. She let him as she couldn't feel any of her limbs, her hand burned still and her mind reeling.

"I've got you, don't worry Little Bird." He whispered to her as they went up the stairs. "I'll be right beside you and you will rise stronger than before."

Lennox

Pain shot up her leg in frequent waves from the stab and broken ankle that refused to heal. Her eyes followed Eden and Holden out of the room and she leaned her back against the cool wall. A searing pain from the long wound between her shoulder blades reminded Lennox of what Holden had done only hours ago. *Such lovely burns, I'd love to hear the story behind them but I think I should add a bit of decoration.* He hadn't been as threatening as Armaros but he definitely was almost as cruel. He had traced the fire dagger in the shape of an 'S' over all of the scars Armaros had left there decades ago, the scar would forever trace like a snake over her spine.

As the memories faded, Lennox turned her attention to Wyatt and scanned him for any cuts left by Eden. Eventually, they went to his chest as it rose and fell ever so slightly and proved he was still alive. The motion sent a wave of relief over her as she finally went still in her spot releasing a long breath and letting her head hang forward. The world was still spinning from the blood loss and pain in her leg and back as she evened her breathing. The sound of metal on metal caught her attention once more as she saw Aron put the weapon he had used to kill the hunter back on the table.

"Is he okay?" His voice crackled from all the times Armaros had spoken.

"He's breathing but we need to get him back to Kappa and I can heal you both up."

"I'll be fine, you need to be healed too. How's your back?"

"I'll be fine." She smirked slightly and threw his words back at him.

"Why did you come here alone?" He asked as he peered around.

"I was going to call Fang, but... Every time I went to I worried that they would just kill him and run. You know Fang and the others. They would have gone right in, so I waited and planned."

A mirrored smirk appeared on his face as hers did. The large wings folded into his back and he let out a soft grunt as they vanished. His own chains still hung from his wrists and gleamed hot orange from his anger. His gaze drifted over to her, his expression softened as he did and examined the chains that still held her in her spot. Hot metal fell to the floor and sizzled in small drips from his hands as the heat was too much for them to take any longer.

"Holy shit!" He laughed and looked at his now burned skin as a few more drops of the iron came off. "We're getting out of here, Len. I have an idea."

After a few seconds they had melted enough for him to open his arm and force the metal the rest of the way from his wrists. A small smile drifted to her face as hope that they would get out of here soon washed over her. Aron hastily wiped his wrists off on his jacket and went over to her. He knelt down and positioned himself directly in front of her and reached up wrapping his hands around the cuffs holding her arms above her head where Holden had latched her.

The view of him over her with his arms over her head brought up the memories of Armaros doing the same to force her powers out. Her hair stood on end but her eyes locked onto his forest eyes and for the first time her body didn't start to shake at the memories. His eyes searched hers and his body was still as if braced for the panic but when it didn't come she felt him relax slightly.

"Look down, okay? It might hurt a little bit." He instructed in a more serious tone.

"It can't be any worse than what we've already been through... I trust you." The last words slipped out as another wave of pain from her shoulder blades stung.

As she felt the metal around her wrists heat up, Lennox ducked her head into his chest, his stained denim jacket covered her view. Her skin started to burn which caused her magic to call itself forward but stopped when the heat faded once more. Aron huffed in frustration above her and felt him adjust his hands.

"I need the big guy's power here... Make him mad."

Lennox froze for a moment, thankful she couldn't see his face as she thought of what she could say. At first she drew a blank, until she remembered the pure hate Armaros had looked at Eden with. As much as she wanted to feel the same after everything that had occurred, she still didn't blame her, not fully. She was a product of the family she was put into all because she left. *In some twisted way, all of this is my fault.* She decided that it was better to unpack later she finally found her words and discovered there was some truth to them, but she would never tell him that.

"Eden isn't to blame, she was manipulated into all of this and I think we should forgive her."

A deep growl reverberated in his chest which brought goosebumps to her arms. The heat returned to her wrists much hotter this time. She clenched her teeth to prevent herself from yelling out. She only glanced up for a split second and saw the black eyes of Armaros looking back at her. His black burned skin from his fingertips to elbow was illuminated by the orange glow inside his veins. For the first time, she didn't pull away as the hot metal melted down their hands onto her arms. Lennox tucked her head back into his chest as the heat became too much against her face.

"Almost there, get ready to pull your hands out." The two men spoke as one as the metal became thin enough he loosened his grip. "Okay Len, pull!"

Lennox did so and wrenched her arms from his hands, the metal fell to either side. Without the resistance of the chains, the muscles in her shoulders gave out and caused her to slump into him. His arms wrapped around and completely engulfed her, his hand held her head to his chest as he slowly helped her to adjust to the freedom of movement again. Her ragged breath slowly evened and her body became still as the adrenaline stopped.

"Thank you."

"Couldn't have done it without you, Lenny." He whispered in her ear as each movement shot new pains through her body.

"Hey there, can I join the group huddle?" Wyatt's voice caused them both to turn their heads.

A soft smile appeared on her face. "Do you even have to ask?"

Wyatt moved over to them, his eyes fell on the strange way her ankle was healing. "Can you make it up the stairs?"

"Can any of us?" She teased as she looked between the two men.

"Better than you," Wyatt smirked. "Come on, let's get out of here."

They helped her to stand and when she stumbled slightly, Aron wrapped a strong arm around her side and led her to the stairs where the door stood open. The three followed the light from the top of the stairs and found themselves in the kitchen. Lennox looked around at the few decorated pine trees down the hall adorned with dried orange slices and holly. It was at that, Lennox remembered what day it was as they made their way to the front door.

"Merry Christmas you two."

Each let out a laugh that brought a smile to her face. "Merry Christmas, Leonard."

"Merry Christmas, Nox."

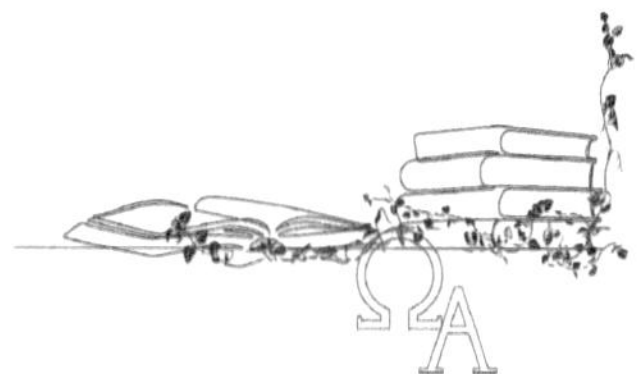

The next day Lennox was responsible for keeping Aron busy at Kappa while Rosalyn and Wyatt supposedly set up for Aron's surprise party. Lennox had received a text from him to tell her that Rosalyn hadn't wanted to help. Though she was sad, she understood why her friend didn't want any part of this. Yet somehow the plan didn't stop. It was easy enough as both were still exhausted and wanted to rest from the night before. Lennox had spent the night in Aron's room since both didn't want to be alone. Though her sleep hadn't been completely peaceful as the moment of Eden's deal haunted her dreams and Aron had woken her up from each one.

Finally able to walk since each of them had taken turns to heal major wounds and wrapped the rest they couldn't, she went and brought up coffee for both of them. Neither of them said much most of the morning that slowly turned to afternoon. Lennox stewed on the memories and how she had done everything she could to prevent Eden from becoming just like her. She had seen the marks of Xemos on her arms and now she had made a deal. Not with just any Crossroads Demon, but Armaros. Not only that, Wyatt himself had known for who knew how long Eden was a hunter and he hadn't said anything all because he fell in love.

"Penny for your thoughts?" Aron's voice interrupted the storm.

"Wyatt knew... He knew who she was and he did nothing."

"No, there's no way he knew."

"I saw it in his face, Aron. The day before you disappeared I was going to warn him after what happened in the hallway. I was going to tell him she was a hunter and he stopped me from speaking." She explained, shifting herself in the rolling chair by his desk.

"That's not like him, we'll have to figure out where he stands." Lennox nodded and peered at her second cup of coffee. "There's something else."

"It's nothing to worry about right now." She tried to brush it off.

"That sucks, I'm worried about it right now." He swung his legs over the side of the bed. "Talk to me."

Lennox fiddled with the sleeves of the hoodie he had lent her as she chewed on her words for a few seconds. Heat filled the tips of her ears as her emotions were shown clearly on her face. It took effort to keep her voice even when she wanted to yell at him. *Not Aron, I want to scream at Armaros... Never thought I'd be able to do that.* However, here she was fully able to give him an ear full and he couldn't do anything about it.

"I'm not mad at you, Aron." She started off and picked her words carefully as she tried to get accustomed to the two demons that shared a body. "The deal... With Eden, Armaros took it... I thought you were done with deals?"

His expression fell slightly and he flinched. His hand rubbed his temple but understanding reflected in his eyes. "We are done with deals, but we did it to stop her from hurting anyone here again. To protect Wyatt, Octavious, Rosalyn, and you."

The word *we* caused her to pause. "That doesn't negate the fact of what it means for her. I fought with everything I had to prevent her from taking on the curse- From becoming me."

Her vision blurred as tears formed just in time to erase the saddened look in his eyes. She turned away to look at the Foreigner poster on his wall, as silly as it seemed she didn't want Armaros to see her cry. The bed creaked as she heard him stand and approach her. Quickly, Lennox slammed her eyes shut as she felt a hand on her knee and another on her upper arm. A new wave of regret that didn't quite match with her own mixed within her.

"Len, you did everything right. She's made her choices and we would have made a deal with whoever was trying to hurt you."

Her heart skipped inside her chest at his words and she looked over to him to find him knelt in front of her but was quickly shoved to the side. "Maybe she had the right to go after me, she's right I should have believed Xemos."

"She has no right to go after a peaceful group of supernatural beings who just want to study." A deeper voice rumbled up from his chest and one of his eyes smoked over and the hand on her arm dropped.

"And you don't get to decide who lives and dies anymore." She snapped directly at Armaros in hopes Aron would understand this wasn't for him.

"And you will not act as if you deserved her cruelty." Armaros insisted.

"You certainly thought I did twenty years ago."

"I've learned differently since then. Eden won't break our deal." His face twisted into a frown, a hint of anger in his darkened eye. "As much distaste I have for the girl if she does she shall not remain as you or Rosalyn did though I think she does deserve it."

"Promise that to me." Lennox held up her pinky which made the demon inside him roll his eyes. Raising an eyebrow at Armaros she motioned to it with her head. "It's stupid to you but it's become a thing and you're going to have to deal with it."

He shook his head and looped his finger through hers. "You are one unique demon, Lennox Cade."

With that Armaros faded away as Aron's eyes returned to normal as he released her hand. The previous frown that he had left shifted into a small smile as he squeezed her knee before he stood.

"Big bad Lenny calling out Armpit. I like this side of you."

She couldn't help but to let out a laugh at his nickname for the very demon that struck fear into mortals. "I'm sorry, Armpit?"

"I thought it was fitting." Aron chuckled.

"You know, you're good with people." The tension they had spent most of the day dispersed within minutes.

"I better be, all the guys come here for advice or to get some shit off their chests."

The two continued their casual conversations and made morbid jokes about the last few days. Lennox hadn't been looking at her phone and ignored all the notifications on her smart watch until she heard the door to Aron and Wyatt's rooms open. Both of them looked over to see Wyatt in Aron's open door frame with his arms over his chest and leaned against the side.

"Hey, you guys got the time?" He looked directly at Lennox with a deliberate let's get going expression.

"Yeah it's like a bit after five I think, why?" Aron raised an eyebrow.

"Oh well some of the girls at Omega wanted to have an end of year meeting with you two."

"Sure, no problem, but can we talk to you for a second?" Aron motioned for Wyatt to join them.

Wyatt pushed himself off the frame and plopped himself on the bed beside Aron with a smile Lennox knew was fake even from her spot in the computer chair. After being best friends for seven years she could see when he pretended that he was okay.

"What's up, Chief?"

"We have to talk about what happened... There's no point in tiptoeing around it but the day before Aron disappeared I tried to warn you about Eden you stopped me... How long have you known about her?"

Wyatts smile sank the moment she started to speak. "Only for a few weeks."

"Why didn't you say anything?" Aron asked.

"She had promised not to hurt anyone else... She was leaving the family and I was trying to help her escape without drawing too much attention until she was ready."

Before Aron or herself could ask any more questions, he went into a long story about how when Eden had been supposedly sick she was actually in a magical coma due to vampire venom. He had gone to make sure she was okay but had been locked up in the very basement she and Aron had been. In turn Aron took over and told the story of how Eden attacked her in the hallway but for now left out the whole Armaros ordeal. Eventually he ended with the story of how Eden got him into the basement with the dagger, a story he had already told her once they got back to Kappa.

"Wait wait wait- You told me you were in a motorcycle accident." Lennox turned to Wyatt once Aron had finished the story.

"Yeahhh, that was a lie." He ran a hand through his hair with a nervous smile.

"You were locked in their basement and you still protected her?" Aron questioned. "I knew love was blind but fuck man I didn't think you were that blind."

"I'm not, I was doing what I do for the people I care about, like I said she was changing. She didn't want to be a part of the cult anymore."

Aron flinched and frowned. "It didn't really seem that way in the end."

"Well, I was hoping things wouldn't go that way." He admitted.

"Yeah well you should have told us just in case they did." Aron's voice rose and deepened slightly. "Lennox was almost killed three times now and myself just last night. Eloise even almost killed you!"

"If I would have known she would do that I would have stopped her!" Wyatt's voice joined his.

"Would you have?"

"Yes! I would have, Aron. I can't look at her for what she did to you guys! To Felix and Rue! How could I forgive her for any of that? I hate her."

The room went silent as Lennox was reminded of their two fallen family members. Lennox watched the regret and deep grief filled Wyatt's tired eyes. She stood and closed the distance to the chair in a few steps. Without a word she sat beside him and wrapped her arms around his torso. In return she felt hands find their way around her as they sat in silence for a second.

"Thank you for showing her that family isn't her only option." She whispered before she pulled away. A grateful smile crossed his face as she let go and turned to both men. "We all have had our fair share of lies and shitshows happen this year. I say no more lies from here on out, agreed?"

Aron shot her a look as if to ask if he should tell him now and she shrugged to tell him it was his choice. "If that's the case, I have some things I need to tell you Wyatt."

Suddenly, the loud ring of an alarm on Wyatt's phone went off. "If we can promise each other no more lies, then it can wait. It's time for that meeting."

"Ugh, fine." Aron gave an exasperated groan and made a show of getting up.

"It's not gonna be that bad," Lennox stood and nudged him as he passed her.

"Listen, for all we know we are being dragged into some sort of drama between Nick and one of your girls."

"Well if you could keep him from harassing my girls, that would solve it."

"I've been giving him lessons on how to be less- Him when flirting." Aron countered as they made their way from the house and into the brisk air.

The three of them were walking in the door of Omega Alpha. When Lennox opened it for them they were welcomed with all the lights shut off and complete silence. Aron looked at them confused as she motioned for him to go inside. Though he gave her a nervous look he stepped through the threshold. The moment he entered the house all the lights flipped on and about two dozen people from both houses popped out from around corners and yelled at the same time.

"Happy Birthday, Aron!" Donnie said as her and Leilani came around from the kitchen with a large sheet cake with guitars as candles.

He jumped at the sudden movement but quickly laughed as he saw everyone. "Hey! This doesn't look like a meeting! Are those guitars!?"

"Wyatt said you'd like them." Donnie smiled brightly interpreting for Leilani.

"Make a wish!" Donnie chimed in.

Aron looked around the room, the largest smile Lennox had ever seen spread across his face. He closed his eyes dramatically and blew as hard as he could before he laughed along with the others as eighties music started to play.

"Hell yeah, this is my jam!"

"There's a bonfire and beers outside!" Octavius called from beside a not so happy and seemingly drunk Rosalyn.

"Say no more!" He pivoted in place, grabbed Lennox's hand and pulled her with him. "Come on! I've gotta see your moves to this one!"

Lennox laughed as she was pulled and shuffled off with him, Wyatt and the others close behind him. The sun fell lower in the sky and the fire kept most of the backyard pretty warm. Lennox drank and danced beside Aron most of the evening, even Celia and Remi came over to join them followed by Octavius, Rosalyn, Donnie, Leilani, and Val. A few songs played as they all sang along loudly and drank as they danced.

"Hey there Lennyboo, how's the party?" Val asked over the music with her usual taunting tone and mischievous glint.

For once, Lennox looked at the very demon who put her in hell and didn't react more than a polite smile. "It's perfect, I'm glad you made it."

Val looked at her in surprise but didn't retort back as Donnie elbowed her. "Stop harassing them, sister."

"I'm not, I'm just chatting. So Lenny, what's the story with you two, hmm? I saw two little love birds sneaking off to the lake recently."

Lennox froze and Aron stepped forward and placed his elbow on Lennox's right shoulder with an entertained smirk. "Friends, Val. You're still nosey."

"I gotta keep up with my friend of course, besides I had to know if the rumors were true."

"You started them, Val." Donnie rolled her eyes as her twin opened her mouth again.

"It means you have a chance-"

Donnie quickly grabbed her sister's arm and pulled her away and said something about needing ten more drinks, Leilani followed behind. The light weight on her shoulder vanished and she peered over to Aron who looked at her perplexed but with a knowing smile.

"What?" She raised her eyebrow at him and put her hands on her hips as the drinks sent the world in slow motion.

"I think someone likes you." He teased motioning to the spot the two demons disappeared from.

"What? No." She shook her head having never even considered the idea. "Donnie and I are friends."

"She seems to think you two could be more."

She paused and let her eyes drift to the spot they had been and familiar grief pulled at her heart. "I'm not interested in anyone for right now. I think I need a vacation first."

"A beach sounds great right now." Aron agreed.

Lennox turned her attention over to the group left behind, Remi and Celia in their own conversation as they danced. Octavius and Rosalyn beside them with her back to Lennox. Her heart sank as she remembered just how damaged their friendship was. It killed her to know she was so angry however justified it was, she wished they would be able to talk it out one day.

Lennox raised her own drink to her lips and added to the healthy buzz she already had going. Her friend stumbled, obviously much more intoxicated than earlier, Octavius easily kept her upright as he motioned toward Aron. *It's fine, neither of them will say anything in front of all these people.* She convinced herself as the two approached.

"Happy birthday, I didn't know it was the day after Christmas!" Octavius laughed.

"What are you, like five thousand years old now?" Rosalyn taunted though Lennox knew she wasn't really asking Aron.

"Not exactly sure, I lost track over the years." Aron seems to also catch it as he flinched.

"I think it's time for presents!" Wyatt appeared from behind the couple and wrapped his arms around both of their shoulders.

Lennox shot him a thankful glance as he led the group back toward the house. Once inside the music was much more manageable and she could hear everyone clearer despite the slight ring. The seven of them went into the living room, kicking the balloons that littered the floor out of their way to where two packages with Aron's name on them sat. She watched him and saw his eyes light up as he looked at the group of them.

His eyes bounced between both packages and he went for the one she had brought. Lennox had wrapped her gift inside a large thin box in bright red paper with a silver bow. Aron made quick work of her immaculate wrapping job to reveal a poster sized frame with a star chart in the center. Planets were labeled and connected in various places and details were written below. As his eyes scanned the chart a bright smile drifted to his face as he looked up at her.

"Len, how did you do this?"

"I made some educated guesses." She smiled. "If it's wrong I can make a new one."

"No, it's perfect." Aron shook his head and wrapped her up in a tight hug.

"Okay, now for the group gift."

Wyatt smiled and held out the small bag. He quickly moved the paper aside and took out a small snow globe with a snowman made of sand on a beach. He looked at it confused and peered into the bag and pulled out a set of seven tickets. His eyes traced the words for a few seconds before he looked around at each of them.

"Cancun?"

"All of us!" Wyatt said excitedly. "It will be the best semester break yet!"

"Hell yeah! We're going to Cancun!" Aron picked up his drink and finished it in one go.

They laughed and the room buzzed with chatter as they all started talking about the trip. A drunken Celia yelled to Aron about how she had been absolutely dying to tell him. Lennox found a smile creep to her face as her gaze fell on each person. Though she was missing two, their little family had somehow managed to gain a few along the way. For the first time since Felix's death, warmth filled her chest. Somehow, they had made it through the daggers and deals of the semester. Once again, they were once again safe behind the iron gates.

 Crossroad Chronicles wasn't always meant to become a book, let alone a series. However, during the height of the Covid-19 pandemic, Kikie P. Akers and Sam Braid met within the Cosplay Discord community. At the time Kikie was running a Harry Potter server. After a few months, June 16, 2020, the original Discord server for what we called SCHUni was created. Within this server friends from across the globe were made, stories were created collaboratively and a family was found. All together they told stories through TikTok and roleplay. An elaborate world filled to the brim with a loved world. After some time of inspiration and creativity, Kikie decided to write Lennox and Eden's story soon followed by Sam. Collaboratively the two create a literary universe to share with the world through the main series and future prequels to come.

To my found family who loved this book with their whole hearts from begin-ning to end. You have shown me true magic and changed my life forever.

I want to give the biggest thank you to those who have supported me during this crazy process. There's a few characters within the world of Crossroad Chronicles as readers know it that I have been lucky enough to use to bring this story to life. Thank you to those who have allowed me to tell the stories of Coyote, Bloodfang, Corvus, Principal Moon, Cathwulf, Donnie and Val Bane. As well as Aron, Armaros, Rosalyn, Andy, Eloise, Leilani, Mort, Wyatt, Celia, Silas, Bastien, and Octavius. These characters wouldn't exist without your excitement and love for this world. Each of you have inspired and have helped bring this book to life. I wouldn't have been able to tell this story without the people who read Crossroads at every and any stage. Your advice and opinions were vital to the story.

To my husband, Kyle who supported me while I wrote. We have had such a rollercoaster in life but I am so excited to look into the future with you as I continue on this journey. Thank you for standing beside me and sharing the milestones of this road. As well as our daughter, Kaydence. You inspire me everyday to continue pushing forward. I hope you always know you can chase your dreams no matter what they are.

To Sam, my Black Dove. The one who started this world with me and loves it just as fiercely as I do. June 2020 was the start of something truly magical and I'm still in awe of the world we put together. I will always remember our first few chats where we shared Lennox and Aron. Created a story, a home. Little would we know what these two would turn into. November 2022, our little home found its way back together one chaotic morning and I will forever be grateful for it. You've been there for my many plot ideas and my rambles about plot holes at six in the morning or midnight. Through over ten covers, a million "what if's", and "Read this and tell me what you think." On those days the words didn't come as easily. You were there to talk through it, inspire or remind me I need to take a break every so often. I couldn't dream of going on this incredible journey fate has put us on with anyone else. Your creativity with Aron, Eloise, Rosalyn, Armaros, and Andromeda is inspiring and I am so thankful you allowed me to tell parts of their stories! Thank you for all the nights in Discord with sprints, lore and so much more. Thank you for being beside me every step of the way. I can't wait to create more together!

To Jamie, my Mushie. You and I may have not gotten close until just over a year ago but I have never met someone so loving, kind, and capable of anything. You are the person who made this book even remotely able to be in anyone's hands. Not only were you one of my biggest cheerleaders, sharing in the excitement of every milestone as I hit it. You were there every step of the way of bringing this book to life. From reading draft after draft with as much detail and care as me. Formatting not only this version, but my first draft to help me celebrate and put it into the hands of our friends. Anything I have possibly needed through this entire process, you have shared. Tools and knowledge that made all of this possible. You are a pillar in the fact this book exists today. Not only because of your willingness to help me, but you inspired me to get back into writing after years of searching for the right story. I had never seen someone successfully publish a book and you showed me just how possible my dream was. You have taught me so much and pushed me to do better. Thank you for letting me tell the stories of Leilani and Mort! Words will never be enough to tell you how much you mean to me.

To Morgan, my Copperhead. I can't believe it's really been four years since I met such a genuine soul. Though life has definitely had its twists and turns I'm so glad to have you beside me on this journey! You have always down to work through roadblocks and cheered me forward. When I say cheered me on, I mean it. The amount of times I thought I couldn't do it and you were there to keep me going. You listened to every complaint about scenes that seemed to drag. Since December of 2022 you have sat with me every night while I bring this to life. Thank you for being the manager I needed. You also were there to remind me when it was time to rest, to keep it simple, pull me out of deep plot holes and so much more. You have always loved this world as much as I do. Your constant support and excitement over every little detail and scene means the world every time I share something new. I can't believe you made it through such a chaotic first draft. It was rough, buddy. Your love for Supernatural Creatures Hidden University and genuine soul shines through Wyatt. It was an absolute honor to write such an amazing character who I fell in love with the moment I saw him! I am so thankful to tell the stories of Celia, Silas, and Wyatt! I couldn't have done this without you.

To Eli, for his passion and unwavering support in my writing. You have been there from the very start of my adult writing career. You edited old stories and told new ones that helped inspire my passion since 2019. Though life gets in the way, you were always there to listen. Every event, plot, quote, and cover. I hope I did Bastien justice. Thank you so much for letting me tell his and Octavius's stories.

Thank you will never be a strong enough word.

9 798218 490300